OF NIGHT AND CHAOS

JENNA WOLFHART

Copyright © 2023 by Jenna Wolfhart

All rights reserved.

No part of this book may be reproduced in any form or by any electronic or mechanical means, including information storage and retrieval systems, without written permission from the author, except for the use of brief quotations in a book review.

Cover Design by The Book Brander

Map by Allison Alexander

Chapter Art by Etheric Designs

Editing by Practical Proofing

Proofreading by Wicked Pen Editorial

Proofreading by Holabird Editing

Hardcover Character Art by Ruby Dian Arts

For every single one of you. Thank you for reading Tessa's story.

Author's Note

This series is intended for adult readers and will contain dark elements. To see a full list of potential triggers, visit www.jennawolfhart.com/books/content or scan the QR code below.

THE FAE OF AESIR

ELITE FAE

All the common fae powers, as well as additional magical abilities related to their bloodline.

COMMON FAE

Immortal life-span. Enhanced senses, strength, and speed.

LIGHT FAE

Power over fire.
Power over light.
Ability to create shields.

SHADOW FAE

Power over mist.
Animal communication.
Telekenesis.

STORM FAE

Power over wind.
Power over rain.
Power over lightning.

The Story So Far

In case you need a refresher...

In book one, Tessa Baran defied cruel King Oberon by stealing his powerful gemstones from the chasm. He caught her and punished her by choosing her to become his next mortal bride. Once he took her from her loved ones, he terrorized her and tricked her into believing he'd killed her sister.

Eventually, she escaped with the help of Morgan, one of Oberon's guards, who secretly works with the Mist King—Kalen Denare.

Kalen found her in the mists and took her back to his kingdom in the mountains. There, he offered her a deal. If she would sneak back across the barrier and kill King Oberon with the Mortal Blade, he would find a safe haven for her people, and he would help her find her family, currently lost somewhere in the mists.

She agreed.

They traveled together, dodging attacks from dangerous monsters and enemies from the Kingdom of

Storms. When they got trapped in a castle in Itchen, they grew closer. But half of the God of Death's power was also trapped in that castle. She offered Tessa the life of her sister in exchange for her release.

Tessa denied her and tried to destroy her as a way to stop the god from muting Kalen's powers any longer. It was the only way she could help him fight the storm fae, who had been attacking them for days.

It worked. Kalen got his powers back, and they survived.

Soon after, a letter arrived from Kalen's kingdom. Tessa's mother and dearest friend had made it there safely, against all odds. Eagerly, she returned to Kalen's homeland to reunite with them, only to discover the note was faked.

Kalen had betrayed her. According to Morgan, her family was trapped in Oberon's dungeons, and Kalen had known about it the entire time they'd been traveling together.

With vengeance in her heart, she stabbed him with the Mortal Blade, and then returned to Albyria where she stabbed Oberon as well.

Unfortunately, she soon discovered the blade was a fake. Oberon didn't die, and neither did the Mist King.

King Oberon then threw her into the dungeons, where she discovered her sister was still alive. That night, when she slept, Kalen visited her dreams.

"Hello, love," he said. "Surprised to see me?"

In book two, Tessa and Kalen reconciled in their dreams. He told her he once made a vow to his mother to destroy anyone who brought back the gods. She also learned her own father had dabbled in the dark magic and that Kalen had been forced to kill him.

Meanwhile, Oberon prepared her for their wedding ceremony once again. His eldest son, Ruari, encouraged Tessa to fight back. So when Oberon took her before his court, she revealed that he no longer had access to his powers. Oberon retaliated by pulling his power back into his body, breaking down his protective barrier and letting in the mist. But his power fought back against him in an explosion of fire. The entire city was consumed by flames.

Tessa fled to Teine with her family, and she discovered writings left behind by her father—evidence that she was a descendent of the God of Death.

Not long after, Kalen and his Mist Guard arrived to save her. The Mist Guard led the mortals of Teine to safety while Tessa and Kalen hunted down Oberon. They investigated the Tower of Crones and found Oberon had left behind his previous mortal brides. When one of them touched Tessa's arm, she gave Tessa a vision. Oberon had been in love with Kalen's mother, Bellicent Denare, and when she got killed, Oberon turned to the God of Death in order to save her. The God of Death agreed and gifted Bellicent with eternal life—by putting her soul into the bodies of others.

After this discovery, Kalen took Tessa to the city of Endir where the other mortals were taking refuge. But Tessa's mother did not trust the Mist King and she attempted to flee with several others. She was slaughtered by the shadowfiends, leaving Tessa bereft. To help her overcome her grief, Kalen trained her to fight.

Meanwhile, Morgan had taken an injured Oberon

and a weary Bellicent Denare to a hidden cave in the mountains. There, Bellicent suggested Oberon transfer her soul into Morgan's body, and Oberon reluctantly agreed. Panicking, Morgan contacted Kalen and asked for his help.

After receiving Morgan's plea for help, Kalen, Tessa, and the Mist Guard left Endir to find Oberon and Morgan. During the journey, Tessa finally remembered her childhood horrors. Her father had known she was a descendent of Andromeda (the God of Death), and he'd left her in the mists to fight the monsters on her own, hoping it would spark her powers to life.

And then Oberon appeared, regretting everything he'd ever done. He dosed the Mist Guard with valerian fog and stole Tessa away to lock her and the necklace in a vault beneath Albyria—to protect the world. When she woke, she fought him and stabbed him with the Mortal Blade. But he had been carrying the gemstone necklace that held the God of Death's essence, and so it was destroyed as well. Andromeda was finally released, and then the comet heralding the return of the gods streaked through the sky.

Tessa searched for Kalen in the mists, but she could not find him.

Where did he go? Did he believe Tessa brought back the gods? If so, did that mean he would soon be forced to kill her?

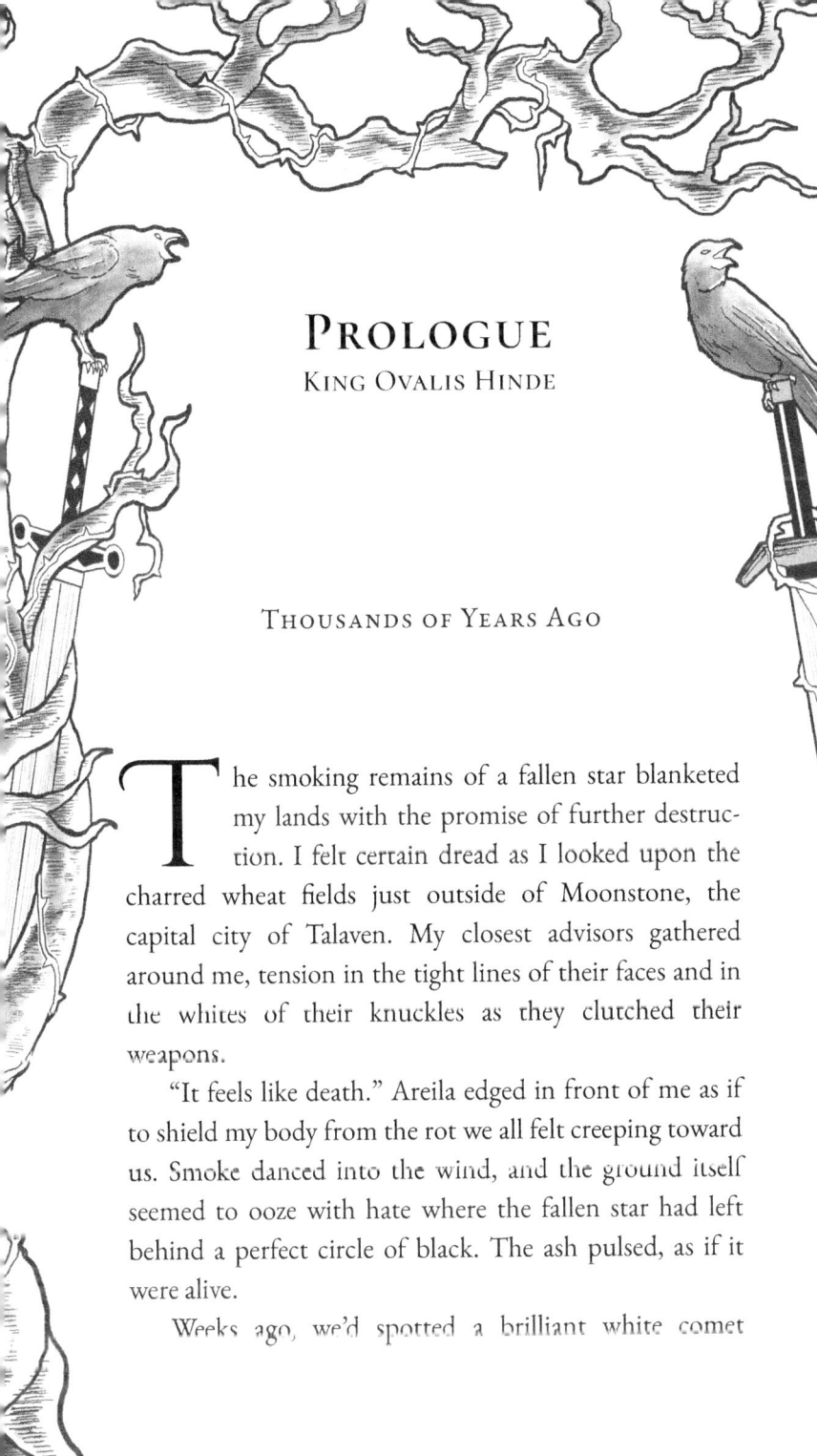

Prologue
King Ovalis Hinde

Thousands of Years Ago

The smoking remains of a fallen star blanketed my lands with the promise of further destruction. I felt certain dread as I looked upon the charred wheat fields just outside of Moonstone, the capital city of Talaven. My closest advisors gathered around me, tension in the tight lines of their faces and in the whites of their knuckles as they clutched their weapons.

"It feels like death." Areila edged in front of me as if to shield my body from the rot we all felt creeping toward us. Smoke danced into the wind, and the ground itself seemed to ooze with hate where the fallen star had left behind a perfect circle of black. The ash pulsed, as if it were alive.

Weeks ago, we'd spotted a brilliant white comet

streaking overhead. We'd thought it nothing more than a curiosity. The astronomers had eagerly charted its path through the sky and predicted the moment it would fade from view.

But it never vanished. It turned its path toward *us*.

"This was no normal falling star." Marrk, the lead astronomer of Moonstone, turned toward me, his golden nose hoops glinting beneath the morning sun. "There is some strange magic in this. I can feel it in my bones."

"As can I," I said tightly.

With a frown, I inched closer to the edge of the blackened ground, my emerald silk robe billowing behind me. We were no strangers to magic in this land, but unlike the fae across the Bantam Sea, we mortals were not born with powers. Any gifts we possessed came from gemstones—the emeralds, moonstones, amethysts, tiger-eyes, and onyx we mined from the mountains that stretched along the western coast of our island kingdom.

Still, magic delivered from the heavens above was a discomforting thing indeed.

"Ovalis," Areila warned as I stepped past her. "Stay away from there. We do not know what it will do."

"Someone must find out," I countered. "The city gates are a mere mile from here. If this is some kind of dark magic, or something that might spread, we need to prepare the people of our city to leave."

Areila paled. "Leave? And go where? There are thousands in the city. Tens of thousands. There's nowhere else in this kingdom that can house them all."

"Which is why someone needs to discover whether this is a danger to them. I do not want to force the people of Moonstone to leave their homes unless need be. And yet, I will not ignore this threat. Someone needs to touch that dust and learn what it is."

I took another step toward the circle of black, readying myself. I was the King of Talaven. This was my responsibility, no matter the weakening of my knees or the tightness in my chest. I would protect my people, even if it killed me. There was no other option.

"Your Majesty," Marrk cut in, casting a nervous glance toward the loyal guards on either side of me. They had not objected, though I saw the fear in my heart reflected in their eyes. I had taken a vow to protect my people, but *they* had taken a vow to protect *me*. Watching me walk toward a circle of potential death went against their every instinct. But they would also cut anyone down who tried to stop me.

"Do not try to talk me out of it, Marrk. You know it must be done."

He nodded, his neck bobbing as he swallowed hard. "I will do it. It should be me."

I paused, my leather sandals only inches from the ring of rot. "You?"

"Your Majesty, if this is indeed a dangerous magic that could destroy an entire kingdom, your people will need you to lead them to safety. You are beloved and trusted. Your death would only cause chaos."

"He has a point, Ovalis," Areila called out. "If our people must flee, let them flee by taking your hand, not your son's."

I closed my eyes at the thought of my son, who had come into this world kicking and screaming and balking against his duty from his very first breath. With a heavy sigh, I nodded. "Very well, then."

Marrk's boots crunched the dead grass just beyond the circle of destruction. I opened my eyes and braced myself as he carefully knelt, splaying his fingers toward the dust and ash. He cast me a nervous glance and then nodded.

"The stars be with me," he whispered.

He pressed his palm to the charred ground. For a moment, nothing happened, but I did not dare blink or even breathe. The only sound was the rustle of my silk robe rippling in the wind. And then the ground pulsed—just once, but it was violent enough to knock me sideways into Areila. My guards shouted and grabbed my arms, hauling me away from the blackened ground.

Marrk sucked in a gasp. His eyes rolled back, and then he collapsed.

Panic clutched my heart. I shook off my guards and rushed toward Marrk, grabbing his ankles and pulling him away from the ash. His body was limp, but his chest still moved—only slightly, as if his lungs struggled to pull in enough air. With glazed eyes, he stared up at me, unseeing.

"Areila!" I shouted. "Go fetch a healer!"

Marrk blinked. Fear rushed across his lined face, and he clutched my hand, pulling me toward him. "No, Your Majesty. Go fetch a scribe."

"A scribe? What are you on about? Are you all right? *What happened*?"

His hand tightened around mine. "I've just seen a vision of things to come. Now, and then again...two thousand years from now or even more. And I know what we must do if we want this world to survive against them. We must create the Daughter of Stars."

My heart pulsed. "Survive against who?"

"Immortal creatures who have come to our world on the back of this fallen star. They'll call themselves our gods."

One
Kalen

Present Day

"What is this place?" Niamh's voice echoed through the cavernous room as we took in the unexpected sight before us. A space had been hollowed in the side of the mountain, and towering shelves lined each wall. Weapons, chains, gemstones, and books were clustered in neat little piles with symbols etched below them. There were also some canteens of water and some dried meats. Someone had spent a long time on this place.

In our efforts to chase down Tessa and Oberon, we'd skirted around the base of the mountain toward the light fae army camping in our way. But just before their camp had risen through the mist, Alastair had spotted a hole in

the rock face. A shortcut through the mountain, we'd hoped. Instead, it had brought us to this room.

Alastair frowned and spun one of his earrings absent-mindedly, as he was wont to do. "It's clearly some kind of hidden hoard. Must have taken years to get all this shit in here."

"Yes, but *whose* hoard?" With gleaming silver eyes, Fenella approached a shelf stuffed with little covered trays of dried herbs. She pulled one from the shelf and held it up, squinting. The darkness and mist had followed us into this place. Without torchlight, there was only so far we could see, even with our fae sight. Fenella wrinkled her nose and put the tray back on the shelf. "This is valerian. Looks like there's piles of it."

"Oberon." Toryn swore beneath his breath and pointed at a pile of chains near the door. "This is how he trapped you. He came here to get his hidden chains and valerian, and then he took you out so he could steal Tessa away without having to fight you. He knew he wouldn't win."

I shook my head and turned back toward the hewn archway leading out of the cave. "We're wasting time. This is a dead end, and we need to turn back. If we don't catch up to them..."

My stomach clenched. I couldn't even bear to speak the words out loud, and my Mist Guard already knew the ending of that sentence without me sharing my thoughts. If we didn't reach them in time, Oberon would kill Tessa, all to keep my mother alive for a little longer. I could never let that happen.

No one objected when I pushed back out into the mists, although Fenella hung back just long enough to stuff some valerian into her pockets, along with a handful of tiger-eye gemstones. Curious that this place would have them, I had to admit. I hadn't seen a tiger-eye in several hundred years. They weren't found in Aesirian mines. Had a mortal from across the Bantam Sea built this place? It couldn't have been Oberon or any fae inside of Albyria—they wouldn't have been able to cross the barrier to get here. But Oberon's one-eyed dragon symbol had been all over the place, and the weapons I'd spotted were light fae swords.

None of that mattered, though. Not as long as Oberon had his hands on Tessa.

Frowning, I squared my shoulders and stared out into the mists. The lilting sound of a fife drifted toward us, but the murmur of voices had died beneath the gentle rumble of a small fire. The people in the camp must have gone to bed for the night, though being the soldiers they were, at least three of them would be standing watch while the others slept. Everyone—even the light fae—knew what lurked in the mists: monsters.

And me.

I turned to my Mist Guard just behind me, all silent and waiting for my order. "We'll have to skirt around them as best we can and then make for the bridge. Toryn, are you certain Oberon was taking Tessa back to the city?"

He gave me a solemn nod.

I frowned. It made little sense. Out of all the moves

he might make, that was one I never would have predicted. His city was nothing more than a burnt husk of ash and embers, full of his enemies. I'd sent my warriors to patrol the streets and hunt for any sign of him. A few of my men even camped outside the Tower of Crones, which still stood even after fire had raged through the streets. Oberon's brides were still alive and waiting for him, but surely he must know he could never show his face there again.

But they *were* his brides. Perhaps somewhere in his twisted heart, he held some sort of lingering affection for them. All those years ago, love had been his downfall. His path to the darkness.

And it would be the downfall of us all if we did not find a way to stop him.

"He must be suffering from delirious desperation," I muttered beneath my breath.

Toryn stepped up beside me. "Boudica saw him badly wounded. He clearly knows he's been defeated."

I nodded. "We need to catch up to him."

Just as we crept out from behind the shadow of the mountain, the sky shuddered as if it had been holding its breath for a very long time and had finally gasped for air. An uneasy sensation whispered across the back of my neck, and I dragged my gaze up from the misty landscape to the night-drenched sky. The ground beneath me seemed to tense as I met the sight I'd been dreading all my life. Even through the murky fog, there was no mistaking it. Blazing hot and as bright as diamonds, a comet speared the inky dark.

Niamh gasped, and Toryn staggered to the side.

"Oh, fuck," Alastair muttered. "He's done it."

"It's here." The word scraped from my throat. Four hundred years ago, my mother had warned me of this very day. The comet heralded the return of the gods, those monstrous immortal beings who would be the end of everything we knew and loved. I'd dreamt of this day, feared for it. My mother had told me so little about the gods—the knowledge had been lost over the years, and even what she'd found in the mortal lands had not been much to go on.

But it had been enough.

They were impossible to kill—immortal like fae, but even beyond our capabilities. There were a few ways to kill us: magic, cutting off our heads, and burning us alive. The gods, on the other hand, were indestructible, and their wickedness knew no bounds. When they'd first arrived in these lands thousands of years ago, they'd brought death, destruction, hunger, pain, and fear with them, along with the beasts that now roamed my mists.

And then they'd turned the humans of this world into nothing more than cattle to be brutally slaughtered whenever they needed their next meal.

"We'll kill Oberon," Alastair growled from my side. "It will put a stop to this, right?"

"It might."

There was still too much I didn't know about the prophecy. Mother had made me vow to kill whoever brought back the gods. She believed it would be impossible to stop them as long as that person remained alive, but she'd never explained more than that. For a time, I thought it was because she didn't know. Now I wasn't so certain.

Regardless, there was only one way forward. Oberon had to die. And I would gladly be the one to wield the sword that cut off his head.

Several hours later, we reached the sagging gates of Albyria. The air tasted of soot, and flecks of ash thickened the mists that had descended upon the crimson buildings. The city still burned. A smattering of small fires lit up the dark, flickering across the stone paths. There was little left for them to burn now, and yet they carried on, powered by the remnants of Oberon's magic.

"This place smells like death," Niamh said, wrinkling her nose at the stench.

She was right. A strange scent clogged the air beneath the haze of soot, a roiling, pungent odor unlike anything I'd ever smelled before, not even during all those months I'd spent at war with Oberon, picking my way through solemn battlefields and ruined cities. The feel of it seeped into my pores and filled my gut with an inescapable dread.

"Be on guard," I said to the others when we slowly edged closer to the open gates. As we approached, three forms solidified in the mists. All decked in black fighting leathers, they tensed at the sound of our footsteps but relaxed when they saw my face.

"Your Majesty." The front guard, a tall fae woman, lowered her sword and dipped her head in respect. "Apologies for the steel. We weren't expecting you."

"You were doing your duty." I nodded to her and the two men who stood with her. "Oberon was spotted heading this way. Have you seen him?"

Alarm flickered across her dark features. "No, Your Majesty. We've been stationed here for the past several hours. No one has come or gone in that time. In fact...no one has come or gone since we got here. This place is cursed."

"Knowing Oberon, he would have found another way inside. But keep an eye out, just in case." I moved past the guards, thanking them for their steady service, and led my Mist Guard toward the broken castle that had once loomed on this hill, glittering in shades of gold and crimson. Now it was nothing more than a black smudge against a dark sky.

"The bastard has to be here somewhere," Niamh said, falling into step beside me. "He's not *invisible*."

"Sometimes it feels like he is." I tried to calm my rising panic. I didn't know what I'd expected. Oberon was not stupid. He wouldn't have waltzed through the front gates with Tessa in his iron grip, but I'd still set all my hopes on finding him here. We'd sent Boudica scouting through the skies while we made the trek around the chasm and across the bridge. Oberon had not backtracked to the mountains, as far as we could tell.

He'd released the god on his way to Albyria. And then what?

What had he done to Tessa?

Rage gripped my heart, and my fingers buzzed from the temptation to loose my brutal power on whoever might stand in my way. Tessa was in danger. And I would tear this city apart, piece by piece, until I found her.

Niamh suddenly grabbed my arm. I lifted my eyes to scan the mists, half-expecting to find Oberon's orange eyes glowing in the darkness while his hand wrapped tightly around Tessa's throat. But all I saw were shadows as thick as storm clouds. Niamh leaned closer and hissed into my ear. "Do you see that?"

Alastair stopped beside us and opened his mouth to ask what she meant, but Niamh quickly pressed a finger to her lips. Delight danced in her eyes. Never a good sign.

Morgan, she mouthed at us.

My hand went to the hilt of the sword strapped to my back, dread curling through me. Silently, I scanned the courtyard. And then, just beside the entrance to the Tower of Crones, came a flash of silver. I ground my teeth together. Morgan was here, the fae who had tricked Tessa into believing I'd betrayed her.

The fae who had worked with Oberon to trap us in the mountains so he could steal Tessa away from me.

I stormed through the mists, my eyes narrowed on her unfamiliar form. Even though I had known her for centuries, I'd never seen more than her face and shoulders. She was tall and built strong—that was clear even beneath her steel-capped armor—just as most guards and warriors typically were, but there was something else in the way she stood. Some hidden strength—or hidden power. But Morgan was a common fae. She had no elite power running through her veins. And yet...

My boots crunched a pile of charred wood, and Morgan spun, her hand flying off the door handle at the base of the Tower of Crones. Her silver eyes flashed wide.

"Where is Oberon? Where is...the queen?" My steel whistled through the air as I pulled it from my scabbard, leveling it before me to prove my point. I didn't know how long Morgan had been working against me or how much Oberon had made her lie. Deep down, I knew none of this was her fault. Oberon had tied her to his will centuries ago. But that did not mean I could trust her.

And if Oberon had done anything to harm Tessa, that didn't mean I could forgive Morgan for her part in it.

Her wide eyes spun from me to take in my Mist Guard flanking me—Alastair and Fenella stood on one side, while Toryn and Niamh stood on the other. She pressed her lips together. "Oberon is dead. They're both dead. The last order he gave me was to send you that fake message. It was meant to lure you to the mountains. To be honest, I'm surprised it worked. I thought you would have realized it was nothing but a trap."

It took a moment for her words to sink in. Oberon... dead? My mother—also dead. My eyes burned. I'd lost her once and had only just discovered she'd survived all these years that I'd been searching for answers and vengeance for her death. A part of me had harbored a secret hope, one I hadn't dared speak aloud.

I'd wanted to see her again, no matter what she'd done.

From beside me, Alastair barked out a laugh. "You really expect us to believe that?"

"What a coward," Niamh sneered, raising her voice so that it echoed through the quiet streets. "You're too scared to face us, aren't you, Oberon? Stop pretending and come out from the shadows."

"This is no trick," Morgan said flatly. "The king is dead. Here, I'll prove it. He ordered me never to speak your name aloud, and yet I can say it now: Kalen Denare."

Fenella inched forward, her twin daggers raised. "He could have revoked that order so you could convince us he's dead."

Morgan cocked her head, as if considering Fenella. There was something odd about the movement, something I couldn't quiet place. It was that feeling of hidden power again. An eerie sensation tickled the back of my neck. Had she been lying to me all these years about being a common fae? It wouldn't surprise me.

Nothing about Morgan would surprise me anymore.

"If Oberon is dead, then who killed him?" Niamh asked, her brow arched. "You?"

A smile tugged at the corners of Morgan's lips. "Oh, no. I never could have harmed a hair on Oberon's head. You want to know who killed him? Think of the one person who wants him dead more than anyone else. Tessa Baran."

My sword dropped, and the end punched the ash. "Tessa?" A painful tightening in my throat made the next words difficult to speak. "Where the fuck is she, Morgan? What have you done with her?"

"She fled. From *you*, I imagine." Morgan's eyes flashed with a cunning cruelty. "Did you not realize what happened when you saw the comet streaking through the skies? Tessa Baran has brought back the gods. And if I recall correctly, that means you have to kill her now."

Two
Tessa

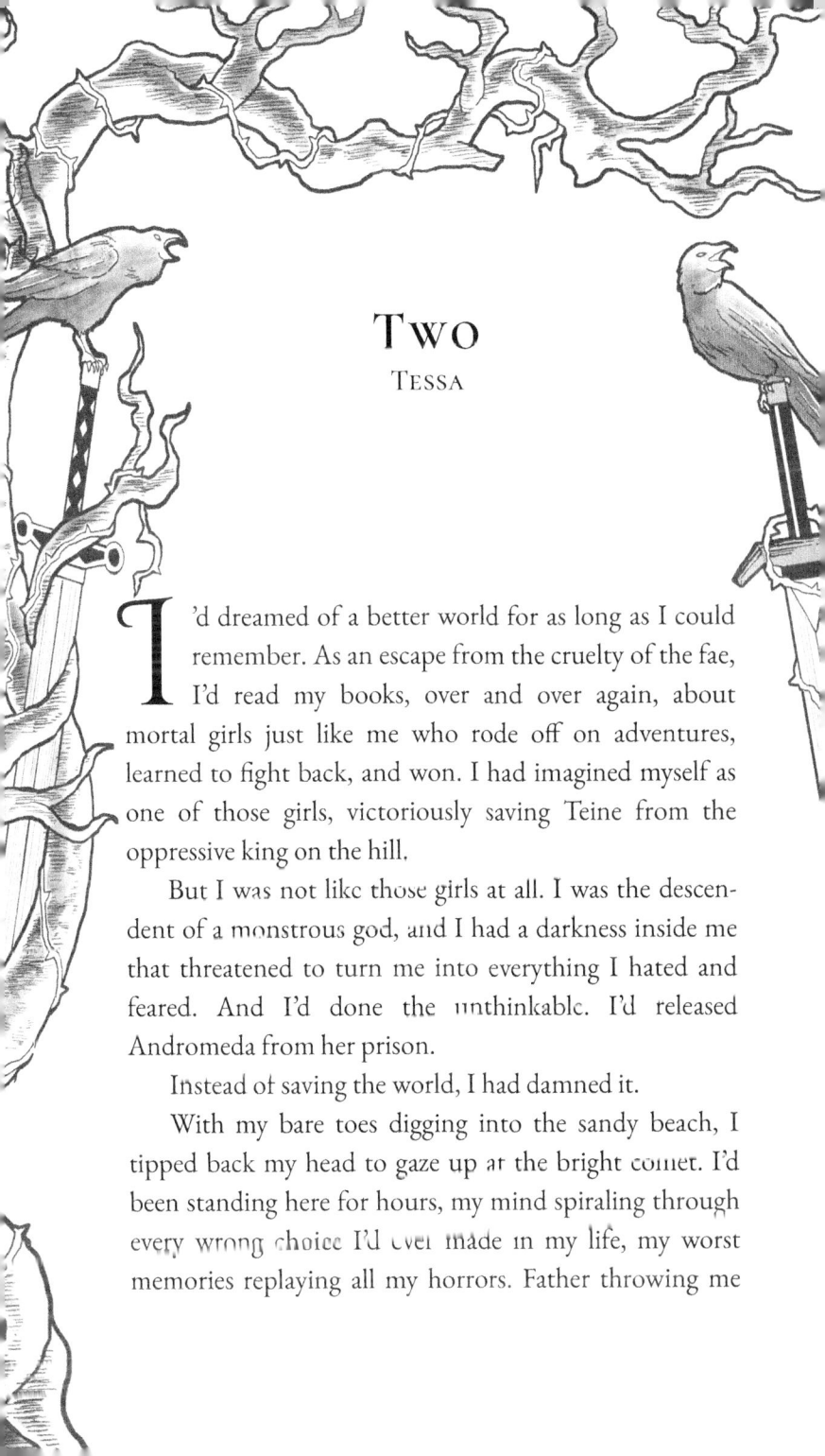

I'd dreamed of a better world for as long as I could remember. As an escape from the cruelty of the fae, I'd read my books, over and over again, about mortal girls just like me who rode off on adventures, learned to fight back, and won. I had imagined myself as one of those girls, victoriously saving Teine from the oppressive king on the hill.

But I was not like those girls at all. I was the descendent of a monstrous god, and I had a darkness inside me that threatened to turn me into everything I hated and feared. And I'd done the unthinkable. I'd released Andromeda from her prison.

Instead of saving the world, I had damned it.

With my bare toes digging into the sandy beach, I tipped back my head to gaze up at the bright comet. I'd been standing here for hours, my mind spiraling through every wrong choice I'd ever made in my life, my worst memories replaying all my horrors. Father throwing me into the mists. Oberon cutting into my skin. And me... piercing Kalen with the Mortal Blade.

My shoulders bowed beneath the weight of it all.

I didn't cry, though a part of me wished I could. My soul was too raw to do anything but give in to the numbness creeping through me.

At every step along the way, I'd only made things worse. All I'd wanted was to save my family—my people. I'd wanted to stop Oberon. It turned out stopping him was the worst thing I could have done. And so maybe he'd been right. Maybe I should be locked up and hidden away in the vault so that I couldn't hurt anyone else ever again. Because now the gods were on their way, and they would destroy everything. Maybe I didn't deserve to be here. Maybe this world would be better off if I wasn't.

I sat hard on the beach, pulled my knees up to my chest, and stared into the mist until all my thoughts were drowned beneath the waves of my self-loathing.

A soft, wet snout nudged my cheek. Startled, I jerked up my head to see Oberon's horse staring down at me with his dark, unblinking eyes. I hadn't noticed him approach. I hadn't even registered he was still here with me. I reached up and placed a hand against his pale gray muzzle. He was probably hungry.

That realization was the only thing that could cut through the fog in my mind. Sighing, I stood.

"Let's find you some food," I said, even knowing he couldn't understand me. Unlike Midnight, this creature was nothing more than a regular horse—at least, I assumed so. Joint eaters could not survive in the sun, and this horse had once belonged to Oberon, which meant he'd lived in Albyria. Still, I could have sworn his ears flicked in anticipation.

"What shall we call you?" I asked him as I led him over to the pack I'd dumped on the ground. When Oberon had taken me, he'd relieved me of my weapons, but he hadn't taken my supplies: a canteen of water, a handful of dried meat, a heel of bread, and two apples, along with some rope and a bedroll. I passed the horse an apple and gave him a once-over.

He was a magnificent beast. Tall and powerful, he towered over me, a protective shield against the chilly breeze. His mane was the color of wheat, and he had a long tail that snapped at the air. I handed him another apple when he finished the first.

"I think you'd like my sister. She loves apples, too."

He nickered, and then chomped his powerful teeth into the fruit. Despite the sorrow weighing me down, I smiled. As he ate his snack, I nibbled on a piece of dried meat and turned my thoughts to the present. I'd been avoiding the truth for as long as possible, but I couldn't ignore it forever.

And the reality was, I needed a plan. I could not stay here on the beach for days on end. I didn't have enough food or any shelter, and eventually, shadowfiends would find me. But where could I go? What in the name of light did I do now?

Returning to Endir did not seem like an option. Kalen would be forced to kill me now, and even though I deserved it, I couldn't bear the thought of him stabbing me in the heart. I lifted my eyes to the misty horizon. There were the human kingdoms, of course. I could journey to Sunport and board a ship to sail away from Aesir.

I could leave it all behind, find someplace rural that only a few people called home, build a little cabin in the woods and then a fence to protect the world from me.

I could abandon everyone.

I closed my eyes, sagging forward. "But I can't do that."

The horse nudged me again. I glanced up at him and frowned as he angled his body to the side, and then lowered his head, facing *away* from the sea, toward Albyria. It was almost as if he were trying to communicate with me...

But that was impossible. He was just a horse, and why would he want to return to that burning city?

"There's nothing for us in Albyria," I said to him. "The streets have been ravaged by flames, and Kalen's warriors are patrolling the city to keep the light fae from retaking it. If we go there, we'll probably both be in trouble. You could get hurt just by being with me."

I could have sworn the horse narrowed his eyes. With a stomp of his front hoof, he nodded east again.

He blinked at me, and I blinked at him. Frowning, I gazed toward the mountains that obscured my view of the burning city. We were too far for me to see Albyria with the naked eye, even if the mountains weren't there, but I looked toward it all the same. What was the point in going to Albyria? What was the point in doing anything at all, other than leaving this continent in the hands of those who would protect it, not ruin it?

The fae would be forced to fight the gods now. The fate of the world was in their hands, and they'd be far better off without me in the way, making matters worse. But *how* would they fight them? Kalen didn't seem to have the answers any more than I did.

But there was another who might know what to do. Kalen's mother.

Something stirred in my chest, sparking in my blood and clearing the fog in my head. Kalen's mother had journeyed to the human kingdoms and heard a prophecy about the future of this world. She knew things about the gods that no one else did—she'd been communicating with half of Andromeda's essence all this time.

"The Crones," I said, sucking in a sharp breath before turning toward the horse. "They gave me that vision of Oberon's past. They know everything...or at the very least, all of it is in their heads. If I could get to them and go through more of their visions..."

Maybe I could find the answer to fighting back.

Maybe I could right my wrongs.

Another flash of pain went through my heart. There was a chance I could fix things, but I was just as likely to do something wrong. Everything I did made things worse. Because the truth was, I was a monster, just like the gods. Their darkness lurked inside me; their destructive power was coursing through my veins. I'd felt it all my life, never knowing what it was. But I knew it now.

I was the Daughter of Death.

The horse stomped his hoof. The thud broke through my dark thoughts. Maybe I was right, and I was too dangerous to stay here while the fae fought the gods. I should leave. And I would. But I had to do something to help before I left this continent. I had to try to give the fae an edge—or at least even the odds. I would find out what I could from the Crones, and then I would pass the information along to Kalen's Mist Guard. It would be my parting gift—the only thing I could give them after dooming them all.

And then I would leave Aesir and never return.

The secret entrance into Albyria still stood among the rubble. I pulled aside the tapestry with its ends charred and curling, and peered into the silent street. A few fires still dotted the cobblestones, but most of the smoke had cleared. I could have heard a pin drop for how quiet it was.

My heart ached as I took in the destruction. The buildings nearest the wall had once been homes, but they were nothing but blackened shells now. How many light fae had died in that fire? Those who had survived, where had they gone? Were they hiding out in the city somewhere, or had they crossed the bridge to brave the mists?

Silver—it seemed the only fitting name—nudged me, and I bit back a sigh. "Yes, all right, all right. I'm going through."

I pushed past the tapestry, holding my breath, and gazed around. Kalen's guards could be anywhere nearby, and they would hear and see me far before I would see them. The last thing I wanted was for them to catch me here. Then they'd be forced to deliver me to their king.

I clamped down the pain that threatened to roar back to life. For a moment in time, it had felt like fate had turned a kind smile on me after so many years of cruelty, pain, and hate. Kalen and I had found each other—twin flames—despite everything, despite the world working against the both of us. I'd thought he'd be by my side for years to come, but fate had a different plan in mind.

Swallowing, I blinked my burning eyes. Now was not the time for those thoughts. It wasn't fate's fault we'd ended up like this. It was mine.

I cast a glance over my shoulder where the tapestry half-covered the hole in the wall. Through the ripped shreds, Silver watched me with a steady stare. "You should move away from there so that no one spots you. I'll be back soon."

Hopefully.

With night and mist drenching the city in darkness, it was easy to hide among the shadows of the buildings. I eased down the nearest street with my eyes trained on the fog, searching for any sign of movement. Kalen's warriors were most likely stationed near the front gates and the castle. Unfortunately, the castle was exactly where I needed to go if I wanted to reach the Tower of Crones.

Soot sprayed from the ground with every step I took closer to the courtyard. Soon, voices drifted toward me on the wind. Achingly familiar voices. Heart in my throat, I threw myself up against the nearest stone wall and didn't dare take a single breath.

"You're lying." Kalen's distant growl ripped through me. My lips parted, my hands tightening into fists.

Kalen was here. How? And why? When I'd found myself alone on the shores of Aesir, I'd assumed his Mist Guard had somehow forced him to return to Endir. They knew the truth about what had happened out there—or so I'd thought.

But he was here now and very much not in Endir.

Which meant...

My heart pounded. Kalen must not know I'd released the god.

"I said..." Morgan's familiar voice sounded hollow—and *wrong*—and tinged with dark, twisted delight. "...your little mortal plaything was the one who caused that comet to appear. Don't look so shocked. You told me about the prophecy centuries ago, and I've been on the lookout for it ever since. For the longest time, just like you, I thought Oberon would be the one to cause it. Looks like we were both wrong."

Well, it seemed he *hadn't* known, but he certainly did now.

I eyed the distance from my hidden spot against the wall to the doorway leading into the Tower of Crones. From here, it was difficult to make out anything other than vague shadows in the mists, but those shadows rose high into the hidden clouds above. Kalen and Morgan blocked my way.

I needed to find shelter somewhere and wait for them to leave.

So with one last glance in Kalen's direction, I spun around the side of the building and ventured into what had once been a tavern full of boisterous laughter, the clinking of tankards, and the lilting songs of bards. Now it was home to nothing but death.

Three
Niamh

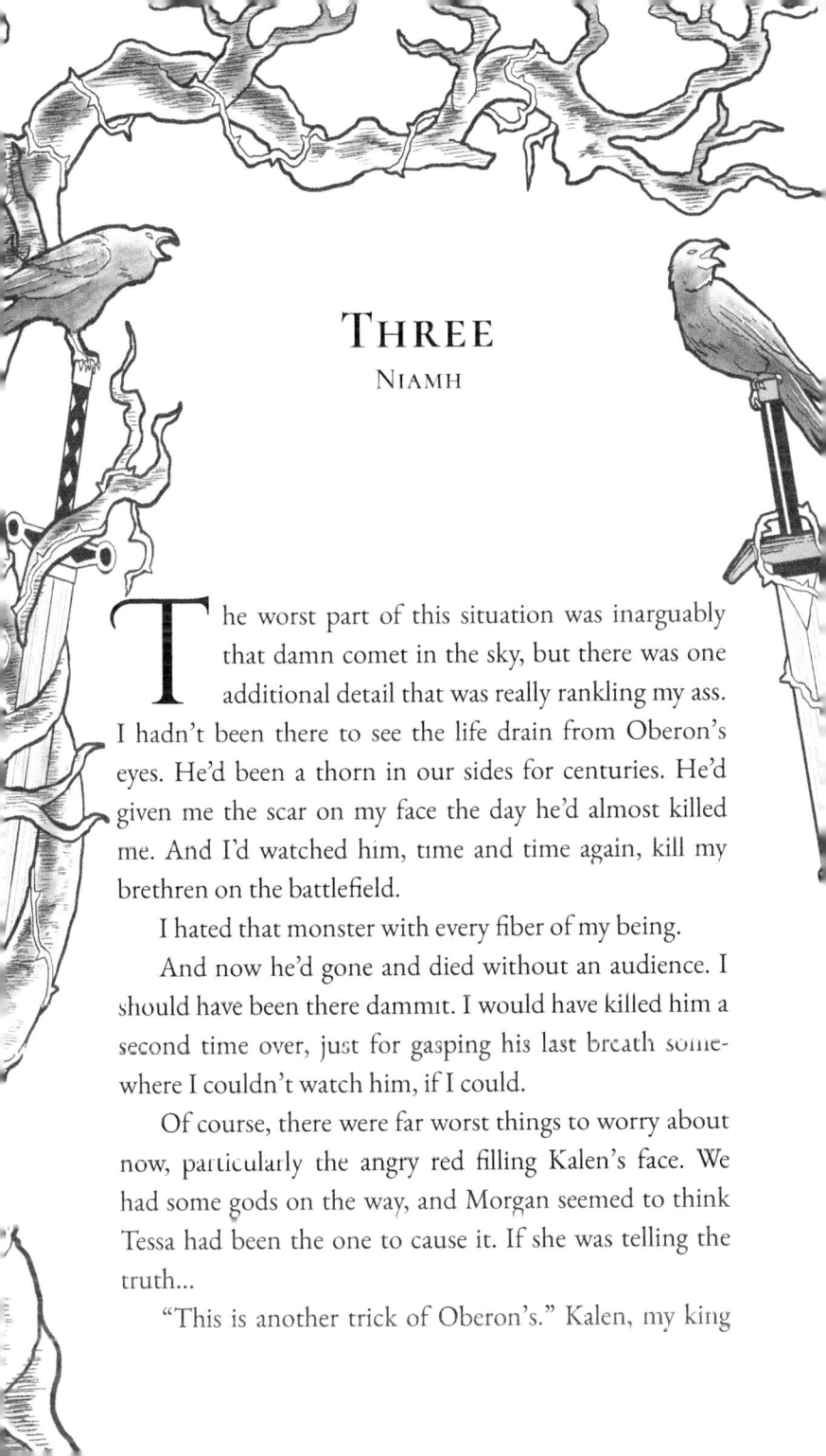

The worst part of this situation was inarguably that damn comet in the sky, but there was one additional detail that was really rankling my ass. I hadn't been there to see the life drain from Oberon's eyes. He'd been a thorn in our sides for centuries. He'd given me the scar on my face the day he'd almost killed me. And I'd watched him, time and time again, kill my brethren on the battlefield.

I hated that monster with every fiber of my being.

And now he'd gone and died without an audience. I should have been there dammit. I would have killed him a second time over, just for gasping his last breath somewhere I couldn't watch, if I could.

Of course, there were far worst things to worry about now, particularly the angry red filling Kalen's face. We had some gods on the way, and Morgan seemed to think Tessa had been the one to cause it. If she was telling the truth...

"This is another trick of Oberon's." Kalen, my king

and closest friend, stormed toward Morgan, who still stood in the doorway of the Tower of Crones, looking eerily unbothered by the whole situation. She did know who she was poking at, right? "Tessa never would have done that. She *knows* what it means." He pointed a finger at the sky. "Tell me the truth. *Now,* Morgan."

Morgan was unarmed, but there was a dangerous glint in her eye—the hint of a threat. With a whistling breath, I slid an arrow from my quiver and notched it in my bow. According to her, she was a common fae, but... well, I no longer trusted a single fucking thing she'd ever said. "You even move your boot an inch, and this arrow will go straight through your skull."

Morgan looked at me then, and something strange passed across her expression. "I've told you nothing but the truth. Search the streets if you don't believe me. Oberon isn't here, and this isn't a trap. But I can see why you'd struggle to believe a word I say, knowing I've been forced to obey him all these years. So search away."

I narrowed my eyes. Since she was fae, it was impossible to scent her truth or her lies. But something about her words didn't sit right with me. Or the way she looked at Kalen, like she was a hunter and he was her prey.

"Move away from the Tower of Crones," Kalen said in a low, dangerous voice.

"Your Mist Guard has made it very clear that I should do no such thing. If I move, Niamh will shoot me."

"Niamh," Kalen called over his shoulder, "search the streets. Take Toryn and Fenella with you."

I opened my mouth to argue, but the tension in Kalen's body practically hummed through the courtyard.

His mist pulsed from his skin, pounding with every thud of his heart. He was teetering on the edge of a very dangerous cliff, his magic likely scraping against his skin, desperate to get out. His anger fueled it—called for it, really. I'd only seen him lose control a handful of times, but it always started like this.

"Careful, Kal," I warned him.

His mists whorled and snapped. "I'm fine, and Alastair will stay with me. Just go."

Frowning, I lowered my bow and hooked my arm into Toryn's elbow. "Come on. Let's go hunt down a light fae bastard."

Toryn gave our king a sidelong glance, but then he nodded, following Fenella and me away from the courtyard where Alastair and Kalen remained to keep an eye on Morgan. I didn't really want to miss a word of the conversation, but if Morgan was lying and Oberon was hiding out somewhere nearby...a delicious excitement whipped through me. I wanted to be the one who found him.

After we rounded the corner, Toryn loosed a tense breath. "What do you think about all that?"

"I think we're fucked."

Fenella scowled. "Do you really think Oberon is dead?"

I pursed my lips and moved toward the nearest building just beyond of the courtyard—a sagging old pub that had been fairly untouched by the fires. "All I know is Morgan is hiding something, but what that might be—"

With a shove, I threw open the door and shot a cursory glance through the darkened building. My fingers tightened on my bow when I spotted the figure leaping up beside a table near the back wall, a wild look in her deep brown eyes. She glanced from me to Toryn to Fenella and back to me again. And when I looked at Tessa Baran's horror-stricken face, I knew—*knew*—that every word Morgan had spoken was the truth.

"Well, shit," I muttered.

Tessa held up her hands. "Wait, listen. It was an accident."

"Tessa?" Toryn started to walk toward her—he'd always had a soft spot for the girl—but Fenella threw out an arm to block him. Seemed she was on the same page as me.

"Let's all just take a moment," I said quietly as I gave Toryn a small nod toward the open door. We'd barely left the courtyard, and Kalen's keen hearing picked up things even I missed at times. We couldn't risk him hearing her voice, not yet. Not until we understood the full situation. If his vow snapped him into action…

Toryn's lips flattened as he understood the direction of my thoughts. "He would never harm her."

"I don't think he has a fucking choice," Fenella muttered.

Tessa paled while Toryn closed the door behind us, hopefully blocking any of our words from reaching the others outside. Tension pounded in my skull. Truth was, outside, I knew I was the portrait of calm confidence. I'd learned to mask my thoughts long ago. I would take control of this situation and make it right somehow—at least, that was the front I presented.

But deep down, I had no idea what the fuck I was going to do about any of this.

If Tessa had really done it, if she'd been the one behind the comet in the sky, there was nothing anyone could do to stop Kalen from enacting his part of the vow. His words—his promise to his mother—were laced in ancient magic that could never be broken. Not by any of us.

Only by Kalen's mother herself. And according to Morgan, she was dead.

Even if Tessa hadn't meant to release the god, it wouldn't matter. Kalen would be forced to go after her. And that might very well be the last crack in his already shattered soul. He'd never said it, of course, but I could read the truth in his eyes, in the way he looked at her. He might not realize it yet, but he'd fallen in love with the girl. And if he killed her, it would *destroy* him.

"Now, I'm going to listen to what you have to say," I started as Toryn edged back up beside me and Fenella, who was staring at Tessa with the same mask of calm I wore, "because I know what this will do to my king when he finds out you're here—"

"You're going to tell him?" Tessa hovered behind the table, keeping the charred wooden furniture between her and us, like that would save her if I had to make a move. And damn it, I might have to. At the end of the day, my loyalty was to my people and my king. I would shoulder his burden if there was no other way.

"I haven't decided what I'm going to do." I lifted my arrow. "Now talk."

Tessa's eyes darted to Toryn, and out of the corner of my eye, I saw him give her an encouraging nod.

"We'll figure this out," he said. "Just tell us what happened."

And then she looked at Fenella. She got no word of encouragement there.

So Tessa blew out a breath. "I know this looks bad, and well...I guess it is. If you're wondering why I vanished, it was because Oberon took me from the camp when we were all sleeping."

"Not sleeping," Fenella corrected, her fingers twitching by the daggers strapped to her side. "He hit us with a dose of valerian fog. Knocked us out for so long, you were halfway to Albyria by the time we woke up, according to Boudica."

Tessa frowned. "That's odd. The valerian only knocked me out for an hour or two."

"How is that possible?" Toryn asked.

"I don't know." Tessa shook her head. "When I woke up, I was on the back of a horse, and Oberon was leading me through the mists. He wanted to bring me back here, to lock me and the gemstone necklace in a vault beneath the castle."

"He wanted to lock you in *a vault*?" I asked incredulously.

"Shockingly, Oberon had a change of heart near the end." Her eyes went distant, and her jaw tightened. "All this time, Oberon knew exactly what I was—the descendent of the God of Death. And he somehow knew that I —far more than Nellie ever has—suffer from that darkness. He wanted to lock me away so I could never use my powers against this world. Me and the necklace." Sighing, she closed her eyes. "Oberon was a monster, but...he tried to fix things in the end. I didn't realize it until it was too late."

I knew some of this, of course. Kalen had confided in all of us after he'd learned the truth about Tessa's heritage. At the time, he hadn't seemed at all concerned. Thousands of years was a very long time, especially for mortals. Generations had come and gone, and the power would be diluted by now. Tessa had never shown any inclination she might have powers, other than a tad more physical strength than most mortals. But that could partly be explained by how much she'd trained to scale that damn chasm wall.

Tessa continued. "He had the gemstone necklace—the one that held half of Andromeda's power—on him, but it was hidden in his cloak. I went to stab him with the Mortal Blade, and..."

My eyes widened, understanding at once. "You stabbed him, which meant he and everything on him turned to ash, including that gemstone. That's how the god was released."

This wasn't good. Morgan had been right. In Tessa's attempt to free herself from Oberon, she'd inadvertently destroyed the gemstone. She was the one who had released the god, which meant...

Sighing, I closed my eyes, and then quickly reopened them as I heard steel slash the air.

"I am sorry, Tessa," Fenella said in a tight voice as she aimed her twin daggers at the poor girl's face. "Kalen will be forced to kill you, and I can't let him do that. It would destroy him. I'll have to kill you myself."

Four
Tessa

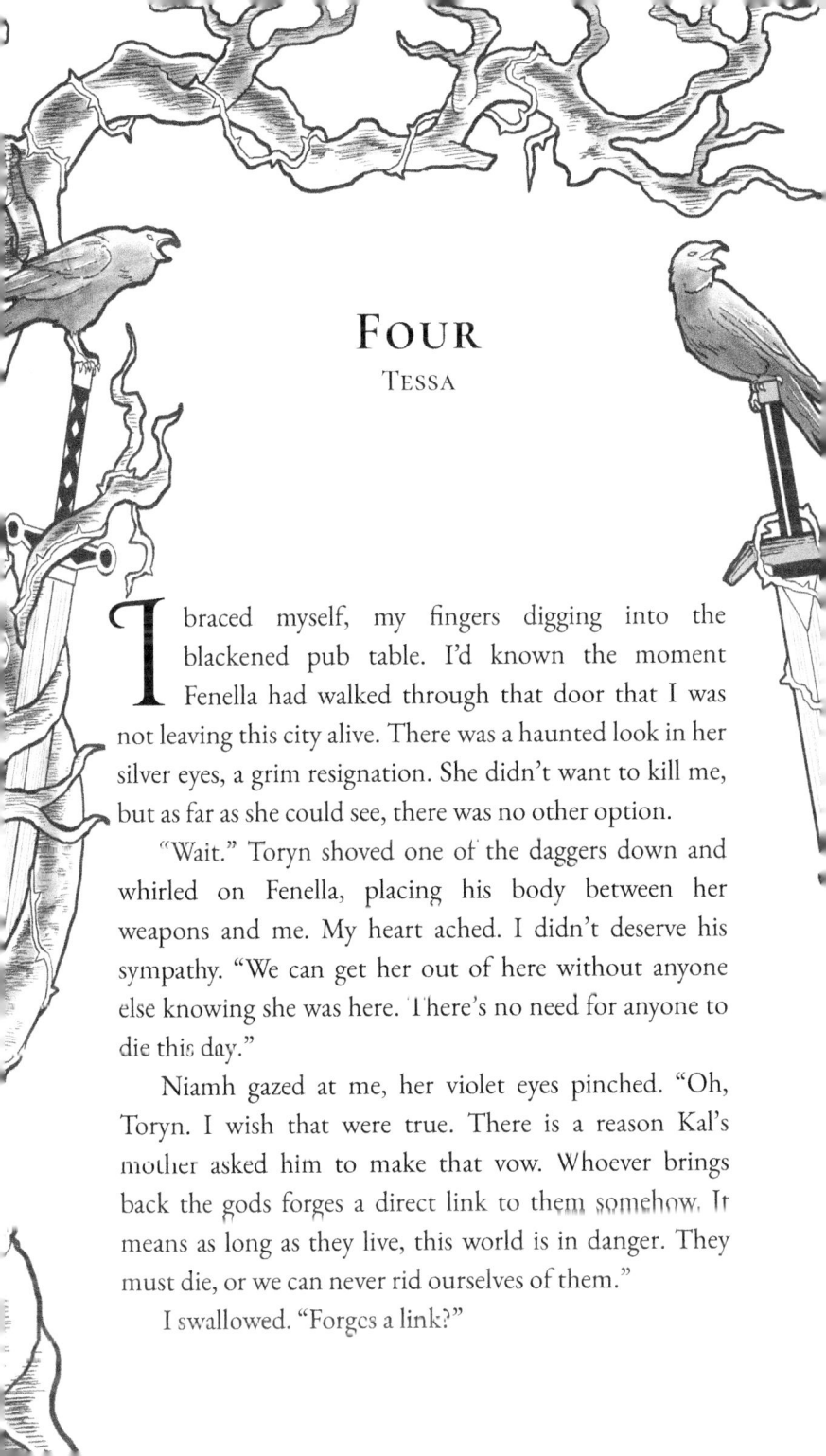

I braced myself, my fingers digging into the blackened pub table. I'd known the moment Fenella had walked through that door that I was not leaving this city alive. There was a haunted look in her silver eyes, a grim resignation. She didn't want to kill me, but as far as she could see, there was no other option.

"Wait." Toryn shoved one of the daggers down and whirled on Fenella, placing his body between her weapons and me. My heart ached. I didn't deserve his sympathy. "We can get her out of here without anyone else knowing she was here. There's no need for anyone to die this day."

Niamh gazed at me, her violet eyes pinched. "Oh, Toryn. I wish that were true. There is a reason Kal's mother asked him to make that vow. Whoever brings back the gods forges a direct link to them somehow. It means as long as they live, this world is in danger. They must die, or we can never rid ourselves of them."

I swallowed. "Forges a link?"

Niamh nodded. "Yes, through magic, much like the forging of a vow. At least, that's what we think."

A question rose from the depths of my sorrow, and the clouds in my mind parted just long enough for a seed of hope to sprout through the mist. "Are you certain about this?"

She frowned. "Well, Bellicent was very vague about most of this, but she was clear about that. Someone will forge a bond with the god, unbreakable in any way other than death."

"I didn't forge a bond," I said quickly, my nails turning black as I dug them into the soot-covered table. "I made a vow once, with Kalen, and I know what it felt like —that magic. I didn't feel anything at all when the gemstone was destroyed. Nothing but regret, but that's beside the point."

Toryn turned toward me then, hope in his eyes, while Fenella still clung to her daggers.

"I stabbed Oberon, yes, but...I actually didn't mean to. Well, I did, but I hesitated. He was acting so strangely and telling me about the vault." I shook my head, the memories rushing through my mind. "He started shouting, and then he stumbled forward. It was like he was... like he was shoved."

Suddenly, the pub door was flung open, and Kalen's powerful, mist-enshrouded figure appeared in the doorframe. Morgan stood just behind him with a strange light dancing in her eyes. I shuddered at the way she looked at me.

But it was nothing compared to the twisted expression on Kalen's face. Fury and despair raged across his features. Those sapphire eyes glowed. Mist spilled from his skin, coating the entire room in a fog so thick, it almost made me choke.

"Kal." Toryn shifted sideways to block Kalen's view of me. But despite his expression, despite knowing he'd likely made an unbreakable vow to destroy me, my heart still leapt at the sight of him. He was terrifying and beautiful and consumed by the mists that had threatened my existence for as long as I could remember. And I loved every single part of him.

"Move out of the way, Toryn," he commanded in that powerful voice of his, pain etched in every word.

Fenella frowned and glanced over her shoulder, though she kept one eye on the place where I still stood, backed against the pub's far wall. "You don't have to put yourself through this, Kal. I can bear this burden for you."

"*No one* is bearing this burden." His voice became a growl as he moved around Fenella and Niamh, his glowing eyes locked on my face. "Did you not listen to what she just said? Tessa didn't kill Oberon. He *killed himself*. None of this is her fault, and she will not die for it." He stepped toward me, his body humming. "No one will lay a hand on her, including me."

My knees nearly buckled with relief. I stared at him, my heart racing, a part of me wondering if I could have heard him wrong. These were the words I'd longed for him to say, but...surely it couldn't be that easy.

"But your vow," Morgan said from the doorframe. "Tessa is the one who brought back the gods, so—"

Kalen's eyes narrowed, and he whipped toward

Morgan. "Fuck the vow. Tessa wasn't the one who brought back the gods. *Oberon* was. He is dead, which means I am finally free from this endless torment. The real question is, who in the moon's name are *you*?"

My heart clenched as Kalen, Niamh, and Fenella stared down Morgan. Just behind her, I spied Alastair widening his stance to block her from any escape attempt. She lifted her chin and stared right back in challenge, and I understood at once what Kalen had meant by his question. I'd been so distracted by the comet and Oberon's death and my fear of what might happen next that I'd forgotten what Morgan had told us when she'd sent that raven.

Oberon had planned to transfer Bellicent into Morgan's fae body. When he'd captured me, it hadn't seemed like he'd gone through with it, but...

What if he *had*? What if this was Bellicent Denare standing in front of us?

"I am Morgan Allanach," she said in a steady voice. "And I am finally free of King Oberon's control over my life, which included, as you well know, lying to you. He forced me to send you that raven so he could set a trap. I don't blame you for not trusting me now, but that's the truth of it. Do you really think he would have allowed me to contact you without his permission?"

"You did contact us for months. Years, even," Niamh said, cocking her head at the silver-haired light fae.

"True." Morgan nodded. "And then he found out what I was doing and forbade me from ever doing it again."

"Prove it," Alastair barked from behind her. "What was your mother's name?"

Morgan paled. "Keira."

Fenella leaned forward and pressed her small blade against Morgan's throat. "That's too easy. Bellicent could know that information. Try something else. Something only Morgan Allanach would know. Something she never would have shared with Oberon or his queen."

Morgan's eyes darted to the side, and she hissed.

Kalen moved to my side and wound his arm around my back, tugging me close. His mist curled around me, a comforting embrace, even as he kept his hard gaze locked on Morgan. It took all my strength not to sag against him. As I'd wandered through the mists, watching the comet streak through the skies, I would have given up *everything* just to see him. One more time. And now, here he was.

"I have an idea," I said, tensing when every eye in the room turned my way. "If Oberon went through with it, Morgan will have that mark on her back. The same one I have—the one-eyed dragon. It's part of the ritual."

Morgan smiled.

There was something in her expression that unnerved me, even though this seemed like a good idea. Oberon had to carve the mark into the vessel's skin with the ancient comet's dust. It created the magic that allowed the transfer to happen. If Morgan was Bellicent, she'd have that mark. But the look in her eye felt wrong—like we'd walked straight into another trap.

Fenella dug her blade into Morgan's neck and hissed into her ear. A trickle of blood dripped down her pale skin. "You hear that? Show us your back."

Morgan held up her hands and met my gaze. "I can't show you my back if you're trying to slice my throat."

"Fenella," Kalen warned.

She huffed and dropped back. "You don't deserve our mercy, especially if you're *her*."

I glanced up at Kalen, taking in the tensing of his jaw and the darkness around his eyes. I could only imagine what he must be feeling right now. Only a few weeks ago, he'd believed his mother had been dead for centuries. Since then, storm cloud after storm cloud of new information had opened the skies above him, drenching him in the truth. His mother was alive—or she had been. And she'd been working with Oberon, using the god's power to prolong her life. Now she might be standing before us, pretending to be someone else entirely.

If it were me, I'd be seconds away from ripping the sky apart.

With steady calm, Morgan slowly unbuckled the bracers around her armor. She slid off the steel and dropped it on the ground, leaving her in a stained tunic that clung to her sweat-drenched skin. She kept her eyes locked on my face as she tugged down the material and showed us her back.

Her skin was clear and smooth. There wasn't a single mark on her.

A whistling breath escaped Kalen's throat, and his grip around my waist tightened. "You're not her," he said, his voice rough. "You're not my mother."

"I'm sorry, Kalen," Morgan said, pulling the shirt back over her shoulder. "Your mother is dead."

His arm trembled where he held me close, but there

was no visible sign of his suffering. I'd heard the disappointment in his voice, though. Despite what it would have meant, a part of him had hoped we'd find that mark on Morgan's shoulder. It would have meant Bellicent was alive. After all these years, he'd be able to speak to her again.

An ache formed in my chest. I understood how he felt more than I wanted to admit. My father had done so many terrible things—things I still hadn't fully processed. Might never process. He had hurt me. He'd hurt Nellie, too. And yet, I couldn't hate him. I still wished I could see him again, if only so I could say goodbye.

If only so I could move on from it all.

"I still don't trust her," Fenella said, grabbing Morgan's arms and twisting them behind her back. A moment later, manacles snapped around her wrists, and Fenella hauled her out of the pub by pulling on a heavy chain. Where had she gotten that? "We'll take her with us and lock her in the dungeons until we can decide what to do with her."

"Kalen," Morgan said sharply, vanishing out into the streets with Niamh and Toryn just behind her. "Surely you don't agree with this."

Kalen closed his eyes, and the door slammed.

And then it was just the two of us in the pub, clinging to one another. A moment passed before I found the words.

"It's a good thing that it's not her," I said softly. "It would have hurt more, if it were."

"I know. Still hurts, though."

A moment passed in silence, my heart twisting into

tangled ribbons of unease. I hated to shatter our reunion, but I couldn't stop the questions that tumbled through my mind. Regardless of what Kalen insisted, I knew what I'd done. I'd destroyed Oberon and the necklace...

"Kalen."

"Hmm?"

"Are you certain I'm not a threat? That I'm not the one the vow was talking about?"

And that was when he opened his eyes, a fierceness returning to his expression. He took me by the shoulders and turned me to face him, his eyes sweeping across every inch of my face. "Listen to me. You did nothing wrong, and I will not listen to anyone who says differently."

"Tell me the vow again. The exact words she said."

He sucked in a breath, and for a moment, I didn't think he would tell me. But then he said, "If you see a comet in the sky, it means a god is returning. You need to kill whoever caused that to happen. That person must die."

I started to speak, but he pressed a finger to my lips.

"You didn't cause it. Oberon did."

I moved his hand aside. "This is a loophole and nothing more."

"No," he growled. "I will not harm you. I will not let *anyone else* harm you, do you hear me? Oberon caused it, and he is dead. My vow has been fulfilled. Do you really think I would be able to stand here and hold you like this if it weren't?"

He had a point, but something did not sit right with me. It seemed too easy when it came to something as terrifying and world-changing as the return of the gods.

To prophecies and centuries-long vows. To gemstone necklaces hidden in vaults, and a comet hurtling through night-drenched skies. It was all so impossibly *big*.

How could it come down to an accident as easily solved as this?

"I hope you're right," was all I said. "Either way, it's clearly not over. That comet is still in the sky."

He palmed my cheek and smiled. "It's not over, but nothing is going to happen to you. I won't let it. We've beaten Oberon. We'll find a way to fight what's next." His words stirred hope in my chest. Maybe he was right. Maybe I couldn't see past the darkness inside me to accept that the worst of it was over.

But then angry shouts rang in the courtyard, and all that hope fell to my feet.

FIVE
RUARI

A few days ago, a little mouse walked into a trap. It wasn't a trap I set, mind you, but I happily cast the net the moment I saw the lost brunette wandering through the mists. She was the answer to all the light fae troubles, including mine. I had done my part, according to the instructions the mortals of Talaven had given me, and now it was time for my reward.

Nellie Baran would get me my city back.

Only a few hundred light fae had escaped from the smoldering ruins of Albyria. Many members of our court had been caught in the initial blast, and the commoners had not fared much better. The screaming, the chaos, the flames licking the sky...that had been terrible on its own. But then the shadowfiends had come.

I'd gone for my brothers and sisters first, and then the many guards who were more family to me than my mother and father ever had been. Eventually, we'd reached the base of the mountain and set up camp. And I'd wondered if we would ever find a home again. Night after night passed—days did, too, but we no longer knew what time it was. Up was down and down was up and everything was covered in a blanket of heavy darkness.

I'd been warned of this, of course, and I'd made preparations for it by squirrelling supplies away in a nearby cave, but experiencing it was far different than anything my imagination had conjured.

Not long after two of our horses had vanished from camp, I'd spotted a slip of a girl creeping along the wooden wall that stood between the light fae camp and Teine. I'd recognized her, even though her form was nothing more than a smudge of shadows. For years, I'd kept an eye on her and her sister for my father—and for the mortals of Talaven.

"Tessa and Nellie Baran are the descendants of a god," my father had told me at least two decades ago, his eyes burning as bright as his flames. "Keep a close watch on them."

"Of a god? Which god?" But I'd already known the answer to that, of course.

"The God of Death."

"How?" I had glanced at the onyx necklace he or my mother always carried. As his eldest son, I was one of the few who knew everything that gemstone represented and what might happen if the god's power ever escaped. Still, he'd continued to use it, despite the risks. All to keep my wicked mother alive.

"I do not know."

"Do the sisters have powers? And what of the other humans? If Tessa and Nellie are descendants, surely that means there's more of them in that village. They've been trapped here for hundreds of years, just as we have."

I had already known the answers to these questions, but I'd needed to find out how much my father knew, how much he suspected. It could have affected everything.

He had shaken his head. "I'm not certain, but I think they're the only ones. Apparently, it can only be passed from father to daughter, and it must have skipped many generations. But the stars have aligned now, and one of them will be the perfect candidate for Bellicent. This might be the final time she has to transfer bodies."

"Of course," I'd said tightly.

And so I had watched the Baran sisters for years. I had memorized their mannerisms and every small shift in their expressions. I'd seen my father dig into Tessa's back, searching for a pair of wings that didn't exist yet, and Nellie bravely brandishing a broom in a sad attempt to help. And I had hidden in the forest shadows, watching Tessa scale the chasm and then pass stolen gemstones through the wall—something I had, to this day, kept to myself.

So when Nellie had appeared after the Breaking of Albyria, I knew her in the darkness.

"Nellie Baran." I approached her by the wall, glad the others were sleeping. The light fae were hungry, angry, and scared. Best to keep them from knowing a "mortal" was in their midst.

She stiffened and whirled toward me, raising her fists. Her fingers were curved like claws, and the nails were sharp and long—longer than anything I'd ever seen before. Her brown eyes were haunted, matching the muddy tunic and trousers she wore, along with the sturdy leather boots. At her waist, she carried a dagger, though I doubted she knew how to use it. She hadn't gone for it when she'd heard my voice, after all. Instead, she showed me her claws. It was difficult for me not to smile at that.

"So my father's theory was true then," I said in a good-natured voice, slinging my hands into my trouser pockets. "You got the raw end of the deal, as far as the god's power is concerned."

She hissed at me, exposing her razor-sharp canines. "Get back."

Nice. I'd been waiting a long time to see this side of her. It was too bad it had to be like this.

"I helped you and your sister escape the dungeons."

"I said get back." She slashed her claws at me.

And so I took a long step back. "I'm not going to hurt you."

"No." She narrowed her eyes. "You're not."

I stared into the face of death and wished I could will my horns away. I knew what Nellie saw when she looked at me—what they all saw. Despite my half-human blood, I was all fae, all *Oberon* to everyone, even though I had far more in common with my mortal birth mother than I had with anyone else in that sun-forsaken city.

Rowena, my birth mother and the first Mortal Queen —the one who had been erased from the history books— was trapped behind enemy lines inside the Tower of Crones. Magic prevented her from ever stepping foot outside that place. She knew too much, Oberon had said. Even if she could not speak it, she could spread her memories—the memories of all the Crones—just with the touch of a hand. And so he had locked her up.

Or Bellicent had. My father had been the king, but he'd never truly been in charge. Not after he'd surrendered himself to the god.

"I'm not going to hurt you," I repeated to Nellie. "But I'm afraid I can't let you go, either."

At that, I had lifted my hand and waved my brothers forward from where they'd been hidden in the mists. They'd easily surrounded the poor girl and snapped manacles around her wrists. As her breath had quickened, her nails and teeth had retracted, and all the fight had gone out of her eyes.

I hated that I was the one to do that to her, but I had no other choice.

I strode right up to the Albyrian gates with twelve of my brothers and sisters flanking me. Mykon, my second, was right beside me, as always. The chain in my hand clanked with every step Nellie took. She hadn't looked at me or spoken to me since we'd left camp, though I occasionally noticed her claws poke through her fingertips when she thought I wasn't paying attention.

Kalen Denare had three shadow fae guards stationed at the entrance to the city, at least that I could see. They all wore black leather armor that was a tad too battered for my taste, but it suggested they'd seen battle before, so

I'd need to take them seriously. Besides, I knew there would be others hidden along the walls. They likely had arrows aimed on my face already.

I gave the guards a pleasant smile when they each drew their sword. "Hello, there. I have a trade I would like to make with your king. Tell him I have his beloved's sister."

Nellie hissed.

One of the guards pierced me with his ice-blue gaze and scanned me to head to toe. "You're one of Oberon's bastards."

"Bastard? No. Technically, I am his trueborn son. His heir, if we're being really specific."

The guard surprised me with a smile. I'd assumed all the shadow fae were grumpy bastards like their king. "Then you made a mistake coming back. Especially with an army." He inclined his head toward the walls where, just as I'd suspected, shadows shifted behind the embrasures. Archers, ready and waiting.

"If this is what you consider an army, then I worry for your people. Twelve warriors? To take an entire city? I hope you never try to do something as senseless as that." I chuckled. "But no, I'm not here to fight. I want to make a trade. Is your king still in Endir? Send a raven. I'll wait."

The guard frowned and glanced at Nellie. "What's her name?"

"Nellie Baran, sister of Tessa Baran. You might not know who that is, but the king certainly does. Send word and—"

"I know who it is," he said in a low growl, his hand

tightening on the hilt of his sword. And then he swore. "You're playing a dangerous game, lad."

I prickled at his condescending tone. As Oberon's eldest son, I'd been breathing in the air of this world for over three hundred years. No doubt I was older than this bastard and had done far more to affect the outcome of this impending catastrophe than he had.

"I have said everything I need to say. Now pass it on to your king, or I will return to my camp with this mortal." I didn't mention what she truly was. No need to go into all that.

The guard clucked his tongue while the others clustered around him. The three of them fell into a hushed conversation, and as much as I strained to listen, I couldn't make out more than a few syllables here and there. Unfortunately, I hadn't inherited my father's keen hearing. Strength? Oh, yes. Healing? Thankfully. The ability to scent lies from mortals? Very much so. But enhanced speed and hearing had evaded me so far.

The lead guard broke free of the others, shot me a sharp glance, and then motioned to my brothers and sisters. "You, come inside with the girl. The others must stay outside the city walls."

"Hmm." I narrowed my eyes. "I think not. I'll wait here until your king arrives."

"His Majesty is already here," the guard countered. "I'll take you to him, but none of the others can join you."

I arched a brow. "Kalen Denare is supposed to be in Endir."

"No, he's here," Nellie finally spoke up, the first

words I'd heard from her since we'd left camp. "That's why I was out there by the wall. I was following them."

"Why, in the name of the sun, would Kalen Denare leave his safe city to return to this burnt husk?"

There was very little that could surprise me. Most of the time, the mortals warned me of events ahead of time—thanks to their prophetic Druids—so I could fulfill my duties to Talaven. They hadn't told me about this, however. A tickle of excitement went through me. I liked being surprised.

"To find your father," Nellie whispered.

I sniffed the air. The girl was telling the truth. Interesting. My father should be long gone by now—off on a ship that would take him to the eastern realms, where he could heal from this ordeal, where he could learn to be Oberon again. That was what the mortals had told me would happen.

But I supposed Kalen Denare would not know about that, and neither would Nellie Baran.

With a slight smile, I whipped my dagger from my belt and pressed the blade to the girl's throat. "Very well. It can be just the two of us. But if any of you guards so much as flinch in my direction, the Baran sister dies."

Nellie growled at me. It was a lovely little sound, and I appreciated her ferocity. It was more than I'd expected from her, to tell the truth, though I'd always hoped for it. She had always seemed meek and calm compared to her older sister. But like Tessa, she had the god's power running through her veins. She had fight in her, too. She just hid it better.

We passed through the gates, and I felt at least a dozen

pairs of eyes lock on my face. Arrows would be trained on my back now. This was a risky move. Unlike my father and other full-blooded light fae, I could die by an arrow to the head. But it was a risk I was willing to take.

We marched through the streets, Nellie finally squirming against her bonds as if the closer we drew to the king, the bolder she became. I kept my hand tight around her chains and the dagger against her neck. Hatred practically boiled off her skin.

She hissed at me *again*. "My sister is going to kill you for this."

"Just like she killed my father after she thought he'd chopped off your head?"

She let out a low, dangerous laugh, her neck bobbing against the blade. "Didn't you know? Kalen didn't journey here alone. My sister came with him, and she brought the Mortal Blade. And if they're in Albyria now instead of still hunting for Oberon in the mountains, that means they've done it. He's dead. By *her* hand, I'm guessing."

A sharp pain went through my abdomen, and the air suddenly grew so thick, I could scarcely breathe. There was no love lost between my father and me—I'd *wanted* Tessa to fight against him, to end his reign once and for all. He'd never treated me with anything other than distant unease. I had his horns and his eyes, but I had my birth mother's smile. And I'd shown it to him at every possible chance. He'd been wicked and cruel. He'd entertained Bellicent's delirium for far too long, and *he* was the reason Andromeda and the other gods would return.

Still, the thought of him dead turned the world on its

side. It seemed impossible. He was indestructible, unbeatable. For five hundred years, he had walked these lands, and I'd grown to believe he'd never fade.

Talaven had told me he'd live. That one day, he would heal from this. But they always communicated through gemstones, which meant I could not scent the truth from them. Had they *lied?*

Numbly, I followed the guards through the streets until we entered the courtyard just outside the castle. And then a furious shout rent the night as spear-wielding fae rushed toward me.

Six
Tessa

I rushed out of the tavern as Toryn's bellow shook the stones. My chest tightened. I'd never heard him even raise his voice before, and the unbridled anger dripping from his roar felt like a punch in the gut. If something made *him*, of all people, sound like that...

Grabbing a dagger, I ran around the corner, Kalen just beside me.

And then I saw what caused him so much anguish. *Nellie.*

Oberon's son, Ruari, stood in the courtyard, surrounded by a dozen of Kalen's guards, with a blank expression on his face, even as Toryn leveled a spear at his gut. He had a blade pressed to my sister's slender neck. Her bottom lip trembled, but her fingers were curled at her sides.

Fingers tipped with claws.

I glanced from her hands to Ruari's face—eerily calm. Now he was smiling.

"I will kill you," I growled, stalking toward him. "Get

your blade off my sister's throat, or I will tear you limb from limb."

Kalen did not try to stop me. None of the Mist Guard did. I walked right up to Toryn's side, pulled out the Mortal Dagger, flipped the blade, and started to lunge toward the orange-horned half-fae. But then—

Ruari pressed his dagger harder against my sister's neck and tsked. "Ah, ah. Careful, now. I don't want to have to cut off her pretty little head. Judging by how you reacted when my father threatened the same, I don't think you want that, either."

Anger thundered in my veins. Darkness crept into the corners of my vision and pulsed against my skin, desperate to get out, desperate to tear the creature before me to shreds. He had a blade on my sister's throat. My blood boiled with a viciousness that made my back begin to ache.

"I swear on the sun above that I will kill you if you don't let her go."

He looked up at the sky. "I'm afraid the sun has abandoned you."

"What do you want?" Toryn demanded from beside me, his spear trembling.

"I want to make a deal with your king," he said as easily as if he wanted to swap some apples for gemstones, not my sister's life. I should have known not to trust him. For sun's sake, I *hadn't* trusted him. I'd seen the glint in his eye when he'd made his plan against his father. I'd known I was nothing more than a pawn in his twisted game. But then he'd vanished after the fire. I'd forgotten all about him, but he hadn't forgotten about us.

And now he had my sister.

Kalen stepped up beside me, sword in hand. "I don't think you'll find me in much of a mood to make a deal when you're threatening the life of someone who is precious to me."

From behind me, I heard the distinct sound of a bowstring pulled tight. Niamh was readying an arrow.

"I doubt you're faster than us," Kalen said, taking a small step toward Ruari. "We can have you disarmed and dead within seconds. All we have to do is wait for you to lose your focus, just for a breath, and it's over."

Uncertainty flashed across Ruari's face. It was gone within a heartbeat, but I'd seen the doubt in his eyes. He was facing four of Kalen's Mist Guard, along with Kalen himself. They were all faster and stronger than any fae I'd ever met. Ruari was strong, yes, but he was nothing compared to them.

"I just want to make a trade," Ruari said slowly. "And if you try to attack me, I'll kill her."

A low growl rumbled from my throat. "If you think you can kill her and make it out of here alive, then you're even more deranged than I thought you were."

His eyes narrowed, and then he turned his gaze to the smoldering buildings that surrounded us. "I don't have much to live for. You've taken everything from me. My home, my people, my family. All I want is a piece of it back."

I frowned. "What do you mean?"

"King Oberon is gone. Isn't that right? So you don't need to worry about him anymore. Most of his court is gone, too. Those of us alive don't want a war with the shadow fae, and we certainly have no plans to ally with the coming gods. We just want to live in our homeland in peace. Albyria and Teine, they're ours. Remove your warriors from our city and give us back our streets, and Nellie can go free."

My lips parted. "You want Albyria back? But the city, it's...dead."

"We'll rebuild it."

"No war?" Kalen asked. "No more fighting? No more deals with the gods?"

Ruari gave a nod.

"How can I be certain you'll uphold your end of this deal? I saw your army camping in the shadow of the mountain. What's to stop you from marching on us once we retreat?"

"If we wanted to march on you, we would have already. I've heard Endir is a pleasant city, even with all the mist everywhere. Safe, too, with that wall. We could have tried to take it from you, but we didn't. We want Albyria back. Albyria and Teine."

"No one lives in Teine anymore," I argued. "All the mortals left."

He lifted a shoulder in a shrug. "Teine has always been part of the Kingdom of Light. Perhaps someone will decide to settle there someday, and the homes will fill with families once more."

"The Kingdom of Light will never have you for their king," Nellie muttered, her eyes bright with anger.

I wanted to tell her not to argue. If this was what Ruari wanted, then so be it. I would gladly hand this city over to him if it meant he'd let her go...but I also knew it wasn't my call. Heart pounding, I turned to Kalen to try to get a read on his thoughts, but his face was a mask. Surely he would agree to this. If not, he'd have to move fast to kill Ruari, and that would put Nellie in too much danger.

"Kalen," I whispered.

"You can have your city back," the King of Shadow began. I sagged in relief until he continued. "If you release Nellie *and* make a vow to me."

My breath stuck in my throat.

Ruari scowled and tightened his hold on my sister. "I don't make vows."

"You say you're against the gods. Prove it. Make a vow to fight beside us when the time comes." Kalen glanced up at the skies. "And it will not be long from now."

My heart pounded as Ruari stared and stared and stared at Kalen. With my eyes locked on my sister, all I could do was pull in desperate breaths, readying myself to spring into action if need be. And if Ruari tightened his grip on her even a little bit more, I didn't think I could hold myself back. The anger raging through me whispered in my ears.

Stab him, stab him, stab him.

"All right," Ruari finally said, and all my breath whooshed out of me. "I vow to fight beside you against the gods if you vow to give me my city and never again try to take it from the light fae."

Kalen's hands tightened into fists. I knew he hated vows—they'd haunted him his entire life. But he was willing to do this to gain another army. We would need it, I realized. Desperately. I didn't know exactly what the gods were capable of, but we needed all the fighters we could find. The shadow fae numbers were low. Even after centuries, they'd struggled to rebuild their army after the war against Oberon.

"I vow it." Kalen did not lower his sword. "Now release your hold on Nellie."

At long last, Ruari whisked his blade away and gave my sister a little push. It was all I could do to keep standing as the overwhelming relief crashed over me like a tidal wave. But she did not run into my open arms. She whirled on her feet and stabbed a finger into Ruari's chest. "You're an absolute monster, just like your father. One day, I'll repay you for this."

And then she sliced her sharp nail across his cheek. A small line of blood dribbled down his face, and I couldn't help but smile.

SEVEN
TESSA

While Kalen rounded up his warriors to prepare for the trek back to Endir, I wrapped my arms around my sister and pulled her close. She hugged me fiercely, her body trembling, but when I pulled back to look into her face, I saw no fear in her eyes. Only anger.

"What happened?" I asked her over the steady thumping of boots as the warriors made their way to the city gates. "How are you even here in Albyria?"

She winced and glanced away. "When Toryn left Endir, he said you all were in trouble. I wanted to help for once."

I blinked. "You could have gotten yourself killed."

She held up her hand, the nails still sharp and long. "I'm strong, too, you know. Claws and fangs, you said."

I took in the sight of her claws, finally understanding. I'd spent a long time in the darkness of my mind but no more. "When I spoke those words, I didn't actually understand what I was saying. I just meant you should fight like an animal, if you had to. Deep down, I must have had an inkling there was more to it than that. The truth about you—and me—was in my subconscious all along."

"And you remember now?" she asked in a soft whisper. "All of it?"

I swallowed. "Yes. Everything, I think. What Father did to me, to you. And about the power he wanted to harness. I remember it now...It's just so hard to reconcile it with the image I've had of him all this time. When he left all those years ago, to go into the mists, he said it was to protect us. He said he'd do anything for us, even go up against a fae king."

"I know," she said, a tear slipping down her cheek. "I think, eventually, he regretted what he did. He wasn't all bad, Tessa. He just wasn't all good, either. At the end, I think he loved us in his own way. And I think he stopped seeing us as tools." She huffed out a breath and took my hands in hers, searching my eyes. "I'm sorry I didn't tell you. Well, I mean, I tried to a few times, but you...you would get so upset and shut me out and run off into the woods. The way your mind locked it all up...I worried if I forced you to face your trauma before you were ready, it would only make it worse. I'm just so sorry."

I squeezed her hand and pressed my forehead against hers. The scent of apples surrounded me like an old, familiar hug. "Don't be sorry. You did the right thing. I needed to remember on my own...but..." I pulled back and lifted her hands—the claws were gone now. "More importantly, you actually have *claws and fangs.*"

Her cheeks turned red, and she shoved her hands into

her trousers as if to whisk them out of sight. "Not inside Oberon's barrier. I saw them once, when Father took me outside the barrier, back before you stepped in and volunteered yourself instead. Twenty years passed without them. And now that Oberon's barrier isn't numbing that power anymore, they're back."

"And you can call them on command?"

"Eh," she said, scrunching up her nose. "My control of them comes and goes. But I've never had what you have. The power to kill by touch, I—"

I sucked in a breath and stepped back. "No. I did that once, but never again. Being inside the barrier muted all that until I lost the power completely. I don't kill by touch. I can't. All right?"

"Tessa," she said softly.

"I can't kill by touch. *I can't.*"

Her gaze turned fierce. "You can't? Or you don't want to?"

"Both. I don't have the power to do that anymore, and I don't want it to come back. That would make me just like Andromeda. Too dangerous for this world."

The thought of it filled my veins with acid. If I could kill by touch, no one around me would be safe. Just a small brush from my skin would be enough to send them to an early grave. And even while I felt something dark stirring within me, I couldn't accept that Death was part of it.

"We could find a way to harness it," she argued. "And use it *against* the gods when they come for us."

"I don't have that power." Gritting my teeth, I turned

away. "Maybe I'm stronger than I should be, and I heal faster, but that's it. There's nothing else."

Nellie pressed her lips together, but she didn't argue anymore. My chest burned from the thought of the god's dark power inside me, my mind flipping through images of my worst nightmares: Nellie dead from my touch; Kalen's eyes rolling back; the world cowering when I rose up with Andromeda's mighty power radiating off my body.

A strong hand pressed into my back, and the images blinked away. Kalen stepped up beside me with a furrowed brow, as if reading my expression. "We're ready to go." His eyes asked, *Are you all right?*

I schooled my features into a mask of calm. "I just need to fetch Silver, and then I'm ready."

"Silver?"

"One of Oberon's horses. He helped me reach Albyria, and I don't want to leave him behind."

His eyes softened. "All right, love. Go get him, and then meet us back here."

Silver still stood on the other side of the hidden passageway, waiting for me. I grabbed his reins and led him back to the courtyard. His hooves clattered against the stone road. I could leave him here with Ruari and the other light fae. Truth be told, he belonged to them, but it felt like he'd chosen me that day in the mists, and I couldn't bear the thought of saying goodbye.

I helped Nellie onto his back, and then we began the journey out of the city, across the bridge, out into the mists, and through the empty countryside toward Endir. It would take a couple of days on foot—the horses we'd taken to reach the mountains were gone now. Boudica swept through the skies overhead, keeping an eye out for shadowfiends. As the hours passed, the large party of warriors and guards settled into an easy rhythm, our boots thudding against the soft earth.

Kalen fell into step beside me, but his eyes were hard and distant. Every now and then, he'd looked up at the comet, and tension would ripple through his body, as if the very sight of it was a gut punch. Guilt thickened in my throat. Even though Kalen blamed it all on Oberon, I still felt at fault. I'd been the one holding the Mortal Blade. I'd been the one to chase Oberon through the mists. If I hadn't fought him—if I'd not taken out my anger on him, desperate for revenge—we wouldn't be in this situation now.

A situation I didn't even fully grasp.

"Kalen?" I finally asked after a long stretch of silence.

"Hmm?"

"What happens now?"

He heaved a sigh that told me he, too, had been focused on this very issue. "We prepare ourselves for the inevitable."

"A war with Andromeda and the other gods."

"That's right," he said. "I don't know how long it will take for them to reach this world, or where, exactly, they're coming from, or what they'll do first when they arrive, but we need fighters. A lot of them. Whatever they have planned, it will not be peace."

My stomach tightened. *War.* It was something I'd never faced—none of us mortals had. We'd heard the tales from fae, of course, or we'd read about the battles in our books. But war had never felt like anything more than a fable, something that didn't happen anymore. Nothing about it felt glorious. It was just blood and death and brutality. And it was coming for us.

"I'm so sorry, Kalen. I—"

"No." He pulled me against him, our footsteps in sync. "As I've said before, if anyone's to blame, it's Oberon. And even then, he did not want this, either. The God of Death—Andromeda—was determined to find a way back, and she put forces into motion that could not be stopped. I see it now. This has been a long time coming."

My heart shuddered in my chest. "You think this is what she planned all along? When she offered Oberon the chance to bring back..." I didn't finish my thought. I knew how Kalen felt about what Oberon had done to his mother, and he still hadn't fully processed it.

"I think she hoped to convince Oberon to release her from that gemstone a long time ago, but he managed to resist. But in the end, yes. It seems like she started this four hundred years ago. To a god, that's only a flicker of time."

"And there's no way to kill them."

"If there is, no one knows it. Thousands of years ago, fae and humans only found a way to banish them—or trap them. Not kill."

And so, if we managed to banish them again, was it only a matter of time before they came here a third time, setting off this cycle once more? The thought weighed heavily on my shoulders. If it was hopeless—if there was no way to win—how much would we have to sacrifice just to give this world a little more time?

Was there any reason to hope at all?

I opened my mouth to confess all these thoughts to Kalen—maybe he'd have a salve for the darkness in my mind. But a bird's screech shattered the silence. Kalen grabbed my arm and jerked us to a stop. His gaze went to the clouds as a pair of black wings swooped toward us. Boudica raced closer, and another screech shot from her open beak.

"What's happening?" I asked, instinctively reaching toward Nellie, who rode on Silver just beside me.

Kalen's sword whistled as he pulled it from his back. "Pookas. They've caught our scent and are heading our way. They have some wraiths with them."

"Wraiths?" I asked sharply. In my time spent in the mists, the only creatures I'd faced had been shadowfiends —or pookas, as Kalen and the shadow fae called them. They were monstrous things—fangs and claws and matted fur, capable of ripping a man into pieces before feasting on his blood and flesh. They were terrifying enough without adding another creature to the fight.

"Wraiths are usually not so brave," he murmured, "and they only like the taste of bloody spines. I imagine they're hoping the pookas will do the work for them, and then they can come in behind to feast on our remains. Watch the ground. They leave poisonous sand behind anything their feet touch."

Bloody spines?

I swallowed and glanced up at Nellie, whose face had gone bone white. "Stay there."

"I won't be a coward," she hissed at me. But she didn't make a move to dismount.

Kalen wound a hand around the back of my neck and gazed at me with fire in his eyes. "Stay in the back here with Niamh. I know you're learning to fight, and you're damn good at it already, but there are too many of them. Let the trained warriors take care of it."

He kissed me fiercely, and then marched toward the front of our party, barking orders at his warriors. They moved into formation, facing the dark mists ahead of us. Those with swords stood in front, while the fae carrying spears, including Toryn, waited just behind them. In the back, Niamh and the other archers readied their arrows. Kalen, to my dismay, was right in the front.

I stood within a cluster of archers, my hand tight around Silver's reins. Silence descended upon us, thick with fear and rage. The moments inched by. Warriors shifted on their feet, but they stayed in position, their weapons raised, their eyes set on the dense fog that swirled around us.

Nellie suddenly leapt off the horse and landed beside me. "I can't stay up there. It's driving me crazy. I feel like my skin is about to jump off my bones."

"It's not any better down here," I muttered. "Why haven't they attacked yet?"

Niamh leaned in from my other side, her violet eyes gleaming in the dark. "The beasts have been changing tactics these past few months. They move in bigger groups now, attacking when they wouldn't have before. Prepare yourselves, and don't leave my fucking side. I have a feeling this is going to get bloody."

My tongue thickened into a lump of sand. With tension wracking my body, I pulled the Mortal Blade from my belt, but Niamh's hand on my wrist brought it back to my side. She shook her head. "Best not. If things turn to chaos, you could scrape one of us, and then we're ash. Take this instead." She handed me the sword I'd lost in the mists near Albyria—the one Kalen had given to me as a gift—and then she glanced at Nellie. "Can you fight?"

As I gratefully took the sword, Nellie pushed the breath from her flared nostrils and then held up her claw-tipped hands. "I have these."

"Good." A ghost of smile flickered across Niamh's lips. "If a beast attacks you, claw their eyes out, and then paint yourself in their blood. They won't be able to see or smell you then."

Nellie grimaced. "That's disgusting."

"Better disgusting than dead."

Thunderous footsteps boomed, shaking the ground and growing louder with every moment that passed, as if a wicked storm were rushing toward us. Gripping my sword, I quickly realized what was so wrong with that sound. The shadowfiends weren't headed toward the front, where the swordsmen waited in perfect fighting formation. They were coming straight for the archers —and me.

And as I whirled on my feet, the beasts leapt from the darkness.

Eight
Tessa

Five shadowfiends raced toward me. Shouting into the night, I grabbed Nellie's arm and yanked her sideways, out of the path of the beasts. The ground slammed into my side. Pain cracked through my shoulder, which was still sore from my recent fight against the shadowfiend in the mountains.

The archers scattered, caught off guard from the direction of the attack. Arrows launched into the sky, but the volley wasn't fast enough. The nearest shadowfiend threw out its vicious paw and slammed it into an archer. The fae flew into the air, screaming as his body vanished into the mists.

"To your feet!" Niamh barked at me as she loosed another arrow. It whistled through the foggy air and punched into the nearest beast, but the creature kept charging forward as if the arrow were nothing more than a pesky fly.

I grabbed Nellie's arm and hauled us up from the ground before throwing myself in front of her. For a moment, the world seemed to slow around me as I took in the chaos. There were at least a dozen shadowfiends—maybe even twenty. Several dark figures shuffled along behind them, their faces hidden in the depths of their cloaks. The ground hissed as they walked, and smoke curled around them like strands of mist. I glanced back at the fae warriors. A third of them had scattered to the right, while another third had launched to the left, where I'd ended up. The rest surrounded Kalen, now at the rear, but there was a gulf of air between us all, right where the shadowfiends were whirling in circles, fighting off any fae who approached.

Through the chaos, I locked eyes with Kalen, just for a moment. Twelve, or fifteen, or even twenty shadowfiends was nothing to him. He'd faced far greater numbers than this. But these shadowfiends were in our midst, which meant Kalen couldn't take them out with his brutal power. If he launched it at them, he'd certainly kill them. But he'd kill everyone else in his path, too. That meant us.

"What do we do?" Nellie whispered from behind me.

I lifted my eyes to the horse, who was neighing and stomping at the ground. "Keep Silver safe."

Swallowing, I lifted my sword, my limbs screaming in protest. Every muscle in my body ached. It had been far too long since I'd had a good sleep, and the past few days had been a blur of agony, fear, and rage. But I would not back down.

A shadowfiend lumbered toward us. Niamh swore as she loosed an arrow, but the beast batted it aside. She grabbed another arrow from her quiver and shot. Again, the beast knocked it aside. As I stared down the snarling creature, I sucked in a breath, then another. My past rose behind me on phantom wings, threatening to remind me just how weak and powerless I was.

But I shoved those thoughts aside. I'd won one fight. I could win another, especially when this time, I wasn't facing one of these monsters alone.

The beast roared and leapt into the air, its claws outstretched. Niamh loosed another arrow. This time, the sharp tip slammed into the shadowfiend's neck. The creature howled in pain, but it just kept coming, its vicious fangs aimed right at my throat.

I swung my sword as it crashed into me. My breath rushed from my lungs as I landed hard on my back. Several more shadowfiends rushed out from the dark, their sights on the fae. Nellie was safely in the middle of a group of archers now, thank the light. It was the only thought I had before the beast swung its claw at my face.

I got my sword up just in time, and the blade sliced into the beast's paw. Its wild eyes zeroed in on me, and thick, rancid blood dripped onto my face. The shadowfiend kept pushing and pushing, as if it didn't notice the pain from the sword cutting into its paw. Suddenly, the blade shifted in my hands, tipping sideways until the blunt side pressed against the claw.

The beast shoved down, even harder now. Tears leaking from my eyes, I released my grip on the sword and rolled to the right. The sharp claws hit the ground right where I'd just been. Sand sprayed into the air, mingling with the mist. Sucking in a shaky breath, I leapt to my feet.

"Tessa!" Kalen roared from somewhere in the distance. But I couldn't look for him, not now. The beast knocked my sword aside and started stalking toward me. I took a step back, swallowing.

Niamh and the other fae warriors were engaged in combat with the rest of the shadowfiends. Kalen was too far away to help me now, blocked by the circle of beasts in the middle of our army. My sword was out of reach. Now it was just me and the creature stalking toward me, snapping its sharp fangs at the air.

I curled my fingers and felt that darkness pulse through my veins, whispering words into my mind.

Use me, it hissed. *Kill the beast.*

My mouth went dry. The power in my veins—the power of a god—was all I had now. But if I gave in and tried to use it, would the darkness claim me, too? I'd seen what had happened to Oberon and to Kalen's mother— what had happened to my own father. The power had twisted them, corrupted them beyond saving.

Yes, Oberon had fought back against it in the end, but it had been too little, too late. He'd died a monster, despite how hard he'd tried to right his wrongs. None of it could undo all his terrible deeds. All his cruelty. All the lives he'd ruined in his quest to extend the life of someone who had become just as twisted as he had.

But if I didn't do something, this shadowfiend was going to kill me.

"Tessa!" Kalen shouted again. "Get your sword!"

I shuddered as the beast took another thunderous step toward me. I glanced behind it, where my sword lay on the sandy ground. If I could just get around the shadowfiend, I could grab my blade. And that would be enough. I wouldn't need to use the power then.

Body coiled tightly, I stepped to the side. The beast growled and inched closer. I shifted to the side again, keeping my gaze locked on its snarling face.

Another step, and it followed. But I was only a few more moves away from the sword now.

And then it lunged.

I threw up my hands as the shadowfiend's fur-coated body slammed into me. My back hit the ground, snapping my neck and sending a storm of stars through my eyes. Its heavy body pinned me in place, and it ran a long, wet snout along my cheek. I ground my teeth, shuddering, memories rushing through my mind. This was just like that night—that horrible moment when I'd been nothing but a helpless child tossed to her death by her own father.

I'd survived then, but only just.

That night had broken me. It had twisted me until I'd become a reckless ball of rage.

My hands shook as they pushed against the beast's rough fur. Tears of terror burned my eyes, but I gritted my teeth, forcing down the fear so I could focus—focus on the place where my hands connected with the shadowfiend. The creature bellowed as it heaved up its massive paw, ready to swipe its claws right through my neck. Its other claw pinned me in place, piercing my fighting leathers and digging into my skin. Venom stormed through me, and my vision began to swim.

I squeezed my eyes shut, calling upon whatever power I had inside me, even as I hated and feared every part of it.

Something stirred in my veins, something dark, electric, and so terrible that it made my teeth slam together. Hissing between my clenched teeth, I *forced* that power into the beast.

But nothing happened.

Sudden certainty of death punched my heart. I opened my eyes and braced myself for the pain.

A sword whistled above my head. Alastair's blood-soaked face appeared as he roared and shoved his blade deep into the shadowfiend's gut. The beast let out a soundless scream. Blood and gore sprayed. The weight left my chest as the creature tumbled sideways and landed heavily on the sand.

My nostrils flared as I sucked in frantic gasps of air. The venom was spreading now, numbing my limbs and silencing the world around me. Alastair fell to my side and brushed back the hair that had pulled free of my braid.

"Little dove, speak to me," he said in an urgent voice. "Tell me what hurts."

I could barely shake my head, unable to speak the words.

"Fuck," he muttered, his eyes finding the wound. My skin felt slick where the beast had punched its claw into me. There was blood. Lots of it. "Can you still feel anything?"

I just stared at up at him, my neck no longer responding to my pleas to move. The world seemed nothing but a dusty haze around me. Gone were the sounds of fighting and the brutality of all that blood and death. All that existed was Alastair's concerned face, his glittering earrings, and that ponytail of midnight hair. Such lovely, silken hair for such a powerful warrior.

It was then I realized the pain was gone. All of it. The aches that had been plaguing me these past few days—my shoulder, my back, the lack of sleep that had pressed heavily on my eyes—gone. But I knew that as good as I felt now, it probably wasn't a good sign.

I must be dying.

Footsteps came closer, and something beside my head hissed. Alastair lifted his eyes and growled at whatever stood beside me now. I tried to follow his line of sight but only caught the vague outline of a towering creature in dark robes. A single hand was outstretched, long and thin and bone white. It pointed a finger right at me.

"Yeah, that's not happening." Alastair stood and raised his sword. "That beast didn't get her, and neither will you."

Dully, I knew I should probably panic at his words, but my fear was gone, just like everything else. Earlier, that shadowfiend had come straight for me. Alastair seemed to think the wraith had, too. Were they targeting me? Could they somehow scent the power in my blood? Did they know I was a descendent of Andromeda?

Steel whistled through the air, but all I could do was lie flat on my back, staring up at the mist that swirled overhead. It was so thick, I couldn't even find the vague outline of the moon anymore. There wasn't the hint of light anywhere. Just endless darkness, so deep it felt as though my soul might drift from my body and get lost in it forever.

But then what was that? My finger twitched, and a

dull pain radiated through my chest where the beast's claw had dug into me. Then my foot shifted, just a flinch and nothing more, and another flash of pain went through my shoulder. Sights and sounds and a million different scents pounded down on me all at once.

Suddenly, it was all so *loud, loud, loud*. The shouting and screaming, the thundering of massive paws, the slice of steel through flesh.

Kalen appeared, his face full of anguish. He dropped to my side and grasped my hand, bringing it to his heart. "Tessa."

Everything within me reached toward him, but my body hurt too much to respond. His face was caked in dirt and blood, and his familiar, Boudica, shivered on his shoulder, but he'd never looked better. He'd survived.

"One of the pookas got her," Alastair said. "And the venom spread. She won't be moving for a while."

"No," I managed to scrape from my throat. "I can move. A little. Don't worry about me. Go fight the shadowfiends. Where's Nellie?"

"Nellie's fine, and the beasts are all dead. The ones we didn't kill have fled," Alastair said with a wolfish smile, his eyes burning brightly. "We defeated the bastards. Even the wraiths. Just be careful where you step when you get up."

"You can move?" Kalen asked, sweeping his eyes across my prone form. Then his sapphire gaze latched on my torn leathers and the wound underneath. "That shouldn't be possible. The venom doesn't wear off for hours."

Alastair had the audacity to grin. "What, did you suck some venom out of her again?"

Groaning, I pushed up from the ground and held my head, ignoring the spinning world around me. My whole body ached—*again*. But I could move. A little. Kalen held onto my arms and helped me stand, confusion in his eyes.

"Is that where the pooka cut you?" he asked, pointing to my sliced leathers.

"Yes, and it hurts like fire."

"I can see the blood." He arched his brow. "But the wound has already closed up. You're healing."

I blinked at him. "I'm sorry, what?"

"Huh." Alastair took a step closer and peered at my chest. "Kal's right. If I hadn't witnessed it with my own eyes, I'd assume you were covered in the pooka's blood, not your own."

Frowning, I pushed the leathers aside and stared at the cut—or where the cut had been only moments ago. Just like Kalen had said, my skin was slick with the bright color of fresh blood, but there was only a small scar. It was barely the length of my thumb.

With my heart thundering, I lifted my eyes to meet Kalen's gaze. "How is that possible?"

"Andromeda's power," he said. "It's starting to come to you."

Nine
Kalen

Tessa paled when I mentioned Andromeda. "That isn't true. I tried using that power against the shadowfiend when it attacked me. Nothing happened."

"It might not come to you all at once," I said as gently as I could. I knew this was hard for her. "But you've shown hints of it before now. You're fast and strong, and you've healed quickly in the past. Just not quite as quickly as this. Perhaps the power needs a little more time to fully manifest."

I could tell by the way her jaw clenched that she wasn't thrilled. Nor could I blame her. More than anyone, I knew what it was like to have a terrifying power—a power that destroyed far more than it healed. When I'd been unable to get to her during the fight, my power had sizzled in my veins, desperate to burst forth. I'd almost lost control. And if I had, my power would have killed everyone.

"I don't know who I am," she whispered, her gaze

drifting to the bloody battlefield behind me. "Not anymore. Between this power and the memories of what my father did to me, I don't know what pieces of me are real."

My hand tightened on hers, and I pulled her fingers to my chest, to my beating heart. "Here's what is real. You are Tessa Baran, and I am yours. That's all that matters."

Pink spread through her cheeks, and for a moment, I wondered if I'd gone too far. We'd shared so much, but there were still so many words left unspoken between us. But then she sighed and leaned against me, and everything felt right in the world for once, even in the midst of so much death. We stood there like that for a moment, steadying ourselves and each other, but then it was time for me to be a king.

After I rounded up our warriors and took stock of the injured, we resumed our trek to Endir. Our party was silent, clearly uneasy after the attack. The pookas were acting abnormally, and so were the wraiths. To come across so many of them as organized as they were...it was odd, to say the least. I'd noticed strange activity from them for the past few months, but this was the worst I'd seen.

I glanced up at the sky as we marched through the mists. The comet was barely visible now, nothing but a smudge of dim light. The pookas weren't the only things changing in Aesir. Here, the mists had thickened so much that it was almost impossible to see more than a few steps ahead. And the wind that whistled past us was stronger than I'd ever felt in the shadow lands. It smelled and felt like storms.

A long march later, we reached the walled city of Endir without enduring another attack. Darkness blanketed the once-lush hills that the city wound through, small bridges connecting one neighborhood to the next. I led the tired party through the silent streets and into the castle, and then the warriors headed to the barracks to get some rest. Weariness weighed on my bones. It had been a long few days. Normally, I needed little rest, but right now, my bed called for me.

But there was too much to do.

I turned to Tessa when we reached the top of the staircase that led to her quarters. "You go on to bed."

"Aren't you coming?"

I rubbed my thumb along her chin. "Oh, I will, but I have a few things to take care of first."

She searched my eyes, reading the direction of my thoughts. "You have to decide what to do with Morgan."

"For one, yes." Morgan had said very little since we'd left Albyria. She'd been kept chained during the fight against the pookas and had survived against all odds. And I did not trust her as far as I could throw her. "But we also need to plan for what's coming. I don't know how long it will take for the gods to appear, now that they're returning. We need to be ready when they do."

"I'll come to the meeting with you," she said, despite the streaks of red in her eyes. "I want to help."

I nodded, half-smiling. "Of course you do."

We called the Mist Guard to the meeting room, and I asked for Druid Balfor to join us as well. He was ancient—even older than I was—and he remembered things that most would forget, such as the color of someone's dress at a ball six hundred years ago, or the scent of the grass that had once covered the hills surrounding this castle. Some believed the Druids had been gifted with enhanced memory at the expense of other senses, like the keen hearing most fae had.

But of course, Druid Balfor had never confirmed or denied this rumor.

Everyone took a seat at the oval table, and I stood with my hands braced against the wood. "I won't mince words. Andromeda will be here soon if she isn't already. With her come the others: Sirius, Perseus, Orion, and Callisto. The five winged gods who will set their sights on the human kingdoms. Out of everything in this world, that's what they'll want most."

Tessa cleared her throat.

I arched a brow. "Yes?"

"Andromeda is the God of Death. I'm certain I won't like the answer to this, but I have to ask: what are the others?"

"Ah." I cast a glance at the others gathered before me. Not everyone here would know this information, I realized. Niamh did because she'd been by my side in the months after my mother's disappearance, and I'd told her everything. But I'd never gone into detail with the others. "Andromeda is their leader, as you know. Her second-in-command is Perseus, the God of Fear. He brings terror to anyone he touches, bringing their worst nightmares alive in their minds until they go insane."

"He sounds lovely." Fenella leaned back in her chair, using a dagger to pick at her fingernails. As soon as we'd returned to Endir, she'd taken a moment to splash water on her face and change into a fresh set of fighting leathers. Her eyes were bright and clear, and she almost looked like she was ready for round two against the pookas.

Gaven was the only other fresh-faced among us, but only because he'd remained here to keep an eye on the Endirians while we'd been gone. The rest of us looked a mess. Our faces were caked in dirt and blood, and we filled the room with the stench of battle. Even Alastair had purple bags beneath his eyes.

"Then we have Sirius, the God of Beasts." I caught Tessa's wide gaze, and I nodded as if to confirm her suspicions. "We believe he may control the pookas, the wraiths, and the joint eaters. He may have controlled other creatures, too. Ones that did not survive when the gods were banished from this world."

"You *believe*?"

"My mother tried to find out as much as she could when she visited the human kingdoms, but much of that information has been lost—or destroyed."

"Well, it makes sense," Alastair said with a nod, twirling one of the rings in his ear. "God of Beasts controls the beasts."

"And Callisto, the God of Pestilence, can spread a plaguelike sickness across the land," I continued. "While Orion, the God of Famine, can turn a person into a pit of hunger. No matter how much food you eat, it will never satiate you. Eventually, you'll starve."

As my words sank in, the room became a gulf of silence. My mother had told me about the gods years ago, but at the time, it had felt like a fairytale. Now the reality was coming for us. Everything the gods touched, they destroyed. And if we didn't find a way to stop them, life as we knew it would cease to exist.

"By touch," Tessa finally said, her soft voice cutting through the pregnant silence. "That's the only way they can use their power?"

I nodded. "As far as the humans know, yes. That does limit their power, but don't let that make you complacent. They're strong and fast and can withstand any attack. Winning against them won't be simple."

Fenella stood, shoving back her chair. She flattened her hands on the table and stared at each of us in turn, her eyes glittering like the miniature dagger necklace she always wore. "Well, the answer is simple. They were banished once. We do it again."

"Absolutely fantastic idea, Fenella," Alastair said with an eye roll as he folded his beefy arms across his chest. "And I suppose you know how to do that?"

She glowered at him. "All right, smartass, what's your idea? Let me guess. Find a brothel and spend the rest of our limited days fucking our brains out?"

He smiled at her, but I didn't miss the sharp glint in his eye. "You offering?"

Gaven chuckled.

I cleared my throat to get everyone's attention back on the task at hand. "If the mortals knew how to banish the gods, they didn't share that information with my mother. Druid Balfor, what can you tell us?"

The pale-faced Druid had chosen to stand along the back wall, and by the uneasy shuffle of his feet, he likely regretted coming to this meeting. The tension was so thick, I could feel it pulsing against my skin. Most of the time, my Mist Guard got along—they'd been friends for centuries. But they could also bicker like siblings when it suited them.

"Well," Balfor said after brushing down the front of his drab robe, "I've spent a lot of time scouring our library here for answers. There are few, I'm afraid. Endir is not an old city, and the Fell predates it. So I'm not terribly surprised we don't have any records from that time."

"The Fell?" Tessa asked.

Druid Balfor cast her a nervous glance. "Er, yes. That's the term the mortals use for that time period, when the gods first arrived here. I've visited their lands, you see. They told me very little, but I do have a bit of insight that might give us an idea of what comes next."

I arched a brow and leaned forward. "And that is?"

Out of the corner of my eye, I saw Tessa lean forward as well, and then I noticed Druid Balfor give her another little glance, as if she made him uneasy. I frowned.

"We have about a month until the comet falls from the sky," Balfor said. "After that, Andromeda will reunite with the others, and they'll work together to enslave the mortals. Anything more than that, I don't know."

"But how do we *banish* them?" Fenella asked sharply.

Balfor shook his head. "The mortals didn't say."

"But they do know how, right?" Toryn asked. "The mortals, I mean."

"I don't know."

Niamh, who had been silently watching the exchange, tsked and leaned back in her chair. "So we have a month."

"That's not much time," Alastair muttered.

"The gods don't have an army," I said, thinking out loud as I began to pace at the head of the table. "There are five of them, but there are hundreds in my army. Ruari vowed his kingdom would fight by our side. That's a few hundred more."

Niamh shook her head. "As much as I love a good battle, I don't like these odds, Kal. We outnumber them, but they're indestructible. And even though they can only spread their shit through touch, if a handful of our warriors came down with pestilence or famine, or even fear, our army could erupt into chaos."

I rubbed my chin, and then turned to Balfor once more. "Niamh is right. We need more than just warriors if we want to survive this. Do the mortals know anything that could help? Would they have insight on how to destroy these immortal beings?"

"I don't know."

Fenella flicked her the edge of her dagger. "I'm sensing a pattern. You're the oldest here, and yet you know little more than the rest of us combined."

"The mortals fear the gods more than we do, and they've been certain of their return for centuries. There will be a reason they didn't tell the fae anything."

I frowned. "What's that supposed to mean?"

"Those of us in Aesir brought them back, didn't we? This is *the fae's* fault." He gave me a strained smile. "The gods corrupt souls. I've always believed the mortals would be more susceptible to their influence than we would. They're weaker physically. But perhaps I had it wrong all this time. Perhaps *the fae* have weaker hearts, and that is why the mortals have kept the truth hidden for so long. They knew Aesir would cause the Second Fell."

Tessa suddenly stood. "It wasn't—"

"You're right," I cut in. "In the end, Oberon was too weak to protect the world from Andromeda and her fellow gods. But what's done is done, and we can only hope the mortals know more than they've shared before now. We need to reach out to them. I'm certain they've seen the comet in the sky, so they'll know what's happened. We're never going to survive this if we don't join our peoples together, just like we did all those centuries ago."

Gaven, who had remained silent during the meeting thus far, finally spoke up. "You mean for us to travel to the mortal lands. What about Endir?"

Tension still lurked in Endir's halls. The fae and humans had come to an uneasy understanding, but peace was a fragile thing. One wrong word from either side, and it could shatter into a million pieces. On top of that, the Kingdom of Storms had been silent in the weeks since my attack against their army, but I knew it was only a matter of time before their queen retaliated. I'd counted their numbers when they'd been camping outside the walls of Dubnos. That had not been their entire army. More would come unless we did something.

And now was not the time for petty battles.

"Only a few of us will go to Talaven. Gaven, unless something happens, you can stay in Endir to ensure peace continues. The rest of us will journey to Gailfean and offer a treaty to the Kingdom of Storms. Perhaps we can make the queen see some sense and join us in our fight against the gods." My gaze moved to Toryn's face. "You don't have to come, of course."

The muscles around Toryn's eyes tightened. "I should go with you. If you attempt to cross the border, she'll have you killed on sight. But not if I'm there."

Niamh scowled. "Have you forgotten she tried to have you killed?"

"No, she tried to send a message." He fisted his hands against the table. "She will not kill me—nor any of us—if we go to her. She wants me by her side too much for that."

"I don't like it," I said in a low voice. I'd seen and heard too much to feel comfortable sending him back to that place, even by my side.

The day Toryn had stumbled across the border, begging me for a safe haven in Dubnos, he'd been bruised and bleeding and so weak, he could barely stand. They had been flesh wounds only, of course—nothing from which a fae couldn't heal. But he'd been so broken, I'd worried for a good long while whether he would ever recover. In his heart, perhaps he finally had.

I met his gaze. "Your mother might not harm you, but your brother most certainly will."

In the Kingdom of Storms, succession was determined in a brutal tournament if the current ruling family had more than one child. In front of the entire court, as well as hundreds of citizens, the potential heirs engaged in a fight to the death when they all came of age. Whoever won was declared the next king or queen. Magic was not permitted in the battle—only daggers, fists, swords, and arrows. Anything that made blood paint the floor.

And so as one of Queen Tatiana's grown children, Toryn had been forced to endure the tournament against his two brothers and two sisters. Only he and Owen had survived the first round, though Toryn had done none of the killing. Just before round two began, Toryn escaped from the arena. He fled to Dubnos to take refuge, refusing to kill his brother. His mother had been trying to get him back ever since. He was her heir, or one of them, at least, and she wanted him and his brother to finish what they'd started all those years ago.

If Toryn crossed that border, his brother would go for him.

"He won't attack me as long as you're with me," Toryn said. "Owen fears the mists. And you. That's why he never followed me here." He rubbed the scar on his cheek. "I need to do this, Kal. After all these years, I need to face them."

My chest tightened, but I nodded. "All right. You and I will go to the Kingdom of Storms. Fenella, you come, too, and ask your cousin Caedmon to join us. Niamh, you and Alastair will visit the mortals."

Niamh sighed but didn't argue.

"If Druid Balfor is right, the people of Talaven might not be happy to have fae visitors now that the comet is in the sky. You'll need a mortal to go with you..." I trailed off and glanced at Tessa, but then I shook my head. I wouldn't part us again. "We'll ask around and see if anyone would like to go on a trip to—"

"What about Val?" Niamh cut in, her eyes locked on the table before her. "Knowing her, she'll want to do something to help."

"Now wait..." Tessa said with a frown.

"Ask her." I gave Niamh a nod and turned my gaze to Gaven. "As I said before, I'd like you to stay in the city. The people of Endir trust you. We'll leave Morgan in the dungeons here. See if you can get any information out of her. She might know more than she's said."

My Mist Guard nodded, agreeing with the plan, though there was a thick cloud of unease clogging up the room. I hated splitting us up again, especially now. Gaven typically stayed in Endir all year round, but things felt different this time. Like this was the last time I'd ever see him or anyone who traveled to Talaven.

I just didn't think we had another option. We had to divide first before we conquered.

I could only hope the gods wouldn't conquer before we did.

Ten
Tessa

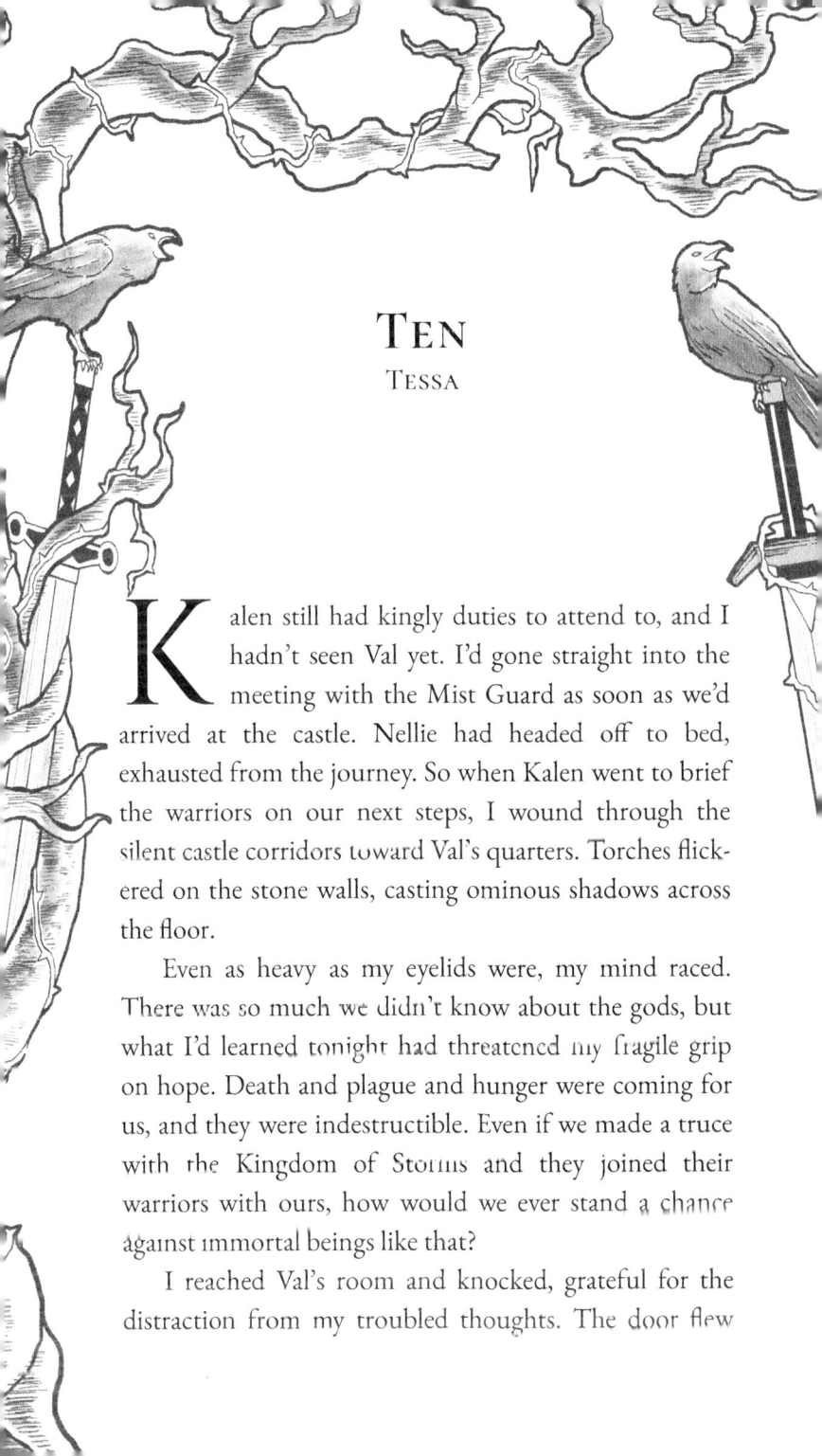

Kalen still had kingly duties to attend to, and I hadn't seen Val yet. I'd gone straight into the meeting with the Mist Guard as soon as we'd arrived at the castle. Nellie had headed off to bed, exhausted from the journey. So when Kalen went to brief the warriors on our next steps, I wound through the silent castle corridors toward Val's quarters. Torches flickered on the stone walls, casting ominous shadows across the floor.

Even as heavy as my eyelids were, my mind raced. There was so much we didn't know about the gods, but what I'd learned tonight had threatened my fragile grip on hope. Death and plague and hunger were coming for us, and they were indestructible. Even if we made a truce with the Kingdom of Storms and they joined their warriors with ours, how would we ever stand a chance against immortal beings like that?

I reached Val's room and knocked, grateful for the distraction from my troubled thoughts. The door flew open a second later, and Val let out a string of curse words that would rattle any sailor. Her flaming red hair hung around her shoulders in loose, frizzy waves, and wrinkles consumed every inch of her pale green tunic. Before I could manage a word of hello, she threw her arms around me and practically dragged me into her room.

"Thank the light. I've been going mad with worry," she whispered fervently as she kicked the door shut with a bare foot. "What happened? You look like shit. Is that blood?"

"It's a long story, but, ah..." I lifted my finger and pointed at the wall beside her dressing cupboard. "Mind telling me one thing first? What the fuck is that?"

A towering pile of books teetered on the floor just below a maze of parchment clippings attached to the wall. One of the clippings held nothing more than a paragraph, while another was an entire page's worth of writing. Several of the papers were connected to each other by bits of twine. My eyes dropped to the stack of books. One of them lay open on the floor. Half of the page had been cut out.

Val grinned and motioned at the mess. "*This* is the answer to everything."

"Please tell me you haven't ripped pages out of books."

"All right. I won't tell you, since you can see it for yourself." Suddenly, her grin vanished. "Before we go into all this, can you please tell me what happened out there? Are you all right? How is everyone else? Is Nellie safe? Niamh...she got back safely, right?"

I gave her a look, noting the flush in her cheeks, and a

slow smile lifted the corners of my lips. "Interesting you should ask about Niamh."

"She's...nice."

"And beautiful."

"And really fucking fierce," Val said with a sparkle in her eye. "Don't you think?"

"Absolutely." I strode over to her and slung my arm around her shoulder, gazing up at the strange array of pages attached to the wall. "And *you* are brave and beautiful and strong. And also...slightly deranged."

Quickly, I filled her in on everything that had happened, making sure to point out Niamh was safe and sound here in Endir. When I was finished, I motioned to the wall. "Now it's your turn. What in the name of light is all this?"

Val laughed. "I swear there's a reason for this. Look— this paragraph here is about Andromeda."

I leaned closer and read the words, squinting in the dull light that emanated from the hearth. "Death will rise from the ashen remains of a great city." Mouth parting, I turned to her. "This sounds like it refers to Albyria burning down. Where did you get this?"

"There are dozens of books in the library that detail the history of the fae world. At first glance, it doesn't seem like any of them cover the period called the Fell. That's what the mortals call it, when the gods came the first time."

I nodded. "That's what Druid Balfor said."

She tapped another note. "See? It's here in these books. It was just harder to find because it's woven in with the rest of the history, and it's rarely directly referenced."

"So you've spent the past few days combing through the library and finding any passage that might connect to what's going on now."

"I had to do something," she said, fisting her hands. "You were out there tracking down Oberon. Nellie was training with Gaven until she ran off."

"Nellie was training?" I asked, surprised. "With what?"

"Her claws and fangs."

That explained a lot.

I turned back to the wall. "We'll need to tell Kalen everything you've learned, although if anyone was going to find this information, it's good it was you."

At that, I explained what the Mist Guard had discussed during the earlier meeting, including her part of the plan. I hated the idea of her sailing to the mortal kingdoms instead of staying by my side, but I had to admit, this was the safest task the Mist Guard could have given her. The journey to the Kingdom of Storms would be dangerous. Staying in Endir might be a better option, but tensions between fae and humans were still high. I didn't want her in the city if things went wrong. And if the shadowfiends decided to launch another attack...next time, they might have even greater numbers than before. They'd never bested Endir's protective walls, but things were changing.

Val sat hard on the high-backed chair beside the hearth, her face pale. "They want *me* to journey to Talaven? As some kind of diplomat?"

"Something like that," I said, taking the chair across

her. "The others are worried Talaven won't want to exchange information with a group of fae. But if Niamh and Alastair have a human with them, perhaps the humans will share what they know. It helps that you've been doing research already. You have some insight."

Val nodded. "What about you?"

"I'm going to the Kingdom of Storms."

She arched a brow. "That's a terrible idea."

"Kalen is going," I said with a shrug. "And where he goes, I go."

Val released a heavy sigh and draped her arms across her knees, leaning forward. "I just wish we could all stay here in Endir and live out the rest of our lives in peace. With good food, good drink, good company. Sure, there's mist everywhere, but it's not so bad most of the time."

"Me too, Val," I said. "But we're the ones who are here for the Second Fell. The only way we'll ever get that better world, where we can live in peace, is to build it ourselves." I held out a hand. "We'll do this. And we'll do it together, even if we're apart, just like we always have."

Val grasped my hand and nodded. "If you fall, I fall."

"If you fall, I fall," I whispered back.

Val left to visit Niamh, so I wandered into the library to see if I could find any more texts that might help us work out the puzzle of the gods. Bed called to me, but my mind buzzed with a thousand different thoughts, and I knew I'd never get sleep, even if I tried. Tomorrow morning, we'd set off on our journey to the Kingdom of Storms. I would see the lands I'd only ever imagined—rolling fields of wind and rain and thunder. It might be a long time before we returned to Endir, depending on how long it took us to convince the storm fae to agree to our truce. But we only had a month before Andromeda appeared, if that.

I held up the gemstone-lit lantern and roamed through the stacks. Dust motes drifted on the stale air, making me cough. As I scanned the spines, I realized I didn't really know what I was looking for. All the information Val had found was hidden in random texts. With a sigh, I grabbed the nearest book and flipped it open.

Footsteps echoed from somewhere nearby. I jumped and I snapped the book shut just as a tall, powerful figure strode from the shadows. Kalen's black hair curled around his face, and the dark look in his sapphire eyes made my heart skip a beat.

"I thought I might find you here," he said, wrapping his hand around the book and holding it up before him. "The Sex Lives of Courtesans. Interesting choice."

"Oh." My chest burned. "I didn't look at the title before I grabbed it."

"Hmm." Smirking, he braced his hands on either side

of my head, his palms against the wooden shelves. "Nice try."

"Val is doing some research."

"I don't think you're going to find the answer to saving the world in a book about sex." Leaning closer, he brushed his lips against my ear. "Although wouldn't that be a lovely way to win?"

"Kal," I said, biting back my moan.

"Hmm?"

"We need to talk." I hated myself for the words, but as much as I wanted to give in to the desire pulsing between my thighs, I needed to clear something up between us. "About your vow."

He pulled back, and those sapphire eyes went flat. "There's nothing to talk about. My vow does not apply to you."

"But what if it does?" I insisted. "I know you're just using Oberon as an excuse. It's a way to put the blame on someone else. And I'll admit, you could be right. It *was* partially Oberon's fault."

"Then I fail to see the issue here, love." He tucked his finger beneath my chin. "He caused it, and he is dead. End of story."

"Except the comet is still in the sky. Killing him didn't stop it."

"And that is where prophecy and unspecific vows cause trouble," he countered. "We do not know what any of this means, and no matter how much Val scours these books for answers, she won't find them here. We don't know how to undo this or stop it or fight our way out of it. And I refuse to believe your death is the answer."

My heart pounded. I palmed his rough cheek and lifted my chin, forcing him to see what I knew he wanted to avoid. "I know what you're trying to say, and I agree with it to an extent. But I think we must prepare ourselves for the possibility."

"What possibility?"

"What if the way to stop them is to kill the person who brought them back?" I whispered.

"*Oberon* brought them back."

"I held the knife. He threw himself forward—or something pushed him—but I still held that fucking knife. We can keep repeating that it doesn't matter. But what we think and say might not matter in the end. Not if there's some kind of magic involved that ties the gods to me."

Kalen pulled back, a muscle ticking in his jaw. "I will never harm you."

"You might not have a choice." I hated that we were having this conversation. I hated this wall of pain between us. It felt impassable, a bigger obstacle than any we'd faced before, and that was saying something. Everything about this felt unavoidable, as if fate were dragging both of us toward the worst possible outcome—one where Kalen would have to rip out my heart.

"There is one way to protect you," he said, his voice growing soft. "I can never be free of my vow to my mother, but there is one thing that supersedes all vows. One way to ensure you will always be safe by my side."

"Kalen," I started.

"A bond. A vow that you are mine, and I am yours."

My heartbeat quickened. "You mean, a marriage vow?"

"A *fae* marriage bond," he said roughly. "It is far more carnal than a human marriage, far more binding. Magic will connect our souls, preventing either of us from harming the other. It is unbreakable. It can never be undone. I will be yours for as long as I draw breath, and I will never take another for as long as I live. I will be linked to you forever."

I stared into his eyes, the words stuck in my throat. He cupped my cheek and rested his forehead against mine, and he breathed me in, as if memorizing my scent, memorizing me. "Are you certain you want to do this? You're fae. I'm mortal. I could die in fifty years, maybe even less. You could live hundreds more years. Do you really want to link yourself to a mortal like this?"

He answered by rubbing his thumb across my jawline, and my core tightened with desire. "You are mine. And I am yours. I vow it."

"Kalen," I whispered, tears flowing down my cheeks. "You can't do this."

"Your turn."

"It's too big a sacrifice."

"For you, I would sacrifice it all."

Heart pounding, I leaned back into the hardwood bookshelf, gazing up into his fiercely glowing eyes. He meant every word, and the determined set of his jaw told me he would not take no for an answer.

"You wouldn't agree to this if it were the other way around," I finally said. "If I were the fae and you were the mortal, you wouldn't want me to be alone for hundreds of years."

"Listen to me," he demanded.

Swallowing hard, I stared into the depths of his eyes.

"I don't know what's to come, but if you're right—if there is even the smallest chance I might be forced to raise my hand against you..." The muscles around his eyes tightened. "It would destroy me. I cannot do it, do you understand me? And so I will gladly bind my soul to yours if there's even a chance this will override the vow I made to my mother. Anything to keep you safe. Do this *for me*, please."

"You really mean it," I said, searching his gaze for any sign he might regret it. But there was nothing there. Nothing but fierce determination and something else that made my heart pound even faster.

"All you have to do is say the words, and I am yours until I take my last breath."

I swallowed. If I spoke these words, there would be no undoing it. But looking up at him, I couldn't help but feel, deep in my bones, like this was right, like this was meant to be, like fate had brought us together just for this.

And so I clutched him tighter, and I said, "I am yours, and you are mine. I will never leave you. I vow it."

Magic pulsed between us, and an invisible hand clutched my throat, choking me. I gasped for air, my eyes going wide. Kalen's expression mirrored mine, and it was as if this unseen power wanted to drown us in our own words—as if it wanted to steal the last breaths we'd sworn to save for each other.

But then, just as quickly as it had come over me, that overpowering magic disappeared.

I pressed my shaking hands to his chest. "What in the name of light was that?"

"The power of the bond. It does not take our vows lightly. Our breaths are now linked." The shelves behind me dug into my back as Kalen leaned closer, his breath hot against my neck. "I am yours now, love. For all the remaining days of my life."

I shivered, melting against him as he dropped his hot mouth against my skin. Curling my fingers around his tunic, I tugged him closer. His voice rumbled against me, a low growl that sent shivers of delight down my spine. I'd felt tired and aching before, but now, I felt impossibly alive.

His mouth found mine, hungry, rough, and hard. My core tightened, and I moaned as his hands dropped down to trace the line of my hips.

"You are mine, and I am yours," he said.

A shiver went through me, my thighs widening instinctively. He inched forward until his hard length pressed against me. Even through the material of our trousers, I could feel his need, matching my own.

Our kiss deepened, and heat seared through me. I reached up and wound my fingers through his silken hair, desperate to pull him closer, to erase every inch of space between us. And when I arched against him, pressing my core harder against his length, he practically purred.

Distantly, I was aware we were in a library and someone could barge through those doors at any moment, but I didn't care. Not when I needed to feel his mouth on my skin, not with that pounding ache between my thighs, not when every part of me now felt linked to every part of him. We were bonded now, and I swore I could *feel* his emotions as if they were my own.

When he pulled back, his scorching gaze burned through me. I untangled my hands from his hair and got to work on his buckle. A moment later, he started on mine, and soon, our trousers were in puddles by our feet, along with his tunic.

And then the King of Shadows knelt, one knee against the wood. With a gentleness that bordered on reverence, he lifted my leg and hooked my thigh around his neck, drinking in the sight of my wetness.

"You are fucking beautiful," he murmured, leaning in to brush his lips across my thigh. I shuddered against him, my body tensing against the shelves. His lips drifted closer —closer and closer, each second tightening the ache until I could barely stand the lack of contact any longer.

Arching against him, I lifted my tunic a little higher, wanting to feel his hands on every inch of me.

With one hand gripping my thigh and the other splayed across my backside, Kalen dragged his tongue across my aching core. I bucked against him as pleasure swept through me. My moans echoed through the silent library stacks. With an answering growl, Kalen pushed his tongue deep between my folds.

I nearly came undone as desperation for more clawed through me.

Every flick of his tongue, every taste he took of my need, was better than it had ever been before, and yet it wasn't enough. I needed all of him. I wanted him to bury himself inside me, feeling every ounce of the pleasure he was giving me right now.

I couldn't help myself. I started to move my hips, grinding myself against his mouth. He growled, his hand tightening against my backside, and I could feel the deep vibrations of that sound beneath me. Moaning, I slid my hands into his hair once more and held on as I bucked against him, faster and faster until everything within me clenched tightly.

He lifted his eyes to mine with his tongue deep inside me. And it was that one look with the fire blazing in his sapphire eyes that shattered me completely.

I bucked against him, coming so hard I nearly screamed. I worried my violent shakes might hurt him, so I tried to pull away. But he held me in place, letting me ride my waves of pleasure against his mouth.

When the last of my quakes subsided, Kalen slowly rose, my need gleaming on his lips. He gave me a feral smile. "I think I'm going to need you to sit on my face more often."

I blushed and palmed his shoulder, marveling in the curves of his muscles. "Your turn."

That feral smile turned electric. "What did you have in mind?"

I turned, presenting my backside to him, and leaned forward to grab the lower shelves. "I need you inside me."

He gripped my hips, and the tip of his cock brushed against my core. Even though I'd just had my release, everything within me clenched once more. His palms massaged the shape of my thighs, my hips, my waist, until his thumbs stilled against those decades-old scars on my lower back.

"You are the most beautiful creature I've ever seen," he murmured, gently pushing his swollen tip inside me. "And such a good fucking girl."

A delicious shudder went through me as he filled me to the hilt. He pulled out and thrust harder this time, causing a rough gasp to pop from my throat.

"Is that all right?" he asked in a low growl, and I could tell he was trying to hold himself back.

"Faster," I whispered, spreading my legs wider. "Harder."

Kalen did not need any more encouragement than that. With a grunt, he thrust deeper into me. I cried out from the delicious sensation that shook through me, no longer caring if anyone heard. Holding tight to the shelf, I rocked against him and met his building need with my own.

Our reverberations shook some of the books loose from the shelf, and they tumbled to the floor. That only seemed to drive Kalen on. He gripped me tighter and pounded into me so hard that stars dotted my eyes.

My pleasure began to build, my walls tightening around him until I couldn't hold on even a second longer. Shaking, I arched against him, getting the angle just right, and—

The world shattered around me. Delicious light spilled through my mind, transforming my entire existence into nothing but stars. Panting, I clung to the shelves, the tremors of my climax more intense than I'd ever felt before.

Kalen roared as he followed in my wake. His cock throbbed between my legs, spilling his seed. Our bodies shook together, and for a brief moment in time, I felt something between us snap tight—a thread, or a coil, winding around his soul and mine. Our breathing was in sync; our orgasms throbbed in time. Even our hearts seemed to beat as one.

And then that sensation flitted away like leaves on the wind, leaving me spent and in desperate need of sleep.

I sagged against the shelves as Kalen slowly pulled out of me. And then he was there, hauling me into his arms and kissing me as if he'd never kissed me before. When he pulled back, his eyes latched onto mine, and that strange thread seemed to tug at me again.

"Never leave my side again," he said, his voice rough. "Stay with me always."

Heart swelling with a strange kind of hope, I palmed his jaw and I smiled. "I'm not going anywhere. I promise."

"Good." He dropped his forehead against mine, and I swore I could still feel the heavy thudding of his heart as if it were mine.

Eleven
Tessa

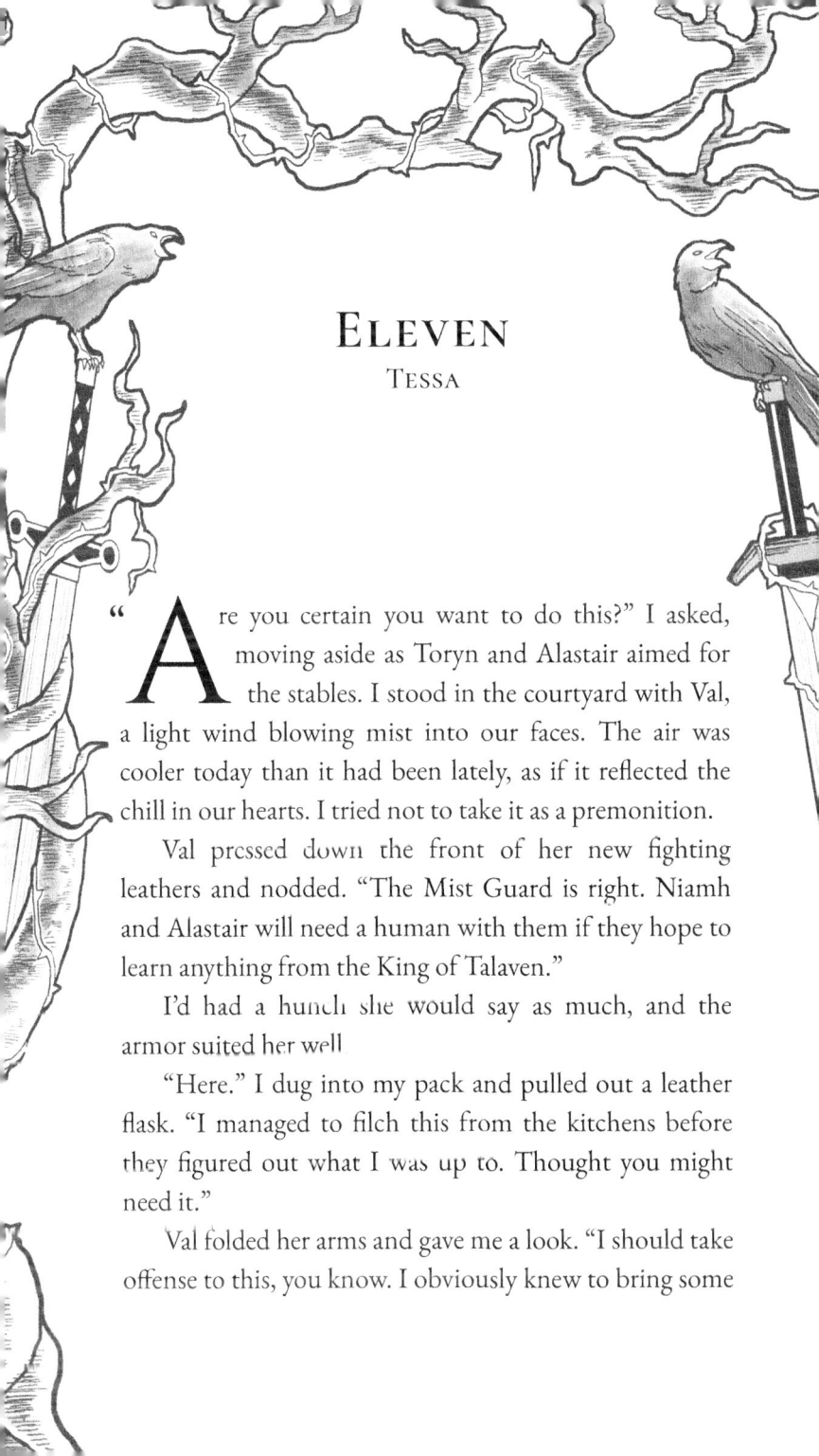

"Are you certain you want to do this?" I asked, moving aside as Toryn and Alastair aimed for the stables. I stood in the courtyard with Val, a light wind blowing mist into our faces. The air was cooler today than it had been lately, as if it reflected the chill in our hearts. I tried not to take it as a premonition.

Val pressed down the front of her new fighting leathers and nodded. "The Mist Guard is right. Niamh and Alastair will need a human with them if they hope to learn anything from the King of Talaven."

I'd had a hunch she would say as much, and the armor suited her well.

"Here." I dug into my pack and pulled out a leather flask. "I managed to filch this from the kitchens before they figured out what I was up to. Thought you might need it."

Val folded her arms and gave me a look. "I should take offense to this, you know. I obviously knew to bring some water on a long journey like this. I have four canteens in my pack."

"It's fion," I said with a grin. "Just in case you need to take the edge off."

She laughed, unscrewed the cap, and then sniffed. "I really do love some fion."

Niamh strode by with an exaggerated swagger and exchanged a glance with Val, who blushed furiously in response. I held back a smile and waited for her to vanish into the stables before I elbowed Val's ribs. "I like the idea of you two spending more time together."

"Me, too. Ah..." Val cleared her throat and pulled a stack of parchment clippings from her bag. She passed them to me. "It's no fion, but I have a gift for you as well. It's everything I found that might connect to the gods and prophecies. Have a read through it. Share it with Kalen. See if you can make sense of it."

"Thanks, Val." Throwing my arms around her, I yanked her close and squeezed her like I'd never again see her face. A part of me worried I never would. We had a month before the enemy descended upon our world. If we hadn't made it back to each other by then... "Take care of yourself, all right?"

She nodded, pulled back, and swiped a tear from her cheek. "I never thanked you, you know."

"For what?"

"After my parents died, you took me into your life like a sister, not just a friend who lived down the road. Without you, I would have never gotten through what Oberon ordered his soldiers to do to my parents. I'm glad you killed the bastard. I don't care if Andromeda corrupted him, and I don't care if he was trying to make things right at the end. He deserved to die for everything he did to us. And I'm so fucking glad you were the one to hold that dagger."

I took her hand in mine and gripped it tightly—my left and her right—like a handshake of promise. "You're not just *like* a sister, Val. You *are* one. And stop talking like this, eh? It's not goodbye. I won't let it be."

A ghost of a smile crossed her face. "Well, if anyone can fight the tides of fate and win, it's you. See you soon, then."

Swallowing down a lump of pain, I nodded. "See you soon."

"Hello, there," I cooed at Silver, who stood in the warm safety of the stables. The others had been leading their mounts into the courtyard when I'd passed by the stall where I'd been told I'd find my ride. The dark beauty was a magnificent creature, just like they all were, but I was drawn yet again to the horse who had followed me through the mists.

Silver nickered and stomped a hoof when I draped my arms over the low wall of his stall. The stablehands had brushed his coat until it gleamed, and the oats they'd given him were reduced to a pile of crumbs now. But his eyes gleamed with excitement, as if he knew exactly why I'd sought him out.

"You've just returned from a journey," I said, passing him a carrot—another thing I'd grabbed from the kitchens. "Really, you should stay here and rest. There are plenty of other horses who are refreshed and ready to go."

His hooves clattered as he stepped right up to me and brushed his snout across my outstretched palm.

"If you want to come, you can, but it's your choice." I hauled open his stable door and waited to see what he'd do. After a moment, he bowed his head and stomped out to join me in the corridor. I rubbed my hand against his neck and smiled. "I'm glad you're joining me. I don't know why, but I feel like you have my back."

Fenella led a horse from a stall at end of the stables and shot me a look as she passed us by. "You're talking to a horse again."

"He understands me."

"I'm sure he does. Just like you healed from that pooka wound within an hour. Your powers are growing." To my surprise, she actually smiled. "Sorry I threatened you with my daggers back in that Albyrian pub."

I nodded, still stroking Silver's snout. "You were doing what you thought you had to do."

"I still might have to do it." She sniffed. "I can smell it, you know. You and Kal made a marriage vow." She held up her hand when I opened my mouth to explain. "You don't have to tell me why. I get it. You two had an unbreakable bond long before you spoke the words to seal it. But just remember,

I've made no such vow. Now, I like you, Tessa. I really do. The thing is, though, I like this world better, and I'm not convinced Oberon's the one Kal's mother warned us about. And if it comes down to it, I'll do what has to be done."

Fenella vanished out the door with her horse. My heart racing, I leaned against the stable wall and steadied my breathing. Just like me, she clearly still thought I might be a threat, if not for my powers then for my link to the gods. When I'd made the bond with Kalen, I hadn't considered what that might mean for the others. They might have to kill me, leaving Kalen alone for the rest of his life.

Regret rolled over me like a boulder that threatened to flatten me to the ground, breaking every bone in my body. In the heat of the moment, I'd wanted to give myself to Kalen Denare, the King of the Shadow Fae. It had felt exhilarating and romantic and *right*. When I looked into his eyes, I felt safe and accepted and cared for in a way I never had before. I wanted to be his. And I wanted him to be mine.

But not like this.

A painful ache formed in my gut as I led Silver out of the stables to join the others. Nellie stood with them, her long chestnut hair blowing in the breeze and a defiant look in her eye. The dark trousers and fitted tunic matched my own, though I'd donned leather armor on top of mine. I walked over to her, leaving Silver with the other horses.

"Let me guess," I said. "You want to come with us."

She lifted her chin. "Val is going with Niamh and

Alastair. She doesn't have any more fight training than I do."

"The mortal kingdoms will be a lot safer than the Kingdom of Storms. We don't even know what we're walking into there."

"I want to help. There must be something I can do."

I sighed. "All right, Nellie. Do you want to go with Val? You could see the world and find answers we desperately need." And it would be safe for her there. Far safer than Endir.

Her jaw clenched. "One day, we will fly away from here like the ravens. We promised each other that, and I always meant that we would do it together. Not you by yourself, leaving me behind to twiddle my thumbs."

"But we did do it, Nellie. We got out of there, away from Oberon and the light fae. That doesn't mean you should fly into something far more dangerous. The storm fae might try to kill us."

"You're going," she pointed out.

"That doesn't mean you should."

"If you leave me here, I'm just going to follow you again." Her eyes flashed with defiance. "I heard what Fenella said to you—that you might still be a threat because you were the one to hold the blade that killed Oberon. You need me with you if something goes wrong. I don't trust her."

I didn't quite know what to say to that.

So Nellie continued. "It's your decision, I suppose. Take me with you now or let me trail behind you in the mists where I'll be traveling all alone. Either way, I'm going to the Kingdom of Storms. I'm not staying behind this time. I want to help."

I heaved a sigh and closed my eyes. "And there's nothing I can say to convince you to go with Val instead?"

"Absolutely not."

I almost had to laugh at that. "You're even more stubborn than I am. Well, all right. I guess I have no other choice. If there's no stopping you, go choose one of the horses. There's a black one in there that I think would like to come. I hope you're prepared for how much your ass is about to hurt."

We set off an hour later, leaving behind the safety of Endir's walls. Toryn and Fenella took the lead, along with her cousin, Caedmon. He was a tall, muscular fae with silver hair shot through with red. As with his cousin, pale blue horns curved out of the top of his head.

The mists clogged the world around us, thicker than I'd ever seen it before. A blanket of unease settled over our silent party as only the clop of horse hooves filled the air. No one dared speak, not after our fight with the shadowfiends the day before. If the beasts were gathering in greater numbers—if they were hunting in ways they never had before—we couldn't risk the sound of our voices drifting toward them.

The hours passed in a blur. When my stomach began to growl and my eyes grew heavy, a familiar smudge rose in the distance. Tall, black, and gleaming, the onyx stone castle stirred a forgotten fear in my gut. Echoes of my days spent in Itchen with Kalen flashed through me. Quiet moments filled with hope and a newfound connection. But over all that sat the understanding that I'd released part of the god's essence that final day we'd been stuck in that castle. If I hadn't done that, if Andromeda's half-spirit hadn't tricked me...well, just like with everything else, I'd messed up.

As before, the city was silent and empty. The last time we'd been here, we'd found evidence of a shadowfiend attack. Anyone who had survived had been chased out of the city, leaving behind an eerie settlement full of empty homes and footprints in the sand.

The only sign of life now was the six shadow fae warriors who stood outside the castle doors. Kalen walked off to speak with them while I set up camp with the others. We chose one of the empty homes and set out our bedrolls in the living space after pushing aside tables and chairs to make room. Camping out in the open, we'd be much more likely to attract undesired attention. So inside it was, even though it felt like a tomb.

I curled up on my soft bedroll, and it didn't take long for the sound of my sister's steady breathing to lull me into sleep. I'd only just drifted into a dream fresh with spring flowers and birdsong when a strong, calloused hand grabbed my shoulder. I sucked in a gasp and leapt to my feet, grabbing the dagger I'd set beside my bedroll. I angled it at the intruder's neck.

Kalen gently moved the blade away from his throat. "Good instincts. Come outside with me."

Tiredly, I blinked at him and lowered the dagger. "What's going on?"

"We need to work on your powers before we reach the Kingdom of Storms." That was all he said before he turned, walked across the creaking floorboards, and pushed out into the shadowy night. Frowning, I glanced around me at the sleeping forms of our companions. Toryn rested on Nellie's other side, while Fenella lay flat on her back on the opposite side of the room with both daggers clasped to her chest. Caedmon looked dead to the world.

I couldn't help but wonder what they would think about this, us sneaking off to tease out the dark magic running through my veins. Would it make Fenella distrust me even more?

With a sigh, I followed Kalen outside and found him pacing at the bottom of the wooden steps. Mist swirled around him, his own power mingling with the ever-present fog that flowed through these lands. He glanced up as I approached and read the tension and uncertainty on my face.

"You need to do this, love," he said before I could voice my arguments. "You healed from the pooka's venom incredibly quickly. The power is coming to you, and you don't know how to control it yet. You need to master it before it masters you."

My hands fisted. "Control what, though, Kalen? Killing people with my touch?"

"Perhaps," he said in a low voice.

Fear burned my heart. I pressed a hand against my chest and breathed deeply, trying to calm my rising panic. Every time I thought about that power—and what it might make me do—I felt like my body might cave in on itself, taken down by the overwhelming thunder of my heart.

"I don't want it," I said in a harsh whisper. "I tried to use it yesterday, against the shadowfiend, but I don't want it."

"I know, love," Kalen said with a sad smile. "But it can be a tool, one for you to wield. It's something I'm forcing myself to face with my own power. It can do monstrous things. It can destroy anything in my path, but perhaps, if I just stop hating it and fearing it and trying to pretend it doesn't exist, then I can use it for good. For once in my life, I want to use it for good."

For a long moment, we stared at each other through the mist. His eyes were full of a wary hope, a contrast to the self-hatred and disgust I'd seen in him every other time he'd spoken of his power.

"What's changed?" I whispered.

He strode through the mist and wound his hand around the back of my neck. "*You.*"

My heart trembled. "What if...what if it *changes* me, the way it changed Oberon?"

"In Oberon's darkest moments, he melted beneath the flames of his despair. He let them burn him up until he was nothing but a husk of the man he'd been before. But you...you grew stronger. You will keep growing stronger. Learn it. Master it. And then, when Andromeda arrives, she will see that *you* are one person she can never control."

His words wormed their way into my heart, and as much as this power scared me, I wanted to believe he was right. Lifting my chin, I looked him square in the eye and said, "Then let's begin."

Twelve
Niamh

It took us a week to reach Sunport. Along the way, we'd narrowly avoided two pooka attacks by jumping in the river to hide our scent. They seemed to be wandering around in big packs now—strange, to say the least. In my long centuries alive in this world, I'd never seen or heard of the beasts behaving this way. As much as they looked like wolves, they weren't pack animals. They were more like the pale white bears in the far northern lands, solitary except for when they sought out a mate. A few would sometimes join together for a hunt, but I'd never seen more than ten in one place until a week ago.

That comet in the sky must be the reason.

Unlike Endir, Sunport felt like a ghost town. The once-bustling port city had lost three-quarters of its residents during the war, and they'd never recovered, even after almost four hundred years. The fae on this side of Oberon's protective barrier hadn't suffered from infertility like those in Albyria, but it was still difficult for fae to reproduce the way humans did. Our rapid healing meant our bodies weren't well suited to it.

On my left, Val slowed as she gazed at the city before us. The buildings were bleached white stone, topped with golden tiled roofs that had once glittered beneath the light of the sun. The cobblestone streets wound through the buildings like a maze that eventually led to the shore, where wooden docks shot off into the sea. Four hundred years ago, there would have been dozens of ships hauling goods, but only a lone ship sat there now, swaying gently in the current.

"Where is everyone?" Val asked, her eyes bright with curiosity, her loose, wavy hair flowing around her shoulders. For the love of the moon, she was beautiful.

Alastair came up beside her. "Inside, where the pookas can't get them."

Val glanced over her shoulder at the dilapidated wooden wall we'd passed through. The gate had been bolted, but it had been easy enough to shove it open. "Pales in comparison to the one in Endir."

"The last one got torn down in the war, and they've struggled to rebuild it," I said. "As I've heard it, the noise attracted the beasts, so they had to make do with this hastily constructed thing."

"Only problem is," Alastair said with a frown, "it's not very good at keeping the beasts out of the city. So the fae who live here spend most of their lives inside. Sad for a place called Sunport."

Val swallowed. "I think that's my cue to head for the docks."

Bow held tightly in my hand, I watched the red-headed mortal sashay in front of us. Her hips swayed from side to side, her curves—

"Watch out," Alastair said with a low chuckle. "You'll get drool on your armor."

Rolling my eyes, I shot a scowl at his back as I followed the two of them to the docks. Truth be told, I hadn't been able to take my eyes off Val from the moment I'd first seen her in Teine. Her long red hair, those bright, bright eyes, and the courageous energy she exuded with every step she took. Not just anyone would be willing to sail off to unknown lands and leave behind everything she knew and loved, just for a little hope of making a difference. And look so good doing it.

Maybe I really did need to watch out for drool.

When we reached the docks at the western edge of the city, the ship was waiting for us. Two human men stood on the docks and watched us approach with frowns that made spiderwebs around their eyes. Their sunburnt faces and shocks of white hair were a surprise. Most of the sailors I'd met from the mortal realms were younger men in search of adventure. The dangerous lands of Aesir were perfect in that regard.

"Captain," I said as we reached the two men, addressing the one who wore a fine tailored coat with three golden braids stitched onto its shoulders. He gave me a once-over before he turned to Val and frowned.

"One mortal. There were supposed to be a hundred," he said in a low, gravelly voice. "What happened to the others?"

"Did you not get our raven?" I asked as I stepped up

beside Val, edging my body in front of hers. "Our plans have changed."

He exchanged a glance with the other man, whose coat designated him as the first mate. "As long as you have the coin, I'll take just the one mortal, but I want to know what's happened to the others. Are they all dead?"

"Most survived. They're in Endir. And when given the choice, they decided to stay in Aesir rather than journey to a foreign land."

His gaze narrowed before he turned to the sailor standing beside him. They were both short and squat, and Alastair and I towered above them, but you wouldn't think it by the way they carried themselves. An air of unwavering confidence lifted their shoulders and told me they were powerful men, wherever they came from.

"I find it difficult to believe that only one mortal from Teine wants to get out of these hellish lands," the captain finally said. "Aesir is full of cruel fae and hideous beasts and so much fucking mist. It's spread even further now, did you know that? It's come into the sea. And that damn comet in the heavens above. That can't mean anything good."

Val started to move toward them, and I pressed a hand against the small of her back to urge caution. If these mortals didn't know the full truth about the comet, then I didn't think we should be the ones to fill them in. They might very well flee from these lands before we could board that ship.

For a moment, I struggled to find the right words, so Val found them for me.

"I'm not here to escape Aesir," she said. "I'm seeking

answers about our past, and answers about the gods and what they did to this world. We worry they're coming back, and we need to know how to fight them. All our answers are lost. We're hoping we can find them in Talaven. It could mean this world surviving. Or not."

I held myself still as the captain and his sailor scanned our trio with hawkish eyes. They didn't trust us, despite Val's words, and I didn't much blame them. We were strangers talking about gods and death, and this had never been part of their ship's plan. They were here to rescue a hundred humans, and those humans weren't here.

"You want passage to Talaven to do research on the gods?" He cocked his head. "With two fae armed to the teeth? One might think you were hoping to find a way to bring them back."

So they truly didn't know what the comet meant, then.

"That's the last thing we want," Val insisted, the sea breeze transforming her hair into a tangle of fluttering red ribbons. "We want to stop them, not help them. And you're the only ones with answers as to how we can do that."

The captain shoved his hands into his pockets and rocked back on his heels, considering the three of us. I didn't like the way he looked at Alastair and me, like we were wild animals that needed to be leashed or else we'd rage through his lands hunting for prey.

"How about the girl here comes with us on her own?" the first mate asked.

Alarm jolted my heart, and I stepped protectively in front of Val. "Absolutely not. I'm not sending her to a foreign land alone, and don't you even dare look at me like that. You wouldn't do it, either."

It was a gamble. They knew we needed the information, and they could easily turn us away. But I would not see Val step on that ship without at least one of us going with her.

Alastair clearly shared my thoughts. He took a step closer, hand on the pommel of his sword and a sneer curling his lips. "One might ask why you're so keen to get her on your ship without us."

The captain's expression remained blank and unreadable, but his throat bobbed as he swallowed hard. "All right, all right, no need to get aggressive. We'll let you come on board, but you're going to have to hand over your weapons."

I narrowed my eyes, but I'd expected as much. After elbowing Alastair in the side, I dropped my bow and arrows into the outstretched arms of the first mate. Alastair followed suit by handing over his sword. Val didn't move, but after a long, lingering look from the captain, she sighed and yanked the dagger out of her back waistband.

"Good." The captain gave us a tight smile. "I'll show you to your cabin."

Alastair took the lead, while I kept Val sandwiched between the two of us. We followed the captain and his sailor across the wooden plank from the dock to the ship, and I braced myself as several sailors stopped what they were doing to stare. I ground my teeth and kept moving forward, choosing to focus on the billowing white sails and the gleaming polished deck.

The captain led us to a cabin in the bowels of the ship. Inside, two bunk beds were built into the walls, and a small basin of water sat in the far corner, along with a wooden table that was only big enough to hold a lantern lit with gemstones.

I fought back a scowl. "You were expecting a hundred humans. You don't have a bigger cabin than this? Or one for each of us instead of making us share?"

"We were going to pile the humans in the cargo hold with bedrolls and sick buckets. If you'd rather spend the journey there, then by all means..."

"This is fine," Val cut in, though she looked about as thrilled by this as I did. "It's only a week, right?"

"Weather permitting," the captain replied. "Could be as long as three if the winds change."

Val blew out a breath and then met my eyes. "A week will be fine. Besides, it's not like we'll have to stay in here the entire journey."

"Of course." The captain smiled, and then stepped out into the corridor. "Enjoy the trip."

But then the door slammed shut, and a lock tumbled. With a sharp breath, I crossed the floor and tried the knob. It wouldn't budge. They'd trapped us inside.

Thirteen
Kalen

Tessa and I stood in the cold dark as she tried to call upon her power. As the minutes stretched into an hour, I could sense her growing frustration. Her power frightened her, but deep down, I knew she was far more afraid of losing control than of using it. So she tried. And tried again—and again and again, until her breath became ragged from the effort of it all.

With a frustrated sigh, she slammed her hand onto a patch of iridescent grass. I waited for the blades to shrivel up and die, but nothing happened. After a long moment, Tessa shook her head and sat back on her heels. Sweat beaded on her forehead.

"It's not going to happen," she whispered. "My father said..." Her voice cracked, but she shook her head and forced herself to continue. "He said the reason *I* had to use the power instead of him was because he'd spent too long behind Oberon's barrier. It somehow numbed whatever magic he had in his veins until it was gone completely. Maybe it's gone from me forever now, too."

"Hmm." I strode toward her, took her arm, and helped her stand. "You're scared, and you're still blaming yourself after everything that's happened."

"Wouldn't you?"

"You know I would. We had twin souls even before we made that bond."

"Then you understand why this power," she said, pointing at her chest, at her heart, "is something I *shouldn't* use. It comes from Andromeda, and I can feel that it does, that it's *wrong*. I think I've always been able to feel it. It's like a dark cloud of anger and viciousness and rage, and it...well, I can't blame it for everything because I'm still me, and it's a part of me. *It is me.* But I know I've been influenced by it, just like Oberon was."

I nodded. "And Oberon tried to hide from it. He tried to pretend he wasn't messing with fire and that everything was fine."

"What are you saying?"

"Accept what you are," I said, taking her hand and pulling it to my thundering heart. "Accept what's inside you. Channel that anger into something good, and *use* it."

"But my anger has led to horrible things. People have died because of it." Her eyes clouded over, as if she were recalling a distant memory.

I had an idea which incident she meant. When Oberon had first taken her to become his next mortal bride, he'd thrown a lavish ball to show Tessa off to his court. Her anger had gotten the better of her when she'd seen what the Albyrian light fae planned to do with one of their unnamed mortal maidservants. And so Tessa had thrown all caution to the wind, stabbing Oberon with a wooden dagger.

It had backfired terribly. Oberon had ordered Morgan to kill the poor maidservant in retaliation.

When Tessa had first told me that story, she'd had a haunted, defeated look in her eyes. Just like now.

"Love," I murmured. She blinked and met my gaze, and her eyes were hollow. "Both of us have done things we regret, but you know what we can't do?"

"Erase the past." Her hand tightened around mine.

"I'll make another deal with you."

She coughed out a strained laugh. "No more deals. No more vows."

"This one won't be bound in magic," I said. "It's just a promise to each other, based on nothing but trust. Let go of your fear and use your anger—*really try*—and I'll do the same. With you. We'll do it together."

It was a hard thing to say, and part of me wanted to reach out into the air, grab those words, and stuff them back inside. Tessa thought her potential power was dangerous, but mine was far, far worse. It had been hundreds of years, and I still didn't know how to fully control it. Because I'd feared it all this time. Because I'd avoided it. Because I thought it best for everyone if I locked it up inside me, never to be used again. Only recently had I dared wield it, when there'd been no other option.

"You'll train your power, too?" she asked.

"You train yours, and I train mine. Together, we'll be unstoppable," I said roughly. No matter what Andromeda and the other gods brought, they would never be able to defeat us if we fought side by side. My power would take out any big army—not that they would have one—and Tessa could kill the gods themselves once they got too close. "I've been thinking a lot about this. Your power might be the only way to stop the gods. *We* cannot kill them, but perhaps you can."

"Oh." Her eyes widened. "*Oh*."

"The power comes from Andromeda. She can kill anything and *anyone* by touch. Surely that includes other gods. And herself."

Tessa sucked in a sharp breath, then loosed it slowly, her entire body tense from the weight of my words. This had been on my mind for a few days, but I hadn't wanted to burden her with my suspicions, not yet. Not until I could be certain. But we didn't have much time. A month, if that.

She paced in front of me. "So I could make it right. I could undo what I did and rid this world of them once and for all."

"What *Oberon* did."

She turned toward me, her eyes flashing. "All right, I'll take that deal. We'll train together. You learn to blast the gods down just long enough for me to get to them. And then I'll kill them all."

Warmth spread through me at her fire. "There it is."

She lifted her chin. "Here it is."

"Now focus on all that anger," I said. "Take it and shove it into the ground. Let's see what you can do, love. Make the stars weep."

Nodding, she knelt again. All her wary unease vanished beneath the furious determination flashing through her eyes. Jaw clenched, she palmed her hands against the glowing iridescent grass, the blades poking between her fingers. She closed her eyes and leaned forward with her knees digging into the ground. I held my breath and waited.

There was no doubt in my mind Tessa Baran could do anything she put her mind to. With the power in her veins, she could rip this world to shreds if she wanted. She truly could make the stars weep. That power should terrify me, especially after what had happened to Oberon. With the flip of a coin, she could yield to the darkness, just like he had.

But deep down, I knew—I just *knew*. Call it intuition. Call it stupidity. Call it love. I knew she'd do the right thing.

A long moment passed. The breeze dusted sand into the air, rustling the grass. Tessa's braid slipped over her shoulder as she leaned further forward, her jaw tensing, her fingers trembling.

"Think of Oberon and his soldiers," I said, hating that I was pushing her to that place. But she had to go there. She had to face it. If she was going to master the anger, she had to fully embrace it. "Think of everything they did to you and your people."

A growl rumbled in the back of her throat.

"Remember everything he did to you. Remember how it made you feel."

Tessa heaved out a breath and then shouted at the ground. Her fingers formed claws as she dug into the soil, her entire body shaking. I had to fight my instinct to rush forward, to hold her in my arms and tell her everything was fine. I hated to see her like this—hurting and angry and shaking from the force of all those emotions churning within her—especially when my words had been the cause. But—

The ground *thumped* like a single drumbeat.

A few blades of grass around Tessa's palms curled, browning, crinkling. Dying. The brown spread from the tips of her fingers past the sides of her hands, forming a perfect circle of rot around her body. When she glanced up at me, tears glassed her eyes, but the smile on her face released the tension around my heart.

"You did it, love. You fucking did it."

Still smiling, she stood and rushed toward me. I opened my arms to lift her from the ground and squeeze her against my chest in a victorious hug. But she stumbled to a stop only inches away, and then held up her hands, grimacing.

"What if..." She stumbled over her words, paling. "Now that I've used it, what if..."

I took her hand and yanked her toward me. "I'm fae, love. Not some blades of grass. You'll have to try a lot harder than that to kill me."

Sighing into me, she slid her arms around my waist. I held her against me, resting my chin on top of her golden head of hair. "I knew you could do it."

"It's a start, at least." She tightened her hold on me. "Andromeda won't expect this, either. She won't know that I've found a way to unlock this power."

"Hmm. She knows you exist, though. I think we can't be—"

The ground rumbled. Frowning, I pulled back and

gazed around, scenting the air for the pungent scent of incoming beasts. But the air was fresh, the breeze full of mist and the cool scent of night. Tessa turned toward the onyx castle where my soldiers still stood, guarding the place. Her faced paled as another rumble shook the earth.

"What is that?" she whispered. "It's not coming from the castle."

"No."

"Shadowfiends?"

"There would have to be an entire host of them to make the ground shake like this," I said, frowning out into the mists. "And there's no scent of them on the wind."

The ground shook—harder this time. It knocked Tessa sideways, and she lurched into me. I grabbed her arms and pulled her against me, her back to my chest. I tightened my hold on her shoulders as I tried to peer through the mists.

One of the castle guards jogged toward me, his face lined with concern. "Your Majesty, do you feel that?"

"Find somewhere safe. Not the castle. Take the guardhouse instead," I ordered.

He nodded and jogged off to warn the others while I turned toward the house we'd chosen to camp in for the night. Toryn appeared in the doorway, his spear in his hands.

"What's happening?" he shouted as Tessa and I jogged toward him.

"I don't know." A crack suddenly appeared before us as the ground shook once more—this time, so hard it knocked me off my feet. Tessa slammed into the sand beside me and rolled to the side as another crack yawned between us.

Tessa scrambled to her feet and leapt over the widening crack, her body slamming into me. I held her close and raced toward the house. Everyone was on their feet now. Caedmon rushed down the steps, Fenella just behind him. She had her daggers out, shielding Nellie, whose pale face rivaled the moon. But weapons would do nothing against whatever this was.

And neither would the house.

"We need to leave," I barked at them. "Grab whatever you can and get out of here. Now!"

The horses screamed from where they were tied to their posts. Before I could stop her, Tessa pulled free of my arms and ran toward the horses. I swore beneath my breath and followed her. Despite my fae speed, she reached them before I did.

With shaking hands, she untied the ropes. She freed Silver first, then the others. The horse started to charge away, but she whispered into the wind. With a wicked scream, he stomped at the ground, eyes wild, teeth bared. But he didn't run. And neither did the others.

A moment later, the rest of our party reached us. The crack beside the house had widened, the split so vast it could swallow an entire building. And then—there. A long, black talon punched up through the crack, larger than two fae put together. My heart slammed my ribs. Something terrible was coming for us.

"Everyone," I said with a lethal calm that betrayed none of the raging emotions inside of me, "get on the fucking horses and ride. Ride like your lives depend on it."

Because they did.

Nellie caught sight of the talon and let out a strangled cry. Fenella glanced over her shoulder, following Nellie's gaze. Her face didn't even flinch, but her throat bobbed. Toryn grabbed Nellie's waist and lifted her onto a horse, and then slapped his hand against the horse's rump.

Nellie screamed as the horse raced into the night. Tessa, eyes focused on her sister, leapt onto Silver and followed quickly. I made certain Toryn, Fenella, and Caedmon left before I ran back to warn the warriors trapped in the guardhouse. They couldn't stay in the city if they wanted to survive.

That was when the ground exploded.

Fourteen
Tessa

The ground shook so hard, my horse stumbled, nickering wildly and tossing his head. Nellie hurtled off into the darkness just ahead of me, her form nothing but a smudge amid the gray. I glanced over my shoulder. The others were gaining quickly, the mists thinning around them. But back in the city, a monster the size of a house stalked toward Kalen.

It was unlike any creature I'd ever seen before, unlike anything I could have dreamed of. Six massive black talons punched the ground, the ends sharper than any steel. Its round black body quivered, and a pair of blood-red eyes swirled this way and that, its pincers clicking together.

Just ahead of it, Kalen raced into the guardhouse without even giving the creature a second glance. When he vanished from sight, Boudica darted madly in the skies.

All the blood in my body stilled.

I tried to turn Silver around, but he bucked against

me. My hands slipped on the reins, and I flew from his back. The wind whipped around me as I fell. The ground raced up to meet me, my teeth knocking together when my backside hit the dirt.

"What are you doing?" Fenella screamed at me as she approached.

Despite the pain, I shoved up from the ground and started running back toward the city. "Kalen went to save the guards. Look after Nellie. I'm going to help him."

It seemed stupid—insane, even. But I could not stop my feet from moving in Kalen's direction. It was as if an invisible rope tugged me forward, despite the danger scuttling closer and closer to the building that Kalen had entered. No one had come out yet. Did they hope to hide from the beast in the guardhouse? It wouldn't work. The creature was big enough that it could smash down those wooden walls if it wanted to.

I just kept running. A moment later, I heard the thundering of hooves once more. I took my eyes off the beast, just for a brief moment, to catch sight of Fenella's horse running beside me. Her face was grim, and she kept swearing into the mist, but any time her horse faltered, she urged him onward.

"Stay back," she called to me. "You're able to heal from a pooka's wounds, but I don't think you can heal from this."

Without another word, she dug her heels into the horse's flank and peeled ahead of me. I ground my teeth and pumped my arms, willing myself to move faster. The creature had reached the guardhouse now and was tapping one of the walls with its vicious talons. My heart nearly stopped when it tapped against a window. The glass shattered like it was made of nothing at all.

Fenella charged toward the beast, lifting Toryn's spear. "Oi! Come get me, you fucking asshole."

The beast whirled toward Fenella. She slowed to a stop, held the spear aloft, and waited for the inevitable. I kept running, moving as fast as I could, but knowing I wouldn't make it in time. One swipe, that was all it would take. One punch of a talon, and Fenella would die. With a click of its pincers, the beast lurched toward the silver-haired fae.

I flicked my gaze to the guardhouse just as the front door flung open. Kalen stepped out into the mists, his hands fisted and his expression hard. "Fenella, get out of here now."

"With all due respect, Your Majesty," she shouted, leveling the spear as the creature, "not until you do."

Narrowing his eyes, he stepped forward. "I can kill it, but not if you're there. Run back to the others. Make sure Tessa is all right."

He hadn't seen me yet, then. I was still running, my legs burning and my lungs aching for air.

Suddenly, the beast lifted a talon and shoved it through Fenella's chest. She tumbled off her horse and fell on the sand. Kalen roared, a sound of pain that slowed my steps. I stumbled, my body shuddering as if his emotions were shattering inside me. My knees hit the dirt.

Tears filled my eyes as I clawed at the ground. I couldn't think. I couldn't breathe. And yet, despite it all, my body kept moving forward. With my hands splayed on the ground, I crawled, desperately trying to get to

Kalen. To the other half of my soul. To the part of me that was dying from the onslaught of his pain.

I lifted my head just in time to see him stride up to the beast. He widened his hands on either side of him, fury written in every line of his face, and then—

"Oh, no," I whispered, realization pounding down on me. He was going to release his power.

My body shaking, I tried to scream out, to warn him that I was here. He hadn't noticed me, and I was in the path of his power. It would hit me if he loosed it on this creature.

But the pain was so great, like my very soul had split in two, that all I could manage was a whimper. I sagged forward and pressed my face into the dirt, breathing in the scent of grass. And then I held on, waiting for it to hit me. At least Toryn had stayed with Nellie. She'd be safe from this. She was far enough away.

Dimly, I thought perhaps this was the vow's twisted way of making Kalen do what he'd promised. He'd tried to outsmart the magic, but in the end, it always won.

Kalen roared. The overwhelming *thump* of his power echoed through the night, and every hair on my body stood on end. I ground my teeth against the force of it and the sensation of that power scraping along my skin, along my bones, along the innermost parts of my heart. And then I took in my last breath and waited for my life to blink out.

This was it, the moment every mortal feared. A strange peace settled over me as my vision filled with stars. The sky above called to me. Beyond this world, there was a place filled with light. A place where stars bathed every soul in a power that soothed even the worst pain until it was nothing more than a distant memory. I smiled.

And the world itself seemed to sigh.

I lifted my head, groaning. My vision blurred. Darkness pulsed around me. Mist still clung to my skin, and my head pounded like an angry drum. Through bleary eyes, I saw Kalen on his knees, holding Fenella's limp body against him. The creature was dead, its talons curled. Somehow, I had survived.

Slowly, I climbed to my feet and stumbled toward Kalen. I could still feel his pain pulsing through me. I could hear the cracking of his voice as he repeated her name, over and over until it was nothing but a hoarse scrape of his throat. He didn't notice me until I was standing just in front of him. Blood painted Fenella's fighting leathers. I looked away from the hole in her chest.

"Kalen," I said.

He looked up at me, and excruciating pain twisted his face. "Fenella is dead. The creature, it—"

"I saw."

His brow slammed down. "You were that close? You shouldn't have—"

"Move aside, Kalen," I said with a calm that I hadn't known I possessed. In fact, I'd never felt like this, as far as I could remember. That strange peace still filled me. Somehow, I knew it would not last long, but while I had it, I knew what I must do. "Let me see Fenella."

He tightened his hold on her.

"It's all right," I whispered to him. "Trust me."

Tension whipped between us. I could feel waves of grief crashing over me, but I let them pound through me, accepting them, letting them do what they must. I knelt beside Fenella as Kalen extracted himself. He stood and paced and jammed his fingers into his hair.

"She's dead. There's nothing you can do." His voice held so much pain that I could hardly think around it. "The talon sliced through her heart. Not even fae can heal from that."

Ignoring him, I placed my hands on her cheeks and closed my eyes. I'd remembered something from Oberon's vision—something that echoed through my mind even now. Andromeda's preferred power was death, but she had life, too. It was how Oberon had been able to grant the mortals of Teine so much protection, using her through the gemstone necklace. And she had been able to bring his love back to life using a vessel.

The only reason she hadn't been able to place Bellicent in her own body was because it had been too late. Days had passed by before Oberon had gone to the vault and asked for help.

It wasn't too late for Fenella.

I focused on peace, on the stars in the sky, on the healing magic I knew lay beyond this world. I didn't understand it, not fully, but I didn't need to. I just needed to feel that hope, that love, that unending kindness that *healed* and never harmed.

"Tessa, what are you doing?" Kalen asked.

The peace rushed through me, filling me up until it cleared my mind and body of pain. My palms pressing into Fenella's skin, I pushed. And then pushed and pushed some more, gritting my teeth, squeezing my eyes so tightly they burned.

All sound snapped away. My head filled with a ringing, a distant call. Everything went starkly, brutally cold, like a river of ice had frozen around me. I tried to pull in a breath and open my eyes, but everything vanished like the sputter of a candle snuffing out.

"Tessa," Kalen murmured into my ear. Warmth flooded my senses, chasing away the ice in my bones. I sucked in a desperate gasp and sat up, blinking at the darkness around me. Strong hands palmed my face and turned my head to the side. Kalen's sapphire eyes lit up the mists. "You're here. You're fine. I've got you."

"Fenella." The word scraped from my throat.

He turned to the side. I followed his gaze to find the silver-haired fae squatting beside me. Blood still painted her armor, but the hole in her chest was gone, and she was...my throat closed up. She was alive.

"You fucking marvelous human," she said in a hoarse voice. "I don't know how you did it, but you saved my life." She touched a hand to her forehead, and then pressed a shaking hand against mine. "I owe you a great debt."

My heart pounded. "You're all right."

"Because of you and whatever crazy magic you have inside you." Her eyes gleamed. "I'm sorry I ever doubted you."

"Trust me, I would have doubted me, too."

She nodded and then stood, gazing back at the dead creature. "Unfortunately, I have a feeling there will be more where that came from."

"What even is that?" I asked.

Kalen frowned. "Nothing I've ever seen before. Some kind of oversized scorpion."

"This, plus the behavior of the pookas." Fenella glanced up at the comet. It looked larger now. "It has something to do with *that*. I'm just glad Kalen's power is what it is. Otherwise, we'd all be dead. *All* of us. And there'd be no coming back."

I pressed my lips together and glanced at Kalen.

His gaze narrowed. "What is it?"

"I turned back when I realized you'd gone for the guards. I couldn't stand the thought of you facing the creature by yourself."

"That's right," Fenella said with a soft laugh. "Stupid and brave, the both of us. Thankfully, your horse got frightened and knocked you off, or it would have been you on the ground and not me. And I've gotta say, there are a lot of things I can do, but I definitely can't bring people back from the dead."

"I got pretty close," I said around the lump in my throat. I still didn't understand exactly what had happened, but... "Close enough that I could see everything, even in the darkness and the mist. What happened to Fenella, the expression on your face, the clenching of your hands when you decided to loose your power."

Kalen's face went pale. "But if you were that close..."

"Your power hit me."

"That's impossible."

"You'd be dead," Fenella said. "Kalen's power crushes anything it hits. I've seen it myself."

"So have I." A pause. "Could this be because of the bond we share now?"

"The marriage vow?" Fenella shook her head. "That only prevents purposeful harm. This would have been an accident."

"It's impossible," Kalen repeated, his voice growing louder. "I couldn't have. It would have killed you. It kills everything."

"Everything," I said with a strained smile, "except for me."

Fenella swore, but then shot me an apologetic smile. "Sorry. I mean, I'm glad you're not dead. But you know what this means, right? If you can survive Kalen hitting you with his power, then..."

Footsteps suddenly sounded beside us. The three of us turned to see Toryn, Caedmon, and Nellie arrive. Their grim expressions matched the dread in my heart.

"I saw it happen," Toryn said. "I was too far away to do anything to stop it, but all of us...we saw your power hit Tessa. Which means...if she can survive it, maybe the gods can, too."

Fifteen
Tessa

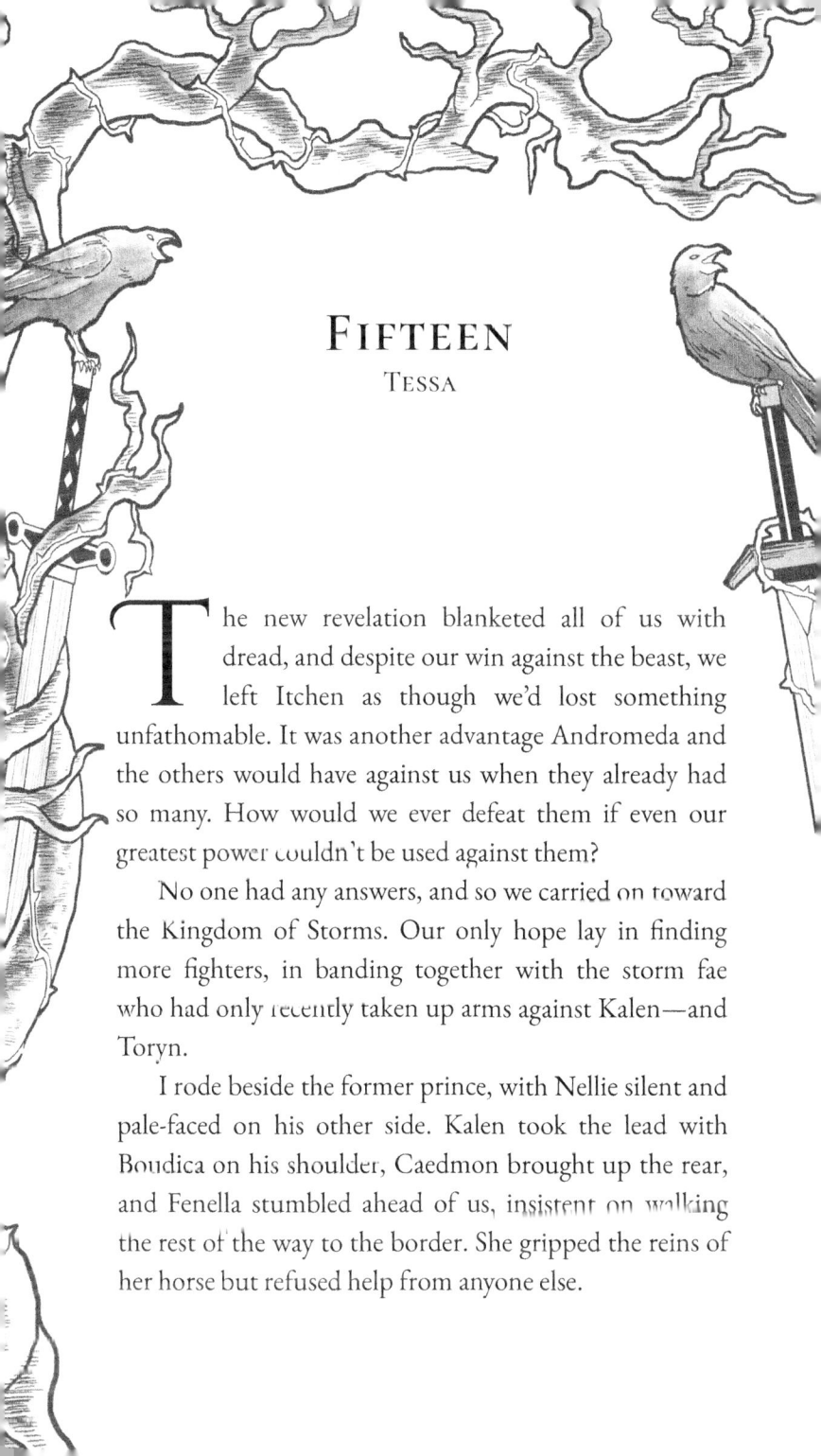

The new revelation blanketed all of us with dread, and despite our win against the beast, we left Itchen as though we'd lost something unfathomable. It was another advantage Andromeda and the others would have against us when they already had so many. How would we ever defeat them if even our greatest power couldn't be used against them?

No one had any answers, and so we carried on toward the Kingdom of Storms. Our only hope lay in finding more fighters, in banding together with the storm fae who had only recently taken up arms against Kalen—and Toryn.

I rode beside the former prince, with Nellie silent and pale-faced on his other side. Kalen took the lead with Boudica on his shoulder, Caedmon brought up the rear, and Fenella stumbled ahead of us, insistent on walking the rest of the way to the border. She gripped the reins of her horse but refused help from anyone else.

"Is she all right?" I asked Toryn. The steady clop of hooves almost drowned out my softly spoken words.

Toryn smiled sadly. "She'll be fine, but she's been through a lot. Sometimes, she struggles beneath the weight of it all. After what happened...I'm sure it brought back a lot of emotions she'd rather forget."

"I get that," I said.

"Just after the war ended and Kalen took control of Endir, not all of the light fae agreed to follow him. They staged a revolt. A lot of people died, including Fenella's husband, Cain. She loved him fiercely."

"Oh." I glanced up ahead at where Fenella stalked through the mists, her fists trembling by her sides. Her horse walked beside her and nudged her shoulder every now and again. His touch seemed to be the only thing keeping her together.

"During the fight, her son, Ilias, almost got killed, too. If it weren't for Kal stepping in and taking the blow for him, he would have—a sword, right in the gut. For Kal, it was only a surface wound that healed quickly. For Ilias, it would have been death, him being half mortal."

"Fenella's husband was a mortal?" I couldn't help but be surprised. "Humans and fae have always mingled so freely in Endir?"

"To an extent," he said with a slight nod.

"How long ago was that?" I asked, turning back to Fenella. It must have been hundreds of years. Even her son would likely be dead now. No wonder she always had such a harsh glint in her eyes. She'd lost so much.

"Just after the war," Toryn said. "So well over three hundred and fifty years ago."

"I see."

"She still loves him as deeply as the day they wed," Toryn said with a wistful smile on his face. "That's how it is for us, you know. Our emotions don't fade with time. If anything, they burn brighter and brighter until they consume us whole. It sometimes means she has a death wish. Living without them both…"

So that explained her willingness to throw herself in front of the beast, practically taunting him. And why she'd urged Kalen to blast away that entire light fae camp when we'd been hunting for Oberon. She had nothing left to live for.

Toryn read my thoughts. "All she has left is her fierce devotion to Kalen. She'd do anything for him, even die. Truth be told, any of his Mist Guard would."

"Something tells me you're speaking of yourself, too. Going back to the Kingdom of Storms must be difficult. I don't know what happened to make you leave, but I heard what Kalen said. It was something to do with your brother."

Toryn's face clouded over. His jaw clenched, and he ripped his gaze away to stare into the mists.

"I'm sorry," I said. "I didn't mean to bring up bad memories."

"Don't be sorry. In a few days' time, I'll have to face them, one way or another. I'm walking right back into the dragon's den, and it was my decision to do this."

I nodded, curious. But I wouldn't ask—I wouldn't push. It wasn't my place to demand answers when they were so clearly bogged down in pain.

But Toryn continued after glancing over at Nellie,

who was listening to our conversation with keen interest. "My mother is the queen of the realm, and while she is a kind and benevolent ruler, she is not so kind where her children are concerned." His face tightened. "There were four of us growing up, my brother and me, and two sisters. I was the eldest, but the line of succession is not decided by birth in the Kingdom of Storms. It's decided by brutality and strength in a much-celebrated fight to the death."

Nellie gasped, and I tensed my hands around the horse's reins. A fight to the death?

"The entire realm comes to watch." Toryn closed his eyes. "My younger brother, Owen, quickly killed Veina, and I horrified everyone by trying to save her and my other sister, Lilia. But it was no use. Owen killed her, too, and then it was just him and me. It was kill or be killed. And so I left, even though I was far stronger than Owen at the time. I would have won if I'd tried. Instead, I ran from the Kingdom of Storms, and Kalen took me in as part of his Mist Guard. My mother has wanted me back ever since. She wants me to finish the fight."

"Oh, Toryn," Nellie whispered. "I had no idea."

I loosed a breath. "What's going to happen when we cross the border? Will she try to make you fight your brother again?"

"Perhaps," he said quietly.

"But you're stronger," Nellie prompted. "You said you would have won."

Toryn reached up and touched the scar on his face from where the storm fae's lightning had almost killed him, and I knew, with certain dread, what he would say. "Not anymore."

T he next few days passed in a blur. We rode through the mist, camping and traveling, and Kalen and I trained as much as we could. We shared stories around the campfire. Caedmon told me about the time he went out hunting in the mist, lost his sword, and had to use his horns to take out a shadowfiend. So I told him about my battle with Oberon. That brought on a story from Fenella, then Toryn, and then Kalen. Nellie listened to us all with wide eyes.

After the trek to the mountain, we stopped only briefly in Dubnos to swap horses and take stock of the city. I hated to leave Silver behind, but he sorely needed rest after riding so hard the past few days. Once Kalen confirmed all was well, he left Boudica with the captain of the guard—a woman named Roisin, who I learned was Niamh's sister.

Then we moved on, trailing down the other side of the mountain and toward the border that would take us into the Kingdom of Storms. It was from the sloping mountain path that curved through the Gaoth Pass that I could finally set eyes on the lands unknown to me until now. Through the misty veil, a bright morning sun beamed down on fields of pink and purple flowers, and tall grass swayed in an insistent breeze. Green was everywhere. On and on and on it went for as far as I could see. The only mark on the brilliant land was an empty war camp at the base of the mountain, where tattered tents and charred fire pits marred the green.

"I thought there'd be more...well, storms," I said to Kalen, who rode quietly by my side. He'd been increasingly quiet the closer we drew to the border, and I couldn't help but wonder if it had something to do with the story Toryn had told me.

"There's always wind," he said, his voice as tense as his body. "The storms occur randomly and without warning, though not this close to the border. I've never seen one happen in that valley for all the years I've stared down at it from the battlements above."

I tipped back my head to gaze up at the towering mountain, where Dubnos perched on top of a large cliff. The castle was a dark smudge hidden in the mists.

"When we cross that border," Kalen said after a moment, "I need you to stay by my side. The storm fae are expert archers. We might not see them before they attack."

A chill tickled the base of my spine, and I glanced over my shoulder, where Toryn and Nellie were deep in conversation just behind us. "What about Toryn?"

Kalen shot me a tense glance. "He told you then."

"What happens if she tries to make him fight again?

"There's no question of it. She will try. But it's never going to happen. I won't let it."

Something told me it wouldn't be quite that easy, but I didn't say it out loud. I didn't need to. I could tell by the darkness swirling in his eyes that he knew it, too.

As we continued down the path and through the foothills, I thought back on everything I knew about the Kingdom of Storms. Like most things, it was very little. Oberon had made it seem as though they were barely surviving, just like us. Just like everyone except for the monstrous Mist King who lurked beyond the bridge, ready to gobble up anyone who dared cross into his lands. The Mist King had destroyed everything, after all. The light fae realm, the human kingdoms beyond the sea. Why wouldn't he have also destroyed the Kingdom of Storms? They were weak and powerless and hardly worth considering, according to Oberon.

But I'd looked into the eyes of those storm fae when they'd trapped Kalen and me in the Itchen castle. They were nothing if not powerful. Andromeda's essence had enhanced those powers then, but I'd seen enough to know they were a deadly force of nature even without her help. And their eyes...there had been something terribly wrong about their eyes.

All that was on my mind when we finally crossed the border—when we stepped out of the mists and into the warmth of the sun. Exhaling from the soothing heat of it all, I tilted my face toward the light and basked in the glow of it. The sun, the beautiful, glorious sun. I hadn't realized how much I'd missed it.

"Oh, in the name of light," Fenella whispered.

I glanced over at where she stood with her arms thrown out on either side of her. She'd closed her eyes and dropped back her head. And for the first time since I'd met her, a genuine smile brightened her face, erasing all the tension, all the anger, all the despair. It was easy to forget she was a light fae at times and that Endir had once existed in the Kingdom of Light. She knew the sun, and yet it must have been centuries since she'd felt its warm rays on her skin.

Kalen smiled fondly at her, and then glanced at Toryn, his brow furrowing as he took in his old friend's tense and wary face. To him, the sun was not a thing to celebrate and enjoy. It meant he was home.

"Come on," Kalen said with an eye on the surrounding hills, "let's get moving."

The smattered war camp lay before us, silent and empty and deadly still, as if the wind around us had been sucked out by the mist pulsing at the edge of the veil. As we walked through it, past the cold fire pits and flattened tents, a chilly dread—the same as before—tickled the base of my spine. I gazed around, my shoulders tensing, and braced myself for signs of the dead. But the camp was empty, and there wasn't a single body anywhere.

"Your Majesty," Caedmon called out. "Didn't you say you battled the army camped here?"

"I'm not sure 'battle' is the right word for what I did, Caedmon," he said quietly.

When I'd been trapped in Oberon's dungeons, the storm fae army had camped at the base of the mountains where Dubnos stood, readying themselves to sack the city. They'd been staging multiple attacks against the Kingdom of Shadow for weeks, even crossing the border at times. Kalen, desperate to end the threat against his people and to reach me before Oberon bound me to his will, had aimed his brutal power on this camp. It had killed them all.

But the only evidence anyone had ever been here was the tents and the blackened fire pits and that eerie sensation creeping along my back.

"Do you feel that?" I whispered to Kalen.

He nodded as we passed another cluster of tents. And then he suddenly stiffened. It was the only warning before dozens of storm fae stood from the swaying grass, their bows taut, their arrows trained on us.

Sixteen
Ruari

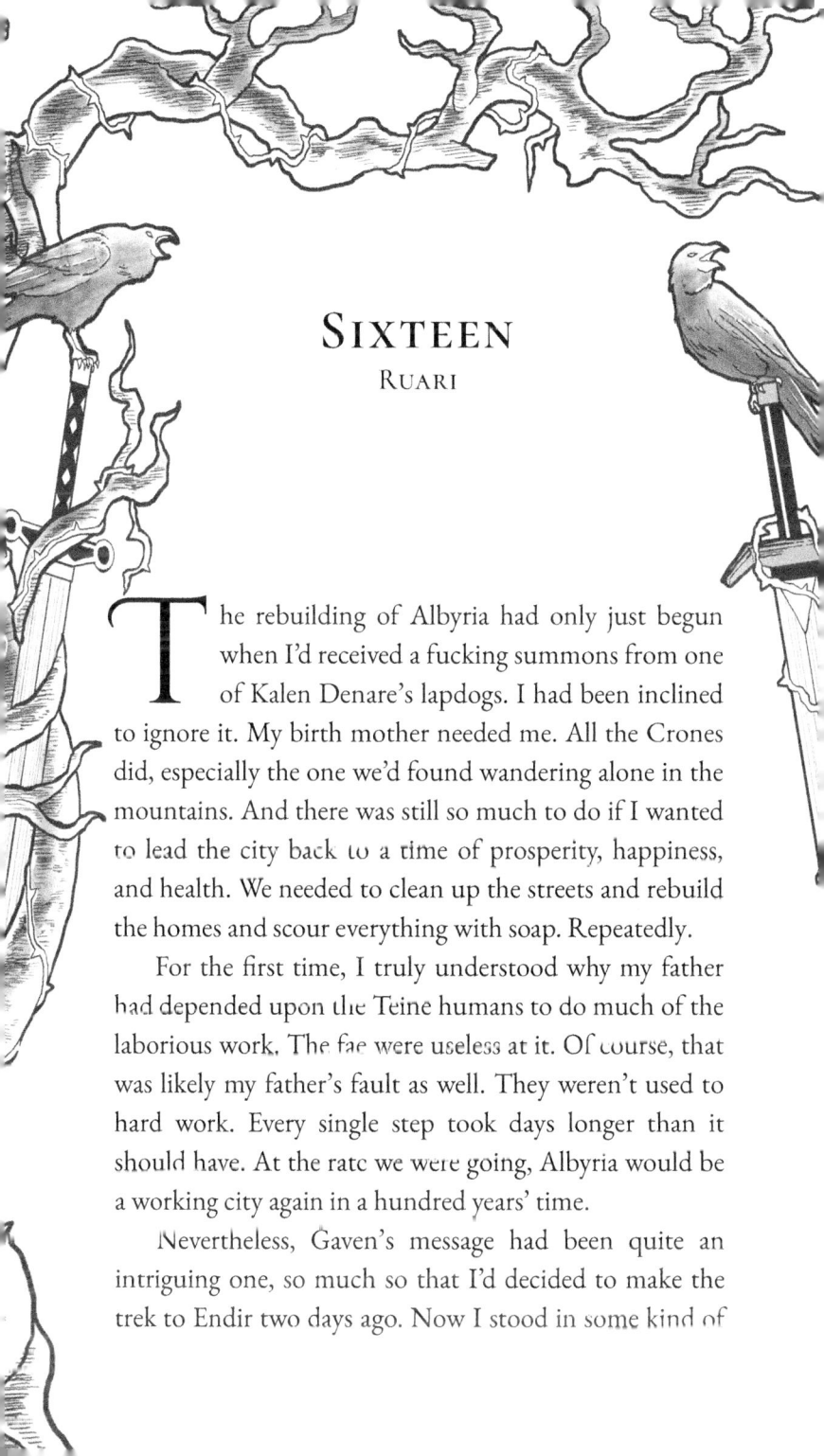

The rebuilding of Albyria had only just begun when I'd received a fucking summons from one of Kalen Denare's lapdogs. I had been inclined to ignore it. My birth mother needed me. All the Crones did, especially the one we'd found wandering alone in the mountains. And there was still so much to do if I wanted to lead the city back to a time of prosperity, happiness, and health. We needed to clean up the streets and rebuild the homes and scour everything with soap. Repeatedly.

For the first time, I truly understood why my father had depended upon the Teine humans to do much of the laborious work. The fae were useless at it. Of course, that was likely my father's fault as well. They weren't used to hard work. Every single step took days longer than it should have. At the rate we were going, Albyria would be a working city again in a hundred years' time.

Nevertheless, Gaven's message had been quite an intriguing one, so much so that I'd decided to make the trek to Endir two days ago. Now I stood in some kind of meeting hall, along with a handful of my own warriors. It was a small space just behind the Great Hall where purple banners decorated the drab stone, the mask-crown symbol of Endir etched in threads of gold. They were proud of their heritage here, despite having been a part of the Kingdom of Shadow for a mere four hundred years.

A small fae sat at an oak table with his leather boots propped on its glossy surface, surveying me with keen silver eyes. He threaded his fingers beneath his chin, each one encircled by glittering rings that contrasted with his dark brown skin. I'd heard of Gaven from my father. One of the Mist Guard, he'd once traded in secrets that helped lead to the downfall of the Kingdom of Light. He'd been loyal to Kalen Denare even before Kalen Denare was his king.

"Are you going to sit?" he finally asked, motioning to the chair across from him. I glanced behind me at my guards and nodded for them to keep an eye on Gaven and the door. Kalen and I had made a vow to each other, but that didn't necessarily extend to anyone else.

Of course, as fucked up as my father had been, he'd taught me a lot of things about surviving in Aesir. For one, you should never let your enemy taste your unease. And so, with a bored smile, I yanked out the chair and sat.

"This better be good, Gaven," I said, scraping my hand along my thickening beard. Most fae didn't approve of facial hair, but I'd become fond of it myself. Mostly because it would have irritated my father. "I came all the way here at the expense of Albyria's rebuild."

Gaven just stared at me with those calculating eyes.

Out of all the members of Kalen Denare's Mist Guard, Gaven was the least well-known. He carried no weapons, which suggested he had elite powers. That, or he was a useless fighter. I knew better than to assume the latter.

"As I said in my message," he finally said, cutting through the tense silence, "Morgan has been asking for you. Insistently. Any idea why?"

"We were never particularly close," I answered, kicking one leg over the other and leaning back in the chair. It creaked beneath my weight, as loud as thunder in the quiet of the meeting room. "She answered to my father."

Gaven arched a perfectly trimmed brow. "You're his firstborn son."

"I guess I shouldn't be surprised your king is passing that information around like the town's gossip."

"I'd hardly call information about the enemy gossip."

"Am I your enemy? And here I thought we'd put aside our differences to ally against the returning gods."

Gaven smiled and laced his fingers behind his head, leaning back with his boots still on the table. "You brought four guards into this room with you when I'm in here all by my lonesome. Is that the behavior of an ally?"

I lifted my hand and signaled my guards, even knowing, deep down, I was falling right into his trap. He'd given me no choice but to send them away or else shatter this tenuous peace. Truth was, if he was as powerful as I suspected, he could kill us all without even breaking a sweat.

"Go on," I said to my guards. "Wait for me outside."

Heavy footsteps echoed through the room, followed

by the sound of the door opening and closing. I tried to still the pounding of my heart, hoping Gaven's hearing wasn't keen enough to hear it. I was alone with a potential enemy now. One far more powerful than me.

"So the truth is," Gaven began, kicking his boots off the table and leaning toward me with his elbows digging into the wood, "we've put Morgan into one of our dungeon cells."

I sat up a little straighter. "What? Why?"

"Your father had a tight grip on her for hundreds of years. She was forced to follow his every command, which eventually led her to betray us. We thought she'd found a way around his orders in secret, but eventually, he found out."

"Yes," I said flatly. "He was always very good at yanking information out of anywhere it might be hiding. Morgan did well to last as long as she did without getting caught. But..." I sucked in a small breath to keep my voice steady. "My father is dead now. Morgan is no longer forced to follow his every whim."

"He could have passed the vow on to someone else," Gaven countered. "Like you, for example."

I laughed, a deep-throated bellow that I felt within my bones. "My father never passed anything to me. Not his crown, not his wealth, and certainly not the most 'loyal' servant he ever had. They had a very twisted relationship, but in his own way, he did care for her. He'd never want anyone else to have her, least of all me."

My heart was roaring in my chest now, and I had to clamp my teeth shut to keep from saying more. I'd said too much already, let my emotions cloud my judgement and spill out of my mouth like a deluge of shit. Gaven tapped the table, and nothing in his expression shifted at all, but he knew—*he knew*. Inside, I was shouting at the wind, desperate for my rage to be heard, rage I'd always tamped down. My father had never wanted any of us, but my mother had. And of course he'd given in to her. She'd been the only one he had always bowed to, no matter what she asked.

Gaven finally sighed and sat back. "Then why, pray tell, is she demanding to see you?"

I held up my hands. "I have no idea."

He sniffed at the air. "Did you know we have a few half mortals here in Endir? Quarter mortals, too. We're a mixed bag, really. In some of them, we can scent lies. Strangely enough, though, we can't in others. I suppose it's one of those traits that's passed down, or it's not."

"I'm afraid, for your sake, I'm not one who inherited that trait. No one can scent my lies."

He arched a brow. "Interesting. You could have pretended you had it. Make me believe everything you just told me is true."

"Everything I told you *is* true."

Gaven nodded, shoved back his chair, and stood. "All right, King Ruari Emed—or is that what I should call you?"

My shoulders tightened. "Just Ruari for now." I had returned our city to my people, but they didn't consider me their king. Yet.

"Well, Ruari, let's go find out what Morgan wants with you."

The stench hit me before the darkness did. Gaven led me down the winding steps to the tunnels beneath the castle while my guards waited for me in the meeting room. He carried a flickering torch that cast dancing shadows on the slick stone walls and illuminated the top of his silver hair. Admittedly, despite the disinterest I'd shown to Gaven, I was curious to find out what Morgan wanted with me. I wouldn't have come all the way here in the middle of the rebuild if I weren't, a fact I was certain Gaven had noted.

I'd told him the truth when I said Morgan and I had never been close. Yes, sometimes she'd done things for my siblings and me—at the request of my father—but normally childcare and nothing more. She looked after us when he was busy with meetings and my mother was feeling dizzy, which had been fairly often. That would have been a maidservant's job in any other castle, but he'd forced it on his most loyal of servants. Sometimes, I'd wondered if it was just to prove a point.

But Morgan had never been particularly fond of me, nor I of her. When she looked at me, I could see the glint of anger, as if she blamed *me* for the trap my father had set for her. And I supposed that was partially true. The tales said that my mother's first pregnancy had paled his face in a way that nothing else ever had. He'd been terrified that something would go horribly, horribly wrong—that it was pushing the boundaries of what the bond between my mother's soul and her foreign mortal body could withstand.

And so he'd whipped Morgan while my mother had been in labor. It had been his cruel way of releasing his pent-up terror, and he hadn't stopped until he knew my mother had survived the delivery.

With a sigh, I followed Gaven the rest of the way down the steps. Morgan had rarely spoken to me in the past few years. I truly couldn't imagine what she wanted with me now. It wouldn't be to offer condolences. For one, she hated my father even more than I did.

We reached the bottom of the stairwell, and Gaven turned down a corridor full of must and sweat and mist. Our booted feet tapped against the stone as we wandered further into the dark. At the first turn, he swung the torch to the left, and the light illuminated a row of barred cells.

They were all empty save one. A shuffle of feet cracked like lightning, and a dirtied pair of hands gripped the bars. As we approached, a woman's face melted into view. Silver hair hung loose and ragged around her shoulders. She was clad in a plain linen tunic—I'd never seen Morgan in anything other than her armor in all the years I'd known her.

That was the first thing to catch me off guard.

But then it was her eyes—those flickering silver eyes—that did me in.

They were more familiar to me than my own, deep-set beneath a thick, furrowed brow. Her eyes roamed across me, taking me in, measuring me up just like she'd always done for as long as I could remember. My hands tensed beside me, but I kept my face blank, holding my breath tight in my throat.

I had seen *her* staring out at me from so many pairs of eyes over the years that I could recognize her no matter what skin she wore.

"Hello, Ruari," she said with a bright, wicked smile that curdled the blood in my veins.

Because the woman who stared at me now, I knew with every bone in my body, was not Morgan. It was Bellicent Denare Emed. *My mother.*

Seventeen
Tessa

"Kalen Denare," a ginger-haired fae said, striding forward from the gathered enemies. Unlike the others, he held no bow, and there was a green pin attached to the collar of his leather armor. An elite fae, then. According to Kalen, the elite storm fae liked to designate themselves as separate from the common fae—those without power. "The infamous Mist King who lurks in the darkness of the mountains above, ready to unleash his monstrous power on us all. For a long time, I thought you were nothing but a tall tale, but..." He gazed around the fallen war camp. "It turns out the stories were true."

Toryn cleared his throat and steered his horse to the front. Bold, considering all those arrows that could be loosed at any moment. "Hello, Finley. It's been a long time."

Finley swept his gaze across Toryn, and his eyes lingered for a moment too long on his face. "Prince

Toryn. I have to admit, I never thought I'd again see you on this side of the border."

"We're here to see my mother."

Finley clucked his tongue. "With *him*?"

"It's important. I'm sure you saw the comet in the sky."

Finley narrowed his eyes, considering Toryn's words. I took a moment to examine him—some kind of captain or leader—and the others. They did not carry that same hollowness in their eyes that I'd seen in the storm fae who had attacked us in Itchen, and their armor was different. The others had been wearing brown leathers topped with silver bracers, but the fae before us now wore dyed leathers in a deep emerald green. They didn't have the branded mark on their necks, either. Odd.

"It's growing larger," Finley finally answered.

"It's a portent of doom, and my mother will want to know exactly what it means. Take us to her."

Finley swore, scowling at Kalen before his gaze slid my way. "You keep odd company these days, Prince Toryn. You've come after all these years, bringing with you our enemy shadow king, two mortals, and..." He sniffed the air and glanced at Fenella and Caedmon. "Two light fae."

Toryn sighed and then dismounted his horse with a grace and speed that rivaled even the most powerful of fae. With determination flashing in his emerald eyes, he strode up to Finley. Where Toryn was the smallest of the Mist Guard, save for Gaven, he towered over Finley now. And there was something about him—an aura of strength—that made the storm fae warrior lower his gaze.

"The comet concerns all of us," Toryn said, raising his voice so his words reached the archers waiting in the swaying grass with their arrows still locked on our party. "Heritage does not matter. Borders do not matter. Grievances must be put into the past. And even if you do not believe any of that—even if you don't care—I am still your prince. Take me to my mother."

Toryn's short speech was all it took to get Finley moving. After he went to command the storm fae archers to stand down, he gathered their cluster of hidden horses and led us away from the eerie war camp and into the grassy fields beyond the foothills blanketed in sapphire flowers. They rode hard, as if a wave of unyielding fire nipped at their heels. It was all I could do to hang on to the horse's reins. My teeth knocked together, and my thighs burned. My eyes blurring from the wind, I almost called out to ask if we could stop to rest when a glorious city rose up before us.

Gailfean, the capital city of the storm fae realm, the largest and most prosperous of them all. A great wall embedded with onyx gemstones circled the maze of teal-roofed buildings, far higher on the western side. And from the strong breeze blowing at our backs, I understood why. It was a protective shield against the storms as much as it was against any invading army.

All the buildings were hewn from glossy stone the

color of bark, including the towering castle and its five spires, which rose like knotty fingers. Moss and vines crept along every surface, determinedly clinging on like residents of the city themselves. It made Gailfean look as though it had sprouted from the ground—a forest of buildings, beautiful and rich and green.

But underneath it all was an eerie feeling that scratched down my spine.

I glanced at Kalen as we slowed and veered toward a lower portion of the wall—on the southern side—where a wooden gate was guarded by spear-bearing warriors. His face betrayed none of his thoughts, but I could still feel dread from him somehow, as if it raced down that invisible string between us.

Walking into the enemy's lair was one thing, but there was something more to this, something *wrong*. I couldn't pinpoint what the feeling meant, but the closer we grew to the city, the harder it dug its way into my skin.

Finley greeted the guards and barked a command. Within moments, the gates opened like the gaping maw of a hungry beast, and the storm fae led us through and into its belly, their city. When the last of us had ridden inside, the wooden gate slammed behind us, and the heavy onyx drawbar thundered into place. I had the eerie sensation that we'd just heard the hammer of our own deaths.

Of Night and Chaos

Vines and wet moss carpeted the castle hallways, sucking at our boots as our party followed Finley toward the Great Hall, where Queen Tatiana would be waiting. He'd sent word ahead, via a raven, about our arrival, and apparently, she had not deemed us worthy of a greeting in the courtyard. Toryn was the only reason we weren't dead, but she clearly detested her son.

She'd tried to have him killed, after all, a fact that had been puzzling me on the thundering ride through the storm fae fields. When I'd first met Kalen, we'd gone on a journey through the misty wastes to find my family, and the storm fae had attacked Toryn. Very specifically, it had seemed. They'd blasted him with their elite powers and then dragged his body behind their horses.

It was a miracle he'd survived.

We approached the looming oak doors, etched with images of the sun, the moon, and the stars. Finley threw open the doors and strode inside, his hands tucked behind his back. A narrow emerald carpet stretched out before us, along a part of the stone floor that had been cleared, between the moss, the vines, and the flowers sprouting through the cracks. The air was heavy and wet against my cheeks as I took in the sight of Queen Tatiana lounging on a throne made of thorns.

With bright, clear eyes, she stared at our party before her razor-edged gaze landed on Toryn. Something dark flashed across her face, but then she smiled and stood. Instead of a gown, she wore rich black trousers that hugged her legs and a tunic that matched, topped with an emerald vest trimmed in gold. A necklace dangled from her dainty throat—golden and glittering and holding an onyx gemstone.

I nearly stumbled as my breath caught in the back of my throat. Queen Tatiana of the Kingdom of Storms wore an onyx gemstone that was similar to the one King Oberon had carried with him until the last moment he'd drawn breath. Tension pounding through my skull, I glanced up at Kalen just as his hand whispered against my back.

A message—*I know. I see it, too.*

Could it be the same kind of stone? Did it hold another god? Was that where they all were—trapped in gemstones scattered throughout the world? If so, where were the other three? The stories always said that the gods had been banished, and Andromeda was the only one who'd been trapped here. How much of that was true?

What would happen if Queen Tatiana was another servant, another fae being used like Oberon? And we'd walked right into her castle.

Queen Tatiana dragged a great sword from where she'd propped it up against her throne. It was almost as tall as she was. She propped her elbow on the hilt and crossed her ankles, flashing a vicious pair of teeth at us, her canines sharp and gleaming.

From beside me, Nellie let out a low growl.

Stiffening, I looked at Tatiana's hands. Black claws extended from her fingertips.

Claws and fangs. She had them, too.

"Toryn," she drawled when we finally reached the end of the carpet, her voice thick and her accent heavy. "My long-lost son. How many years has it been since you've come to see your mother?"

"I haven't kept count," he said flatly.

"Three hundred eighty-one." Her voice was hard. "I *have* kept count, you see."

"You always did."

She flashed her teeth again.

Finley cleared his throat, shifting uneasily. "Your Majesty, I found them in the war camp just near the border, sniffing around."

Fenella scoffed. "We weren't *sniffing around*."

"Silence," Queen Tatiana said with a glare. "In my castle, you will not speak out of turn."

Fenella looked like she'd not only speak out of turn if she damn well pleased, but she'd also take her twin daggers and bury them in Queen Tatiana's eyes. Frankly, I didn't blame her. I was feeling a little itchy for a fight myself, as if the angry, rage-filled beast inside me had roused from its temporary slumber. Ever since we'd left Itchen, I'd felt peace from the boiling in my veins, from the ever-present thoughts of vengeance and violence and hating those who'd wronged me.

But stepping into the enemy's halls, seeing that necklace, and remembering exactly what we faced had brought it all back. Plus, I just plain didn't like the smug look on her face.

Finley gave us a tight smile, and then turned back to his queen. "As I said, I found them near the border. They said they're here to give us a warning about the comet. They seem to think they know what it means."

"We do know what it means," Toryn cut in.

"Ah, I see. Four hundred years pass, and it's stargazing that brings you back to me, not your sense of duty or love for your family."

"The family who kill each other."

"You always were too sentimental about your siblings," she said, tapping a sharp nail against the blunt side of the sword. "But what about *me*? And your father? Your grandmother and—"

"*You*?" Toryn gazed at her incredulously. "You tried to have me killed when your men rode across the border and attacked me."

At that, the wicked smile dropped, and her eyes clouded over. "That wasn't me. It was your brother. I tried to stop him, but he wants the throne, and I told him he can't have it until the two of you decide which of you will be my heir."

Toryn stalked toward her, and Finley made a move to block him. But Queen Tatiana held up a hand, letting her son approach. "I *have* decided, Mother. Owen can have the damn kingdom. The last thing I want is to sit on that throne and have a brood of children who will be expected to murder each other while the entire realm looks on and cheers. This isn't my fate anymore. And that's not why I've come here. The comet in the sky means the gods are returning to this world, and we need your help to stop them."

Queen Tatiana fixed her son with a cool stare. There

was no sign of surprise in her expression. "I see. And how, exactly, will we do that?"

"We will join our armies—I know you have far more men than those who tried to take Dubnos recently—and we will destroy the gods before they destroy us."

She arched a brow. "They're immortal. They cannot be destroyed."

Toryn glanced my way. I had the uneasy sensation that hundreds of eyes were on me, even though we were alone in the Great Hall, save our party and Finley. "We might have a way."

"Hmm." Her attention moved to Kalen. "And I'm to join my army with the one that flattened my son's men, unprovoked?"

"Owen's men?" Toryn asked, alarmed.

She frowned. "I told you, he's the one who keeps attacking you. The last thing I want is to kill you, my son. I want you to *win the throne*. I thought you knew that."

"If you want me on your throne, you should have just named me heir instead of throwing me into an arena and trying to force me to murder the siblings I loved more than anything in this world."

"That is how it is done in the Kingdom of Storms," she said with no remorse.

Toryn closed his eyes, tension bracketing his mouth.

"I should call for Owen and have you fight it out here and now," she said with a sly smile. "Fortunately for you, he is in Malroch for the month. Stay until he returns, and I'll consider joining my army with...his." She flicked her fingers at Kalen.

A month? We didn't have a month. Traveling and

camping and stopping by Dubnos had eaten away two of the weeks we had. Every day, the comet grew larger in the sky. *Andromeda* grew closer. And if we did not prepare our armies quickly, she would arrive to a defenseless land ripe for the taking.

Eighteen
Tessa

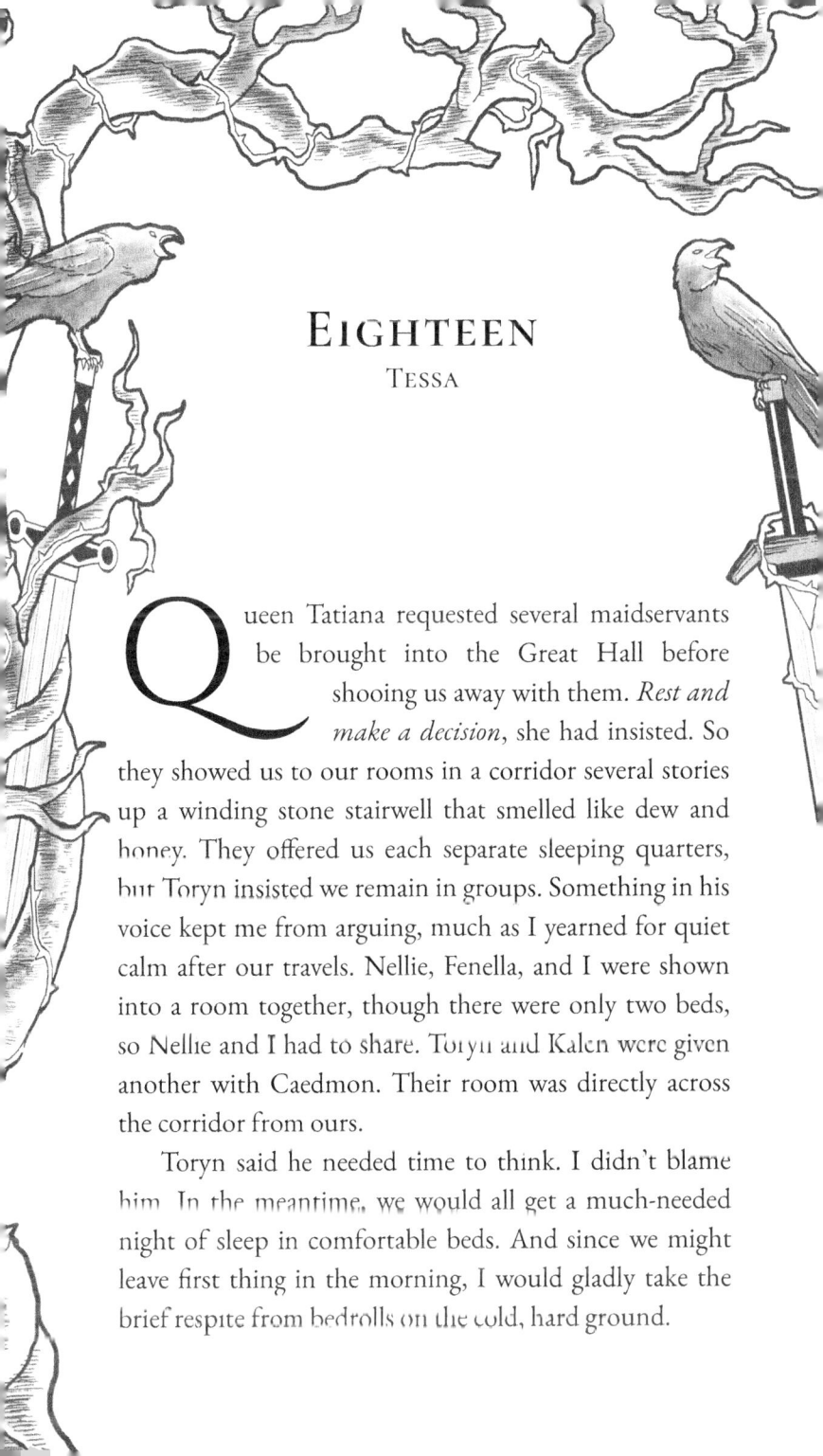

Queen Tatiana requested several maidservants be brought into the Great Hall before shooing us away with them. *Rest and make a decision*, she had insisted. So they showed us to our rooms in a corridor several stories up a winding stone stairwell that smelled like dew and honey. They offered us each separate sleeping quarters, but Toryn insisted we remain in groups. Something in his voice kept me from arguing, much as I yearned for quiet calm after our travels. Nellie, Fenella, and I were shown into a room together, though there were only two beds, so Nellie and I had to share. Toryn and Kalen were given another with Caedmon. Their room was directly across the corridor from ours.

Toryn said he needed time to think. I didn't blame him. In the meantime, we would all get a much-needed night of sleep in comfortable beds. And since we might leave first thing in the morning, I would gladly take the brief respite from bedrolls on the cold, hard ground.

Much like they did in the crooked castle hallways and the Great Hall itself, vines engulfed our quarters. Leaves spiraled across the stone floor and wound up the side of a wooden armoire that was empty save for a few woolen blankets I was certain we wouldn't need. Teine had always been warm due to the eversun baking the buildings all day and night. But the heat in Gailfean was stifling, the humidity so thick it felt as though a sticky film coated my skin.

Thankful for my braid keeping my hair off my neck, I examined the quarters while Fenella flopped onto her bed, still clad in her boots and leathers, and Nellie rustled around in the armoire. I passed through a doorway that led into a bathing chamber, where rich green moss blanketed the floor. Majestic flowers dotted the space, and their scent of blossoms curled through the air. A claw-footed tub sat beside a window—the only window in the quarters—overlooking the city beyond, and a thick slab of stone stood beside it. It was on small wheels that ran by way of a track—the biggest window shutter I'd ever set eyes on. Clearly, it was meant to keep out the storms.

After padding back into the main room and asking a maidservant for some hot water, I waited as three women filled the tub. They left behind scented soap and towels. I closed the door and peeled off my soiled clothes. Blood and dirt and sweat had soaked into the leathers from long days spent traveling. Releasing my braided hair, I eased into the tub and exhaled as the soothing water engulfed me.

The heat infused my skin and unknotted the muscles

in my back. It didn't take long for my eyes to drift shut and for sleep to take me away into a world full of dreams.

Kalen stood waiting for me in the middle of Endir's decorated hall. Music piped through the room, and fae swirled around us as they laughed and danced and clinked their glasses of fion. I raised my brow as I glanced down at my attire. I wore the gorgeous sapphire gown from the night of the ball—the night when things had gone so horribly wrong.

But for a moment, that night had been magic, filling my heart with warmth and light that echoed the glow of the lanterns all around us.

"You're here," I said to Kalen, my heart thumping at the spark in his eyes—flickering from ice-blue to sapphire back to ice blue again. Always so strange how they changed in the dreams sometimes.

Kalen approached me with a smile. His crown was perched on top of his head, twisting silver branches embedded with glittering diamonds that looked like stars. "I always come to your dreams when you call."

"Did I conjure this memory, or did you?"

"I followed you wherever you wanted to go, love. This night is not one I would have chosen, despite how happy it was before...everything."

My soul ached as he wound his arms around me and pulled me to his chest. I leaned my head against him and listened to the pounding of his heart. Closing my eyes, I inhaled his scent. Snow and mist, darkness and leather. It was such a familiar scent to me now that it chased away the pain. The night of the ball had been magical...until it hadn't been. One of the light fae had threatened my life, and Kalen had killed the bastard right then and there. A statement to everyone else. I was under his protection.

Some of the mortals, including my mother, had taken it as a sign that King Kalen Denare was just as vicious and cruel as King Oberon. And so they'd fled into the mists beyond the safety of Endir's walls, and a group of shadowfiends had slaughtered them.

The grief I'd felt at losing my mother had been almost insurmountable. A fist had closed around me and yanked me into the darkness. I hadn't been able see any way out of it, and for a time, I'd thought it might hold me there forever. If it hadn't been for Kalen's steady kindness, the gentle way he'd treated me, and how he'd spent hours enduring—no, *encouraging*—my frantic need to train my body, that grief might have eventually consumed me completely.

"It was one of the worst nights of my life," I said, closing my eyes as he held me, "but there were a few moments before it all went wrong, moments when we stood like this, dancing, when everything felt right. I was happy."

He sighed and tightened his hold on me, his muscles shifting against my body. "*Was* happy. I wish you were happy now, love. I hate that the world keeps taking that feeling away from you."

But as he said the words, I looked inside myself and

saw that he was mistaken. "I am happy, Kalen. Well, part of me is. Even though everything is going horribly wrong, you're here with me, and when I'm with you, I feel..."

Contentment, excitement...love.

My cheeks flamed with heat, and suddenly, I felt subconscious about my words. He clearly cared for me. He'd fought so hard to reach me, and he'd made a *marriage bond* with me just to keep me safe. Kalen had claimed me as his, and yet it still felt as if there was so much left unsaid between us. He had not told me he loved me, and I hadn't spoken those words, either. Not yet.

"I know," he murmured against top of my head. "I feel it, too. And we need to celebrate it. When all this is over, we'll have a ceremony like this with lanterns and dancing and fion, where we'll announce our bond to the realm. We'll have it all."

I lifted my eyes to his face. "A wedding?"

"Only if you'd like one, of course."

Warmth rushed through me, and together, we swayed to a soundless tune, basking in the feel of each other for as long as we could. But the moment couldn't last forever—it never could. And so, after a time, I slowly pulled myself out of his arms and met his knowing gaze. We needed to talk about what we'd seen and heard so far in this strange kingdom. I'd called him here because of it.

"I take it you saw the onyx gemstone on Queen Tatiana's throat," I finally said, folding my arms and wishing I could take the words back. Just for another moment, just for a little longer, where none of this existed at all. But we couldn't ignore this. We had two weeks at best before the world changed forever and Andromeda and her fellow gods took these lands as theirs.

"I'll admit, it does look like Oberon's." He frowned. "And I could tell from the look on your face earlier that you feel the...sense of wrongness."

"I felt it at their war camp first. It's here, too. What do you think is going on? Does that gemstone hold another one of the gods? I thought the rest of them were banished, not trapped."

He paced in front of me, his silver crown glittering beneath the warm glow of the lanterns. "So did I."

"The mortals will know, won't they? In Talaven?"

"I should hope so."

"Have you heard from Niamh tonight?"

Kalen had heard from Niamh a few days ago. They'd boarded the ship, but then the mortals had locked the three of them in a cabin. Kalen didn't seem particularly alarmed. In fact, it seemed like he'd expected it.

"No, I'm sure their situation hasn't changed," he said in a dark voice. "I don't want them to waste a stone telling me they're still stuck in that cabin."

"I never should have let Val go." My voice cracked.

"If the humans decide to trust Niamh and Alastair and share what they know, it will be because Val is with them. I know you're worried, but she'll be fine. The mortals were caught off guard by the change of plan, and the comet likely hasn't helped. They're just taking precautions."

"You're eerily calm about this."

"The humans allowed them on board and are taking them to see their king. If they didn't want to do that, they would have sailed off at the first sign of trouble." He sighed and ran a hand through his hair, the strands curling around his fingers. "We, however, are in a much worse situation. If Queen Tatiana has given herself over to the darkness, she'll never let us leave here alive, and she'll certainly never become our ally against the gods."

I let out a shuddering breath. I'd suspected the same. "We could leave the castle now. We just got here. She won't expect it."

"She'll have guards stationed throughout the castle to prevent us from leaving. Even if she isn't in the thrall of a god, she just got her son back. She's not letting Toryn go anywhere until he's fulfilled his duty."

My blood curdled in my veins. "I can't believe this kingdom is just as wicked as Oberon's was."

"Wicked or not, we need them," he said tightly. "Tomorrow, we'll try to find out what's going on inside this castle. We'll ask for a tour and keep an eye out for any signs that something is off."

"Like what?" I frowned. "There weren't any signs with Oberon other than that damn necklace."

"He took it from a vault, though. If Tatiana has another god-prison necklace, perhaps there's a vault here, too. Perhaps there are more of them around the world where the others are held."

It was a good idea. Oberon's gemstone necklace had been locked up by his ancestors thousands of years ago. The vault had been meant to protect the world from the god's essence. His father, the king before him, had shown it to Oberon with a warning: never open the vault, never use it. And yet, when Oberon's desperation had reached a crescendo, he'd done the only thing he thought he could.

So maybe there was another vault, and it was here. That might explain the weird feeling that scraped through me at times.

"Oh, love, I hate that we have to do all this," Kalen said, taking my hand and tugging me back to him. He cupped my cheek and ran his lips along my collarbone, sending a cascade of shivers down my spine. "All I want is to take you to my bed and spend hours ravishing every inch of your body."

My core clenched as he ran his hand down my shoulder, across my back, and then softly against my backside. Leaning in, I pressed against him, and my nipples hardened and ached. His lips brushed across my ear, sending a wave of pleasure crashing through me, and a desperate moan escaped from my mouth.

"I wonder," he murmured against my ear, "what it would feel like to fuck you in your dreams."

A hungry need took control of me. Winding my arms around his neck, I lifted myself into his arms and wrapped my legs around his hips. The hard length of his cock pressed against me, reflecting the aching desire clenching the delicate spot between my thighs.

He chuckled against my ear and pulled back. His eyes dropped to my parted lips and darkened. "Tell me you want me."

"I want you inside me," I breathed, dropping my hand to my thighs. "Here." And then I dragged my finger up to my mouth. "And here."

"Is that so?" he practically purred.

A jolt of desire tightened my core, and a slow, seductive smile curved my lips. "I've been wondering how you taste."

The ballroom faded away as I knelt before him and unbuckled his belt. In its place, a cave shimmered around us, filled with the warm light of a crackling fire. Through an arched stone wall that led outside, I spied a brilliant night sky lit with stars. There wasn't a hint of mist anywhere, except the soft fog that drifted from Kalen's skin.

Kalen groaned as I wrapped my hand around his length, gently stroking from the hilt to the tip. He gripped my braid in his fist and shuddered against me, and the sound and feel of his pleasure formed an ache between my thighs. Deep down, I knew all this was happening inside our own minds, but it felt heart-shakingly real.

And so I leaned forward and took his swollen tip in my mouth. He tasted of salt and of mist, an intoxicating mixture that made my toes curl. With one hand still stroking him, I dragged my tongue across his head, teasing and sucking and tasting as much of him as I could.

"Fuck," he groaned when I gripped him harder.

I looked up to find him gazing down at me with a heat that nearly seared my soul. Need curling through me, I took his cock deeper into my mouth. I was rewarded with a roar.

Beneath my dress, I could feel my wetness coating my thighs. The more he rocked against my mouth, the more I craved him, the more I ached to feel him filling me with every exquisite inch of his cock. His tip hit my throat, and still I took him deeper, stroking him faster and faster until his release poured into my mouth and his growl echoed down the cavernous halls behind us.

I swallowed every last drop, holding on to him until his throbs began to slow.

A moment later, he collected me in his arms and carried me over to the fire, where he gently laid me on a blanket that seemed to appear from thin air. Heart pounding, I gazed up at him as he slowly undid the clasps around my shoulders and slid the dress off my body. He took his time, gently removing my undergarments until there was no longer anything between us but the warm, soothing air from the campfire.

With a tender touch, he began to trace his finger along my collarbone in slow and steady circles. There was something different in this moment, something softer than what had come before. As his caress moved to my breast, he lowered his lips to mine. And this kiss—this one stolen moment in the depths of our dreams—made every fear and every hurt drift away.

I ran my fingers along the ridges of his abs as he shifted his body on top of mine. He pulled back, and something tightened in my throat from the look in his eye. Somehow, I knew exactly what he was thinking. I could read every word he did not want to speak out loud, and I felt those words echo in the once-hollow parts of my heart.

I smiled up at him, my eyes suddenly glazed with unshed tears.

He shuddered and slowly slid inside me. "So fucking good."

My nails dug into his shoulders as he shifted back and then thrust once more, burying his cock inside me. I arched against him and cried out. He stretched my walls wide, and the tip of him reached the very depths of me.

The bond snapped tight, and I knew I would never again be the same. Kalen Denare had dreamt his way into my life, and he had changed me. Judging by the look in his eye, I'd changed him, too.

His forehead against mine, he thrust into me, the rhythm matching the beating of our hearts. With one hand, he cupped my cheek. The other held tight to my hip, his fingers digging into my skin. I could barely breathe as I got lost in the feel of his length pushing into me, my slick walls tightening around him, and his mist caressing every inch of my skin.

Suddenly, the cave dropped out from under us, but Kalen did not so much as blink. He just held tightly to me as the world around us changed. Snow-drenched mountains flew past us, followed by fields of flowing wheat, and then I could smell the briny air above the sea. With every mile that passed, Kalen's gaze never left my face. He just held me close, and I held him, and the groans of his pleasure filled the ever-changing air. And then...then we were *there*. A forest full of birds rose behind the soft grassy fields where we found ourselves. Stars twinkled in a clear night sky, and a soothing breeze swirled around us, dusting Kalen's mist.

We were there, in that place where we'd first met. Where I had called for him and he had answered. Where

I'd finally found hope after a lifetime of certainty that I'd never escape the torment of life under Oberon's cruel reign.

"Kalen." I moaned his name as he took me deeper, harder, the intensity of his love-making greater with every moment that passed. And as if the sound of his name on my lips broke the last shred of self-control holding him together, he dug his fingers harder into my hip and pounded into me with a roar.

I came undone.

My climax crashed over me in deep, all-encompassing shudders that shook me to my soul. For a brief moment in time, the world around me seemed to vanish entirely. All that existed was Kalen, his own release, and the dark night that swallowed us whole.

When I blinked the stars out of my eyes, the sight of the cave and its flickering fire roared back in around me. Kalen stretched out beside me on his back, the light illuminating his glorious, six-foot-five frame of pure muscle and power. He was absolutely mesmerizing.

"Come here," he murmured, holding out his arm.

With a sigh of contentment, I curled up on his chest. It was surprisingly comfortable, despite his appearance—he looked like he was carved from stone. And then we lay like that for a good long while, watching the stars that twinkled outside the cave and listening to the soft crackle of the fire. My cheeks were damp with tears.

"As long as dreams remain, so do the stars," I whispered.

He dropped a kiss to my forehead. "And so do we."

Nineteen
Tessa

After my *bath*, I toweled off and put on clean undergarments and a fresh tunic from my pack before joining the others in the bedroom. When I walked back in, Fenella and Nellie were fast asleep, their arms and legs tangled in the thin linen sheets. Several lanterns still lit the room. I went around and pulled the silver gemstones out of the iron holders in the center of each lantern, dousing the light, and then climbed into bed myself. I stared up at the vines that wound across the ceiling, unable to stop the thoughts from spinning through my head like a million different threads on a loom.

Eventually, I found sleep, but when a heavy thump jolted me awake, my puffy eyes felt as if they'd shut only moments before. I rubbed at my face and groaned before climbing from the bed, annoyed at the steady hammer of a fist on the door.

Fenella barked out a swear and covered her head with a pillow

I yanked open the door to find Queen Tatiana beaming before me. Her eyes were bright, and her hair was perfectly coiled on top of her head. She wore another set of fine fighting leathers that practically gleamed. "Good morning. Apologies for waking you. I didn't think you'd still be asleep at this hour."

A thinly veiled jab. Two could play at this game.

"We expended a lot of effort to reach you, which meant little rest these past two weeks. But I understand you wouldn't know just how much hard work can take it out of you."

Her eyes flashed. "Ah, yes, roughing it in the wild. When you're someone of little importance, I understand that's necessary. Someone like me travels in much more luxurious conditions."

"You must have such soft, smooth hands," I said with a smile.

Fenella groaned from the bed. "Can you two stop chattering?"

Tatiana narrowed her eyes. "I came to let you know my court and I are breaking fast in the Great Hall. If you're hungry, you're welcome to join. As esteemed guests."

I wanted to reject her invitation and crawl back into bed for a few more hours of much-needed sleep, but my stomach growled its objection. Besides, it would be good to get a look at the others in her court and find out if they had those glassy eyes I'd seen from the storm fae in Itchen.

And so I forced myself to nod. "Thank you. We'll be there shortly."

"Good. I've already informed your men across the hall."

Once we'd dressed, the six of us met in the corridor. Kalen had donned a silken pair of trousers and a dark tunic embroidered with silver moons along the collar. A leather belt cinched his waist, and his crown sat atop his glossy dark hair. A statement, I realized. A reminder of who he was.

It was difficult for me not to stare at his broad shoulders and the way the silk brushed against his corded muscles as we took off down the corridor toward the Great Hall. And his eyes...there was something about his crown that picked up their bright, piercing color. Even though last night had only been in our dreams, the memory of it felt real—the sensation of his mouth on my skin had felt very, very real. With a wicked smile, he caught my gaze and winked. Biting back a smile, I gave him a look that let him know exactly what I was thinking about.

"You've got to be kidding me," Fenella muttered. "Can you two stop making sex eyes at each other when we're about to walk into a roomful of enemies?"

Nellie coughed, and I know I should feel embarrassed, but I just turned to Fenella with a smile.

"That sounds boring," I said.

Toryn chuckled from where he strode ahead of us at

the front of our party, but the laughter quickly died as the looming oak doors came into view. They were partly open this morning, and the sounds of murmuring voices and clinking dishes drifted toward us. Light beamed in from overhead skylights, filling the space with morning sun.

Toryn swallowed and opened the doors wider. Inside, a few wooden tables sat in a row. Finely dressed storm fae crowded the benches placed beside the tables, and crystal trays held an array of food the fae were ladling onto their plates. My stomach grumbled at the sight and scent of so much food—we'd been surviving on stale bread, dried shadowfiend meat, and soups made from boiled shadowgrass. Here, the storm fae had fried eggs, crispy bacon, glistening strips of potatoes that looked like they'd been fried, roasted tomatoes, and bowls upon bowls of fruit.

"Apples," Nellie whispered. "So many apples."

Queen Tatiana stood and motioned us over to the head table, which she shared with five other fae. We piled in on the bench across from her, and several maidservants hurried in with plates that had been warmed in the oven.

"Please dig in," Queen Tatiana said in a pleasant enough voice, quite the contrast to the viciousness she'd shown us on our arrival. "Make yourselves at *home*." Her eyes flicked to Toryn down the row.

Ah.

As I filled my plate, Queen Tatiana introduced us to her companions. They were a family come to visit from Dalvar, a coastal port city on the far eastern side of Aesir. A lord and lady and their three grown children, all with brilliant silver hair. I quietly observed them, searching for any sign of that eerie darkness I'd felt from the other storm fae, but everything about them seemed normal. If anything, they were unexpectedly normal. Their tunics were emerald green and embroidered with fine gold thread along the collars, but the material was standard cotton instead of more expensive silk. And by the nervous glances they kept giving their queen, I didn't think they were used to being in her company like this.

"Lord Byrne here," Queen Tatiana said with a wicked glint in her eye, "was just telling me the most interesting story. Weren't you, Lord Byrne?"

Kalen, who sat beside me, took a long, slow bite of his eggs while Lord Byrne fiddled uneasily with his fork.

"Yes, Your Majesty," the lord said in a quiet voice I could barely hear over the din of the Great Hall. "There've been encounters with strange creatures in the harbor, you see. They destroyed two of our ships a couple months past. Killed every fae on board. We'd never seen anything like it."

I sat up a little straighter. Strange beasts? "What did they look like?" I couldn't help but ask. "Did they resemble a scorpion?"

He shook his head. "Oh, no. Giant octopuses, more like, with spikes on each and every tentacle."

I fought the urge to shudder.

Toryn put down his fork and frowned. "A giant octopus? But we haven't even seen a normal octopus in our waters in centuries. We thought they'd died out."

"*We?*" Tatiana's teeth flashed as delight flashed in her eyes. "*Our* waters? Toryn, my love, it sounds as though your heart is more with us than you'd like me to believe."

Sighing, Toryn stood. He glared down at his mother as a muscle worked in his jaw. "This is some sort of trick of yours, isn't it? You bring a lord in front of me who has an impossible problem to make me want to step in and help. But I can only do that if this realm is mine, right? If I take my position as your heir. I won't do it, Mother. I will not murder my brother."

The lord sucked in a breath and paled.

And with that, Toryn stalked out of the Great Hall without another word or even a parting glance over his shoulder. A moment passed in strained silence. Nellie dropped her napkin beside her plate and clutched my shoulder.

"I'm going to go speak with him," she whispered to me.

"You do not need to whisper on my behalf, girl," the queen said with a roll of her eyes. "I am not a weakling mortal who can't hear words spoken right in front of me."

Nellie's face reddened, but she didn't take the bait like I would have. Instead, she climbed over the bench and followed Toryn out the door. I was not my sister, though.

I turned back to the queen with narrowed eyes. "I wonder why the gods deemed it necessary to give the fae enhanced hearing. Perhaps it was because they realized you wouldn't be able to survive without it."

The table went eerily silent. Caedmon coughed.

But Tatiana just laughed even as the lord beside her grew paler. "Oberon told me a great deal of what he did to you silly Teine mortals. All those tales he wove of the world beyond the Bridge to Death. Funny how you still believe them, even after being free of him. The gods did not give the fae our gifts, girl. They've been ours since the dawning of time."

I found that hard to believe. "You're right. Oberon did lie to us, but I'd be careful assuming you know much more than we lowly Teine mortals do, especially when it comes to the gods."

Tension thrummed through the Great Hall, and as the queen set her glittering eyes on me, I noticed the voices from the other tables had hushed, too. But that wasn't the only thing I noticed. The anger inside me was scraping against my skin, desperate to reach out and slice that wicked smile off Tatiana's face. I'd been so focused on the queen and Toryn and my sister and the weird humming down my spine, I'd forgotten to rein myself in —rein that darkness in. I fisted my hands and forced it back down, but the darkness did not like that.

Queen Tatiana gripped her knife and shoved it into a fried potato slice. "I know who you are, Tessa Baran of Teine. Oberon told me a great deal about you and your attempt to kill him in his own castle."

A few gasps peppered the air, and I tried not to wince beneath the weight of a hundred stares.

Tatiana continued. "He offered me an alliance on the condition I track you down and deliver you to his rotten little bridge. Do you know what I said?" She leaned forward with a fierce little smile. "I said, 'Fuck you, Oberon.' And then I prayed to the stars in the sky that you might forever evade him just to make him sweat. In the end, it sounds like you killed him, so well done."

From down the table, Caedmon folded his arms and let out a chuckle. "This is getting good."

But all I could do was stare at the Queen of Storms. That had been the last thing I'd expected to hear her say.

"I don't understand," I said, my heart thudding angrily against my ribs. If Queen Tatiana had rejected Oberon's offer, if she knew who I was and had wanted me to win, then why had she been so vicious to us since the moment we'd stepped through those castle doors?

As if reading my mind, she clucked her tongue. "After I turned his offer down, Oberon contacted my son. Owen was more than happy to ally with him. I believe he sent some elite fae to Itchen, where they tried to trap you with a storm. Didn't work, though, if you're here and they're not."

Owen. Again.

Kalen continued to eat with lethal calm, his eyes locked on Tatiana's face. He didn't say a word, but he didn't need to. I could feel his anger, feel it seeping out of him.

"If all this is true," I said, palming the table on either side of my plate, "then why the cold reception?"

"Cold?" She let out a tinkling laugh and motioned at the banquet spread before us. "I provided you with warm, cozy beds, pails of hot water for baths, and a delicious spread of breakfast foods to refresh yourselves after your long journey."

At the far end of the table, Fenella scraped her fork against her empty plate and pounded her chest before letting out a burp. Then she shot the queen a glittering smile that could rival her own. "You wield your words as weapons. We know you aren't happy to have us here, probably because we were forced to kill some of your son's men. Men who were threatening our people, I might add. That, or you're in league with the gods. Truth be told, I'm not sure which one it is. Shall I flip a coin?"

"In league with the gods?" Lord Byrne finally piped up, his voice rough with emotion. He turned to his queen. "Your Majesty, what is all this talk of the gods? They've been repeatedly mentioned this morning, and with the creatures stirring in the depths of the ocean...is there something we should know?"

Tatiana patted the lord's hand. "No need to worry, Lord Byrne. If there is any threat—and I'm not convinced there is—I'm certain the Mist King here will take care of it."

When Kalen stiffened—the only reaction he'd shown to her words so far—the queen cocked her head.

"It's true, is it not? Your power can flatten entire armies. You really have no need for scores of warriors or elite fae who can call upon thunder and wind. You can easily deal with any threat we might face. Kalen Denare is the greatest weapon this world has ever seen."

There was something in her voice, something in the flashing of her eyes, that sent another slice of unease down my spine. Did she know Kalen's power was useless against me—and likely useless against Andromeda, too? But how?

My eyes dropped to her necklace. I focused on it, bracing myself for the feel of its power. When I'd gone into the cave beneath Itchen and when I'd been near Oberon's gemstone necklace, I'd felt the magic of it. It had been unmistakable, thick and dark and *eager*. But there was nothing coming from that stone.

Kalen lifted his napkin from his lap and dropped it onto the table. "Thank you for your generous meal this morning, Queen Tatiana. Now, if you'll excuse me, I'm eager to see the rest of the castle. It has such a unique style, so unlike the castles in the shadow fae realm." He stood.

Queen Tatiana launched to her feet before he could move away from the table. Her cheeks tightened. "Of course. You must have a tour at once. I will have my personal guard escort you."

"That's hardly necessary," he replied with a frank, knowing smile that was just as barbed as the queen's words had been all morning. She clearly didn't want us wandering around alone. Was she worried we might find something she was trying to hide? Or was it merely distrust of the enemy fae king who had killed so many of her son's people?

"Nonsense." She snapped her finger at an armed guard who stood along the wall nearest our table. "I can't very well let my esteemed guests find themselves lost. These corridors are a maze, you see. My guard will make sure you see everything you need to see and then return you safely to your rooms."

Esteemed guests? I couldn't help but wonder. *Or prisoners?*

Twenty
Niamh

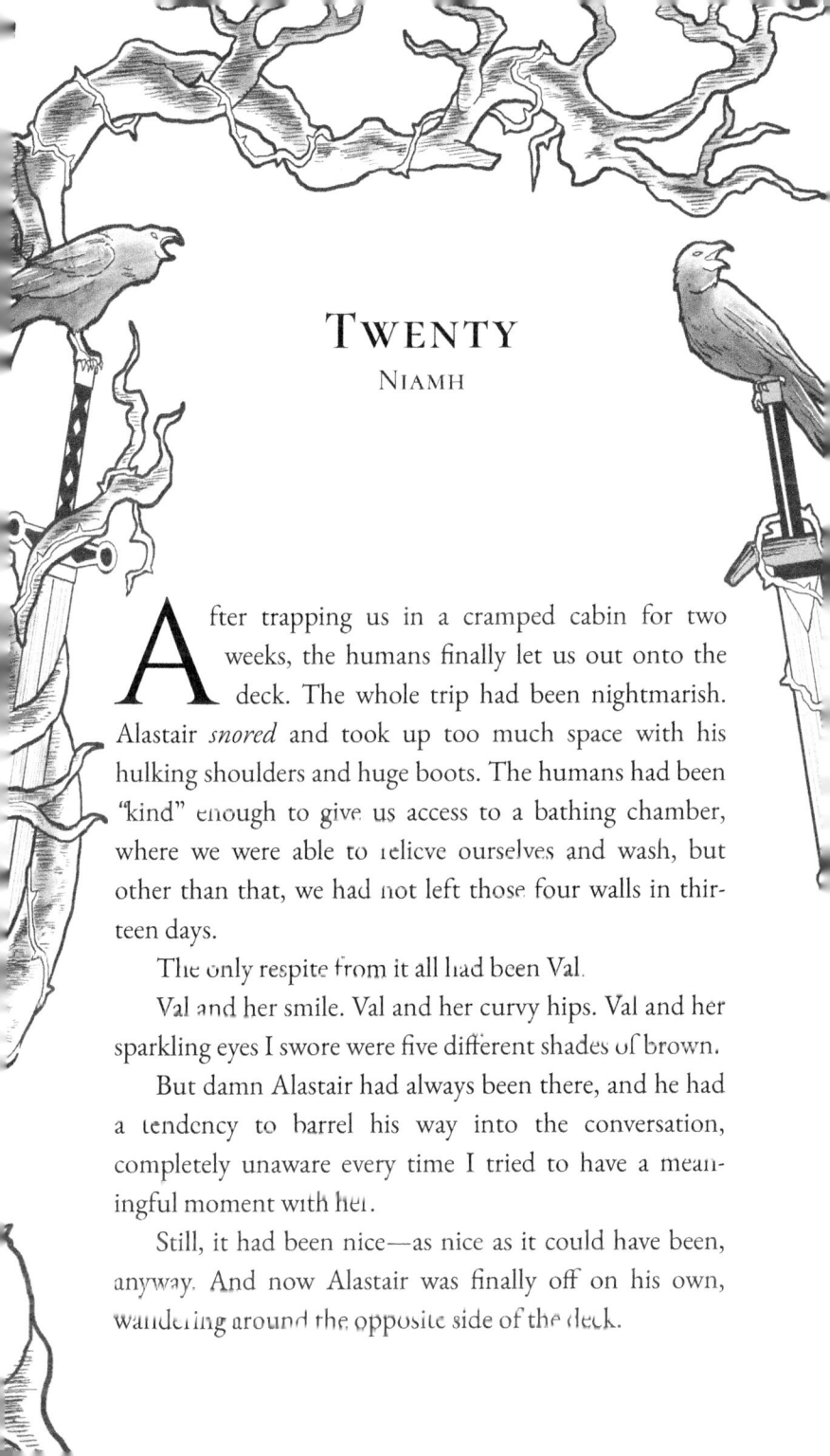

After trapping us in a cramped cabin for two weeks, the humans finally let us out onto the deck. The whole trip had been nightmarish. Alastair *snored* and took up too much space with his hulking shoulders and huge boots. The humans had been "kind" enough to give us access to a bathing chamber, where we were able to relieve ourselves and wash, but other than that, we had not left those four walls in thirteen days.

The only respite from it all had been Val.

Val and her smile. Val and her curvy hips. Val and her sparkling eyes I swore were five different shades of brown.

But damn Alastair had always been there, and he had a tendency to barrel his way into the conversation, completely unaware every time I tried to have a meaningful moment with her.

Still, it had been nice—as nice as it could have been, anyway. And now Alastair was finally off on his own, wandering around the opposite side of the deck.

Val gripped the side of the ship, tossed back her head, and breathed in the salt-scented air. Her wild ginger hair tumbled around her face, and something in my chest flipped over. It instantly made me forget just how pissed off I was about this whole thing.

Until the captain swaggered up to us, surrounded by his sailors, with his hand on the pommel of the sword strapped to his side. I narrowed my eyes and faced him, anger churning in my gut. The bastards had locked us up for two fucking weeks.

"Glad to see you're well," the captain said with a tight smile.

"No thanks to you," I snapped. "Mind telling me what's going on? Why have you let us out? You plan on tossing us overboard now?"

"We're a few hours from the shores of Talaven, and once we arrive, we'll take you straight to our king."

"That makes little sense. If you're taking us to him, why'd you trap us in that damn cabin?"

He gazed at me with deep, impenetrable eyes, his lips pressed into a thin line. And then he spoke. "I do not trust you. There was a plan to take at least a hundred humans to safety. You must understand why I would be wary when that plan changed. Now we're to take two fae and one human to speak with our king about a comet in the sky? It's all very odd."

"There are only three of us," I countered. "What, exactly, did you think we would do?"

"At least two of you might have powers that could sink this ship. Maybe three. The girl there could be a half fae and lucky enough to have inherited an elite power.

One can never be too careful," he said evenly. "Now, I don't know why you would want to attack us, but I didn't want to find out. That cabin down there was lined in iron. If you'd tried to use your powers against us, nothing would have happened."

I barked out a laugh as bitter irony twisted around me like chains. "Oh, if I had elite powers, I would incinerate you right now."

"Lucky for me, you don't. We've been watching and listening. You may be strong fighters, but you can't burn down this ship. So you may take in some fresh air until we dock."

I narrowed my gaze and stalked toward him, but he pulled his sword half from his scabbard in warning. "Careful."

"We came to you in peace. To ally with your people."

"Against the threat of that comet?" He released his grip on his sword and pointed up at the sky. It was broad daylight now, and the comet was nothing more than a faint streak of white against the cloudy blue. But it was larger now than it had been two weeks ago. "Against the return of the gods?"

Shock went through me. It must have reflected on my face because the captain gave me a grim smile. "That's right. We know about the comet and the gods. And we know that you fae are the ones who brought them back."

The bastards put us in iron chains when we left the ship. The three of us were locked together once more, our shoulders jostling, our legs knocking into each other. Down on the docks of Clearwater, one of Talaven's coastal towns, humans stopped whatever they were doing to stare. I supposed we made quite the sight with Alastair's hulking form dwarfing everyone around us. I was trapped by his side with my wicked facial scar. And then there was Val—oh, Val. Her eyes flamed with an anger that burned as brightly as her hair.

Just beyond the docks, a gorgeous city glimmered beneath the soft heat of the sun. Here, it was what the humans called springtime, the season between the cold winter months and the humid heat of summer. Even with all the dirt-packed streets and the buildings crafted from timber and wood, the city was abundant with blooming flowers that perfumed the air. Only a short wooden wall circled the city, and there were no battlements or fortifications in sight.

The human captain said very little as he led us through the streets, past a bustling market square, and down a dirt road, where a wagon waited beyond the town's wall. Our captors threw the three of us inside the cramped wagon lined with bars, and then we were off again, the ground jolting my skull every time it hit a rut or a stray rock.

As the hours crept along, the realm passed us by. There were farm fields and tiny villages here and there, but most of the landscape was unremarkable, except to

Val. She had never seen the world beyond the chasm, let alone past the sea.

She pressed her face against the bars, gazing out with rapturous attention, no doubt drinking in every detail she could. It was difficult not to smile. Even though we were prisoners, Val could still appreciate this moment when a brand new world was spread out before her. I supposed that was a human thing—perhaps a *Teine* human thing. Their lives had been marked with an end point since birth. Under Oberon's rule, they had precisely one hundred years. No doubt they celebrated each and every one of them.

And now, I thought sadly, Val would likely have far fewer than that. Oberon had been a bastard and an idiot. He'd unwittingly caused the doom he'd tried to prevent. But one hundred years...that was a long time for a mortal. I wished I could give those years back to Val.

The wagon jostled as it slowed. I twisted my head to see Moonstone growing larger in the distance. This city was much more like I'd expected. An onyx stone wall topped with battlements stretched around roads packed tightly with buildings, all leading up a hill to a towering, glittering castle hewn from tiger-eye stones. The fabled gemstones only found in the mortal realm were the strongest material of which to craft a building, specifically a castle. The only issue, of course, was in its rarity. It was only found deep within the earth, and mining the gemstones was a dangerous proposition. Many humans had died in in the effort.

Still, the mortal kings of old had persisted long enough to build the capital's castle. And as I gazed up at it, I could see why. Power seemed to ripple across the surface of it—waves of magic that could protect anyone who stood within.

"That's incredible," Val breathed.

Alastair grunted. "Might be more incredible if we weren't"—he tipped back his head and shouted his next words—"fucking prisoners!"

Poor Alastair. He liked to puff out his chest and shout obscenities when he was scared. That, or he'd joke around so no one would guess the truth, but I knew him better than I knew my own damn self. He'd been a prisoner of war during Kalen's battles against Oberon. For months, he'd been stuck inside the enemy's cages. The things he'd seen...He'd never told us, but his eyes had looked haunted for decades. And I knew being inside this cage must be bringing it all to the surface.

Val shot Alastair a smile, shoved away from the bars, and leaned against the opposite side of the cage. "They won't be able to hear you over the rattling of the wagon."

"Fucking mortal ears," he muttered.

"Here," Val said, digging into her pocket. She pulled out a tiny piece of dried pooka meat. How long had she had that thing tucked away in there? "Hungry?"

"Famished." Alastair grabbed the meat and stuffed it into his mouth. He grew silent as he chewed, glowering at the city that drew ever closer.

Val cut her eyes my way, and I smiled gratefully. She didn't know about Alastair's past, but she must have sensed there was something more behind his words.

"Now, listen," I said to her. "I don't know what's going to happen when we get there, but if they separate us, don't concern yourself with Alastair and me. We'll be fine. Just do what you can to get answers and find a way to communicate with Kalen as soon as you can. You still have a gray gemstone left?"

Val kicked out a leg and pulled the other to her chest, where she rested her chin on her knee. "How about, instead of all that, I convince the king he has nothing to worry about when it comes to the two of you."

Not a question. A statement.

"Val, they clearly have a problem with us fae. You do what you can. Worry about us later. Getting answers is more important than keeping Alastair and me out of whatever cage they think will hold us."

"Um, no. I think I'm with Val on this one," Alastair said, still chewing. "No more locked rooms for Alastair, thank you very much."

"I don't like it, either," I said. "But if Val puts up too much of a fight, they'll throw her in with us and refuse to give her any answers."

But Val was Val, and I knew she'd do whatever the fuck she wanted.

After the wagon entered the city gates and made its way through the maze of streets, it settled to a stop outside the castle itself. Val put on her best glare before she was even ushered out of the cage, while Alastair and I were locked up again. I watched as two guards led her to a middle-aged man whose mousy brown hair was topped with a golden crown embedded with onyx and tiger-eye gemstones. An emerald silk robe engulfed his wiry frame, and a light wind dusted the bottom hem away from his feet to reveal a pair of rough leather sandals. Interesting attire for a king.

Concern clenched my heart when the guards forced Val to her knees, but she didn't so much as flinch. She wouldn't give them the satisfaction.

"You'd better be careful," Alastair murmured.

I dragged my gaze from Val. "Me?"

"Yeah, or all that steel around your heart is going to melt." He cracked a grin and shot me a wink he usually reserved for all the women he liked to romance—opting for jokes now instead of shouted swears. He must *really* be struggling to hold on to his composure.

"I don't have steel around my heart."

"No? When's the last time you did something fun?"

I shot him a smile full of teeth. "Couple of weeks ago. When we fought all those beasts. If you don't remember, I'm more than happy to show you how much fun I can have with a weapon."

He just chuckled. "Who're you going to fight? That king over there? Because if we want answers, I don't think shooting an arrow through his head is the right approach, although I can't say I don't see the appeal."

"He's going to take Val away," I said through gritted teeth, shifting my eyes back to her blazing red hair. The guards had stepped away from her now, and she spoke quietly and fervently to the king. I tried to make out her words, but they stood just out of earshot, even for me. I wondered if the king had planned it that way. These mortals seemed to know far more about fae than I'd given them credit for.

But then Val turned to us with a victorious glint in

her eye that was nothing short of breathtaking. Something in my chest warmed.

"Fuck," I muttered. "You might be right."

The king ordered the guards to release us from our chains, and then he led us inside to his grand Great Hall, where his throne perched on a bedrock of more amber-colored tiger-eyes. The hall was empty and silent save a handful of courtiers, who bustled out of the room as soon as they got a look at Alastair and me. I wasn't sure if it was our pointed ears, our dirtied faces, or our red-streaked eyes. Maybe all of the above.

It had been a long, irritating journey, and I wore its imprints like a fucking scar.

As the king settled onto his gaudy throne, I touched the spot on my cheek that had never healed. Oberon, the bastard, had almost killed me that day on the battlefield. Some people looked at me with pity when they saw my scar—mostly fae. Humans understood that kind of thing more than fae did. But what *no one* understood was that I was glad for it. My scar was a daily reminder of everything we fought for and everything we fought against.

And it was what had brought me here to this mortal kingdom beyond the mist-enshrouded shores of Aesir. We had to find a way to save this world against inevitable doom.

"So," Duncan Hinde, the King of Talaven, said as he

laced his fingers together in his lap, "your friend here, Valerie—"

"Val," she cut in. "Just Val."

"Right," he said, trying—and failing—to hide his irritation at being interrupted. "Val here told me you've come about the comet. And that you plan to fight against the creatures who call themselves our gods. She insists you've had nothing to do with their return?"

I arched a brow. There was something so odd in the way he spoke about this—so matter-of-factly. "You don't seem alarmed or particularly surprised."

He cocked his head as if measuring his words before he spoke. "We've been anticipating their return for a very long time. Thousands of years, in fact."

"We thought as much, which is why we're here. We need to know everything you can tell us about the prophecy that foretells their return."

"I see. Unfortunately, we don't share the prophecy with fae."

A low growl rumbled from Alastair's throat, but I held up a hand to shut him up. "You already told one of us. Her name was Bellicent Denare. I realize you weren't alive back then. It was...what?" I glanced at Alastair. "Close to four hundred years ago now."

"Ah, yes." The king's voice went hard. "*Queen* Bellicent Denare. And you're the Queen's Shadow, are you not?"

How did he...?

"I am the *King's* Shadow now," I corrected him. "Though Kalen doesn't really like that term. He doesn't think his people should stand in the shadow of anyone."

The King of Talaven arched a brow. "And this king of yours? He has great power, yes?"

"That's right."

He folded his arms over his robe and nodded. "He is the son of Queen Bellicent Denare, and we did *not* share our prophecy with her. We turned her down and then made the mistake of offering her hospitality, as we would any ruler visiting our great kingdom. And then she sneaked into our library, stole a book, and ran." He gave us a wan smile. "The thing is, she only got half the story and half the prophecy. And I bet the half she told you is about that comet up there."

My stomach twisted into knots. "She wouldn't have done that. My queen was many things, but a thief was not one of them."

"Your loyalty is admirable." The king shifted his eyes to Alastair, who was practically humming with annoyance, and then he moved on to Val. "Tell me, what stories has Bellicent Denare been spreading through the fae lands?"

As much as I wanted to answer, I kept my mouth shut. He'd asked Val, and I knew we'd get nowhere if I interjected when I hadn't been addressed.

Val stared at the king for a long moment before she spoke. "She only told one person the full story. Her son."

"Interesting," the king murmured.

"She said the gods would soon return and to look out for a white comet streaking through the sky. That would signal their imminent arrival. That's why we're here."

He pursed his lips. "And that's all? Nothing else?"

Val hesitated, and I understood why. If the king

found out Tessa was involved, would he put the blame on her rather than on Oberon? According to him, we didn't know the full story. Perhaps the details he shared would point the finger right at Val's best friend, at the woman my king was surely falling in love with. And if that were the case, it would destroy them both.

Finally, Val found her voice, though her face had gone a shade paler. "She said a specific person would be behind the gods' return, and whoever it was needed to die if we wanted to have any chance of survival."

The king tapped his chin and nodded. "And did she say who?"

Val exchanged a nervous glance with me. "No."

Bellicent had never told Kalen who it was. But she must have had some idea—an inkling, at least. She'd insisted Kalen bind his will to hers when she'd never made a single vow in her life before that—not even to her idiot husband.

"Of course she didn't," the king murmured. "She realized just what we did, although it was too late on our part, you see. If we'd put the pieces together a little sooner, we never would have let her go."

Unease prickled the back of my neck. "What are you saying?"

But I already had a hunch. Before we'd left Endir to track down Oberon when he was hiding out in the cave, Kalen had confided in me. He'd been tormented when he'd learned his mother's fate and what she had been doing to stay alive. And so he'd suspected...maybe she was the one. Maybe she had made him vow to kill *her*. Since then, he'd dismissed the idea. She was dead now, after all.

The king's eyes sparked as he leaned forward, draping an arm across his robed knee. "The person we need to kill is Bellicent Denare herself. She brought this upon us all when she made a deal with a god."

Val started, and I felt my breath lodge in my throat.

"Well, there you're wrong. Bellicent Denare is dead," Alastair said.

Shaking his head, the King of Talaven pointed up— up at the ceiling, up at the sky beyond. "The comet says otherwise. She serves as Andromeda's anchor, and as long as she lives, death will come for us all."

Twenty-One
Kalen

The guard led us out of the Great Hall without offering up her name or any conversation at all, but I took the brief moment to assess our would-be opponent, if it came to that. Her silver hair was twisted on top of her head, revealing the points of her ears lined with black earrings. Onyx, I couldn't help but note, like the gemstone necklace her queen wore. She carried a broadsword on her back and two daggers at her hips, and she was tall and broad, much like Morgan.

She reminded me a great deal of Morgan, in fact, especially with that defiant spark in her eye that dared anyone to oppose her. Even in the throes of her vow, Morgan had never lost that spark.

I frowned at the thought of the light fae Oberon had forced into his service. She hadn't been thrilled when we'd left her in a dungeon cell. Her reaction had been so intense, I wouldn't be surprised if she tried to claw her way out of the stone. I supposed after so long spent in invisible chains, she struggled with another cage. More bonds, more barriers to freedom. But I couldn't trust her, not yet. Until I was certain she wasn't still somehow working against us, she would have to remain in that dungeon, just like anyone else.

I would reach out to Gaven when I returned to my room, just to ensure that everything was ticking along without issue in Endir.

But right now, I needed to focus on the task at hand. Tatiana clearly didn't want us roaming through her castle halls unaccompanied, which only confirmed that she was hiding something. A vault, perhaps? One we would find empty since she'd extracted her own gemstone necklace so that she could use the power of a god? The only question was, *which* god?

Callisto of Pestilence? No, that seemed far too messy for her. Orion of Famine? After seeing the breakfast spread, I had to admit she was too fond of food and drink to embrace that.

That only left Perseus of Fear and Sirius of Beasts. Lord Byrne had mentioned strange creatures in his harbor, but after our own encounter with that scorpion-like beast in Itchen, I couldn't be certain Lord Byrne's monster had any connection to Tatiana and her gemstone necklace. The beasts were everywhere in Aesir now, not just in the Kingdom of Storms and their waters.

But Perseus—it could be him. Fear was stealthy. It crept up behind you, attacking when you least expected it. This city didn't *feel* drenched in fear, but that didn't mean it wasn't. Perseus could be lurking in wait, biding his time until Andromeda returned. And there was that strange sense of wrongness that seemed to pepper the air, so thick I could taste it.

Just ahead of us, the guard reached up and rubbed her earrings before her hand drifted down to the pommel of her sword.

We rounded a corner and stumbled upon Toryn and Nellie, who were deep in conversation. My old friend sagged against the wall with his eyes closed. Nellie held his hand in hers, and the softness in her expression almost shattered my heart. Not many people in Toryn's life had ever been gentle with him, and right now, he could sorely use it. I would have to thank Tessa's sister when none of the other storm fae were around.

Toryn lifted his gaze, and his eyes cleared as he spotted the guard. "Enid. Still serving my mother, I see."

"I'm the Queen's Shadow. I will serve her until the day I die."

He shook his head and let out a bitter laugh. "Even though you loved my sister dearly and my mother made Owen murder her while the realm cheered him on?"

Enid tensed and turned to stare down the length of the corridor. When she spoke, her words were clipped. "I'm taking your *king* on a tour of the castle. If you'd like to join us, I'd prefer you avoid spewing treasonous statements. Otherwise, I will not hesitate to drag you back before your mother so she can chain you up until Owen returns from his journey. That way, you can finish what you should have ended four hundred years ago."

Anger flashed across Toryn's face, echoing the roaring emotion in my chest. Nellie gripped his arm and leaned into him. Almost instantly, the tension in his body relaxed. "I'm more than capable of taking my companions on a tour without your help. I did grow up in these halls, same as you."

"By my queen's orders," was all Enid said. Then she stood there waiting for Toryn to make his choice. It felt like a silent challenge, like she wanted to rile him up so he would say something she could use against him. I understood what was happening far too well. She could not challenge him directly. That would make her queen angry, and she couldn't have that. But she would gladly relish anything he said or did that would put him in hot water—any excuse to force him to fight his brother.

All to spill some royal blood.

Toryn had explained their brutal ritual. It was about more than determining the strongest leader, more than the excitement of the roaring crowds. The storm fae believed royal blood must be spilled in the arena, as a sacrifice to nature itself. It was their way of thanking the earth for protecting them from the harrowing storms.

It had already been so long since the last sacrifice. The queen was eager to pass the crown on to her heir, partly so he could breed the next line of royals and the sacrifices to nature could continue. Toryn and I often wondered, though...if she was so eager for more royals, why hadn't she just named Owen her heir? If she had, he would already have a family by now.

After a long moment of silence, Toryn pushed away from the wall and walked over to us with Nellie's hand tucked into the crook of his elbow. He smiled blandly at Enid, and it stretched the burn scar on his cheek. "Very well. Where shall we go first? The library?"

Beside me, Tessa brightened. I couldn't hold back my fond smile. Her love of books knew no end. She'd even tucked one away in her travel pack, forsaking an extra change of clothing just so it could fit. Back in Endir, I'd noticed she'd begun dusting the stacks and moving tables around to create a cozy reading nook. In a different world, she would have been happy in a place like that.

Heaviness settled over me, weighing down those thoughts. We did not live in a different world. This one was full of danger, darkness, and death. But I would do my damnedest to get us through this, if only so I could see her smile again in that library. Fuck, I would build a new one from scratch, if that was what it took.

"To the library." Something in my heart stirred at that bright, bright smile. "Right, my love?"

"Absolutely."

Enid led us through the library. It was less impressive than I'd hoped, but Tessa gazed at it with delight. Smaller than the one in Endir, it still boasted the world's largest collection on fauna and flora with a specialty in the many species of plants that could be found inside the Kingdom of Storms. There were no windows here. The darkness was broken by soft lanterns that stood at intervals upon the carpet of moss. We were able to cross from one side to the other in less than a minute.

Still, Tessa seemed to enjoy it. After she'd perused the shelves, we moved on to the inner courtyard. When we stepped outside, I noticed the sky overhead had turned an alarming orange. Everyone lifted their eyes to gaze at the eerie sight rather than look at the lush gardens just ahead.

"Ah, yes," Enid said with a frown. "That is our five-minute warning. Best get back inside and return to your quarters at once."

Toryn let out a low whistle. "That's a level three storm. It could be worse, but...Enid is right. We'll need to cut the tour short."

I frowned. We'd hardly seen any of the castle, let alone something that might give us an indication of what was going on here.

"And with a color like that, this storm could last for days," Enid added.

"Days?" I asked sharply, and the storm fae guard nodded. If I didn't know better, I'd think Tatiana had brought upon the storm herself as a way to keep us in our rooms until Owen returned.

Fenella scowled. "Mind telling me why *storm* fae are so afraid of storms?"

"You're welcome to stay out here in the courtyard to find out," Enid replied with a lethal smile.

"You joining me?" A challenge.

"Come on, Fenella," Tessa said, hooking an arm through hers. "We don't want to stay out in this dreary garden anyway."

But she shot me a sad smile as she moved to the doors, and I scented the lie on her. She would have loved to stay out here for hours with the blooming flowers, elaborately shorn hedges, and archways made from vines. But underneath all the beauty was that strange, creeping sensation, like a pair of fangs that scraped along your skin, ready to dig in with a venomous bite. One that would kill you before you could take your next breath.

Enid led us back to our quarters, but we all gathered inside Tessa's room after the storm fae vanished down the corridor. Nellie sat on the bed with her legs pulled up to her chest, while Fenella paced with a scowl. Caedmon stood with his ear to the door and a hand on the pommel of his sword—ever the dutiful guard.

Tessa vanished through a doorway that emitted an orange light. Toryn and I followed just behind her. The room was a bathing chamber, and a single floor-to-ceiling window looked out onto the city and its moss-covered rooftops. From here, the streets looked empty, and a whistling wind already kicked up dirt, discarded scraps of parchment, and small rocks that clinked against the sides of buildings. The orange glow of the sky had deepened, the horizon fading into a black that was almost as dark as the misty night itself.

Toryn moved over to a stone slab and started moving it across the window. "You don't want to be standing in front of glass when the storm hits."

I helped him slide the stone shutter into place and

locked it with a chain. All the light blinked out, save that from the lanterns Nellie had begun to light in the bedroom. "Couldn't we just close the bathing chamber's door? If the glass cracks, it cracks. The stone isn't going to stop that from happening."

"We might be here for a while," Toryn said in a tight voice. "Best to have access to the bathing chamber if the storm lasts for days."

"And what is the likelihood of that?" I asked as we returned to the bedroom.

He rubbed his jaw. "With deep orange? Half of those storms are over within a few hours. The other half can last days. At least it isn't a red storm. Those are much worse."

With a scowl, Tessa motioned in the general direction of the sky. "We don't have days to waste. Andromeda will be here soon, and what have we accomplished? *Nothing*."

"No, not nothing," Toryn said, surprising me with a chuckle. "You're speaking to a rebellious royal son who never stayed in his rooms when there was a storm. Now, I don't know where the tunnels are, exactly, but I have a few ideas."

Fenella stopped pacing, Nellie lifted her chin from her knees, and Tessa arched a brow.

"Most fae don't dare venture out of their quarters when there's a storm as strong as an orange," he continued. "So if we want to search the castle, now is the time to do it."

Twenty-Two
Tessa

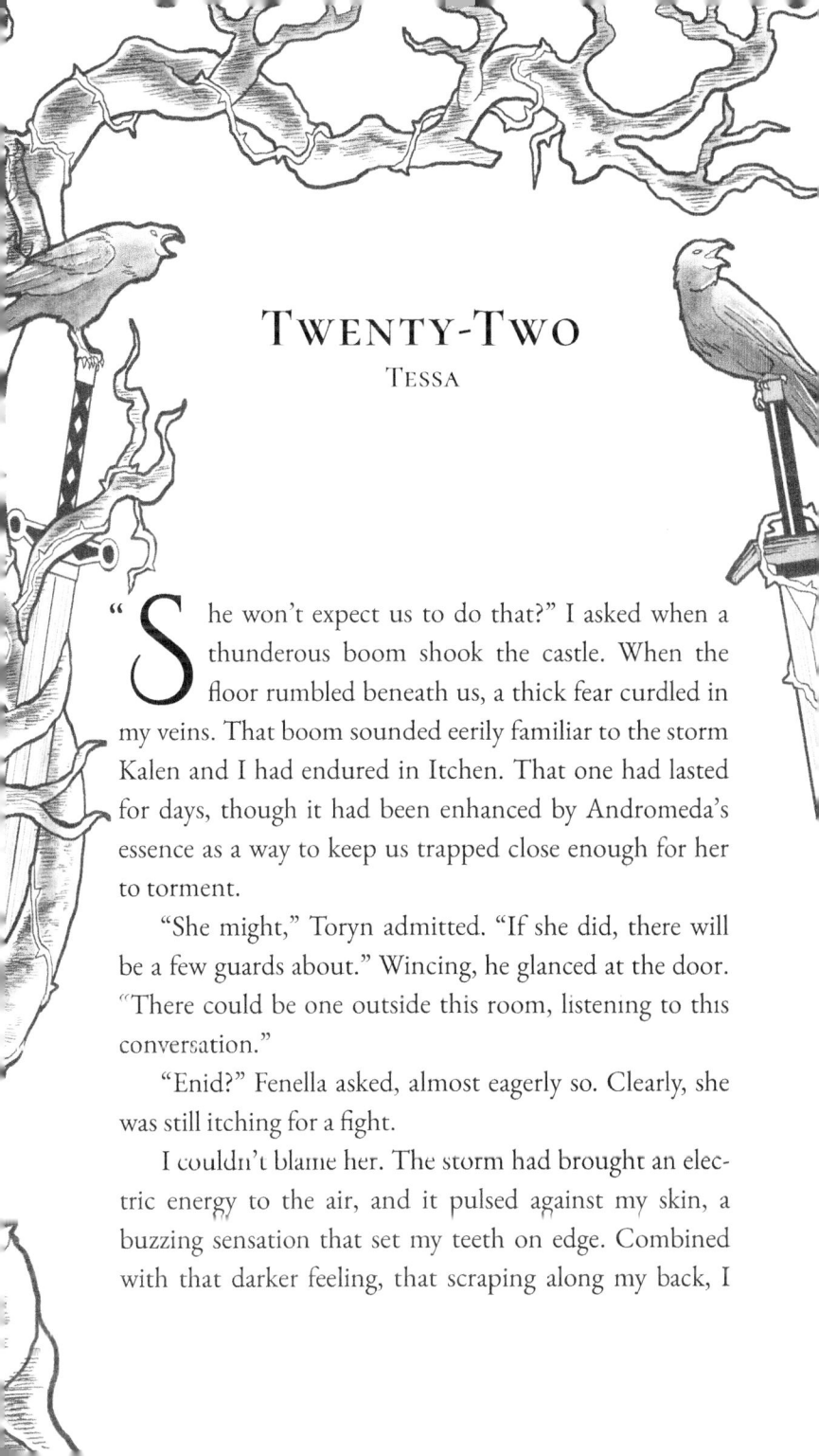

"She won't expect us to do that?" I asked when a thunderous boom shook the castle. When the floor rumbled beneath us, a thick fear curdled in my veins. That boom sounded eerily familiar to the storm Kalen and I had endured in Itchen. That one had lasted for days, though it had been enhanced by Andromeda's essence as a way to keep us trapped close enough for her to torment.

"She might," Toryn admitted. "If she did, there will be a few guards about." Wincing, he glanced at the door. "There could be one outside this room, listening to this conversation."

"Enid?" Fenella asked, almost eagerly so. Clearly, she was still itching for a fight.

I couldn't blame her. The storm had brought an electric energy to the air, and it pulsed against my skin, a buzzing sensation that set my teeth on edge. Combined with that darker feeling, that scraping along my back, I didn't know how I could manage to sit still, much less sleep.

I needed to do something. Prowling through the castle seemed like an excellent way to burn off this energy, particularly if we got to fight some guards.

"Enid is the Queen's Shadow. She's precious to my mother," Toryn said quietly. "Mother would not allow her in the corridors during a storm."

"But why not?" Nellie asked. "There are no windows in the corridors."

Toryn ran a hand along the top of his hair, longer now that we'd been traveling without access to a razor. "There are two weaknesses in the castle walls where wind can break through whenever there's a storm as strong as an orange. No matter how hard the storm fae have tried to fix it over the years, it always breaks down. And it creates a brutal tunnel of wind in the corridors."

Fenella dropped a heavy hand to her side. "Oh, I see. While everyone is being smart and staying safe in their rooms, we're going to wander around in a *brutal tunnel of wind*."

"We have a few hours before that starts, at least." Toryn gave her a wolfish smile. "Of course, you're welcome to stay in here, if you'd like. We can go without you."

"Ha." Fenella rolled her eyes. "You know you need me. Stealth has never been your strong point."

I gazed around at the five of them—even Nellie who had begun to climb from the bed. I didn't much like the idea of her coming with us, but I equally disliked the thought of her staying alone in a strange bedroom while a powerful storm beat at the walls.

"How long do we really have, Toryn?" I asked. "And how many guards do you think will be out there?"

"It's hard to say. Even within an orange band, the severity of the storm is difficult to predict. How fast it comes on, how strong the winds will be. It's impossible to know ahead of time."

"Give us your best guess," Kalen said.

"To stay on the safe side, we should be back inside this room no longer than two hours from now."

"And the guards?" Caedmon asked.

"Harder to predict. Mother doesn't know I used to creep around the hallways during storms. She might not know how far we're willing to go." Toryn moved to the door and placed an ear against the wood. "So there should only be a few guards in the corridors until the winds pick up. Even they'll take shelter once the storm really hits."

Caedmon ran a hand down his tired face. "Dare I ask if we should wait for the winds?"

"The winds would kill us if we did," Toryn said with a quick glance at Nellie. "It's too dangerous."

Ah. Well, that was settled then.

Kalen caught Toryn's eye and inclined his head toward the door. Toryn nodded, which could only mean there was indeed a guard on the other side. How much had he overheard? A sick feeling burned the back of my throat, even as the darkness inside me stirred in anticipation. These storm fae guards were only following the orders of their queen. They were only doing their duty, and we hadn't truly confirmed the queen was in league with the gods. That necklace could just be a necklace.

And if we were wrong, how could we ever expect her to ally her army with ours if we killed her guards?

As if reading my mind, Toryn nodded toward Fenella, who was polishing one of her twin daggers, the steel glinting beneath the light of our lanterns. "Put those away. You know what we need you to do."

She huffed out a breath. "Is that truly necessary? I thought we'd get to have a little fun."

"Yes," Toryn and Caedmon insisted in unison. But she looked to her king, whose solemn expression held no room for argument. With pursed lips, she shoved her blades back into their sheaths at her hips.

"Fine, but I'm not leaving them in here."

She crossed the room and held her ear to the door before nodding.

"What's she going to do?" I whispered to Kalen.

"Just watch," he said with a small smile.

Fenella yanked open the door, and the guard outside stood facing us with a hand on the pommel of his sword. Steel encased every inch of his body, including the helmet that engulfed his head. Only his glittering golden eyes showed through his armor, narrow and tense.

"Hmm." Fenella grabbed his arm and tugged. He stumbled forward into the room. Toryn slammed the door behind him and stood to block the way while the storm fae guard let out a grunt of surprise.

"This isn't ideal," Caedmon said. "Someone take off his helmet."

The guard shoved Fenella back. The sound of steel sang in the air as he dragged his sword from its scabbard and then held it up before him. A deadly glint lit his eyes. "I knew you lot would be trouble. Allies, my ass."

"We just want to look around the castle," Fenella said sweetly. "Since we aren't prisoners, I'm not sure why a fully armored guard is trying to fight us with a sword. Some might say we're merely protecting ourselves from *your* act of war."

The guard shifted on his feet. As he weighed Fenella's words, I noticed Caedmon closing in beside him. A second later, the guard's helmet was off his head and Fenella's fingers were on the back of his neck. And then one second after that, he was unconscious on the floor.

With a smug smile, Fenella brushed her hands together. "It's been a long time since I got to do that. I forgot how much fun it is."

Nellie gaped at her with an appreciative glint in her eye. "What in the name of light was that?"

"A pressure point," Fenella replied. "Sneak up behind a man—or woman—and push as hard as you can right *there*, and he'll lose consciousness. He'll only be out for a few moments, so we'd best get moving."

After we rushed into the silent corridor and shoved a chair under the door to slow the guard down when he awoke, I fell into step beside Fenella. "I need you to teach me that," I said.

She arched a brow. "Can't you already do enough damage with those hands of yours?"

Frowning, I shoved said hands deep into my pockets.

"Trust me, I would rather maim than kill, especially in a situation like that."

She flashed her silver eyes my way and then touched one of the miniature daggers at her neck. "You've been given a gift. I know it doesn't feel like one, but that's what it is. And it's a gift you can never give back. The only way to conquer your fear of it is to bend it to your will."

"I know," I said, almost taken aback by the bluntness of her words, though I should have expected as much, coming from her. "I've been trying."

Caedmon fell into step beside me. "Fenella is right. I've seen you training with Kalen, but you're still not trying hard enough. Your fear is holding you back."

It wasn't fear, not like he meant. It was everything else that came with the power. The truth of where it came from and how it had first manifested in my hands. My father's furrowed, red-cheeked face flashed in my mind, and his voice echoed through me.

Stop fighting me! You have the power to save the people of Teine!

And he'd been right. If I had learned to harness my power back then, I could have put my hands on Oberon long ago, ending his brutal reign in an instant. I could have killed him before he had Val's parents executed and before my father was driven to seek out the god's power in Itchen. And far, far before Oberon had tried to make me his bride.

Even still, there was one thing that haunted me more than all of that.

It was the image of my father's face in my mind. The memory of that feeling when he'd thrown me over the wall and left me to fend for myself against a beast that could have killed me. The father I'd thought loved me. The father who once told me he'd do anything for me, even go against a fae king.

That man had been a lie. And the pain of it all was too fresh. I'd locked it away for so long and had only just remembered it a few weeks ago. I couldn't yet shake that feeling—that grief.

I fell silent as we crossed into the next corridor. Wind howled from outside, loud even through the stone walls. Rain hammered the roof, and the humid air thickened around us until it felt like we were swimming through the halls.

We came to another corner, and Toryn slowed to a stop at the front of our group. He held a finger to his lips. A guard was up ahead, then. He tapped his head. And the guard had a helmet, just like the other one had.

Kalen spoke in a low voice. "Can we go another way?"

Quietly, Toryn replied, "If she's hiding something, it will be in the tunnels below the castle. And there can only be one reason why that door is being guarded."

Suddenly, Nellie winced. With wide and fearful eyes, she held shaking hands up before her. Sharp talons had pierced through the tips of her fingers, and bright blood dripped down her skin.

"What's happened?" I took her hand and examined the claws. They were longer and sharper than they had been before, and the blood was a first.

"I don't know. They just came out. And my teeth." Shuddering, she rubbed her other hand across her jaw, careful not to cut her face with her claws. "They really ache."

"Hmm," Caedmon said. "It's likely your fangs coming out. Don't worry, though, Nellie. You'll be fine."

I shot him a grateful smile even as dread curled around my heart. "How are you feeling other than that?"

Nellie's breathing quickened. "Hungry. Really, really hungry."

Caedmon placed a hand on her back. "Don't panic."

"Kalen," I said, trying to hold my worry at bay. If I lost my calm and gave in to the terror that threatened to knock down my control, I would only scare my sister. For her sake, I needed to believe everything was fine. This only meant her body was getting used to the magic. These claws and fangs had been hidden because of Oberon's protective barrier. Now that she was outside it, of course they would manifest more often.

That was it. There was *nothing* to be concerned about.

"Just give it a moment," I said to her. "The claws are getting longer, and so it only makes sense for there to be a little pain. Like Caedmon said, it's going to be all right."

She gritted her teeth, and something dark passed through her eyes. "No, I feel…I need to get out of here, Tessa. *Please.*"

Concern crashed into me like a storm-tossed wave. I looked over her, at her pale face and shaking hands, and I knew that no matter how hard I tried to will it out of existence, those claws—*that power*—had started to close over her head, drowning her.

"All right." I nodded to the others. "You carry on. I'm

going to take Nellie back to the room. Just be careful, all right?" I met Kalen's intense gaze, and part of me—that deep part tied to his soul—shuddered as I started to turn away from him. "Try not to let those guards see you."

"It's a bit too late for that," a voice called from behind us.

TWENTY-THREE
TESSA

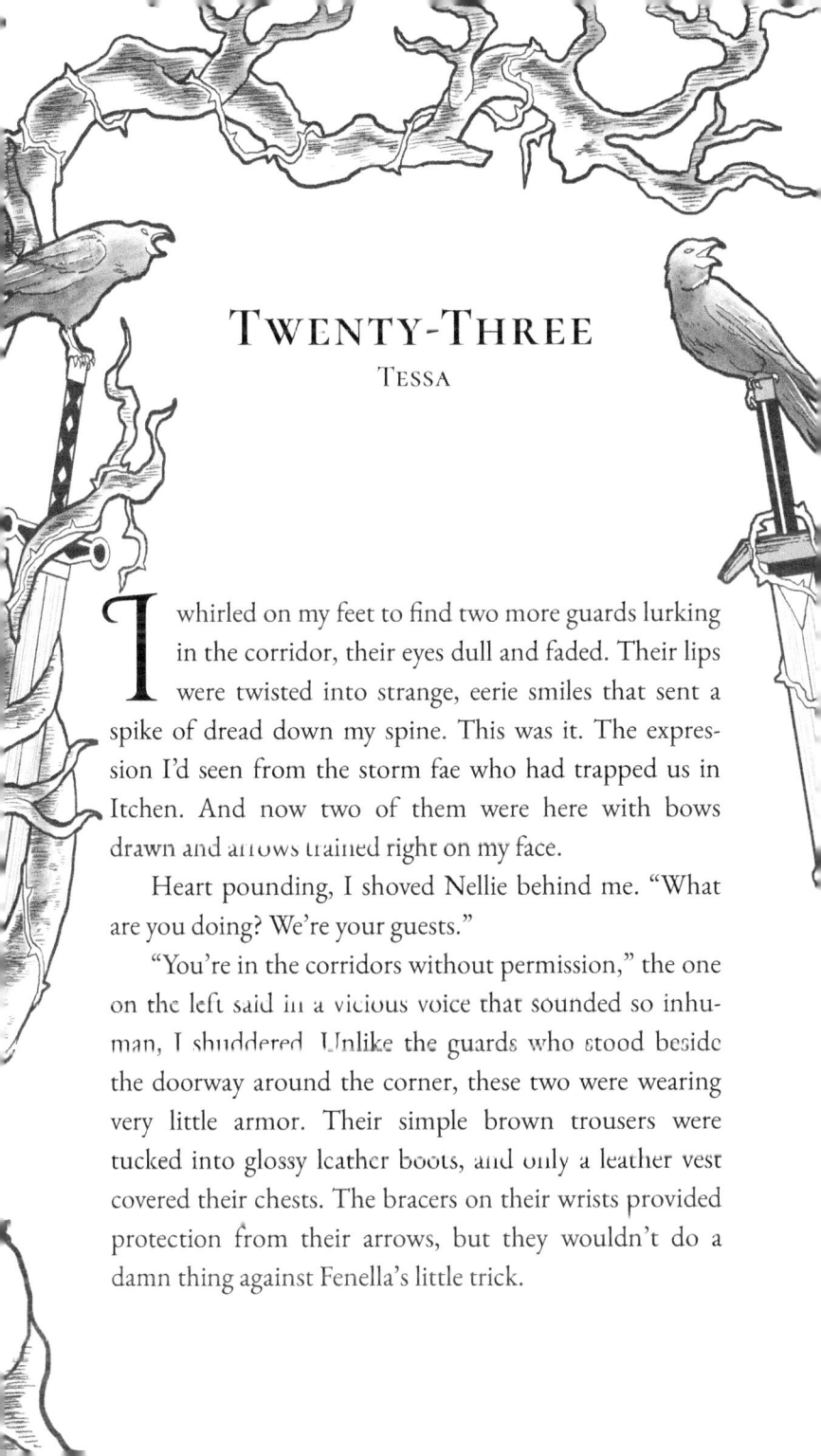

I whirled on my feet to find two more guards lurking in the corridor, their eyes dull and faded. Their lips were twisted into strange, eerie smiles that sent a spike of dread down my spine. This was it. The expression I'd seen from the storm fae who had trapped us in Itchen. And now two of them were here with bows drawn and arrows trained right on my face.

Heart pounding, I shoved Nellie behind me. "What are you doing? We're your guests."

"You're in the corridors without permission," the one on the left said in a vicious voice that sounded so inhuman, I shuddered. Unlike the guards who stood beside the doorway around the corner, these two were wearing very little armor. Their simple brown trousers were tucked into glossy leather boots, and only a leather vest covered their chests. The bracers on their wrists provided protection from their arrows, but they wouldn't do a damn thing against Fenella's little trick.

Unfortunately, Fenella would have to get behind them first.

"We need permission?" I asked.

"Tessa," Kalen said in the same voice he'd used when Asher had threatened my life at the ball. He sounded like he was two seconds away from ripping their limbs off. "Get behind me."

The one on the left, a fae man with mossy hair, sneered. "Take one step, and I will bury this arrow in your skull."

My heart pulsed, and Nellie gripped the back of my tunic, hissing in my ear. Wetting my lips, I held up my hands. "Everyone stay calm. There's just been a misunderstanding, that's all. Look who we're with. It's Toryn, your prince. He was just showing us around the castle."

"*Owen* is our prince," the woman on the right said in a monotone voice, her eyes vacant and cold. "Toryn abandoned us."

"You're not supposed to be in the corridors," the other one snapped, lifting his eyes in Toryn's direction. "We're taking you back to your rooms. Now."

I swallowed. We clearly had no other choice. They'd sneaked up on us from behind and caught us unaware, and with the arrows trained on us, there was little way for us to fight back. Through my strange bond with Kalen, I reached out to sense his emotions or seek his thoughts. If only we could communicate with each other, if only we could make some kind of *plan*, then perhaps we could outmaneuver these guards long enough for at least one of us to get to that locked door down the hall.

Of course, there were two more guards over there to

deal with, too. Had they heard this commotion? Were they readying themselves for a fight? It was highly likely at this point.

This was not going well. At all.

Toryn moved past us and angled his body just in front of mine, forcing the guards to inch back a few steps. He stood tall and commanding, his shoulders thrown back and his chin held high. With a confidence and control that only a king could possess, he spoke to the guards before us in a deadly, threatening calm.

"I have a better idea." His voice was as loud as the thunder booming against the walls. "I'll take you to the queen and see what she thinks about you threatening the life of her son. Her *heir*. Because you serve me just as you do her."

The guards frowned—the only crack in their inhuman expressions—and exchanged a quick glance. And then, the brown-haired fae on the left said, "We serve Owen and no one else."

Toryn just smiled. "That's a treasonous statement. Shall I repeat it to my mother for you?"

The guards exchanged another glance. And then to my surprise, they lowered their bows and took off down the hall, their boots slapping against the stone. They were at the end of the corridor and around the corner so quickly that it seemed as if the wind itself had carried them away.

Toryn chuckled and turned to face us, his eyes dancing with amusement. "Cowards."

"How did you know?" Nellie asked, her hands still holding tight to the back of my shirt.

"That they'd run? They kept mentioning Owen, and they're not dressed like my mother's guards. Plus, they had an odd look in their eye. They smell odd, too, like..."

"Like lightning," Kalen finished for him. "That look in their eyes, it's what we saw from the storm fae in Itchen. There's something not right with them."

The smile on Toryn's face dimmed. "It's Owen. He's always been...strange. I think it's why Mother never handed him the crown, even after I left. She needs an heir, and she does not want it to be him. And truth be told, as much as I want to blame her, I can't. Not when I know what he's like."

"Then just kill the bastard," Fenella muttered.

"He's my *brother*," Toryn said with a vehemence I'd rarely heard from him.

I glanced at Nellie, who hovered behind me, understanding his emotion far more than I could ever explain. My sister was a kind, beautiful soul, but even if she weren't, even if she were as monstrous as Oberon himself, I could never harm her, much less be the one to end her life.

I would rip out my own heart before I'd pluck a single hair from her head.

"Come," Toryn said, motioning toward the corridor just around the corner, where the guarded door sat waiting. "That took up precious time. We need to move quickly if we want to find out what's behind that door."

That was my cue to leave.

"All right." I nodded. "Let's get you back to the room, Nellie."

But instead of leaning into me like she'd done before,

she released her hold on my shirt and stepped up beside me. She was no longer unsteady on her feet. "I feel all right now, actually. And I don't want to miss this."

Toryn reached out and brushed her hands. Gently, he lifted her fingers before his eyes. The tips were stained a dark red, but the claws were gone. "How's the pain?"

"It's there, but it's not too bad."

"Your choice," he said softly. "No one would think poorly of you if you'd like to go get some rest."

"I'm here now. I want to help."

He smiled. "Good. Just stay behind me until we dispatch these guards."

She rolled her eyes and pulled her hand from his. Suddenly, the claws shot right back out. Nellie didn't even wince. "I think I'll be all right."

An appreciative gleam lit his eyes. "You are one of a kind, Nellie Baran."

Fenella coughed. "Can we get on with this, for the love of the moon, the stars, the sun, and every other damn power that's out there? *Please.*"

And as Toryn turned to lead us around the corner, I caught Nellie's blush. Now was definitely not the time, but I couldn't help myself. I'd never seen my sister react to *anyone* quite like this. While the others went ahead, I caught her arm and whispered into her ear. "Is there something you need to tell me?"

Nellie answered with a quick shake of her head, and I knew that was all I was going to get out of her now.

Toryn stepped around the corner, and the rest of us followed suit. The two guards had drifted closer and stood facing our direction. Both were covered in thick steel and held their swords before them, their stances firm and unyielding.

"We could hear every fucking word you said, and you're not getting through this door," a muffled voice came from one of the helmets. "Go back to your rooms."

"I command you to stand down," Toryn called out. "Or shall I repeat what I said to the others? I will take this before your queen."

"Our queen is the one who gave us our orders," came the reply. "We are not to let anyone near this door. Including you, Your Grace."

"Come, now." Toryn took a long, slow step toward the guards. "You aren't really going to fight me, are you? And risk killing me? My mother would chop off your head and display it on a spike for all the realm to see."

But the guards did not back down, not even when Toryn took another step closer to them. Whatever was in that room was clearly worth dying for if they were willing to fight the queen's beloved son—if they were willing to kill him to protect its secret. My stomach twisted into knots as I looked past the guards and at the door.

It was just a normal wooden door, so unassuming that none of us would have suspected what lay beyond it if heavily armored guards had not been stationed outside. Toryn hadn't really seemed to have any idea where to go until we'd approached the corridor and seen the guards protecting it. Frowning, I cocked my head, listening, feeling, trying to find that undercurrent of *wrongness* that had plagued us from the moment we'd stepped foot inside this castle. It was still there, of course, but weaker. Like it was somewhere far away from where we stood.

I sucked in a breath. This was the wrong door. It was nothing but a decoy. The queen had suspected we'd go prowling the castle during the storm, and so she'd set a little trap. I appreciated the cleverness of it, even though we'd fallen for it.

Kalen stood beside me. I placed a hand on his elbow and waited for him to glance in my direction. When he did, I shook my head, hoping he'd catch my meaning. He frowned and raised a brow in question. I shook my head more emphatically, and then flicked my eyes toward where Toryn had started advancing on the guards with his spear held at the ready.

"No," I finally hissed between my clamped teeth.

Confusion rippled across his face. For a moment, I thought he might not listen, not without an explanation. But then he lifted his gaze, cleared his throat, and called out, "Toryn. I'm feeling the wind pick up. We need to return to our rooms."

Toryn froze in place, his entire body stiffening. Corded back muscles shifted beneath his linen tunic, and the blaze of the nearby torches flashed across his tense face as he shot a glance over his shoulder at us. Anger furrowed his brow and etched itself in the lines that bracketed his mouth, anger I understood. Since he'd arrived in this wretched place he'd thought he'd left behind, his mother—the woman who had raised him—had poked and prodded and tried her level best to provoke him. He'd done well to let it roll off his back until now, but this was his opportunity to fight back. And we wanted him to stand down.

I thought he might very well refuse to listen. After

what I'd seen in this place, I wouldn't really blame him, even if killing these guards meant losing any hope of peace between the fae kingdoms.

But Toryn was more level-headed than me. He heaved a sigh and lowered his spear. The guards shifted—clearly relieved—and their steel armor clanked.

Toryn walked back over to us. I caught sight of how his spear shook, just a little, from where he held it clamped in his fist. "Come on then. Let's go back."

Fenella clucked her tongue, but she didn't argue. Neither did Caedmon, even though he grumbled. As the guards shuffled back over to the door, their steels clinking and clacking away, we retraced our steps around the corner and back the way we came. No one said a word for a long while, not even Toryn, who kept shooting questioning glances our way. Only a light wind dusted around us now and again, so he knew we'd made up an excuse to get out of that hallway.

Finally, when we'd made it halfway to our chambers, Toryn stopped and gripped Kalen's shoulder. "What in the name of the moon was that, Kal?"

"You'll have to ask Tessa," Kalen drawled. Then every single one of them, including my sister, narrowed their gazes at me.

Fenella waved emphatically in the vague direction of the guarded door. "We were almost there. All we needed was a few more minutes, and we would have been through that door. We would have found out what the queen is hiding."

"Except Toryn said he doesn't actually know how to

get into the dungeons." I turned to him and lifted a brow. "You had a few ideas, but you weren't certain. Right?"

"Well...yes. But that door was being guarded. It stands to reason that..." He clenched his jaw, realization dawning in his eyes. "My mother knew we might try this and that we wouldn't have much time to explore the castle before the winds would drive us back into our rooms. And she would never risk us actually reaching the tunnels if she were truly hiding something. That's not the door, is it? She lured us there on purpose to make us waste time."

"It was a decoy," I said. "One that worked. Wherever the real entrance to the tunnels is, it's not there."

"Oh, I think I know where it is now," he said grimly. "But it means we'll never get through it, at least not right now."

We all waited for the hammer to drop.

"The entrance to the tunnels is inside the queen's chambers."

Twenty-Four
Tessa

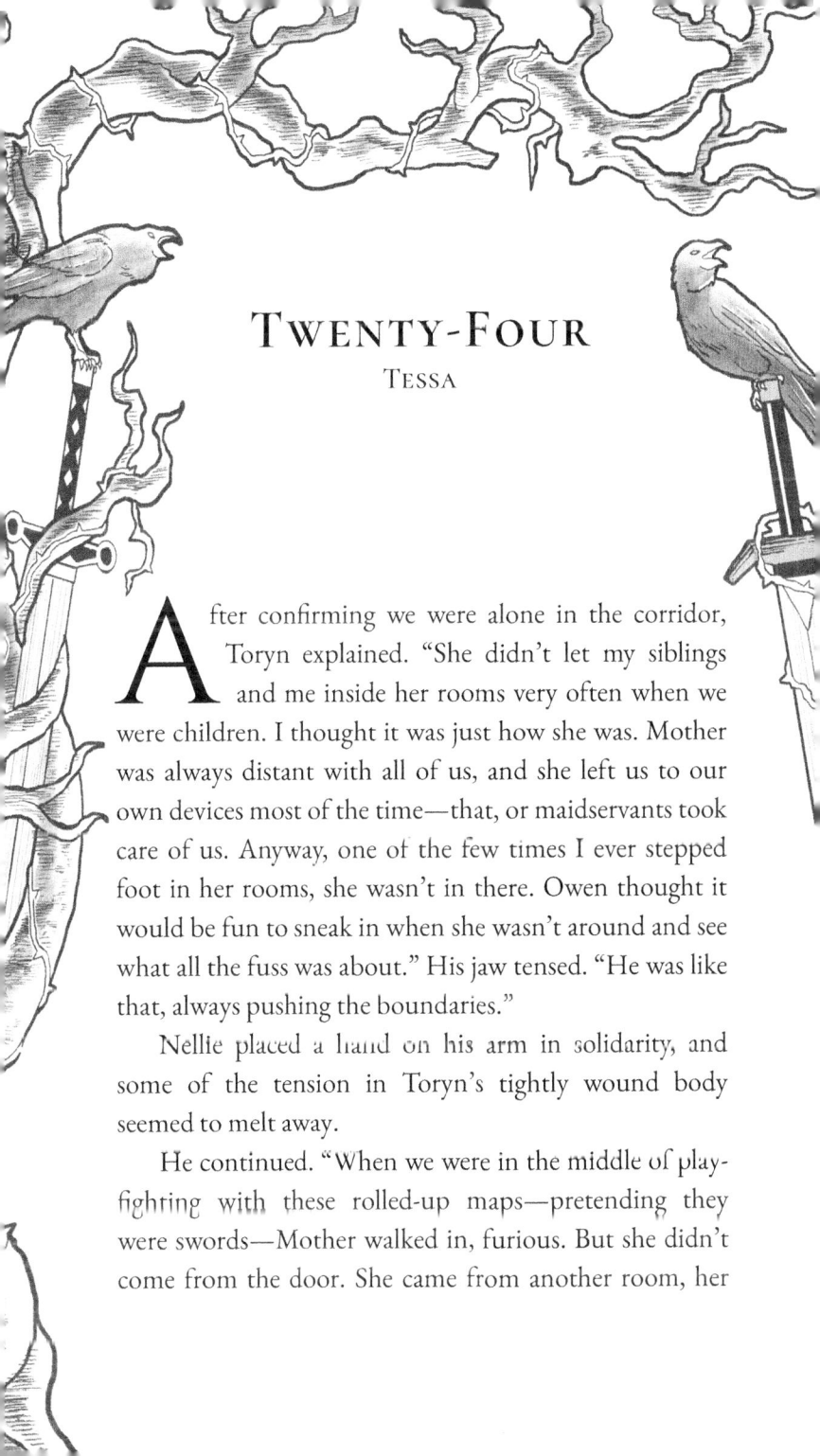

After confirming we were alone in the corridor, Toryn explained. "She didn't let my siblings and me inside her rooms very often when we were children. I thought it was just how she was. Mother was always distant with all of us, and she left us to our own devices most of the time—that, or maidservants took care of us. Anyway, one of the few times I ever stepped foot in her rooms, she wasn't in there. Owen thought it would be fun to sneak in when she wasn't around and see what all the fuss was about." His jaw tensed. "He was like that, always pushing the boundaries."

Nellie placed a hand on his arm in solidarity, and some of the tension in Toryn's tightly wound body seemed to melt away.

He continued. "When we were in the middle of play-fighting with these rolled-up maps—pretending they were swords—Mother walked in, furious. But she didn't come from the door. She came from another room, her bedroom. We'd checked there before we started messing around in her living room, and both of us swore up and down for days afterward that she'd never been inside that room. For a long time, I thought she had some hidden power that no one knew about, some kind of ability to shift through space and time. But after I left the Kingdom of Storms and she never appeared in Dubnos, even after decades and decades went by, I realized Owen and I were wrong. I thought maybe she'd been in the room the whole time, but now..."

"There's a hidden passage leading out of her room," Nellie said, her voice soft.

"And I'm assuming she won't just let us walk in and check it out for ourselves," Fenella said dryly.

"No." Toryn's expression darkened. "Although I imagine she would show me what she's hiding if I won the trial against Owen."

"Toryn," Kalen said sharply. "Don't think like that. There will be another way."

With a grimace, Toryn turned to gaze down the corridor, as if he were imagining the path to the Queen's rooms, where the answers to our questions hid behind a secret bookcase or false wall. If he were to officially win the title of heir, if he were to take over and become the storm fae king, then she would no doubt share the secrets of the realm with him. But Kalen was right. There *must* be another way. To wait for Owen's return would mean allowing the comet to arrive before we joined our armies. By then, it might be too late.

More than that, I didn't think any of us wanted to put Toryn through this trial.

"We'll just have to get inside her quarters when she isn't there," I said, voicing the words I knew everyone else was thinking. "The trial isn't an option, so let's not even consider it."

"I have run from my fate for so long, Tessa," Toryn said. He sounded achingly weary. "Perhaps it's time for me to stop running."

"Speaking of running," Fenella suddenly said, her voice as loud as thunder. "We need to get out of this hallway. *Now.*"

I turned her way just as a bitter blast of wind slammed into us. Like an invisible hammer of war, it swept me off my feet and sent me crashing hard onto the floor. My teeth cracked together; my backside smacked the stone so hard that I was momentarily stunned. A cascade of stars swirled through my vision.

As I blinked and tried to steady myself, the powerful wind rushed against me, keeping me pinned to the ground. My hair snapped free of my braid and swirled around my face, into my eyes, and against my throat. The strands even slid into my mouth.

Groaning, I rolled onto my stomach and faced the opposite direction, finding a small measure of relief. The wind beat against my back, but at least I could see now. Just ahead of me, Nellie was bracing herself in the frame of a door, her long talons sinking into the wood. She met my gaze, grimacing. I sucked in a sharp breath at the deep crimson that burned in her eyes. She looked down at her feet and then at me, nibbling on her lip as if she were contemplating dragging me over to her.

"Stay there!" I shouted at her, unsure if she could

even hear me over the wind. "Can you go inside that room?"

She shook her head. "It's locked!"

"Then claw the damn thing open!" Fenella shouted as she crawled up beside me, her elbows digging into the stone floor. She huffed and tried to push the tangle of silver hair out of her eyes, but the wind was relentless.

"Where are the others?" I asked, trying to cast a glance over my shoulder, but the wind was so harsh against my eyes that I couldn't see a damn thing.

A thump of Kalen's power was my answer. His mist washed over me, sinking into my skin, even though he'd thrown it in the opposite direction from where we huddled on the floor. I ground my teeth against the force of it, my fingers curved against the stone to keep me steady. A moment later, the wind died, and strong hands hauled me from the floor.

"Let's go," he said into my ear. "Run."

The stone beneath me cracked, splintered. Around us, chunks of the ceiling rained down, remnants from the blast of Kalen's power. Heart pounding, I reached for Nellie's hand. She grabbed hold, her nails piercing my skin, but I ignored the flash of pain as we ran. A moment later, we were inside our quarters with the door barred, and the wind blasted through the hall once more. The roar of it was deafening, as if it were possessed by the very gods themselves.

Kalen paced in front of the door liked a caged animal. He'd explained he'd used his power against the wind to stop it just long enough for us to get back to our rooms, but it hadn't worked quite as well as he'd hoped, which troubled him. His power wasn't *dampened,* necessarily, not like when the god had held a choking grip on it. But something about it had felt wrong.

And so, for the last several hours, he'd paced.

I knew some of that pent-up energy was about more than just his power. It was fear for the rest of us. The wind and thunder sounded as if it could shake the very bones of this castle until the walls flattened around us. His power might be the only thing to stop it from getting inside this room, but if the rest of the castle went, there was little he could do to stop the storm from taking us, too.

"Relax, Kal," Toryn said as he dug through a small compartment I hadn't noticed before. A wood-paneled cubby was set into the wall just beside the armoire, and it held an array of drinks and snacks, as well as a handful of small bottles of spirits. He pulled out a bottle of dark amber liquid and held it up. "Here, this might take the edge off."

"I do not want to take the edge off," Kalen snapped as he continued to pace. And then his dark eyes flashed to me, where I stood very tensely beside my sister. As soon as we'd returned to the room, she'd climbed into the bed and fallen into an exhausted sleep.

Fenella cocked her head. She'd kicked off her boots, pulled a chair up beside the bed, and leaned back with her feet propped up on the mattress as she flipped through Val's clippings. "Something strange is going on between you two. Stranger than normal, I mean. You're acting like a man possessed."

Kalen stopped pacing and narrowed his eyes. "We almost died out there."

"Oh, please. We got knocked down and blown around a bit. I'd hardly say we were in any real danger." She rolled her eyes and turned her attention back to the clippings. I hadn't had a chance to look through them yet myself. There'd been too much going on.

Kalen shifted his gaze to me, and something indescribable passed between us. It was as if his very soul reached toward me, wound itself around my heart, and tugged. My breathing went shallow as the overwhelming scent of mist and shadow invaded my senses, as if the very core of his power now flowed through my veins, our hearts pumping in rhythm—as one. And if I could feel all this—all his worry and anger and *protectiveness*—what could he feel from me? Could he feel Andromeda's power? Could he sense death?

Bottles clattered. The sound jolted through me, reminding me that we were not alone in this room.

"For the love of the moon," Toryn said, though he was smiling. "You two made a marriage bond."

Fenella glanced up again. "Of course they did. I've been able to smell it since the morning we left Endir. But it's more than that. Look at him."

Kalen seemed to have to force himself to look away from me. "It's not your concern."

"You made a marriage bond with a mortal?" Caedmon pushed away from the wall. "No offense to Tessa, but what the fuck were you thinking?"

"I was thinking," Kalen ground out, "that I will protect her from anyone who threatens her life, including myself."

"The fucking vow," Caedmon shook his head. "Of course. I should have known. You brushed aside your promise to your mother so easily. I thought it was strange—you shouldn't have been able to resist it. But now it makes sense. This is how. You made certain it wouldn't be a threat, even though that meant tying your life to a mortal's. You'll be nothing but a husk when she dies in a few years."

I shuddered. Hearing Caedmon say it out loud made it feel all that much more real. Was that what happened to fae when their spouses died? I'd heard tall tales of it over the years, but I'd never seen it for myself, not even with Oberon. Though, I supposed, his true wife had never died, not until the end.

Centuries stretched out before Kalen. He had so many years ahead of him. I wouldn't survive my old age, and this bond meant he would be in pain for centuries.

I should never have agreed to this.

As if reading my mind, Caedmon whirled toward me with fire in his eyes. "You say you care for him. How could you do this?"

"I didn't fully understand what I was doing," I tried, but the words sounded hollow. "Not until now."

He scoffed, as he rightly should have. "You agreed to a marriage bond without fully understanding it? How stupid do you have to be?"

"Caedmon," Kalen warned. "Do not take this out on Tessa. This was my decision. My choice. I'm the one who gets to decide what kind of life I lead."

"No, you aren't." Caedmon took a step closer. "You are supposed to be a king. *Our* king. And we depend on you. When you made a marriage bond with Tessa, the *descendent of a god*, did you stop to think about us at all? What will happen to your kingdom when she dies and you're left bereft, like Fenella? What about your heirs?"

"Excuse me, cousin," Fenella snapped. "Don't you fucking speak that way about me. Or Tessa. It's Kalen's bloody decision who he marries."

"There's always been a risk with the succession," Kalen continued evenly, though I felt the pulse of his irritation through our bond. "A risk I could die in a battle or be captured by the enemy. Niamh agreed long ago to be my heir if I have no children. If anything happens, she'll become your queen, and she is the best person in the whole gods-damned world for it."

The room fell into a tense silence. Only Nellie was saved from it all. She hadn't even stirred during the argument. Kalen went back to pacing beside the bed, while Toryn helped himself to a drink and some dried meat. Fenella leaned back in her chair, scowling at Caedmon, who leaned against the wall with folded arms. There wasn't much for any of us to do but wait.

With a sigh, I found a spot on the floor and braced

my back against the wall. And then we all listened as the pounding rain, roaring thunder, and screaming wind tore down the world around us.

Twenty-Five
Tessa

Two days passed before the wind died. We took turns sleeping, rotating among guard duty by the door, snacking on what we could, bathing in the cold water that ran down from a hole in the ceiling every day, and resting as best we could. Still, I couldn't sleep for more than a couple hours at a time. Every time I began to doze, the screaming wind jolted me awake.

Toryn seemed to be able to track the passing of the hours. On the third morning we'd been holed up in the room, the thunderous sounds faded so suddenly, it almost felt like a dream that they'd ever existed.

Kalen, who had been doing his pacing, yanked open the door and walked into the hallway. The rest of us followed close behind him. The corridor was a wreck. Carpets and tapestries were shredded. Chunks of broken wood littered the ground, along with a few piles of stone here and there that had somehow chipped off the walls.

Other than that, excruciating silence was our only

answer until noise exploded all around us. Cheers echoed through the castle as the court celebrated the end of another deadly storm.

***

The rest of the day passed quickly. We joined the storm fae in their efforts to clean up. We cleared away the debris, boarded up holes, and replaced tapestries with freshly woven ones. The Queen's Shadow circled past once to check on us, but we didn't see the queen herself until that night.

The Great Hall was packed full for the nightly feast. After days spent trapped inside their rooms, the storm fae of Gailfean were eager to drink and eat the night away and celebrate their continued survival. A dozen tables were crammed inside, and hundreds of fae filled the benches. Booming laughter, clinking glasses, and the enthusiastic scraping of knives against plates echoed through the cavernous room. And just above it all, at her private table on the elevated dais, the queen watched.

She had invited us to join her, though she'd hardly gifted us with a word since we'd sat at her table. I was sandwiched between Toryn, who sat beside his mother, and Nellie. Kalen and Fenella were further down the table with Caedmon, who had kept his mouth shut since the argument. We all faced forward, looking down at the feast.

"Your people are happy here, my son," the queen murmured on Toryn's other side.

"Of course they are. They survived, and now they're being fed until they burst," he said. "Anyone would be happy in this situation."

"Except you."

"I'm glad everyone is safe. I take it there were no casualties?"

I watched as she slid her gaze sideways. "Only one was wounded. The guard who attempted to stop you from leaving your rooms."

"We didn't wound him." He gave her a tense smile in return. "Besides, just as we told him, we aren't prisoners in this castle. I am the prince. We wanted to have a quick wander before the winds shook the halls. It was our last chance to stretch our legs. And we were glad of it when the storm lasted for days."

"If you're going to throw around your title, you need to do something to back it up, my dear son. Either you're a prince or you're not. Which is it?"

Nellie suddenly coughed, a hacking, jagged sound that made several of the fae at a nearby table stop eating and stare.

"You all right?" I asked, worry flickering through me. Oberon had always warned us about disease, but the mortals of Teine had never endured it. Illness had never ravaged our bodies or left us weak in our beds. That only happened due to exhaustion after all the toiling in the fields—exhaustion and fear.

But Oberon's protective barrier was gone now. Out

here, in the real world, we were susceptible to light knew what, and I'd been so focused on violent threats—shadowfiends, storms, the gods raining destruction on our heads—that I'd forgotten all about disease. The fae did not need to worry about it, of course, but we mortals did.

Nellie's eyes watered, and she leaned forward to speak around me. "Queen Tatiana, Toryn has told me so much about your healing powers. This cough, it sounds like illness, does it not? Can you help?"

I frowned.

The queen's brows arched into a thin line on her smooth forehead. "Yes. Although I have to say, I'm surprised he mentioned that to you. He hasn't acknowledged my healing magic in years."

"I just thought she should understand the irony of your power," he replied with a tight smile. "You're so keen for your children to destroy each other. Meanwhile, you have the magic to heal us all."

"Healing?" I did not glance at the queen's onyx necklace, though I'd noted it when we joined the table. As always, she wore it this night. "That's a unique gift."

It was so achingly familiar to the power Oberon had possessed with his gemstone necklace. He had only been able to extend lives and provide protection to the mortals because Andromeda's essence had been split in two, and he controlled the half with the power to heal. So where did the queen gain this kind of magic? Could that gemstone necklace hold another piece of Andromeda instead of a different god? The thought made my knees turn to jelly.

Queen Tatiana merely smiled. "Indeed."

Nellie coughed again, louder this time. "A unique gift, one I will sorely need if this is some kind of human disease. Or could the storm have made me ill, Your Grace?"

Toryn stood, his chair scraping against the stone. He took Nellie's hand and pulled her to her feet. "Let me take you back to your room. I'm sure I can find a tonic that will help—"

"Nonsense," the queen snapped. She quickly stood and offered her hand to Nellie. "Come with me. I will make sure you're all sorted out."

"I should come with—" I started.

"Nonsense," the queen said, cutting me off. "Stay and enjoy the feast. I will take care of your sister, and she will be as good as new within an hour's time."

The queen bustled off with my sister latched to her arm. I frowned, watching the shuffle of Nellie's feet, the hunch of her shoulders. Her cheeks were a vivid pink, and just before she walked through the Great Hall's open door, she shot a quick glance over her shoulder, met my eyes, and winked.

I swore.

"Don't worry," Toryn said, sitting on the bench with a frown. "My mother is...well, you've seen how she is. But despite all that, she is a good healer. Nellie will be fine."

"Yes, she will be fine." I pressed my lips together and scanned the crowd. A few fae had stopped their raucous meal to watch the queen pass by with my sister, but they'd all returned to their food and drinks now. Most were deep in conversation, swapping adventurous tales or trading the latest gossip. Still, I had spent a long time around fae, and there was one thing you never did: speak in their presence about *anything* you didn't want them to overhear.

I stood. "I'm feeling a little funny myself. Toryn, can you help me back to my room, please?"

"Tessa, what's wrong?" Kalen was on his feet within an instant, his body poised to strike down anyone who so much as looked at me wrong.

Caedmon stayed right where he was, but I heard his grumble. Something about the king and his bloody marriage bond.

"Ah..." I trailed off. If I lied, any fae paying attention would be able to scent it. How had Nellie managed to fool the queen? I thought through what she'd said and realized Nellie had never actually *said* she was ill at all. She'd only implied it by asking questions. Smart girl. "If Nellie is ill, then I will have likely caught whatever it is as well, don't you think?"

"Are you feeling unwell? You haven't coughed," Kalen said.

"I'm feeling like I want to leave the Great Hall."

Toryn frowned, but then gently took my arm and steered me away from the table. "All right. Come on. I'll get you back to your room."

Kalen followed, but Caedmon remained in his chair, along with Fenella.

She glanced up as we passed. "I think you can manage without me. I'll stay here and enjoy my meal, not that anyone asked what I want." To punctuate her statement, she grabbed a roasted chicken leg and took a big bite of it.

Juice dripped down her cheek as she flashed us a wicked smile.

After Toryn and Kalen—fussing over me like idiots—practically carried me into the corridor, I smacked their hands and extracted myself from them both. "I'm fine. I don't have a sickness. Nellie doesn't, either. She did that to draw your mother away from the feast. I'm guessing it's to give us a chance to search her quarters for the entrance to the tunnels."

Toryn lifted a brow. "Nellie can't lie. Neither can you."

Frowning, Kalen took a step toward me. "Love, are you sure you're not feverish and—"

"I am *fine*," I repeated. "Now come on. We likely don't have long before she returns to the feast, and she'll wonder where we've gone."

Kalen wrapped his arm around me as the three of us took off down the corridor, Toryn leading the way to the queen's rooms. "You scared me half to death, you know. I thought there was something wrong with you both, and we'd have no idea how to fix you. I wish you'd told the rest of us what you'd planned."

"We didn't plan a damn thing," I whispered, even as our boots tapped loudly against the stone floor. I didn't want to risk our words reaching any fae who might be in one of the rooms we passed by. "Nellie cooked this whole thing up all by herself, and then she winked at me just before she left the Great Hall. I had to improvise."

Kalen chuckled. "Nellie is far more like you than you led me to believe."

"That does *not* sound like a compliment."

He merely chuckled again.

We reached the queen's quarters without incident. She lived inside the Keep—the central tower surrounded by a second fortified wall, not just to protect her from enemy attackers but from the storms as well. The tower itself was a small, squat thing, as sturdy as a tower could be, I supposed. Moss blanketed the stone stairwell we descended until we reached the floor where she lived deep inside the earth. There were no windows here, no gorgeous views of the city and fields that lay beyond. Queen Tatiana preferred to live in a tomb.

"This isn't what I expected," I said as Toryn pulled a keyring from his pocket and unlocked the door. "Where'd you get that?"

He smiled. "The guards were distracted today while everyone was clearing up after the storm. I managed to slip this off one of them when they weren't paying attention. I knew eventually we'd try to get inside this room. I just didn't know Nellie had decided to take matters into her own hands so that we could do it so soon."

Toryn twisted the brass knob, and the door swung open in front of us, revealing a room overflowing with tropical plants and flowers in at least a dozen different colors. They topped tables that were crammed against the walls, they sat on bookshelves and the arms of sofas, and they stood in clusters on the floor. I went to a nearby flower. Its luminescent petals glowed green, and the scent of saltwater seemed to pour over me.

"This is incredible. How are they alive in here?" I lifted my hand to feel the glossy leaves. When my finger brushed a petal, the green turned black, like a coating of dust had consumed it. I sucked in a sharp breath and yanked my hand back. "Fuck."

In my haste to pull away, I stumbled on a root that seemed to grow out of the floor, and I had to catch myself on the wall to keep from falling. The wall was covered in ivy. As soon as my fingers touched the leaves, the dust consumed them, too, leaving behind a dead smudge. Tears in my eyes, I pulled my hand away.

Kalen was by my side in an instant. "Did you mean to do that?"

I shook my head emphatically. This was everything I'd feared. "No."

"All right. Don't panic." He rustled around in his pockets before extracting a pair of thin leather gloves. "Wear these, just for now."

A horrible, terrifying sensation snaked through me—the feeling of no control. When the leaves had died, I had not been thinking about my power at all. I had no intense emotions rattling through me. I felt...fine. If I hadn't seen it with my own eyes, I wouldn't believe I'd done it.

The death magic was seeping out of me. I couldn't touch anyone without risking their life.

My heart rattled. I couldn't even touch Kalen.

Swallowing hard around the intense pain in my chest, I took a large step away from the man I loved, hating every inch of separation between us. "You need to stay away from me."

"It was only a small plant. No need to panic," he said, his voice even and calm. "But just to be safe, wear the gloves until we can figure out a way for you to regain control."

Regain control. I'd never truly been in control in the first place. A memory flashed through my mind, a moment in time I'd scarcely thought of since. When I'd first met Kalen and we'd traveled through the mists to find my mother, we had stopped in the woods outside a little village called Vere. He and the others had left me with the horses—which I now knew had been powerful joint eaters—while they fought a group of storm fae.

A strange little creature, something like a scorpion, had crawled onto my hand. As soon as it had touched me, it had curled up into a ball and fallen onto the ground, seemingly dead. In fact, for a moment, I'd been *certain* it was dead. But then I'd poked it, and it had come back to life and scuttled away.

It had been such a strange moment. I'd meant to ask Kalen about it at the time, but then the storm fae had almost killed Toryn, and I'd forgotten all about the strange little scorpion. Now the moment lit up in my mind like the eversun's brutal, incessant rays. I had touched that creature, and it had died. And then I'd somehow caused it to come back to life, just like I'd done to Fenella.

I hadn't been in control then, and I wasn't in control now. I couldn't risk touching anything.

And so I slipped on the gloves, unshed tears burning my eyes.

From across the room, Toryn wore a knowing smile, but he didn't say anything. For that, I was grateful. I didn't want to talk about this, not yet. And I certainly didn't want to hear empty words. *It'll be all right. You'll find a way to control it. Your powers aren't terrifying at all, Tessa.*

We didn't know if any of that was true, and if I wasn't careful, I could turn this entire realm to dust even before Andromeda arrived.

Twenty-Six
Tessa

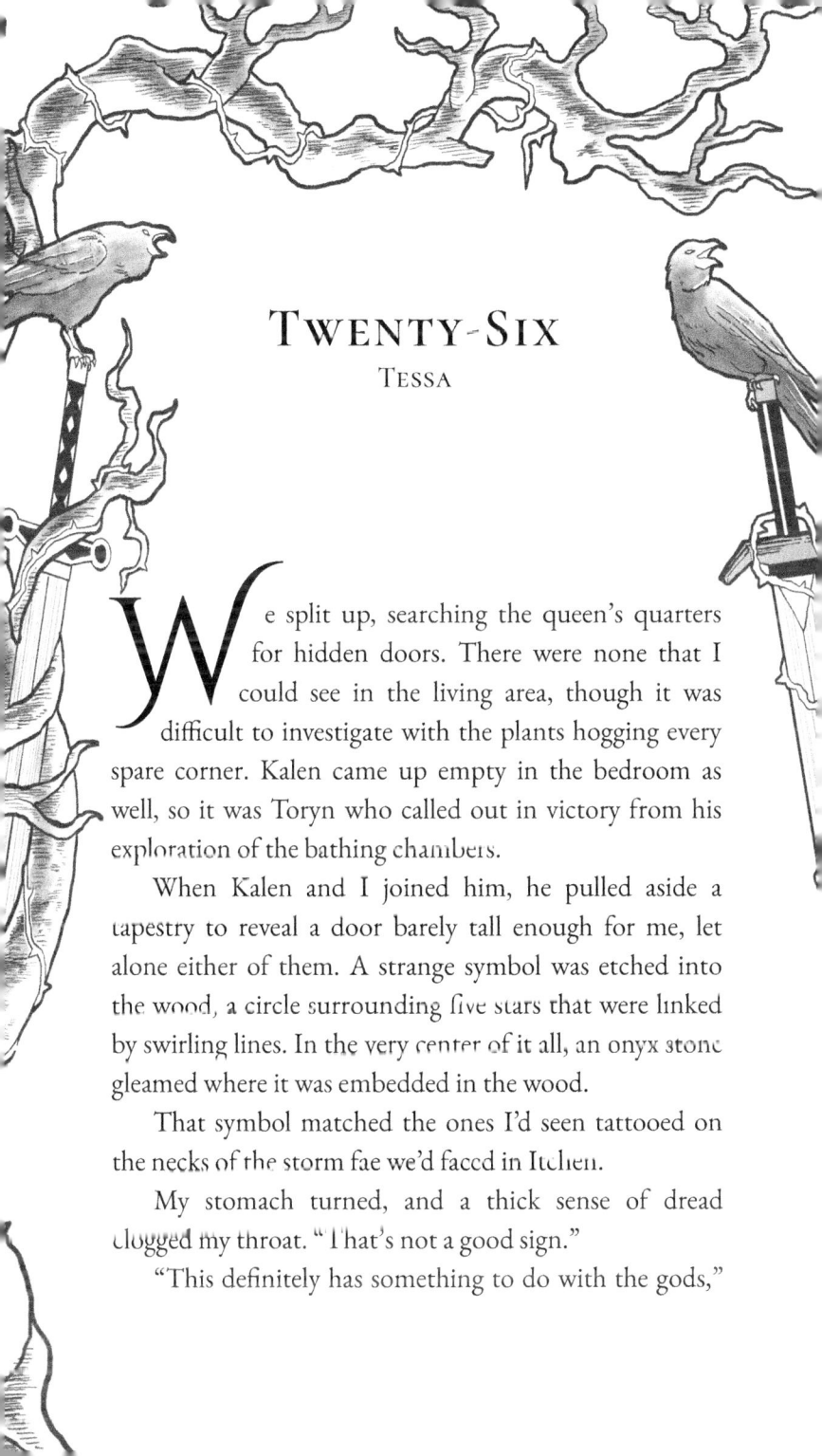

We split up, searching the queen's quarters for hidden doors. There were none that I could see in the living area, though it was difficult to investigate with the plants hogging every spare corner. Kalen came up empty in the bedroom as well, so it was Toryn who called out in victory from his exploration of the bathing chambers.

When Kalen and I joined him, he pulled aside a tapestry to reveal a door barely tall enough for me, let alone either of them. A strange symbol was etched into the wood, a circle surrounding five stars that were linked by swirling lines. In the very center of it all, an onyx stone gleamed where it was embedded in the wood.

That symbol matched the ones I'd seen tattooed on the necks of the storm fae we'd faced in Itchen.

My stomach turned, and a thick sense of dread clogged my throat. "That's not a good sign."

"This definitely has something to do with the gods,"

Kalen murmured, his eyes on Toryn's paling face. "I'm so sorry. I hoped it would turn out we were wrong."

Toryn's entire body exhaled his next breath. "Of course she's involved. Only a queen loyal to the gods would want her children to murder each other."

I pressed my lips together. There truly was nothing to say to that. He was right, of course. Oberon's cruelty had been more abundant than Queen Tatiana's, but hers was more intimate, more personal than his had ever been. At least he had been trying to protect the person he loved most in the world. Queen Tatiana, on the other hand, was quite the opposite.

But the wicked truth of it all was that maybe they could have been different. Maybe neither one of them would have been this twisted if not for the corrupting power of the gods.

It was clear that having that power nearby, or using it in any way, got into your heart and warped it until you were nothing but an unrecognizable shell of who you'd once been—one so capable of monstrous deeds that any scrap of humanity you'd once had was gone.

And this—this *wickedness*—was what I had to look forward to if I did not get my power under control.

"Shall we see what's down here?" Kalen said, drawing his sword.

Toryn nodded and pushed the door open. The hinges squealed as it swung inward, and a yawning pit of black nothingness glared back at us. A harsh wind rushed into our faces, bringing with it the overwhelming stench of *wrongness*. I ground my teeth and braced myself against the force of it. A deep, dark power seemed to vibrate through the very bones of the castle, of the city itself. And it came from the tunnel we were about to enter.

"Kalen, do you feel that?" I whispered.

"Unfortunately," he said, tightening the grip on his steel—though I had to wonder, would a sword do much good against whatever made the air taste like death, sickness, and fear? What kind of weapon could we wield against *that*? "I'll go first. Stay behind me."

Toryn opened his mouth to argue, but Kalen shot him a quick glare. The fae of his Mist Guard were his closest friends—they were his family—and he accepted a lot of attitude from them that he wouldn't from others. But in this moment, King Kalen Denare had taken over, and he had ordered us to stay back. And despite everything, I couldn't help the flush that filled me with an intoxicating heat. He was the most magnificent being I'd ever seen in my life.

Kalen strode into the dark tunnel without a hint of fear on his face. I fell in behind him, while Toryn took the rear. The fae had to stoop, ducking beneath the low ceiling that skimmed the top of my head. Inside, the thundering sensation of *wrongness* only grew stronger. And as we inched forward, I had to grind my teeth against the desire to turn around and run back the way we'd come.

Every single step made it worse. Every whisper of that wind against my face made certain doom thunder in my heart. It felt as though we were walking straight into the pits of the underworld, never to escape again.

Never to see light again.

The mists of the Kingdom of Shadow were nothing

compared to this. Out there, even on the darkest night, a haze of light crept through the fog. This was nothing but black, so all-encompassing and endless, I could not even see the vague shape of Kalen in front of me. I could not hear anything, either, only my ragged breathing and my own boots scraping against the stone.

All I could hear was myself.

A sudden blast of panic slammed into me.

With a gloved hand, I reached out and found his waist, firm beneath my touch. Kalen was there. Instantly, the panic subsided. He was still with me. I was not alone in this place, lost forever to the darkness.

I didn't know how long we walked like that. The moments felt like hours or even days. Time seemed to lose all meaning. I started to wonder if the gods had come and gone, destroying the world completely while the three of us were lost in the halls made of night.

A distant glow curved around a corner up ahead, and my entire body exhaled in relief as my vision began to clear. Kalen continued to trek ever forward, his sword held before him. I glanced over my shoulder to check on Toryn. He was still there with a grim set to his jaw. His eyes looked as haunted as my heart felt.

We rounded the corner and came to the entrance of a cave. The glow brightened, originating from a bleached white stone perched on a raised dais, and illuminated the moss-covered ceiling above it. Water dripped onto the jagged rocks all around us.

Kalen let out a low whistle, and the sound echoed, and echoed, and echoed, growing further and further away as if the caves tunneled deep into the dark earth.

There was nothing else in this place other than that white stone and the steps leading up to the dais just ahead of us. Something in my gut told me we should turn around now and leave, never to return. That feeling of wrongness permeated the air and sank into my skin, like the humidity itself was coated in it. We'd found what we'd come here for—there was a stone that likely held a god, just like the onyx stone back in Itchen had, like the stone in Oberon's necklace had. We didn't need to know anything more than that.

Toryn jerked his head toward the stone. "There's something else up there. Looks like some sort of bench or seat has been carved into the dais."

I followed his gaze, my heart thumping. Along the edge of the dais, there were indeed two flat sides of stone that were squared off on the tops. It was difficult to see more than that, but it clearly wasn't natural. Someone had made those seats, but my mind screamed that we did not want to know any more than that.

"I think we should leave," I said as the thickening fear washed over me.

Leave, leave, leave echoed all around us. A shiver scraped down my spine, tingling right where Oberon had cut into my skin all those years ago—where my father had first cut, desperate to release my wings. Wings I'd always been certain I would never have.

But now...after touching that flower and being down here...

"We need to leave," I said, louder this time, turning to Kalen with pleading eyes. "This place is wrong. We should not be here."

"I know." He gazed up at the dais. "But we need to see what's up there. It could be important."

I clutched his arm when he made a move toward the steps. "You once held out your hand to me when we stood at the edge of a cliff, and you asked if I trusted you. Do you remember? In that dream? And then I took your hand, and we leapt. I tumbled into a chasm with you. I trusted you when you said we should jump. Trust me now, Kalen. We need to leave."

Kalen lowered his sword, searching my eyes for answers I did not have. How could I explain this deep-seated feeling inside of me? How could I ask him to leave before we got all our answers? We'd likely never again find the opportunity to come down here. The queen was hiding something big, something to do with the gods. Whatever it was waited up on that dais, only steps away from us now.

But we had to get out of here or something terrible was going to happen.

He reached out to palm my cheek, as he'd done a dozen times or more, but I hissed and stepped out of his reach. We didn't know the extent of my power or if skin-to-skin contact of any kind was dangerous. I would not risk his life testing it.

His jaw clenched. "Are you certain of this?"

"More certain than I've ever been of anything. We should not be here, Kalen. *Please*."

He nodded and traced an invisible line in the air, as if he were imagining running his finger along the edge of my jaw. "Of course I trust you. If you're that certain we should leave, we'll leave."

I exhaled in relief. There was no reason he should turn away from that dais, but here he was, trusting me despite that. I yearned to reach out and pull him in close, but instead, I turned to go. And then I caught a blur of movement in the corner of my eye as Toryn rushed up the steps.

Kalen swore.

"I'm sorry, Kal," Toryn called out behind him. "I can't leave this place, not until I have my answers. I need to know what she's been hiding all these years."

A shuddering breath escaped my throat, but despite my growing sense of dread, I couldn't blame Toryn. Would I have done the same thing in his place? If this were about my father, or Nellie, or Val, would I have been able to walk away from it? Likely not. The desperation for answers would taste like ash, and I'd never be able to wash it away until I understood everything. I'd been there, when it came to my father. When I'd finally faced it, when I'd *needed* to know the truth, I'd forced myself to watch it all play out in front of me, even though it felt like the claws of shadowfiends scraping through my soul.

Kalen's face nearly crumpled. Fear shot through the bond, so thick and potent I found it hard to breathe. "Toryn, don't do this. Come on. There's something wrong with this place, and Tessa can feel it far better than we can. She's right. We need to leave."

"I just need to know what this is." Toryn reached the top of the steps and spun in a slow circle, the light from the glowing gemstone bathing his face in silver.

With a sigh, Kalen took my gloved hand. "I trust you

more than anything, love, but we can't let him do this alone."

And with that, Kalen started up those steps toward whatever dread awaited us.

My heart kicked my ribs. Steeling myself, I climbed the steps beside him, unable to walk away now. The closer I drew to the top of that dais, the worse my body felt. My back screamed in agony, and my teeth ached as if they wanted to pull themselves out of my mouth so they could scatter onto the bottom of the cave floor and get away from here, away from *this*.

Boots scuffing the smooth stone at the top of the dais, I joined Kalen and Toryn where they gazed at what awaited us. The terror within me was almost too great for me to look, but I forced myself to meet my fate. And then...I cocked my head, frowning.

Four rectangular compartments filled the space around us, backing up onto the edge of the almost perfectly square dais. Hewn from onyx, they would have looked like fairly unremarkable sarcophaguses if not for the five buzzing gemstones inlaid on the surface of each one. In the very center of those stones was the only carving—a unique constellation of stars, different on each of the four. And as we stared, every now and then, those stones shook. It was just a rattle, but it was enough to make me take a wide step back toward the white stone in the middle of the dais.

"What the fuck is this?" I whispered.

Footsteps echoed through the cavernous space. Heart in my throat, I whirled toward the sound. Queen Tatiana walked inside with a tight grip on Nellie's arm. My sister shot me an apologetic look, and even though she looked none the worse for wear, a familiar rage stirred inside me, desperate to spill the queen's blood just for touching her.

Dizziness washed through me, blurring the sight of the queen scowling up at us. I shook my head and gritted my teeth, and then shoved my hands behind my back to keep myself from doing something stupid.

Something about this place—it felt like Andromeda. And the overwhelming stench of it was calling to the power inside of me. I could feel it. It was like it *recognized* me, and the magic in my veins was desperate to answer the only way it knew how, with rage and hate.

Rage toward the fae who gripped my sister.

I fisted my hands and tried to shove it away.

"Mother, what is this?" Toryn demanded, striding toward the edge of the dais. "Let go of Nellie."

Sighing, Queen Tatiana released her grip on my sister. Nellie stumbled forward, her wide eyes trained on the three of us. She started toward the steps, as if she planned to join us up here.

My heart leapt into my throat. "No, Nellie. Stay back. Don't come up here."

Nellie stopped, confusion rippling across her gentle features.

"That's right," Queen Tatiana said. "You don't want to go up there. Because that's where the gods are waiting."

TWENTY-SEVEN
TESSA

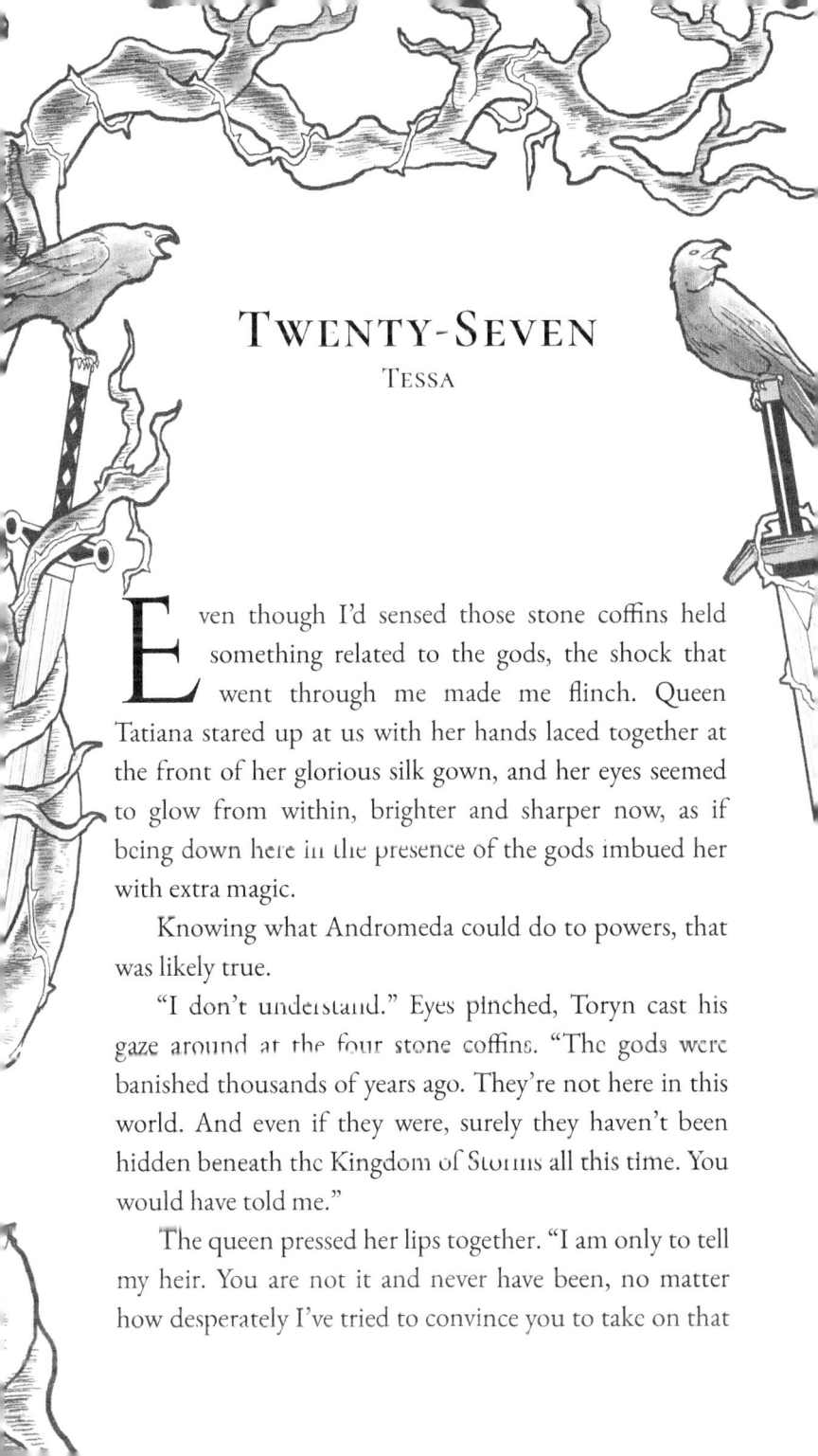

Even though I'd sensed those stone coffins held something related to the gods, the shock that went through me made me flinch. Queen Tatiana stared up at us with her hands laced together at the front of her glorious silk gown, and her eyes seemed to glow from within, brighter and sharper now, as if being down here in the presence of the gods imbued her with extra magic.

Knowing what Andromeda could do to powers, that was likely true.

"I don't understand." Eyes pinched, Toryn cast his gaze around at the four stone coffins. "The gods were banished thousands of years ago. They're not here in this world. And even if they were, surely they haven't been hidden beneath the Kingdom of Storms all this time. You would have told me."

The queen pressed her lips together. "I am only to tell my heir. You are not it and never have been, no matter how desperately I've tried to convince you to take on that title. *This* is part of the reason why. Knowing about these gods...Toryn, I should not be the only one who has this information, but I swore a vow long ago to my father. I had to prevent anyone else from discovering they were here. And I couldn't tell *you* unless you won the trial. Or, I suppose, if you found this cave yourself, as you've done now."

Kalen pressed a hand to the small of my back, and the warmth of him curled through me, chasing away the rage I still felt churning through my veins and the red that bled into the corners of my eyes. He urged me toward the steps. "We need to go."

Queen Tatiana's eyes zeroed in on me. "You can feel it, can't you? Their desperation to get out?"

Wetting my lips, I nodded, but when I tried to speak, I couldn't find the words. The sensation of the gods bore down on me too much, like a heavy weight that pressed upon my mind.

"I thought as much," she said with a sad smile. "You see, it's been getting worse."

The stone sarcophagi rumbled once more, and the force of it sent another wave of rage washing through me. I winced and pressed my hand to my head.

"Ever since that comet arrived in the sky," the queen continued, "they've been...shifting."

"Shifting?" Toryn's alarmed voice rang against the stone but was soon drowned out by another deep rumble. "What do you mean, *shifting*?"

"If I were to guess?" she said with an arched brow. "I'd say it means they're awakening."

"I think we need to have this conversation somewhere

else," I said through gritted teeth. The pounding in my skull was growing louder, that dread growing even more oppressive. The longer we stood here, the worse it got. And I didn't want to be in this cave to find out what happened if the gods inside these coffins truly did wake.

"They were banished," Kalen said from behind me, a steady presence amid the heavy gloom. "Even my mother agreed with that, and she went to Talaven to ask them questions about the gods. The humans told her this directly. She would have been able to scent if they were lying."

"Oh, yes, they were banished." The queen's eyes flicked to the coffins. "But to where? Did they tell her that?"

I could tell by the tensing of his body that no, the humans hadn't divulged the details to Queen Bellicent Denare. They'd only told her just enough to convince her to force her son into a vow against an enemy she couldn't — or wouldn't — name.

"There's no killing the gods, you see," Queen Tatiana continued, reaching up to touch her necklace with a shaking finger. "There's no ridding this world of them or forcing them off these lands. They're too powerful. We're too weak. All we could do was force them in those stone coffins and separate them from Andromeda. Because when she gets near them, they grow stronger. Soon, they'll be strong enough to break free, no matter what wards we've put into place to prevent them from escaping."

I glanced at the onyx gemstone necklace, understanding at once. It *wasn't* a sign of loyalty to the gods at all. It was a way for the queen to protect herself and her people from the influence of them, and to stop the gods from leaving their coffins. But if what she said was true—and the rumbles indicated that it was—none of that would matter soon.

Shoving down my blinding rage, I stepped to the edge of the dais to meet her steady gaze. "You need to get out of here. You need to take all the people of Gailfean and run."

"I cannot," she said with a sad smile. "I told you, I swore a vow when I learned of this place. I have to stay here in Gailfean and stand guard against the enemies when they rise. My power may not be strong enough to kill them, but it will slow them down. It will be enough for *you* to get my people out of here in time."

"Mother," Toryn said, his voice hoarse. "You don't mean that. You can't just stay here and die."

"I can, and I will." She motioned Toryn forward. "Someone needs to hold them back long enough to get the people of Gailfean safely out of this city. I'm only glad that you sought out this place. Deep down, I knew you were still the stubborn, curious boy you've always been."

Toryn shook his head and jogged down the steps. When he reached his mother, he took her hands in his and dropped his forehead to hers. "Mother. I'm so sorry I doubted you all this time. I should have listened to you. I should have—"

"Shh, my son," she whispered, staring up at him with glassy eyes. "How were you to know? I was tasked with keeping this a secret from everyone, including you. You had no reason to suspect anything more was going on than what you knew."

"This isn't fair," he ground out. "You can't do this. You can't sacrifice yourself, not like this. I've spent the last four hundred years angry with you. And now that I know the truth...we need more *time*."

She smiled up at him and palmed his scarred cheek. "It is a gift to have any time at all. Take what is given to you and use it wisely, just as I will now. Get our people out of here, Toryn. Make certain you wear the onyx and pass around as many gemstones as you can to everyone else. There's a stash of them in my quarters. They will protect you from the influence of the gods."

She lifted her necklace over her head and hung it around his neck.

"I can't take this from you," he said.

"You must. I've seen what happens to fae who are not protected from the influence of the gods. They become a twisted version of themselves."

"Owen," Toryn said.

She palmed his scarred face. "I am so sorry for what he did to you. Now, go. Hurry. We don't know how much longer we have before the gods awake and tear this city down."

As if angered by her words, the ground beneath our feet jolted us sideways. Kalen took my gloved hand and pulled me along behind him, rushing down the steps. Toryn was embracing his mother when we reached the cave floor, while Nellie looked on with a sad, distant look in her eyes, no doubt remembering the last times we'd seen our mother and father.

After Queen Tatiana pulled away from Toryn and motioned him toward the tunnel, she caught my arm before I could follow. There was a knowing glint in her eye. "I've spent a lot of time in this cave and a lot of time near these gods. They even tried tempting me to their side by gifting me with these claws and a host of other powers. Bribes, you see. So I know what they smell like, and you reek of them."

Heart thundering, I opened my mouth to try to explain, but she cut me off before I could find the words. And then she took my gloved hand in hers and lifted it before her eyes.

"I did wonder when Oberon got so obsessed with getting you back to Albyria," she murmured, a line pinched between her brow. "He was quite frantic, really. Far more concerned about you than he'd ever been about those other brides of his. Why, I couldn't help but wonder. Was there something special about you? You've appeared normal enough so far, though your smell is a tad off. At first, I couldn't put my finger on it. Not until just now when I found one of my beloved flowers covered in a layer of dust. Dead."

"I...that was an accident."

"I'm certain it was," she said in a tight voice, reaching out to brush a few wayward strands of my golden hair away from my face, though she was careful not to touch my skin. "I heard a prophecy once upon a time. It said the gods will one day return, and they will crush this world beneath their boots unless we find a way to turn their own power against them. It also said there is only one person strong enough to do that. I wonder, could that one person be you?"

I let out a tense laugh. "If there's one person strong enough to do that, it's Kalen Denare. Even his own mother thought so."

"Ah, Bellicent Denare." Her voice went razor sharp. "The woman Oberon killed when she refused his proposal. The humans told her something that scared the living moonlight out of her, according to her letters. Something about mist and shadow." She took a step closer, and the scent of wine drifted from her lips. "And death."

She didn't know the truth about Bellicent, then.

The ground suddenly shook, but the queen hardly seemed to notice as she continued her speech. "Bellicent mentioned the prophecy in a few letters. Whatever the mortals told her, I think it led her to suspect I harbored secrets myself. Me as well as Oberon. I believe she intended to visit me after her trip to Albyria. But she never returned. I wonder, what did she learn there? What was Oberon hiding?"

"You know what he was hiding," I said around the lump of nausea lodged in my throat. "Andromeda."

"Anything else?" she asked in a whisper, her bright eyes eager.

I glanced behind me at the rumbling stone sarcophaguses and toward the tunnel entrance where the others waited. There was no time for stories, but there was a desperation in her voice, a plea. As if she had wondered all her life what Oberon had been doing, and she feared she'd have to die without ever knowing the answer.

And so I said the only thing I could. "He was in a lot of pain, and he couldn't endure it. So he used the god's power to save the only woman he ever loved. I think you know who that was."

The queen's eyes widened in understanding, and then she clutched my arm. "Thank you. It explains so much. Now go."

I gave Queen Tatiana one last look, taking in her emerald eyes and her pale brown hair and the defiant set of her jaw. I committed every single part of her to memory, and I swore to myself and to everything I was that the world would one day know her sacrifice. If we survived whatever came next, I would make certain there were songs written about this queen. I would make certain that her name was not forgotten—that she would be written into the stars.

As if reading my thoughts, her grip tightened on my arm, and she hissed her final words. "For Aesir, for the land of magic and fae, I will face these creatures. The first thing they see when they wake will be me and my great power. I will make them understand they have made a grave mistake in targeting this world again. May the realm never break."

"May the realm never break," I murmured back to her.

And then I joined the others and ran.

Twenty-Eight
Tessa

The floor's violent shaking told me we did not have much time, and there was no stopping it now. Toryn led the way back through the tunnels and into his mother's chambers, his jaw clenching as he took one last look around the rooms filled with so much life. Soon, all these plants, which had clearly been lovingly cared for, would be crushed beneath the rubble.

And so would his mother.

The pain etched into his face was evident. I could even see it in the way he breathed, as if his lungs struggled to find the air he needed in order to keep moving.

"Toryn." Kalen clapped his hand on the storm fae's shoulder. "We're all here. You don't have to do this alone."

He met Kalen's eyes with an unflinching gaze. "I know. But I have to play the role of prince now, which means I have to be the one to take charge. The only way we're going to get the storm fae to leave this city is if I order them to do it. It's their home, the only place most of them have ever known."

With my heart wrenching at the pain in his eyes, I reached out to him, but then let my hand drop to my side. "Trust me, they'll be all right when they realize you've saved them from this."

"Where will you take them?" Nellie asked. "Is there another city nearby?"

Toryn steadied himself against the wall as the floor jolted beneath us once again. Once it ceased, he went to the stash of gemstones that Queen Tatiana had left out in several large sacks—like she'd expected someone to need them this day.

"The closest city is Dubnos, but the storm fae won't want to go into enemy territory," Toryn said, hauling one of the sacks from the floor.

"I am the enemy, and I'm standing right here," Kalen argued. "Surely they've seen that we're allies now. There's no reason for them to fear the shadow fae."

"It's not the fae they fear," Nellie said softly. "I heard them talking earlier at the feast. It's the mist. It terrifies them. They think it's full of monsters."

"To be fair, it *is* full of monsters," I had to admit.

"Either way, most of them won't want to go." With a heavy sigh, Toryn ran a hand down his tired face and grabbed the next sack. "The only way to be certain of everyone's safety is to take them somewhere else. Otherwise, some will insist on staying. And they will die here."

"Where to, then?" Kalen asked as he passed me a sack of gemstones and then grabbed another. "Malroch?"

Toryn grimaced. "It's the closest storm fae city, and

their walls are impenetrable." But then he sighed. "It's a two-week journey traveling by horse. To get everyone there, we'll need wagons and supplies. Some will have to walk. At that rate, plus finding shelter to stay safe during any oncoming storm...it could take upward of a month or longer if the weather works against us."

Kalen clenched his jaw. "The gods will be awake by then."

I glanced down at the stones beneath my feet, where the violent shakes were growing in frequency. Even as we'd stood here gathering the gemstones, they'd gotten so much worse. Dread crept through me. "How long has it been since we left Albyria? I've lost track of the days."

"About a month," Kalen replied.

Nellie gasped. "A month? Then the gods will wake any moment now, won't they? Andromeda could be here now." When no one answered, she shook her head and started backing toward the door. "You can't take them to this other city, Toryn. You have to come with us, back to Dubnos."

The ground suddenly bucked, and the stone cracked wide. Nellie grabbed my arm and held on tight as the four of us stood there in the depths of the Keep, waiting for the tremor to subside. It took a good ten minutes for it to fade, and even then, I could still feel the vibrations through the soles of my leather boots.

"We must go." Kalen grabbed the final sack, and moved to the door and yanked it open. "Toryn, your people are welcome in Dubnos. And you know I'd rather you be by my side than anywhere else in this godforsaken world. But it's your choice, and you should do what you must."

Pain flashed through Toryn's eyes as he followed Kalen into the corridor that led up the stairwell to the rest of the castle. As we climbed, the floor kept shaking, and the stone threatened to crumble down around us.

But when we reached the top of the stairwell and pushed out onto the main floor, an eerie stillness whispered through the rest of the castle.

Here, we could no longer feel the shaking from the great depths. It was as if nothing was happening at all. The people of this city had no idea what danger lurked in the caves beneath their feet, the evil that was awakening and readying itself to swallow them whole.

"The Great Hall," Nellie whispered. "They're all in there feasting. They have no idea."

We took off at a run and raced through the silent corridors. The further we got from the Keep, the less I felt that all-consuming darkness that pulsed from the cave. The gods weren't awake—not yet. But I did not think we had long before they broke through their stone prisons.

Panting with exertion, I followed the others into the Great Hall. Someone had started to play the flute, and another fae had grabbed a handful of drums. Music swirled through the air, upbeat and full of hope, mingling with laughter, booming voices, and the magic of the celebration. My heart ached to gaze upon the happy faces. They'd just survived another storm, and they thought they were safe, at least for a little while longer.

They had no idea what was coming for them.

No one paid us much attention as we strode toward

the raised dais where Fenella still lounged in her chair, her feet kicked up on the table beside a brooding Caedmon. She gave us a wry grin as we approached, but then her eyes flashed across our faces, and her smile died. She lowered her feet to the floor and stood. "Toryn, you look like death. What's happening?"

Toryn leaned in and whispered into her ear. It was a risk speaking so publicly like this, but the storm fae would soon find out, regardless. When he was done filling her in, she sat hard in her chair, lifted the bottle of fion from the table, and gulped it down until there was nothing left of it.

"Fuck me," she breathed before passing another bottle to Caedmon and filling him in on what she'd learned. The silver-haired fae paled at her words.

The Prince of the Kingdom of Storms gazed out at his people, his jaw hard. But his eyes were soft, unlike the eyes of the mother he'd long believed had hardened her heart toward everyone, including him. He ran his hand along the top of his head, the strands longer and wavier now. He looked less like a warrior and more like all those regular storm fae down there just trying to live their lives.

Just trying to survive.

"You've got this, my old friend," Kalen murmured.

Toryn nodded, and before our very eyes, we watched him change. It started with his chin—he held it just a tad higher. His shoulders were next. Squaring them, lifting them, filling his chest with breath, he stood half a hand taller than he had moments before. He ran his palms down the front of his tunic and then centered his belt. Nellie inched in, pressed up onto her toes, and then clasped something onto his lapel. When she pulled back, the emerald gleam of his kingdom's sigil matched his own hardening eyes.

The Toryn I'd met that day in the dungeons beneath Dubnos had worn an easy smile and carried lightness in his eyes. But now the weight of entire kingdom had settled onto his shoulders. And he did not bend.

With a quick breath, Toryn lifted a chalice from the table and clinked his fork against the glass. The fae at the table nearest us immediately hushed, and then a murmur spread through the crowd. Within moments, the entire room went silent. Every eye in the Great Hall was aimed on Toryn's unyielding face. I gazed across the crowd, at the curious yet rapt expressions. Despite turning down his chance to become his mother's heir, Toryn was their prince, and they would listen to him.

He'd always been their prince.

It was a good thing Owen was not here.

"Good people of Gailfean," Toryn began, his voice booming through the vast hall. "You have always been a strong city made of strong fae who suffer the storms and survive. And you've just survived another."

A celebratory cheer rippled through the room. Tankards clanked, beer sloshed, hands were thrown into the air. The uneasy sense of doom curdled in my stomach, but it wasn't from the gods down in the caverns this time. It came from the aching regret at seeing the happiness in all these fae. They thought Toryn was making a speech of triumph to mark the occasion of surviving another storm without a single casualty. The people of Gailfean were safe until another one hit, and just like this one, they would face it head-on and make it through. They always did.

But their lives were about to be irrevocably changed. I wished there was something we could do, some way to keep those gods locked up tight. But there was no way, not unless Niamh, Alastair, and Val found the answers in the human kingdoms. And they had not sent word in days.

There was no option but to run. A tear spilled down my cheek.

Toryn gave the fae a moment before he pounded a fist on the table, a heavy, dark sound that sent another hush through the crowd. I saw his throat bob. It was the only piece of his kingly mask that gave way.

"I'm afraid that a greater threat has arrived, and I need everyone to stay silent until I tell you to move," he said, his voice growing hard. The fae shifted on their seats, and a few gasped. "You may have seen the comet in the sky. It foretells of—"

"The comet is no longer in the sky, Your Grace," one of the ladies sitting at the head table murmured up at him. "I went onto the balcony a moment ago for some fresh air. The comet is gone. It's not there."

Toryn's jaw went rigid, and a few whispers sounded from nearby. Heart pounding, I turned to Kalen. His eyes were wild and held an intensity that shook my soul. Our worst suspicions were confirmed. Andromeda was here, and the gods below would awaken at any moment. We didn't have time to explain things to the storm fae. They couldn't pack their belongings or calmly walk out of this castle and into the city streets beyond.

They needed to flee *now*.

Toryn held up a hand. "I need everyone to leave this castle immediately. Do not take anything with you. Do not return to your rooms unless it's to get your children or anyone who didn't attend this feast. Go, as fast as you can, and gather in the market courtyard along the southern wall. Call out to every building you pass. Tell the people of Gailfean they need to run. The gods have returned."

And then the Great Hall exploded into chaos.

Twenty-Nine
Kalen

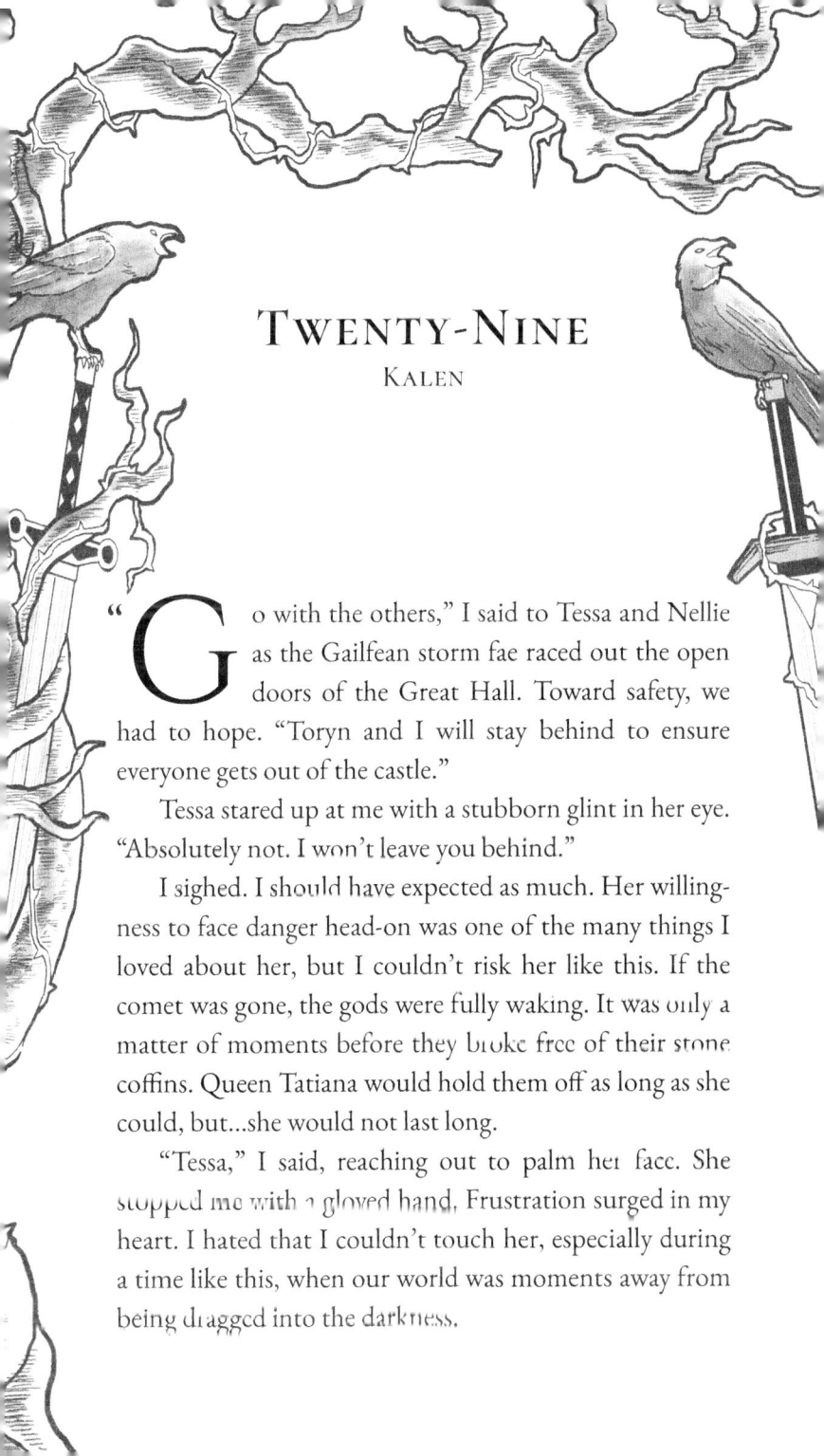

"Go with the others," I said to Tessa and Nellie as the Gailfean storm fae raced out the open doors of the Great Hall. Toward safety, we had to hope. "Toryn and I will stay behind to ensure everyone gets out of the castle."

Tessa stared up at me with a stubborn glint in her eye. "Absolutely not. I won't leave you behind."

I sighed. I should have expected as much. Her willingness to face danger head-on was one of the many things I loved about her, but I couldn't risk her like this. If the comet was gone, the gods were fully waking. It was only a matter of moments before they broke free of their stone coffins. Queen Tatiana would hold them off as long as she could, but...she would not last long.

"Tessa," I said, reaching out to palm her face. She stopped me with a gloved hand. Frustration surged in my heart. I hated that I couldn't touch her, especially during a time like this, when our world was moments away from being dragged into the darkness.

"We are a team now, Kalen," she whispered up at me, unblinking. "I can't go without you."

"And your sister?"

A tense line formed between Tessa's brows, and then she turned to Fenella, who was watching the screaming, fleeing fae with blatant unease. Her hands clutched both her daggers. "Fenella, can you go to the courtyard and take Nellie with you? Caedmon, too."

"We can manage that."

Caedmon gave a nod, his jaw tight. "Don't worry. We'll get her somewhere safe."

Nellie didn't even argue as Tessa threw her arms around her, hugged her goodbye, and then sent her on her way. I'd been impressed with Nellie's bravery—she'd faced far more than most humans ever would in their lifetime. But I could see by the paling of her face and the trembling of her hands that she knew this was not a time to be bold.

It was a time to run.

The Gailfean fae continued to stream out the open doors, their desperation causing them to push and shove and claw their way toward the front of the crowd. One fae got knocked to the floor, a smaller man with black hair and terrified eyes, who struggled to get back on his feet. Toryn saw and left the dais at once, pushing through the crowd to help the man.

I took Tessa's gloved hand and pulled her to my chest. "Tessa, there's something I need to tell you."

She dropped back her head to gaze up at me. Unshed tears glazed her eyes, but they weren't for her own fear, her own sorrow. I could feel her emotions surging through the bond—even her thoughts. This was where it all ended, where it all changed. From this moment on, peace and happiness would be forgotten things. How would we survive? Perhaps we wouldn't. It seemed impossible that we could win against five powerful beings who could never die.

But beneath her grief, there was another emotion that softened the hard edges she displayed to the world. An emotion that swelled in my own chest. One I'd yet to voice aloud.

But I needed to. If this was where it all ended, I wanted Tessa to know.

Suddenly, the floor rumbled, shaking down the length of the Great Hall. Fae screamed, and the thunder of their footsteps grew so loud that it almost drowned out the sound of the gods awakening in the cavern beneath the castle.

Tessa leaned into me, her gloved hands splayed across my chest. And I held her tightly to me, unwilling to let her go. As much as I would have preferred she leave with her sister and go to the safety of the courtyard outside, I was glad she was here by my side. Here, with me, when we faced the end of it all.

Sighing, I tugged the end of her braid. Those soft brown eyes gazed up at me, and my heart clenched. I'd always been a damn fool when I looked into those eyes. They were the color of a gemstone, the tiger-eye. Such a shockingly golden brown. And in them, I saw the other half of my soul.

"Tessa," I said in a rough voice. "No matter what happens next, I want you to know—"

"Wait." Her expression softened even more, and she traced her gloved finger across my chin, ignoring the rumbling that grew ever louder. "Not here, not like this. Don't talk like this is the end because it's not. We can do this. We can fight those gods. May the realm never break."

I clasped her hand in mine and held it against my heart. Emotion surged within me, hers and mine combined. "May the realm never break."

And then the dais beneath our feet splintered.

Tessa cried out and leapt across the crack that widened between us. Her body slammed into me, knocking me sideways. I caught her arms and steadied myself, and her eyes met mine. Something passed between us then—an understanding, a bone-deep realization that we would either get through this together or we would never again see the sky.

"To the stars," I told her.

She nodded.

I took her gloved hand in mine, and we ran to where Toryn was herding the last remaining fae out of the Great Hall. After he helped a woman and her crying child pass across the shaking floor, he turned to us with tired eyes. "It's done. They're all out of this hall. But we should check the bedrooms and make certain no one in the court has been left behind." His voice was weary, and his crumpled face displayed the truth of his thoughts now that he no longer had to put on a brave and powerful show.

Tankards clattered off a nearby table and onto the floor as the rumbles transformed the entire room into an avalanche of destruction. A chunk of rock slammed down beside us, and I looked up at the ceiling to see a jagged crack in the stone high above. On the wall to our right, a storm fae tapestry ripped in two as the walls began to separate.

I pushed Tessa through the door first, and then shoved Toryn just behind her. We made it into the corridor just as hundreds of rocks rained down from above. The entire Great Hall collapsed.

"Go!" Toryn shouted, motioning us in front of him. "We'll check the rooms on our way out."

Hand in hand, Tessa and I ran through the corridors, stumbling when the ground lurched beneath us. We traced the path from the Great Hall toward the front of the castle, where we'd find safety—for a little while at least—and checked the rooms along the way.

But when we reached the main corridor, a strange sensation prickled the back of my neck. Tessa sucked in a sharp gasp and yanked on my hand. She'd felt something behind us.

"Sun above," she muttered, and her fear punched into me through our bond. "It's Sirius. He's found us."

Tension pounded in my skull as I slowly turned to face the enemy. Darkness engulfed the other end of the hallway, pitch black and gleaming like the onyx gemstones that were scattered throughout the castle. A deep, dark dread pulsed toward us, as if pushed forward on the wind by invisible wings.

And then the shadows shifted. A large form strode from the darkness with a pair of eyes that glowed red.

For a moment, all I could do was stare. He was broader than I'd imagined, and at least half a foot taller than even the largest of the fae. Short crimson hair curled around his pointed ears, both of which had been pierced with an onyx gemstone earring. Shooting us a wicked smile that displayed his sharp, protruding canines, he reached up to his ear, yanked out the stone, and tossed it across the floor. It clattered as it scuttled toward us.

From beside me, Tessa shuddered.

The god seemed to sense her slight movement, just in tune with her every breath as I was. A possessiveness I'd never felt rose inside me as Sirius turned his flaming eyes on my wife, the other half of my soul. He cocked his head and sniffed.

His smile stretched wide. "Such an interesting little creature."

Rage surged through me, and I drew my sword. "You touch one hair on her head, and I will relish tearing you apart again and again until all you know is pain."

He chuckled, a rotten, hollow sound, and then he sniffed again. "Ah, fae. So easily corruptible. You live such long lives, it doesn't take much to make you forget what you once were when there's so much more that you can be. I can give you that—the power you crave."

I tightened my grip on my sword and sneered. "I crave nothing you can give me."

"Ah, ah." With flashing eyes, he took a step closer and drew a sword from the scabbard at his side. "I can sense it in you. You're a king, a proud one at that. Your reign...it's a burden. But it's one you enjoy. You bask in the adoration of your subjects." And then his smile dropped. "Give us the girl, and you can have all of Aesir. We don't want these wretched fae lands. All we care about is Talaven."

Heart clenching, I angled my body in front of Tessa's. "I will never let you touch her."

"Oh, no?" The god laughed. "And how do you plan to stop me?"

My power might not harm the gods, but it could still stun them. It could shake through the very foundations of this castle and bury them beneath a pile of rubble. And that would give us time—time enough to get everyone out of the city. The gods would have to crawl through the rubble, pushing aside rock after rock...

It wouldn't be our victory, but it would be enough for now. Enough for us to survive until we heard from Niamh and Val. If they didn't already, they would soon have an audience with the mortals. They would find the answers to defeating the gods. For now, we just needed to slow the enemy down.

"Toryn, Tessa, get behind me."

Sirius let out a delighted laugh. "What's this, now? You're actually going to attempt to fight me? Well, this is a first. The last time we were awake in these lands, everyone fled when they laid eyes on us. But I see time has eroded your brains just as much as it has eroded your magic."

Eroded our magic?

I didn't take the bait. Clearly, the god wanted to keep me talking as he slowly stalked down the corridor, carefully stepping around the cracks in the stone. The other gods must still be trapped in that cave, perhaps fighting Queen Tatiana. And Sirius was stalling for time.

I would not give it to him.

Tessa grabbed Toryn's arm and tugged him to the

floor. I called upon the dark power inside me, that magic I'd always hated and feared. Every time I'd used it, I'd only done so because I'd had no other choice—or the power had been forced out of me. This time, though, I relished what I could do. There was nothing human about the creature who stood before me with his red, gleaming eyes and a voice that sounded like shards of glass.

I called upon that power, and I launched it at the towering god.

Nothing happened.

A whistling wind echoed down the silent corridor, and Sirius's thin lips widened into a smile. Frowning, I reached for my power again, searching for any sign of it, for that all-consuming hole of blackness I'd hated all these long years. But gone was any trace of it. It was as if it had never even been there.

"Did you truly believe you could use your fae magic against *us*?" The god asked with a bitter laugh. "Your power is useless." He stormed down the corridor, his footsteps quicker now. "You are ours to command. Now *yield* and give me the girl."

Sirius threw all his weight behind his raised sword. I got my weapon up just in time, but the force of his blow threw me off my feet. I slammed into the wall, my head knocking against the stone. Tessa's terror—and my horror—tangled around my heart, and as I tried to reach out, to do anything I could to save her, darkness consumed me.

Thirty
Tessa

I screamed when Kalen hit the wall. His head snapped back, and he collapsed into a heap on the floor. My heart ripping in two, I rushed toward him, but Sirius grabbed the back of my neck and threw me in the opposite direction.

Toryn lunged toward the god, his spear raised. But Sirius knocked him out of the way as if he were nothing, and the god's crimson gaze zeroed in on me. My back against the wall, I slowly pushed to my feet, my breathing shallow and desperate. I didn't know what to do. I didn't know what I *could* do. Kalen was hurt. Toryn was scrambling to his feet down the corridor, but even if he reached me in time, his spear would do nothing but irritate the god. I saw it now, as clear as a new day in Teine. We were nothing but insects to him. Flies buzzing about, pesky and annoying. And easy enough to smash.

Sirius stopped just before me, only a breath away. He smelled like incense and blood and dirt. Up close, I could see the depths of red in his eyes. The bright crimson was marred with flecks of black and gold, and his skin was as smooth as glass. He leaned close, sniffed, and cocked his head.

"Oh, Andromeda is going to enjoy meeting you," he said in a voice that slithered down my spine. "How, exactly, is it that you came to be?"

"I don't know what you're talking about," I breathed.

"Don't play dumb. You're part mortal, and you smell of lies."

So the gods could smell the truth in mortals, just as the fae could. That might be useful knowledge in the future, if I got out of this without being flayed alive.

"You're coming with me," he hissed.

Sirius reached for my neck, but I ducked down and yanked my glove from my fingers. As his hand made contact with the wall, I reached up and brushed my fingers across his face. A part of me didn't want it to work—death by touch still horrified me—but there was no other way out of this. He was too strong for us to fight any other way.

A jolt of surprise flickered across his face, but he did not even shudder against my power, let alone take his last breath. Instead, he grabbed me by the throat and slammed me against the wall. Pain lanced through my skull, and my windpipe seemed crushed beneath the force of his grip.

"Did you just try to give me the gift of death?" he hissed into my ear, his breath hot against my neck. "Oh, yes. Such a lovely little toy for Andromeda to play with.

She might even give me an entire herd of mortals when she sees what I've found for her."

I shuddered, my teeth grinding as I tried to recoil from the god. But I had nowhere to go, nowhere to hide. He had me trapped, and he knew it. My power was useless against him. *Everyone's* powers were. And he was only one of the immortal beings we had to face. There were four more, including the worst of them—Andromeda herself.

All of this...it was impossible. The world had no hope of defeating them. I could see it now, the future a vision in the back of my mind. The gods would destroy Aesir in their quest to stomp down any opposition. They did not care how many fae they had to kill if it meant conquering this world.

And then they would move on to the mortal kingdoms, their true desire. They would take control of all the cities and burn down whichever ones resisted them, just as they'd done before. The mortals would bow to them as their gods, and then offer themselves up—their blood, their flesh, their bones, until there was nothing left, and then the gods would move on at last.

I saw all this in Sirius's gleaming red eyes, as if he were somehow showing me exactly what he and the others intended to do to my world.

And it made me weep.

"There, there, little one," he murmured, tracing a finger down my cheek. He snatched a tear and brought it to his lips, tasting my grief. "You don't need to fear us. None of that will happen to you. You will stand by Andromeda's side, you see. You will be one of us."

"Never," I growled, and then I spat in his face. A glob of saliva splattered onto his glass-like skin, and I had the satisfaction of seeing him flinch. Baring my teeth, I smiled at him. "I would rather die than become one of you."

I expected anger or some retaliation, a brutal response like Oberon would have given. Instead, Sirius smiled. "Little vicious thing. You are so much like your mother."

My blood chilled. "Andromeda is not my mother."

He tightened his grip on my throat. "In every way that matters, you are Andromeda's daughter, and there's no sense fighting it. You even look like her. But more importantly, you have her rage."

I fought the urge to punch him in the face. He'd probably like that, too. Instead, I clamped my mouth shut and sought a way out of this. On the far wall, Kalen had begun to stir, thank the light. But Toryn...there was no sign of him. Furrowing my brow, I flicked my gaze around the corridor, noticing that the rumbling had ceased—probably not a good sign.

A blur of motion came from my left. I turned in unison with Sirius. Toryn raced down the corridor with his spear raised, angry determination twisting his face into a scowl. Sirius released his grip on my throat to face Toryn. I sagged against the wall, sucking in deep breaths of air, bracing myself on the stone.

And then a feral shriek rent the air.

A bundle of fur and fangs flew from the depths of the castle. Sirius whirled toward the creature a second too late. The beast slammed into his body and knocked him off his feet. When the creature, a small, wolflike beast, landed on top of him, it sliced its claws across his throat.

Sirius let out a wordless cry, and blood spilled from his neck. The red light in his eyes suddenly dimmed.

Trembling, I shoved away from the wall and reached for Toryn's hand. He was on the other side of the beast. Right now, it was distracted by Sirius, but if it lifted its head, even just the slightest bit, it would see Toryn standing there and looking at it in...

Awe.

He did not look afraid. Instead, he practically beamed as the beast launched off the god's chest and sat on its haunches, blinking at me.

What in the name of light was going on?

Toryn knelt beside Sirius and peered into his vacant eyes. "He's unconscious for now, but it won't take long for these wounds to heal. We need to get out of here before they do."

"Toryn." I pointed a shaky finger at the wolf. It was licking its claws now. Licking the blood, I realized, my stomach turning. "What is that? Where did it come from? Is it...some kind of miniature shadowfiend?"

But despite the claws and the fangs and the fur, the monster looked little like those shadowfiends that stalked the mists and haunted my dreams. Its gleaming brown eyes were achingly familiar, and its chestnut fur was smooth and lush, its little ears twitching as if it listened and understood every word I said.

My breath shuddered out of me. "Nellie?"

But then Kalen was there, his hand on my face, on my arms, on my chest, and then on the back of my head. His eyes glowed with a ferocity that made my toes curl, and he drank me in like a parched man drinks in water.

"Tessa." His voice was a shudder, and I swore every muscle in his body tensed. He looked two seconds away from slamming his fists into the wall to bring the castle down. "Tell me you're all right. Tell me he didn't harm you."

"I'm fine," I whispered, reaching up to palm his face with my gloved hand. "See? I'm right here. I'm fine."

"I will fucking kill him." He turned to the god sprawled across the floor. His blood no longer leaked from the wound Nellie had given him. Not likely a good sign. But then Kalen *moved* with lethal grace, raising his sword above his head and bringing it down on Sirius's neck. The blade sliced through the air, through flesh and bone, but when Kalen pulled back, there was no sign of any wound.

It was as if the blade hadn't even touched him.

"What the fuck?" Toryn muttered, gazing down at the god in horrified awe.

"Our weapons don't work against them," Fenella called out from behind us. We turned to find her heaving in the next corridor, her face and hands covered in soot and blood. *Her* blood, judging by the gaping wound in her side where her leather armor had once protected her stomach. She pressed a shaking hand to the wound and stumbled toward us. "We have to get out of here. *Now*. They're coming."

Kalen took one last look at the god. His lip curled back as a low growl emanated from the back of his throat. And then he sheathed his sword, gave me a look that I understood all too well—*run*—and collected Fenella in his arms. Together, we raced down the corridor with Toryn and Nellie just behind us. The open castle doors ahead revealed a gray sky pregnant with clouds. Before we could reach them, a boom shook the castle, reverberating through the floor. I stumbled, but then Nellie was there. *Nellie.* She ran beside me in some kind of wolf form, pressing her body against mine to keep me from falling.

Something like awe went through me. Claws and fangs, indeed.

We reached the castle doors and ran down the steps leading into the courtyard where the rest of the castle denizens were awaiting us. Thousands of terrified fae stumbled toward the streets beyond, ushered forward by a grim-faced Caedmon. Many fell silent and looked at Toryn. Their prince—or their king now, I supposed, at least until his brother came along to challenge him for the title. And now, once again, Toryn had wiped away any sign of fear or uncertainty from his face. Instead, he moved toward them with a sense of calm purpose, as if four of the most powerful creatures in the world weren't behind us, coming to kill us all.

As Toryn called out words of assurance to his people and motioned for them to follow Caedmon, I turned to gaze upon the vine-covered castle one last time. Kalen had set Fenella down. She was kneeling with her eyes closed—calling upon her magic, no doubt, to heal her wound. Nellie sat on her haunches, blinking up at Kalen as he focused his power on the castle. If anything would stop the gods, it was that brutal power he carried within him.

And yet nothing happened.

"Come on!" he shouted. "For once, I truly need you!"

He stared up at the crumbling building, his fists shaking. Anguish pushed into me through the bond.

"Kalen?" I called out. "What's happening?"

He turned to me, and the look in his eye made my stomach drop. "My power is gone. Sirius can mute it, just like Andromeda has in the past. We must run."

THIRTY-ONE
TESSA

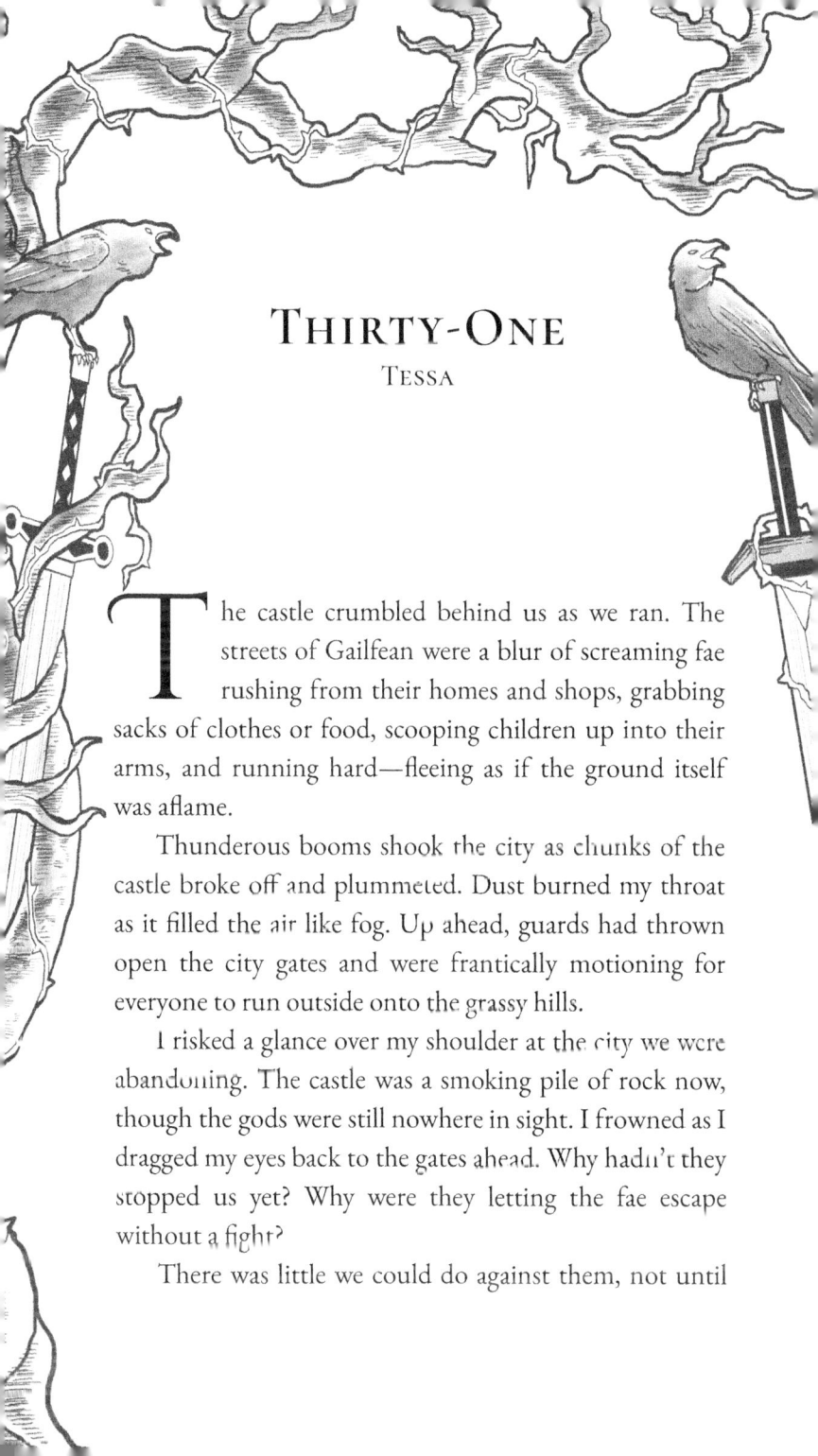

The castle crumbled behind us as we ran. The streets of Gailfean were a blur of screaming fae rushing from their homes and shops, grabbing sacks of clothes or food, scooping children up into their arms, and running hard—fleeing as if the ground itself was aflame.

Thunderous booms shook the city as chunks of the castle broke off and plummeted. Dust burned my throat as it filled the air like fog. Up ahead, guards had thrown open the city gates and were frantically motioning for everyone to run outside onto the grassy hills.

I risked a glance over my shoulder at the city we were abandoning. The castle was a smoking pile of rock now, though the gods were still nowhere in sight. I frowned as I dragged my eyes back to the gates ahead. Why hadn't they stopped us yet? Why were they letting the fae escape without a fight?

There was little we could do against them, not until

we heard from the mortal kingdoms. And they knew it. So why were they holding back?

There was no time to ponder those questions. Because when we finally made it through the gates, we found a world drowned in mist. Screams of panic filled the humid, night-drenched air. Heart pounding, I gazed up at the sky. Gone was the sun, there only a moment before. Now a pale moon pressed a vague light onto the lands, highlighting a vast expanse of nothingness. A familiar panic curled in my gut. Even after all my time spent in the mists, even after everything I'd survived—or maybe because of it—my blood went cold.

Some of the storm fae started to run. Toryn barked at the guards to stop them, frantically trying to maintain order. But there were thousands here, a swarming mass of panic. They had no idea what was happening or why. All they knew was that their city was crumbling and the mists had finally come for them.

Kalen strode toward his friend and clapped his hand onto his shoulder. "There's too much panic. You'll never get to them to the coast like this. Bring them to Dubnos. We'll find beds for them all."

Toryn shook his head, but then he swore as another cluster of storm fae broke past the guards and fled into the night. "If you can help me calm them the fuck down, I will. Otherwise, none of them will make it away from this city."

Kalen nodded before glancing at me. "Brace yourself."

I only had a brief moment to slide my arm around Nellie's furry shoulder.

And then he roared. The sound was as loud as thunder, booming over the screams, the crumbling castle inside the gates, and the pounding of so many frantic footsteps. The gods may have muted his telekinetic strength, but they had not dampened the power of his voice. It shook through me, right to my bones. Even my teeth seemed to rattle.

All around us, the fae stilled, stunned.

Terror and awe crept across their faces as they turned our way. They stared at the Mist King, their long-feared enemy from beyond the shadowy border. A few of them fell to their knees, splaying their hands against the ground as if in prayer. I knew at any moment they'd start running again, but for now, he held their rapt attention.

"Your king will lead you to safety," he called out, and then he nodded to Toryn.

With a grateful smile, Toryn nodded to his old friend and then strode to his people. And despite their white knuckles and their pinched mouths and their widened eyes, they listened to him.

"I'm leading you to Dubnos," he told them. "It's the nearest city. You will find refuge there. I know you are afraid, but the Mist King is here, and he is helping you."

No one argued. Not even a single one. Because the booming sound of the crumbling castle grew ever louder, and there was no more time for talking. And so the storm fae fell behind Toryn as he led them away from their dying city.

Hours later, we arrived at Dubnos, exhausted. The gods had done nothing to stop us from fleeing the Kingdom of Storms, a fact that did not sit well in my gut. Most of the Gailfean fae had followed Toryn as he led them across the mist-drenched lands, too scared to do anything else. We hadn't stopped to rest, not once, but not a single soul had complained. The terror of the gods nipping at our heels was enough to keep everyone moving.

And so we descended upon Dubnos with thousands of hungry, tired, and wide-eyed fae who had nowhere else to go. Many shadow fae ventured outside to see the procession through their streets, and then they welcomed whom they could into their homes, even if it was just for a pallet on their living room floor. Even with the threat of Sirius and the others looming over us like a storm cloud, my heart filled with hope. The people of Dubnos were stepping up to do what they could.

Still, there weren't enough homes to go around, so a couple hundred fae followed us into the castle. Kalen had the maidservants transform the Great Hall into one big shelter, using blankets and bedrolls that had once belonged to his mother's army, back before the war and all the losses it had brought to the shadow fae numbers.

I stood with Toryn in the doorway, watching the fae

settle into the Great Hall. An eerie hush had fallen over the room. Shock, I supposed. My heart ached for them.

He heaved out a sigh and leaned against the doorway. His face still wore that mask of calm, but I could see the exhaustion in his emerald eyes. "It is done."

"You did well, Toryn," I felt compelled to say.

His face tightened. "Some of them ran. I sent warriors to find them, but they're gone. They'll struggle to survive out there in the mist."

"You did what you could."

"It wasn't enough." Clenching his hands, he gazed at the storm fae gathered in the Great Hall. "I just...I don't understand how all this happened. How are we *here*? What can we even do now?" And then he turned to me, his mask finally slipping. Terror roared across his expression. "And what I can't stop asking myself is this: why didn't the gods stop us from leaving the city? They could have. I know they could have. Did you see what Kalen's sword did to Sirius? *Nothing*."

"I've been wondering the same damn thing."

Footsteps sounded behind us, and Fenella joined us in the doorway. "Nellie's fast asleep by the hearth."

Kalen had offered Nellie the room just beside his. I'd spent a good, long while trying to talk her into shifting back into herself as she prowled around the space like a cat, her claws ticking against the stone floor. When I realized she wouldn't—or couldn't—I left Fenella to sit with her while I helped set up the Great Hall for the storm fae.

"Finally," I said. "She hasn't shifted back yet, I'm guessing?"

"That would be a no."

"What in the name of light happened? You were with her when it happened, right?"

In our haste to escape the Kingdom of Storms, we'd had little time to talk. Plus, I hadn't wanted to ask her about my wolf sister when we'd been surrounded by terrified storm fae. They were still within hearing range now, but most were asleep.

"One of the gods burst through the stone. Not sure which one." Fenella leaned against the wall and spun one of the miniature daggers along her necklace, deep in thought. "I told Nellie to run, and then I put myself between the god and her, thinking I was the stronger of us. But I didn't stand a chance. The god slid his sword into my gut. Next thing I knew, Nellie was a wolf, and she was launching past me. You know how she said she has claws and fangs? Well, she wasn't fucking joking. She did the same thing you saw—tore through the god's neck with her claws. I think she caught him off guard. Anyway, it worked, and we ran. She saved my life, I suppose. Now I owe you both."

I shook my head and opened my mouth to respond, but the words had left me.

"You didn't know she could do that, I'm guessing," Fenella said.

"No, Fenella. My sister has never shifted into a wolf before. Not that I've seen." And she wouldn't have kept something that big from me.

"It must have been Oberon's barrier," Toryn said. "It muted her powers like it muted yours."

"But then wouldn't you think *I* could shift into a wolf, too? She's my sister."

"She's never shown any indication she can, er, kill things with her touch," Fenella said with an apologetic smile, flicking her eyes to my leather gloves. "Your powers are showing up in different ways."

I nodded, though it didn't make sense. As far as I knew, neither Andromeda nor any of the others had ever transformed into a wolf. But of course, we still knew precious little about them and what they could do, and even less about how to stop them.

"The important thing is," Fenella said with a wicked smile, "her claws can rip through their fucking necks. Doesn't kill them, but...she might come in handy again at some point."

I narrowed my eyes. "My sister is not a weapon."

"She's all we have."

"You must be mad if you think I'm going to send my baby sister to fight five immortal beings when she can't even kill them." I shook my head and took a large step back. "I'm going to go check on her. Don't bring this up again."

I whirled on my feet and strode out of the Great Hall. Fenella's voice rang out behind me. "She's not a baby anymore, Tessa."

But I just gritted my teeth and kept moving. Nellie's pale face flashed in my mind, along with her fearful eyes from the day Oberon had grabbed me outside our house and pinned me to the ground. I thought of all the times I'd shouted at her to hide and all the times she'd listened.

And I thought of the way she'd cried that day, twenty years before. I remembered it so clearly now when before, it had been nothing but vague shadows in my mind. The day my father had thrown *her* into the mists first and forced her to call upon her powers.

She'd shown me her hands then, dripping with blood where the claws had punched through her skin.

That day, I swore I would never again let anyone harm her, especially our father. And so I had volunteered to take her place as his experiment.

All this time, those memories had been lost to me, but they hadn't been lost to my sister. How long had she suffered because of what he'd done to her? How difficult had it been for her to keep her lips shut when I broke down, my wounded heart and soul and mind refusing to see the truth? No wonder she'd never told me. She knew how much it hurt, and she'd wanted to spare me from it.

She had always been so much stronger than I'd given her credit for.

And yet I would not send her out there as some kind of weapon. I would rather die.

I reached her room and cracked open the door. Inside, she lay curled up on a rug before the hearth, sound asleep. The light of the flames danced across her peaceful face. Even in this strange wolf form, I could see her. I could understand her. She was still Nellie. With a sigh, I closed the door and leaned against the wall, brushing aside the stray tears that had fallen to my cheeks.

"She'll be all right," a deep voice said from beside me.

Kalen. The tightness in my chest unfurled as his warmth and his mists pressed against me. He joined me in my spot against the wall, his shoulder brushing mine. For a long time, neither of us spoke. We didn't need to. The past few days had been long and hard, and for a brief moment in time, we just took this chance to breathe.

After the stillness seeped into my bones, Kalen shifted toward me. "I'm so sorry, love."

Frowning, I tipped back my head to gaze up at him. "You have nothing to be sorry for."

"I let him touch you." He slammed his palm against the wall, his jaw tense and hard. "He could have *killed* you, and yet I did nothing to stop him."

"That's not your fault," I whispered, taken aback by the ferocity in his voice—not to me but *for* me. "You did what you could."

"I am meant to protect you," he said in a lethal hiss. "I would rather rip out my own fucking heart than let anyone even *touch* you."

And then suddenly, I understood. With my gloved hand, I carefully wrapped my fingers around his wrist and pulled him away from the wall. It looked like he was seconds away from trying to punch a hole through it.

"It's the marriage bond, Kalen," I said. "The magic of it, it's making you feel this way."

"It's not the fucking magic."

"It is. I—"

He wrapped his hands around my waist and lifted me into his arms. I didn't resist as he carried me across the hall, kicked open his door, and took me into his chambers. When he lowered me onto the bed, I could scarcely breathe from the intensity in his eyes.

"What's going on?" I whispered, gazing up at him.

"Fenella." He shifted to lean on his side, facing me. "While you were helping Toryn with the Great Hall, she brought Val's clippings to me. She's been studying them during our travels. She said we needed to take a look at them ourselves."

Val's clippings. I'd forgotten all about them, too consumed by everything else going on. Fenella had been shuffling through them in Gailfean, but she'd never mentioned anything about their contents.

"All right," I said slowly, watching Kalen pull a few folded scraps from his pocket. He passed me a handful of clippings and started flipping through some himself. "Any idea what this is about?"

"I think it has something to do with us," he said, his voice rough and his eyes bright. "We're experiencing something far beyond what's normal for a marriage bond, and Fenella noticed it. I can sense everything you feel, love. And I know you get the same thing from me."

Silence fell upon us as we read through Val's clippings. Only the shuffle of paper broke the tension. I carefully read each scrap, searching for anything that might have grabbed Fenella's attention. Most of it seemed useless.

One of the clippings said that four hundred years ago, mortals from Talaven had been spotted creeping around Sunport and asking if anyone wanted a prized blade forged in the Iron Mountains. It had a spot in the hilt for a special gemstone. That sounded a lot like the Mortal Blade to me, but as intriguing as the story was, it wouldn't help us now.

But then my eyes landed on the words that shifted the very fabric of my world.

An ancient prophecy must be fulfilled, the clipping said. *Two broken souls will be bound by powerful magic. Mates, blessed by the stars. They will find each other when one calls for help. The other will have no choice but to answer.*

A tremor went through me.

"Kalen," I whispered, passing the clipping to him. Val had seen this and suspected it was important, but she hadn't truly understood. She didn't know I'd pleaded for help in my dreams, begging for someone to save the mortals of Teine.

"This is it," he said as his eyes scanned the paper. "This is what Fenella found. We're bound by far more than just our vows to each other. We always have been."

"But I don't understand." My heart pounded as I tried to make sense of his words. "I thought the ancient prophecy was about the return of the gods. The mortals have that information, not us. So what in the name of light is *this*?"

"I think it's all one and the same, and Val found a piece of it in Endir's library."

"But..."

"You called for me, love." He leaned in and murmured against my skin. "All those months ago, you were in Teine and I was in Endir, and I heard your voice in my dreams."

"I thought you only answered because of Oberon," I whispered. "You wanted to use me to get to him."

"Yes. And no." He pulled back, and there was something in his eyes. Something feral and electric. "No one has ever called for me in a dream. Or if they have, I haven't heard them. You were able to speak to me in a way that no one has before. And I felt this...tug. An irresistible urge to answer."

"But that would mean..."

"Val's clipping is right."

The stars had aligned and brought us into existence at the same time. I came four hundred years later, of course, but still. We were here, *alive*, at the same time.

I gazed into his eyes. "I still don't understand how this has anything to do with the return of the gods."

"Perhaps it has to do with your power and mine." He took my hand in his. "But regardless of all that, I feel it deeply, Tessa. You are made of the same stuff I am. You are my reflection, my star. Back in Gailfean, when Sirius had his hands on you, I felt more than just the rage of a fae protective of his wife. I wanted to tear a hole in the very fabric of the universe. You are my soulmate in every sense of the word. At long last, I have found you."

I trembled, basking in the intensity of his heated gaze. Memories of his past words echoed in my mind, words from when we'd been stuck inside that Itchen castle while the storms had raged beyond the walls. I could still hear his voice in my head when he'd said them.

Mates are a forever thing. It is a bond that cannot be broken. It transcends even death. I do not want anything less than the deepest connection I could ever find. I want— no, I need—*someone whose soul matches mine.*

"All this time," I whispered up at him, "you've believed you had a soulmate out there somewhere."

"No, just hoped." His thumb caressed my cheek, and I did not think to stop him from touching my skin this time. "And my hopes have been answered. Because you are here, and you are mine."

Thirty-Two
Tessa

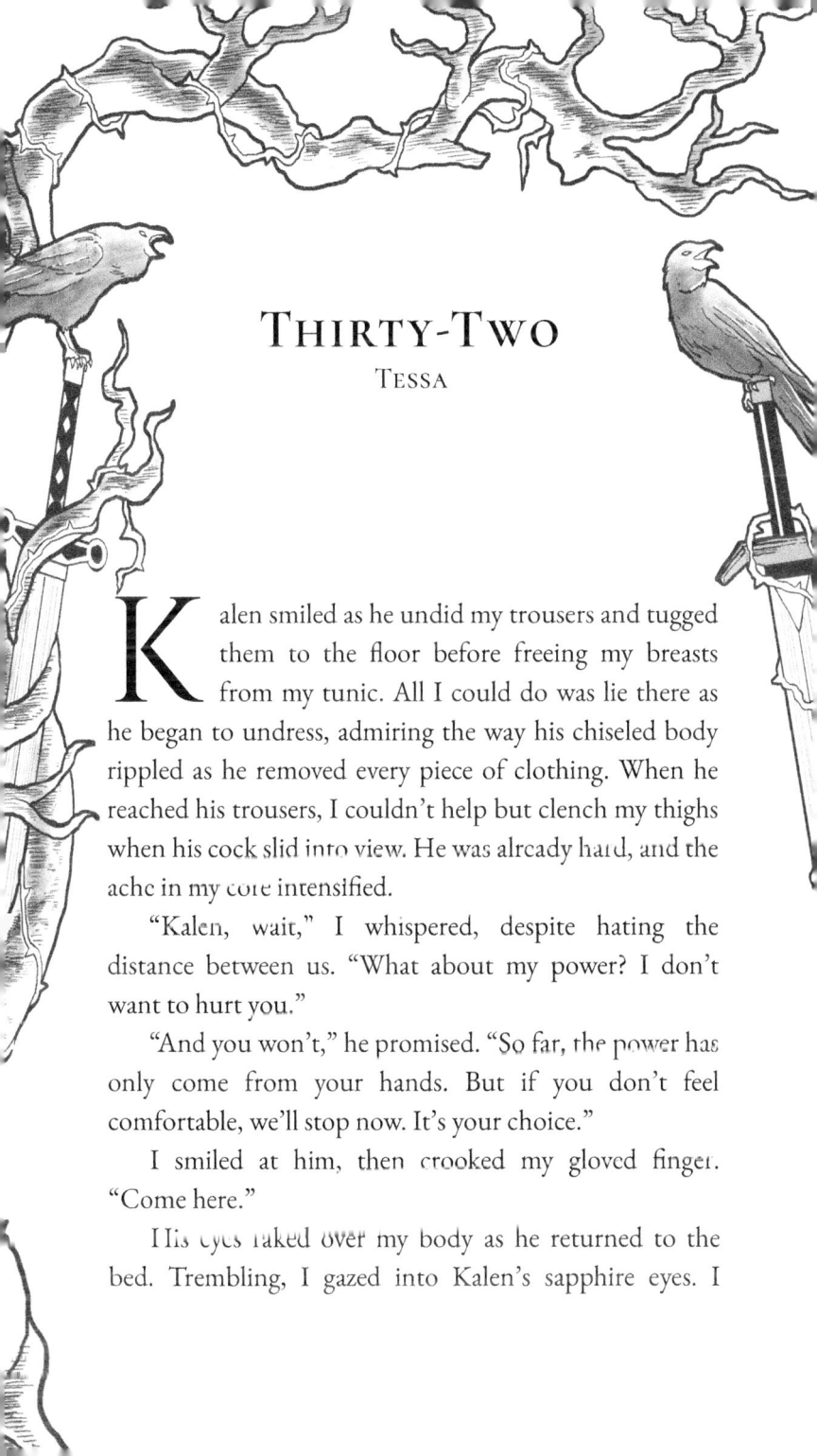

Kalen smiled as he undid my trousers and tugged them to the floor before freeing my breasts from my tunic. All I could do was lie there as he began to undress, admiring the way his chiseled body rippled as he removed every piece of clothing. When he reached his trousers, I couldn't help but clench my thighs when his cock slid into view. He was already hard, and the ache in my core intensified.

"Kalen, wait," I whispered, despite hating the distance between us. "What about my power? I don't want to hurt you."

"And you won't," he promised. "So far, the power has only come from your hands. But if you don't feel comfortable, we'll stop now. It's your choice."

I smiled at him, then crooked my gloved finger. "Come here."

His eyes raked over my body as he returned to the bed. Trembling, I gazed into Kalen's sapphire eyes. I wanted him. I needed him. Nothing else mattered right now.

His hand found my breast, a soft caress until he squeezed tightly. I cried out, both in agony and in pleasure, my nipples hard and swollen under his touch. He leaned in and teased my nipple with his tongue. I dropped my head against the bed and moaned. Kalen growled, and his breath tickled my hot skin.

"Eager, are we?" he murmured as he moved his mouth down my stomach, pausing once he reached the sex between my thighs. His mouth brushed my skin, licking me, tasting me, sending shockwaves of pleasure through my trembling body. I gasped and pushed my hands against the headboard, digging my gloved fingers into the wood.

"I love the way you taste," Kalen murmured as he moved back up my stomach, leaving me aching for more.

I opened my mouth to respond, but the words that echoed in my mind were ones we'd yet to say. *I love you, I love you, I love you.*

As if sensing my hesitation, he paused, not understanding that it had nothing to do with his touch and everything to do with my mounting feelings for him.

"Tell me what you want," he said. I opened my eyes and looked into his, spreading my legs as I wrapped my thighs around him. The fire and passion were still there in his expression, but his face held a spark of something else. Something far deeper than that. Something that made my heart pound even harder.

"You, Kalen," I whispered. "All I want is you."

He sighed against me, squeezing my thighs with his strong hands. Slowly, he filled me, inch by exquisite inch. I let go of everything that had happened in the past few weeks—of all the fear, of all the doubt, of all the pain. I gave in to the sensation of Kalen's body on mine. And I just let myself *feel*. I loved him, desperately so. And even if I hadn't said it yet, I could tell him with my touch.

I wrapped my arms around his neck as he pushed inside me once again. My back slid against the sheets as he began to thrust harder, but his arms held me against his chest. As we wrapped ourselves around each other, it felt as if we'd become one body, moving in rhythm as our need for each other increased with each passing beat. That thread between us tugged so tightly, it felt as though whatever this was between us, whatever we'd become, it would be a part of me until I took my last breath.

Until all the stars vanished from the night sky.

I shook in his arms, pleasure and emotion building inside me. Kalen groaned as I tightened around him, and he took my mouth in his as I crested the top. Shuddering, my orgasm crashed over me like a wave. My arms and legs tightened around Kalen as he followed in my wake. His roars echoed through the castle through the city itself.

I was his, and he was mine.

Kalen pulled me to his chest after his climax finished. I curled up against him, like his body might shield me from the outside world for just a little while longer. Tomorrow, we would have to face what was coming for us. We would need to find a way to fight a power far greater than any of us, even combined.

But for now, I just breathed him in, relishing in the soft brush of mist and his steady heartbeat and that lingering cord that kept us linked.

If I might die soon, at least I spent my final moments with him.

Thirty-Three
Niamh

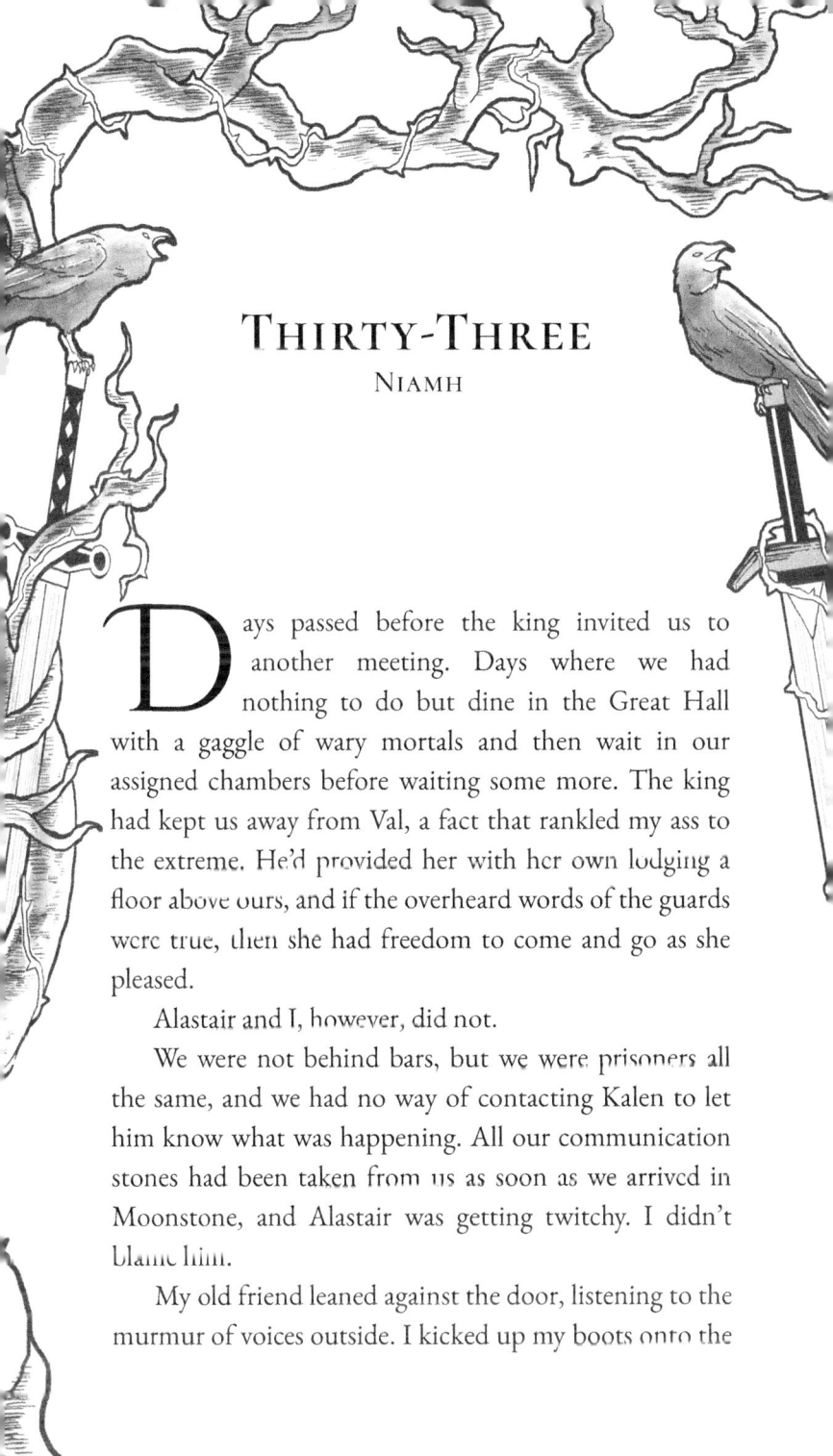

Days passed before the king invited us to another meeting. Days where we had nothing to do but dine in the Great Hall with a gaggle of wary mortals and then wait in our assigned chambers before waiting some more. The king had kept us away from Val, a fact that rankled my ass to the extreme. He'd provided her with her own lodging a floor above ours, and if the overheard words of the guards were true, then she had freedom to come and go as she pleased.

Alastair and I, however, did not.

We were not behind bars, but we were prisoners all the same, and we had no way of contacting Kalen to let him know what was happening. All our communication stones had been taken from us as soon as we arrived in Moonstone, and Alastair was getting twitchy. I didn't blame him.

My old friend leaned against the door, listening to the murmur of voices outside. I kicked up my boots onto the desk along the back wall, scowling at him. The room itself was large and held two beds, but that was the extent of it. As much as I loved my brother of the Mist Guard, I was sick of seeing his face every waking moment of every damn day.

"Just sit down. They know about our hearing." The chair creaked as I leaned back. "They're not dumb enough to talk about anything important this close to us."

He arched a brow. "People can be dumb."

"Suit yourself. If you want to spend all day with your ear glued to the door, by all means."

"It's better than what you're doing."

"I'm not doing a damn thing."

He shot me a wolfish smile. "Exactly."

I rolled my eyes. "At least I'm preserving my energy."

"Yes. You need a lot of energy for all that scowling you're doing over there."

I shook my head and turned to the window. At least we had a view—a glorious one at that. Rolling fields of green stretched toward a horizon bathed in blue. It was a clear day without a cloud in the sky, and the brilliance of it was almost blinding. Even days later, my eyes still hadn't adjusted to the daylight. For so long, I'd known nothing but night. The Kingdom of Shadow had not always existed in impenetrable darkness and mist. We'd had sunlight once. Short sunny days, of course, but we'd had them. And there'd often been a light mist—a fog. Nothing like it was now, as if the mist itself were a living, breathing thing that sought to choke out all life.

"I wonder what Kal and the others are up to," Alastair said, cutting through the silence. I sighed. The man couldn't go more than five minutes without interrupting my thoughts.

"Knowing the storm fae, I imagine he's probably stuck inside a room like we are."

He grunted. "Not for long."

I turned just as Alastair stepped back and the door swung wide. Duncan Hinde, the King of Talaven, stood in the corridor beyond our room with his hands tucked behind his back. His emerald robe swished around his feet as he gave us a quick nod and walked off. "Come along."

Eyes narrowing, I shoved up from the chair. "You have no right to order us to 'come along' after locking us away for days, both now and on your bloody ship."

Alastair chuckled. "I think he's already halfway down the hall and didn't hear you."

With a shrug, he followed the king. I clenched my hands. I'd meant what I said. All of this, the journey by ship and then across the realm in a cage, it was too much. I had no more patience for games. The mortals of Talaven had treated us horribly, and for what? We'd come to ally our realm with theirs. Well, fuck that.

I stormed into the hallway, ready to give the king a piece of my mind and drag Alastair and Val out of here if I had to. The mortals had taken our weapons, but I was still a damn good fighter. Alastair was several steps ahead of me, and I had to jog to catch up to him. I was only seconds away from telling him my plan when we swung around the corner to find the king standing before an open set of doors leading into a gold-drenched library, the gaudy color matching the crown on his head.

Val was just inside, seated at a table and flipping through a mound of books. She didn't seem to notice us, but she looked well, clad in a silk robe much like the king's. Relief shuddered through me. I'd known she was fine, but still. Seeing her sitting in there among a sprawl of books with her brilliant hair flowing around her shoulders...my heart squeezed. She was okay. Still, I couldn't let the king see my relief.

"What's this?" I snapped at him.

At that, Val lifted her head and met my eyes. Her face brightened, and she stood. "Niamh."

I smiled. "Good to see you're all right."

Her cheeks turned a shade pinker. "Yeah, I could say the same to you."

The king cleared his throat. "Val is reading everything we have on the prophecy and the history of the Fell. Though I must warn you, it was a dark time, and you will not enjoy hearing about it."

Alastair moved into the library and approached Val's table, but I didn't follow him in, not yet. I needed more information. "You just kept us locked in a room for days, and now you bring us here without an explanation. Why?"

"I had to speak with your friend there," he said, inclining his head toward Val, "and then consult my notes and the Druids."

"Druids?"

"That's not a foreign term to you, is it? I thought you had them in Aesir."

"We do. It's just…they're very much fae. Elite fae who have chosen not to use their powers."

He frowned. "Ah, yes. 'Elite' fae. I've never liked that term. It makes it sound as if anyone who isn't born with power is somehow less than those who are."

I agreed with him on that, but… "Do your Druids have powers?"

"Not fae powers, but they do have a power of their own." Shifting on his sandaled feet, he glanced at the table where Val was showing Alastair one of the many books. "We have the remains of a comet—the first comet that came here—not far from our city walls. There are those who can touch its dust and see visions of things that will come to pass."

"And that's where your prophecies come from."

The king nodded. "When the star fell, King Ovalis Hinde took some of his men to investigate. One of his men—an astronomer named Marrk—knelt before the black dust and brushed his fingers against it. It gave him a vision, a powerful one at that. It showed him the near future and a future thousands of years later. Since then, others have continued to touch the comet, though the power of it has faded over the years. Now our visions are quite murky. For example, we did not see you coming here. But I sent a few Druids to the comet to ask about you and Alastair. They saw you will not become a threat to us. We can share the truth with you now."

I drew back, my eyes flashing across his face. "You can see visions of us? Our future?"

"Not exactly. It's not that clear these days," he said with a sad smile. "It's only a feeling now. Less of a vision, more of a...sensation. We just know you are on our side and that you had nothing to do with the coming of the Second Fell. So we'll share our knowledge with you, and I apologize for our paranoia."

Alastair folded his massive arms over his chest, his attention shifting from Val's books to my conversation with King Duncan Hinde. "We came in peace from a kingdom that is not your enemy. Some might believe the way you've treated us is an act of war."

The King of Talaven did not flinch, not even when confronted with a towering fae who scowled down at him. I couldn't help the flicker of appreciation that went through me at that. "And will you see it that way? Will your king?"

Alastair huffed out a breath. "I suppose not, but you'd better fucking make it up to us. After you tell us all you know about this prophecy, you need to ready your army, put them on ships, and sail with us back to Aesir. We can fight these gods side by side. Together."

The king started to turn away.

Frowning, I shifted to block his path, and the guards just beside us dropped their hands to their swords, but they made no move against us.

"There's something more you're not saying," I said to him, narrowing my eyes. "You're not going to send your ships, are you?"

"There are certain events that must come to pass first, and until they do, we cannot make a move."

I pointed up at the ceiling, at the sky beyond the castle roof. "The gods—"

"They are creatures who call themselves our gods,"

the king said. "But they are not true gods, not in the least."

"What in the name of the moon are they, then?"

"The word we've heard from the comet is *Lamiae*. They are eternal, but they need man's flesh and blood to thrive. They can even survive among the stars. And we cannot make a move against them until the only one who can destroy them finds the power within her to fight. The one who was born to fulfill an ancient promise to a fae king. One whose own blood flows with the Lamiae's magic."

I sucked in a sharp breath. "You mean a descendent. Are you talking about Tessa Baran?"

His eyes were pools of glass, as if his mind had drifted far away. "Tessa Baran has not yet spread her wings. Until she does, she is not the Daughter of Stars, and we cannot help her. If we go too soon, we risk everything."

THIRTY-FOUR
NIAMH

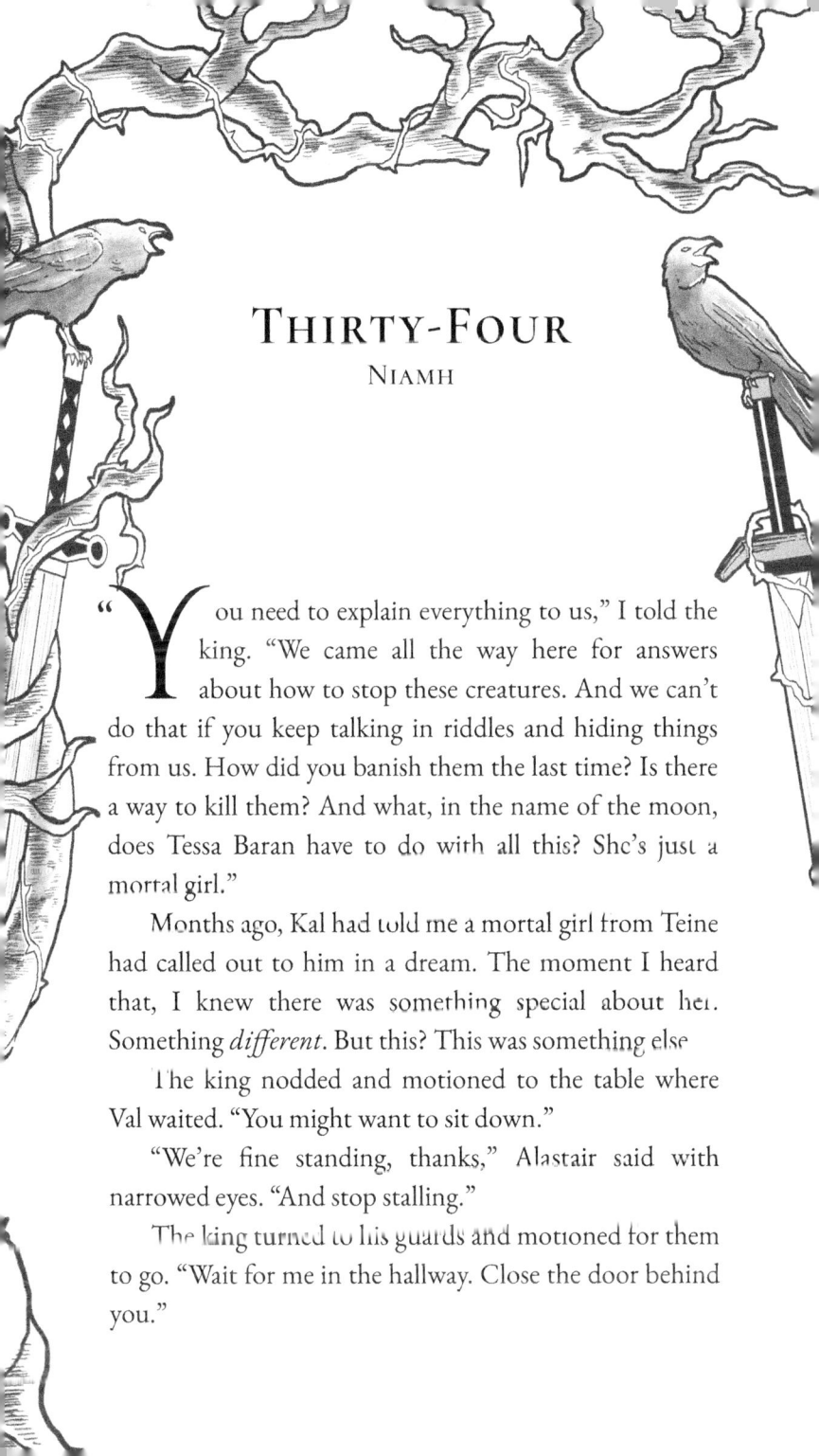

"You need to explain everything to us," I told the king. "We came all the way here for answers about how to stop these creatures. And we can't do that if you keep talking in riddles and hiding things from us. How did you banish them the last time? Is there a way to kill them? And what, in the name of the moon, does Tessa Baran have to do with all this? She's just a mortal girl."

Months ago, Kal had told me a mortal girl from Teine had called out to him in a dream. The moment I heard that, I knew there was something special about her. Something *different*. But this? This was something else.

The king nodded and motioned to the table where Val waited. "You might want to sit down."

"We're fine standing, thanks," Alastair said with narrowed eyes. "And stop stalling."

The king turned to his guards and motioned for them to go. "Wait for me in the hallway. Close the door behind you."

"Your Majesty," one of the guards said with a frown.

"They will not harm me. Now go."

When the door closed, the king paced the floor, and then he began. "When these creatures first arrived in our lands, we quickly discovered they could twist the minds of men, fae and mortal alike. They have some kind of power of manipulation. If you listen to them speak for long enough, you begin to see things as they do. And they carry with them this vicious rage. It can infect you."

I exchanged a glance with Val. "That tracks with everything we know about them."

He nodded. "You'll be thinking of King Oberon and his descent into cruelty. He held out far better than most others have. His will was strong. It's a shame Andromeda still broke him in the end."

"It's not a shame," Val cut in. "He tortured us. He had innocents killed. He was a *monster*."

"The Lamiae are the monsters," the king countered. "And you'll do well to remember that. They can twist the souls of even the brightest and kindest among us. But the comet showed us there was one thing in our world, one element, that could protect us against them. Onyx gemstones."

Val stood and moved to my side. "Oberon's necklace. It was made of onyx."

"That's right. But even with the gemstone protecting him and his bride, Bellicent, they spent far too much time in Andromeda's presence. Centuries, in fact. And the onyx weakened every time he used the power to save his wife."

"That explains a lot," Alastair said with a nod.

"The onyx can also *trap* the Lamiae. We were able to do it once, using the comet to guide us on the right path. We caught them unawares and locked them inside sarcophaguses we'd embedded with powerful onyx. It worked. Temporarily, of course, and it was only meant to last as long as Andromeda, in her full form, was not here. But the comet is no longer in the sky, and they gain their strength from her presence. Her return will mean the others have managed to escape."

"Wait." Alastair frowned. "I thought the fae and mortals banished them all."

"That was nothing but lies meant to hide the truth. The gods have been here all this time," the king said quietly. "There was only enough power to banish one of them, and even then, we could only get rid of her physical form, not her essence. As you well know, Andromeda's essence has been here all these years, split in two and trapped in onyx."

"Wait, you mentioned a power. What power?" Val asked in a hushed voice. And I knew what she was thinking. The king had called Tessa the Daughter of Stars. Did he mean *her* power? Could *she* banish the gods?

"Ironically, the power to banish them came with the very fallen star that brought them here. There was a gemstone hidden among the comet's remains. We call it Dochas. It is not of this world, and it is strong enough to banish a Lamiae. Or rip a chasm in the earth."

I sucked in a sharp breath and stepped back. A *chasm*. Like Kalen's chasm. "What are you saying?"

"My ancestors discovered mortals were not strong enough to use the power of the Dochas. If they held the gemstone, it killed them," the king continued, his face unreadable. "And so we called upon the aid of a fae king. Aodhan Grenat, who at the time ruled over all of Aesir, back before the kingdoms were split into three. Ovalis, the King of Talaven, showed Aodhan everything that would come to be and everything they needed to do to save the future world. And they saw there was only one way this would work. Aodhan, as a fae and strong enough to wield the gemstone's power, would use it to split Andromeda in two and send her body back to the stars, where it would remain for thousands of years. But Ovalis and Aodhan knew she would one day return and that she would not be caught unawares a second time. She can mute any power a fae wields, you see, but even if she couldn't, she found a way to protect herself from the Dochas. Andromeda is very good at adapting. An attack against her only works once. Never a second time."

"Why didn't they just banish all of the bitch back then?" Alastair demanded. "They had one shot at this, and you're telling me they fucked it up?"

"The power of the Dochas came with the gods. It's foreign to these lands. Mortals cannot use it at all, and while fae can, they still cannot call upon its full strength. King Aodhan did his best. It just wasn't enough."

"So then what is enough?" Val whispered.

"We carved the gemstone into pieces. There's enough left for another attempt. A fae must be the one to hold the Dochas, but that person will not be able to wield it against the gods. Not this time. Someone else must channel the power *through* the fae who carries it. Someone powerful enough to call upon the full force of its magic. Someone neither fae nor fully mortal. She must be a descendent of Andromeda. The Daughter of Stars."

My voice had left me. I needed to sit down.

"The gemstone," Alastair said, his face paling, as if realizing the same thing I had. There was only one person with enough power to rip a chasm in the earth. "What color is it?"

"A deep sapphire blue," the king said.

The color of Kal's eyes.

I stumbled sideways, and Val grabbed my arm to hold me steady.

The king continued. "Kalen Denare was born with ice-blue eyes. We asked Druid Balfor to perform the surgery when he was only a year old, when Bellicent was called away on an urgent mission to deal with some fires in Star Isles. She had no idea why his eyes had changed during her absence, not until she came to visit us all those years later, demanding answers."

Druid Balfor? He'd known all this time? All I could do was stare. The roaring in my ears grew louder.

"You fucking bastards," Alastair breathed. "You ripped out a child's eyes and replaced them with *fucking gemstones?*"

I pressed my hand to my throat. *His eyes.* Kalen had mentioned that for a while, his eyes had appeared as ice-blue in his dreams with Tessa, though he'd made a conscious effort to change them back to sapphire once he knew.

But he hadn't understood what it meant. Kalen did not know about any of this.

"It was the only way. The bearer has to be fae,"

Duncan Hinde said without a hint of remorse in his voice. "The power bonded with him, grew with him. It became bigger and stronger. Now Tessa Baran can channel it through her own body, as long as he is near her side. Andromeda cannot mute it because Tessa is not fae. This will *save* us. It's the only way to defeat the Lamiae."

Alastair let out a low growl. "You've used Kalen like a puppet. You've used us all."

The king lifted his chin. "I will not apologize for any of this. None of it was my decision. It started thousands of years ago and—"

"But you kept it secret all this time," Alastair cut in, striding up to the king. He towered over him, a bundle of muscle-bound power. "You've been moving your little pieces around the board, sitting here in the safety of your castle while *real lives* are being affected. People have died because of this."

The King of Talaven lifted his eyes to Alastair's face, and he did not back down. "And if I had not done that, far more lives would end in the coming war. King Ovalis Hinde began this by making a promise to a fae king, and that promise will be the thing that ends it. So long as Tessa Baran chooses right."

"What was the promise?" Val whispered.

The king turned his eyes on Val. "Aodhan saw that using the gemstone's power would kill him. To do this, he would have to sacrifice himself. And so he agreed to do his part only if Ovalis made a vow to do *his,* as unpleasant as it was. He had to find a way into Andromeda's heart so that he could sire her half-mortal son."

"The true beginning," I murmured.

"Oh, yes," the king said with sad smile. "It was the beginning of her line. One that has suffered through the years, as if the world itself worked against them. Most of her descendants did not live long enough to keep their branches of the line going. Even now, Tessa and Nellie are her only living descendants. Did you know her grandfather wasn't born in Teine? He was born here in Talaven. We had our fae contact in Albyria smuggle him in and make up a story about his birth. You likely know of our contact. His name is Ruari, Oberon's firstborn son."

"What? *Ruari* smuggled Tessa's grandfather into Teine?" Val's jaw dropped. "But...that's...but *why*?"

"We needed Tessa to suffer in Albyria beneath Oberon's reign," the king said. "It was the only way for her to end up in the arms of Kalen Denare. Her promised *mate*."

Understanding washed over me all at once.

"For the love of the fucking moon, that's why they're so obsessed with each other. That's how she'll be able to channel his power, isn't it?" Alastair said. "Because they have some kind of magical bond."

"Magic is a wondrous thing. The stars blessed those two, bonding them so that they might save this world."

I just shook my head, speechless.

Val, on the other hand, looked incensed. "You've known everything this entire time, and you've kept it to yourself. Do you know how much heartache you could have saved everyone if you'd shared this information with Kalen and Tessa and all the Mist Guard?"

"If we'd told you, Andromeda would have discovered the truth, too. As it stands, she's only heard part of the prophecy. She believes Kalen is the one who might destroy her one day, but she has no idea it's Tessa instead. She can never find out, not until we put the rest of the pieces into play. Otherwise, she will rip the two of them apart, and this world will never know peace." He smiled. "I'm afraid that means I cannot allow you to contact them until we know Tessa has made the right choice. Now, do you have any more questions?"

I didn't even know where to begin.

Thirty-Five
Tessa

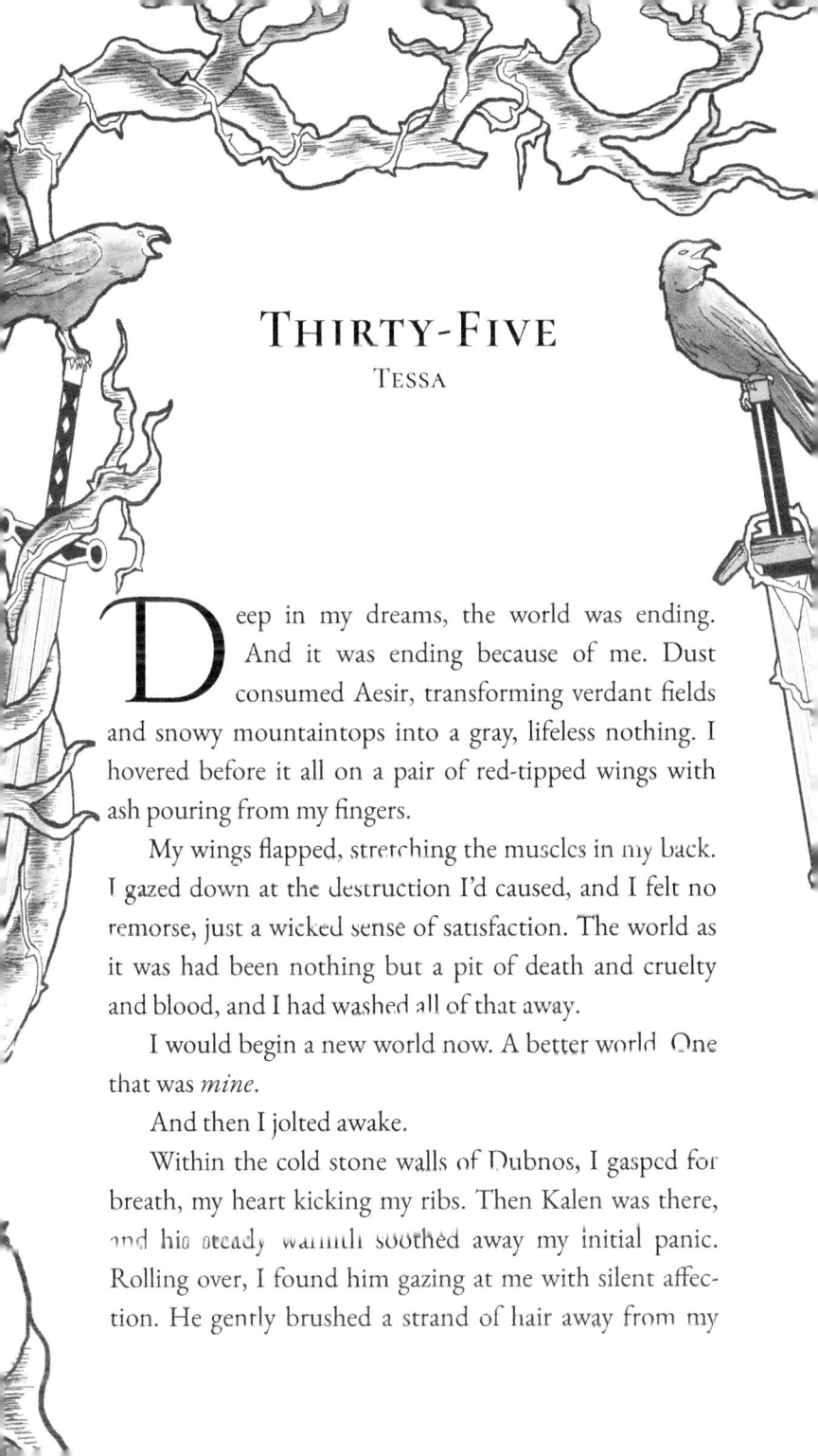

Deep in my dreams, the world was ending. And it was ending because of me. Dust consumed Aesir, transforming verdant fields and snowy mountaintops into a gray, lifeless nothing. I hovered before it all on a pair of red-tipped wings with ash pouring from my fingers.

My wings flapped, stretching the muscles in my back. I gazed down at the destruction I'd caused, and I felt no remorse, just a wicked sense of satisfaction. The world as it was had been nothing but a pit of death and cruelty and blood, and I had washed all of that away.

I would begin a new world now. A better world. One that was *mine*.

And then I jolted awake.

Within the cold stone walls of Dubnos, I gasped for breath, my heart kicking my ribs. Then Kalen was there, and his steady warmth soothed away my initial panic. Rolling over, I found him gazing at me with silent affection. He gently brushed a strand of hair away from my sweat-soaked forehead. "Breathe, Tessa. You had a nightmare."

But I could feel his apprehension through our bond.

"Were you there?" I asked him after I'd calmed my breaths. "Did you see what I saw?"

"No, I wasn't there, but I can still feel it somehow. The image is in my head."

I searched his eyes. "Did you see the destruction? What if it's some kind of warning of what's to come?"

"Relax, my love. It was just a dream. Everything is going to be all right. I wouldn't tell you unless I believed it. There will be no more secrets between us." Leaning in, he brushed a kiss across my forehead. Sighing, I settled into the crook of his arm and basked in the warmth of him just for a little longer, though I could not shake the unease closing in around me.

I wished I could be as certain as he was. I wished we'd heard from Niamh and Val and Alastair. We needed to know more about the prophecy. We needed to hear the words that had given Bellicent Denare such a fright. If we knew all that, we might be able to determine our next steps. As it was, the gods were in our world once more. We'd somehow escaped them, but it would only be a matter of time before they came for us. Right now, we had no idea how to fight them, but I knew one thing for certain. We would have to face them sooner or later.

We needed a plan.

After taking a lukewarm bath, I dressed in a clean pair of black trousers and a soft periwinkle tunic. Just like always, I braided my hair. I was getting better at weaving the strands together myself, though Kalen moved in to help when I lost my hold on a section. He'd taken a quick bath himself, scrubbing away the grime from our rushed journey back to Dubnos. His damp, wavy hair curled around the sharp tips of his ears, and droplets of water dripped onto his finely tailored black shirt, which was embroidered with silver crescent moons along the collar. The glittering silver matched the crown on his head—twisting silver branches embedded with diamonds. Today, he was not the brutal warrior. He was a king.

He tucked his finger beneath my chin, still comfortable with touching my skin, despite everything. "Are you ready?"

I nodded.

Together, we walked hand in hand to the war room, where the others were waiting for us. Toryn and Fenella were chatting quietly and motioning at the wooden map carved into the table. The two of them fell silent when we entered the room, casting a quick glance toward Nellie, who sat beside the blazing hearth, flicking her tail. She looked alert, and there was a keenness in her eyes that told me she understood everything, even in wolf form.

"Are you all right, Nellie?" I asked her.

She flicked her ears. I had to assume that meant she was fine.

Kalen strode toward the war table, and his very essence seemed to take up the entire room. He went around to the side of the map where Gailfean sat, and then he gently tipped over the figurine of their castle. Toryn's jaw tightened.

"Have the scouts returned?" the King of Shadow asked.

"No," Fenella said in a tense voice. "They should have returned hours ago. I think we can assume they won't be coming back."

Kalen palmed the table and stared down at the map. It was a beautiful piece of artwork. I'd never seen anything like it before. Someone had spent weeks—months, even—crafting this thing. Every mountain pass was carved as a precise miniature replica of the real thing. The bend of every river was there, snaking through Aesir's once-glorious lands. Even the chasm was represented with painstaking accuracy. And from this vantage point, Gailfean looked so very close to where we now stood. Such a small distance to cross, especially for winged, immortal gods.

"How many did you send?" Kalen asked in a hard voice.

"At first, we sent three, thinking a small party would be more likely to avoid detection. When they didn't return, I sent a larger party of six. I thought the others might have encountered pookas or wraiths. Or one of those scorpion things we faced in Itchen."

"And not a single soul has returned." He closed his eyes. "We can't risk trying again. I will not send my men to certain death."

"Death is coming for us, Kal," Fenella replied with a sigh. "We'll all have to face it, one way or another."

"I've been thinking," Toryn said, pacing from one side of the war table to the other, arms folded, head cocked. Now that his people were safe, he looked more like himself again, though there was a heaviness in his expression that hadn't been there before. "They let us escape, and Sirius—" He shuddered. "Sirius said all they care about is Talaven, and they don't want the fae lands. Perhaps they don't plan to come for us at all."

"They just want the human kingdoms," Fenella murmured.

My heart pounded. "It doesn't matter if they want Aesir or not. We can't let them reach Talaven. We can't let them enslave the humans and use them as food or whatever it is they do to them."

"And how will we stop them, eh? With our swords? That doesn't work. Neither do Kalen's powers."

"We can't just *let* them do this." My voice dropped to a hiss.

Fenella sighed. "Look, I want to fight them just as much as anyone, but we can't throw ourselves into the line of fire and expect good results. We need a plan. One that will work. You get us one of those, and I will gladly fight by your side."

I fell silent, my cheeks heating, hating that she was right. We had no plan. We had no weapon that could destroy them. Nothing that could even harm them. Nothing but...Nellie. But even if her claws could wound the gods, we couldn't send her up against five of them. She wouldn't survive.

And even if we did send her, then what? The gods would only heal themselves if she harmed them, and then they'd continue on their path of destruction. We needed something else. Something *permanent*.

Suddenly, a muffled voice cut through the silence. "Your Majesty!"

Kalen stiffened and pulled a pale gray communication

stone from his pocket. Within seconds, he'd lit a flame beneath it, and a face flashed across the stone's surface. A dark-haired fae—bloodied and dirtied and bruised—looked out at us.

"It's one of the scouts," Fenella hissed, coming around to Kalen's side. "Kerr, what's happening?"

The scout heaved, his face twisted in pain. Even from here, I could clearly see the lines that bracketed his mouth. "We went across the border, just like you asked. There are—"

Kerr screamed, and blood sprayed. The communication stone went dead.

Kalen swore and dropped the stone on the table. It thudded against the surface, a heavy noise that reflected the pounding of my heart. My mouth dry, I tried to blink away the image. So much blood. Whatever had killed him...he'd been ripped to shreds.

Had it been the gods? Or something else?

Truth be told, which was worse?

"That settles it, then," Kalen said grimly. "If the gods were heading to the mortal kingdoms, they would have moved north toward the coast. If they're this close to the border, I think we can assume they plan to destroy Dubnos."

"We could be in their way," Toryn pointed out. "If they want to reach Talaven, they might plan to sail from Star Isles or even Sunport. That means going through Dubnos first."

"They have wings," I said, gazing around at all of them. "Don't they? Why would they need a ship?"

Kalen traced a path along the table from Gailfean to

the coast. "We're just reaching around in the dark and hoping to find purchase. But truth be told, we have no idea what will happen next. So we need to prepare as if the gods are on their way to attack this city. It's time to reach out to Ruari and Gaven. We need them both if we're going to win this battle."

While Kalen contacted Ruari through another stone, I went over to Nellie's side and sat. Idly, I stroked her fur. It was so soft, as soft as her mane of chestnut hair. I tried to find the words to say, but how do you ask your wolf sister what you can do to help her shift back into her human form? War was coming. I did not know how much longer we'd be alive. I needed to look into the face of my sister—the *human* face—and know that she was all right. At least for now. At least until the end of it all raced toward us from the darkness.

"Have you tried to shift back?" I finally asked her. "Or are you staying like this because you want to?"

The wolf gazed deeply into my eyes and just blinked.

I heaved out a sigh. "Come on. I know you understand me. Nod if you want to come back to me. Nod if you want to be human again."

But Nellie wasn't fully human. She never had been and never would be. And even though I still thought of myself as mortal, I wasn't, either. Sirius had known it, too. I hadn't mentioned it to Kalen and his Mist Guard, but I knew I might be the reason the gods wanted to come here—to find me and take me to Andromeda.

This city was full of innocents who did not deserve to die, least of all for me.

Kalen finished speaking with Ruari and tossed the

broken gemstone onto the war table. It skittered across the surface, knocking aside crowns and buildings that stood in the way of its violent path. An ominous sight.

"Bad news?" I hated to ask.

He continued to stare down at the map. "He's mobilizing his army, but it will take two weeks for him to get here. One week if they move quickly, but they'll likely face battles of their own out there. Pookas and whatever else attacks them will catch the scent of an army easily enough."

"You think the beasts would attack an entire army? That seems suicidal."

"If the pookas remain in small groups? Unlikely." His gaze went dark. "But I would not put it past them to form their own army now if they're being controlled by the gods, like I think they are. An army of hundreds."

Thirty-Six
Tessa

A cool wind whistled through the battlements. Archers patrolled the stretch of stone that faced the border and the silent valley below, but mostly, I stood alone up here, my hair unbound and blowing in the breeze. I pulled the mist into my lungs and memorized the smell of it—the feel of it. There was darkness in it. Darkness and cold. But it also smelled like... silver and snow. There was a hint of pine and sage, even a little salt. The scent of it enveloped me, and the mist caressed my skin, soothing away the clamminess of my hands, free of their gloves now.

Up here, with no one around, I placed my naked palms on the stone ledge and just *breathed*.

I was alive, and somewhere high above, hidden by the dense mist, the stars sparkled in the sky. They endured, their light refusing to blink out despite the darkness that tried to swallow them. If only those of us down here could be like those stars.

Instead, death was coming for us. This beautiful,

glorious, twisted world...I would be gone from it. *Everyone* in Dubnos would be gone if the gods were truly on their way here. The reality of it all choked the breath from my lungs. My fingers gripped the stone.

I did not want to die.

The thought echoed in my mind with sudden clarity.

"I do not want to die," I whispered to the mists.

For so long, I had been careless with my life. I'd barreled into danger with hardly a thought to the consequences. Anger and defiance had been my fuel, and it had burned me up inside, making me throw all caution to the wind. Because deep down, perhaps I hadn't truly cared about my own existence. It had meant so very little to me.

Somewhere along the way, that had changed.

I glanced down at the bundle of flowers I'd asked one of the maidservants to bring me. I'd brought them up here when I'd still been wearing my gloves, but now that my fingers were free—now that my power was free—I needed to see if I could control it.

I *had* to control it.

Kneeling on the stone, I held my breath and forced myself to focus on the thread of magic that wound through me. I reached out and tapped one of the petals. The flower wilted instantly, and dust swarmed across the surface, choking all the life from it. I clenched my hands into fists in frustration, but then shook it away and focused. Andromeda gave death, but she could give life, too. It was the only reason I'd been able to save Fenella. I'd found control then. I could again. And so I tried to call upon that side of me and I tapped the flower once more.

Nothing happened.

With a heavy sigh, I sat back on my heels and shoved my gloves onto my hands.

Boots tapped the stones, and I glanced up as Kalen walked toward me with Boudica perched on his shoulder. He'd changed into a simple tunic, the top buttons open to reveal his perfectly sculpted chest. Gone were his crown and kingly gait. He was just another fae taking a stroll, as if the world weren't hurtling toward doom.

"Any luck?" he asked.

I pressed up from the ground and shook my head. "I still can't control it."

"You'll figure it out."

"We might not live long enough for that," I said, turning to gaze in the direction of the Kingdom of Storms. But all I saw were twisting shadows. The mists were so thick, it was impossible to see much else. "Has Boudica managed to see how close the gods are to Dubnos?"

He shook his head. "She's found nothing, and I don't want to send out any more scouts. All the others have died."

"So we just wait." Wait for death. Wait for the attack that would end everything. Without being able to scout ahead, we had no way of knowing what moment might be the one when everything changed. We could try to be prepared, but it was impossible when we didn't truly know what was coming for us.

A muscle in Kalen's jaw ticked, and a strange sensation flowed toward me through the bond. I had the sudden understanding that something big was on his mind, something he did not want to tell me.

I turned to him and folded my arms. "You're hiding something. Just this morning, you said we'll have no more secrets between us. We tell each other everything."

"And I will tell you. I just want you to promise to stay calm."

I arched a brow. "I will promise no such thing."

His lips twisted into a smile, and he chuckled. "I suppose not. You wouldn't be you if you did."

"So what is it, then? Does it have something to do with Nellie? Because as I already told Fenella, we will not use her as a weapon. I know her claws can stop the gods temporarily, but that's the problem. It's just temporary. More importantly, there's only one of her. I won't risk her like that. I won't."

"I would never ask such a thing." He let out a heavy sigh and turned to gaze at the kingdom just beyond the wall. "I'm going to scout ahead myself. We have no idea what is coming for us or what the gods are planning. We need to at least know how close they are and if they've gathered an army. Preparation is our only chance of survival."

I took a step back with my heart roaring in my ears. "But all the scouts have died."

"Which is why I will be going myself."

"With Toryn and Fenella? And Caedmon?"

"Fenella and Caedmon are busy preparing the city, and Toryn's people need him here. I go alone."

"No," I said roughly. "*Your* people need you, too. You're the king. You're not supposed to be your own scout. It's too dangerous. Too risky."

"I've never operated like that, and you know it."

Gently, he brushed my hair over my shoulder, but his gaze was hard, unwavering. He had been thinking a lot about this. "I would never send my men to do something I wasn't willing to do myself. And I would certainly never send them to certain death."

"Then I'm coming with you."

"Tessa, love…"

"If you're going, I'm going. You and me, we face this together. I won't let you go out there alone, not when your power doesn't work against the enemy. At least my hands can do some damage, if it comes to that."

"So brave," he murmured, his sapphire eyes raking across my face. "*Always* so brave."

"Brave and reckless," I said, thinking back to my earlier revelation. "But I don't want either of us to come close to dying, so you'd better have a good plan."

His wolfish smile lit up the dark. "Oh, that I do."

Thirty-Seven
Ruari

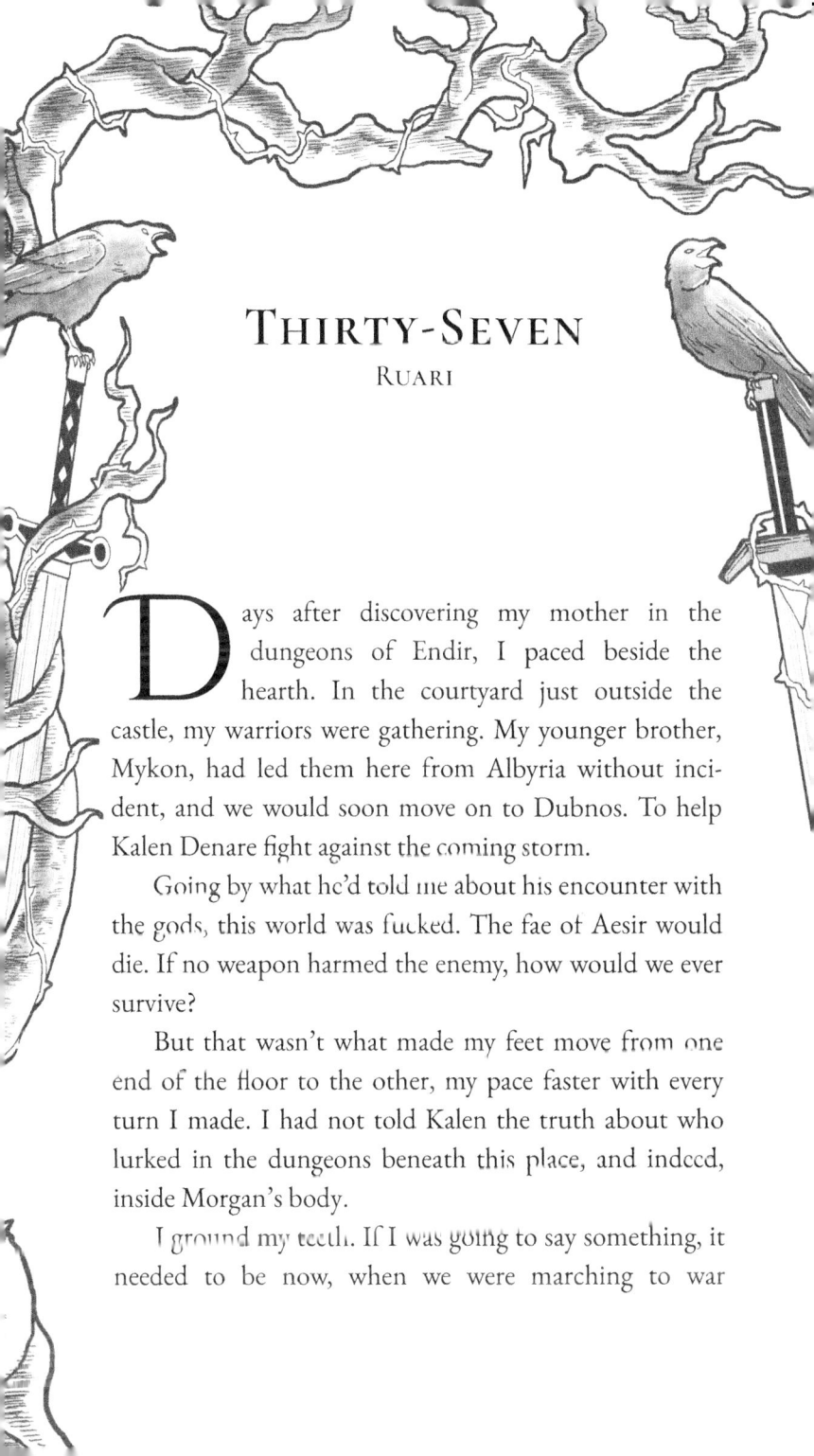

Days after discovering my mother in the dungeons of Endir, I paced beside the hearth. In the courtyard just outside the castle, my warriors were gathering. My younger brother, Mykon, had led them here from Albyria without incident, and we would soon move on to Dubnos. To help Kalen Denare fight against the coming storm.

Going by what he'd told me about his encounter with the gods, this world was fucked. The fae of Aesir would die. If no weapon harmed the enemy, how would we ever survive?

But that wasn't what made my feet move from one end of the floor to the other, my pace faster with every turn I made. I had not told Kalen the truth about who lurked in the dungeons beneath this place, and indeed, inside Morgan's body.

I ground my teeth. If I was going to say something, it needed to be now, when we were marching to war together. The only thing that stopped me was not knowing what he would do with that information. Would he want to kill her, or would he want to let her go?

The worst part was, I didn't know which of those *I* wanted to happen.

I'd tried contacting the mortals, of course, to ask them. As always, they ignored me. I was to never summon them—only the other way around. So for one of the first times in my life, I truly did not know what to do. It was my choice, I supposed. I wasn't used to that.

I could go down there and end this, take my dagger and plunge it into her ever-beating heart. But that was just it, wasn't it? That heart was not hers to beat. She'd stolen it from someone else, someone my father had enslaved for centuries. And even then, whoever she'd been before—Bellicent Denare, the queen who had loved her people, loved her sons—was gone now. The magic of Andromeda had corrupted her until she was nothing but a twisted version of that woman.

She was not my mother, not truly. And judging by the keen glint I'd seen in her eye when I'd visited her in the dungeon, she had something else planned. I needed to stop her. Or Kalen did.

I hated that I could not bring myself to do it.

A knock sounded on my door. I stopped pacing, as if whoever stood on the other side of the door would be able to read my mind by my hurried footsteps. Sucking in a sharp breath, I pressed down the front of my orange tunic, strode to the door, and flung it open.

Gaven stood on the other side with his silver hair

pulled back into a bun. Arms folded, he leaned against the doorframe, a slight smile curving his lips. "Are you quite all right in here, Ruari?"

"Fine," I snapped. "Are your men ready to march?"

"They're preparing. As you should be."

"I'm prepared."

"Have you ever faced a pooka?" he asked, cocking his head.

"As a matter of fact, I have." For years, I'd sneaked in and out of Albyria to hide supplies in one of the caves near the base of the western mountains, knowing one day, I would need them. I'd tried to be as stealthy as possible, but even then, those creatures had far more of a heightened sense of smell than I'd given them credit for at first. I'd been forced to fight them on more than one occasion. Luckily, my father had made certain I knew how to wield a sword.

One of the few things he'd ever done right, at least where his sons were concerned.

Gaven had the nerve to look surprised. "Good. Perhaps you'll make it to Dubnos after all. Unless you betray us, of course."

"Well, I have no other choice but to fight by your side, do I? I made a vow."

"And that's a problem?"

"I see what you're trying to do. You want to catch me out in some kind of lie, or you want to get me to admit I have plans to move against you."

"Do you blame me?" Gaven looked me up and down, noting my orange tunic—my father's color. "You have been our enemy for a very long time, and your father was a fucking bastard who fell under Andromeda's thrall. For all I know, you have, too."

"My father never let me anywhere near that necklace unless he was wearing it. Even then, he hardly paid attention to me, to any of my brothers or sisters. He didn't like..." I snapped my mouth shut.

Gaven's eyes flashed across my face. I didn't like the way he was staring at me now, like he could read my every thought. Like he knew *exactly* what I'd been about to say. *He didn't like that we didn't look like Bellicent Denare. We looked like the human women who had birthed us.*

"I'm sure it must have been difficult," he said more softly than I'd expected.

I shook my head and turned away. "I'm not having this conversation with you."

"Then tell me what Morgan wanted."

Ah, so there it was. The real reason for his visit. Before we left to battle our way to Dubnos, Gaven wanted to know what his prized prisoner had said to me. I gnawed on the inside of my cheek. If I told him, what would he do with her?

"Let me ask you a question," he said when a few moments of silence had passed. "Whatever she said, did it have anything to do with what we might face? Is there anything we need to know, Ruari? Are we walking into something we can't survive?"

I relaxed just a bit. That, I could answer honestly. "She just wanted me to let her out."

"And can you control her, like your father could?"

"No."

"All right." He nodded, as if satisfied by my answers, though I wouldn't have been if I were him. But then a wolfish smile crossed his face, so achingly familiar, I almost flinched. My father often got that look on his face before he said something he knew someone wouldn't like. "That's too bad. I would have been curious to find out if Oberon's power over her still worked, even though she's not Morgan in there now."

I started. *Fuck*.

"How did you find out?" I asked, trying to keep my voice steady even as my heart pounded against my ribs. I had known it would only be a matter of time before the truth slipped out or someone would piece it all together. Of course it had been Gaven. Quiet, calculating Gaven. And even though I was not sure I wanted to protect her, to keep her safe after everything she'd done...she was still my mother. My horrible, brutal mother.

I didn't want them to kill her.

"Well, Kalen and the others suspected it at first, seeing how Morgan sent that call for help and then showed up in Albyria seemingly unharmed." He arched a silver brow, bright against his brown skin. "It was so strange and made very little sense. But to complete the ritual to transfer Bellicent's soul into another's body, a mark must be carved into the vessel's skin. A tattoo of sorts. Tessa has one from when Oberon prepped her for the ritual."

I pressed my lips together, knowing where this was going.

"The thing is, Morgan showed her back to the others,

and she didn't have one of those marks. So everyone accepted her story."

"They still didn't trust her," I pointed out. "Kalen put her in the dungeons."

"Kalen was worried she still served Oberon in some capacity." Gaven took a step forward, the light from the hearth glinted in his silver eyes. "But I could not get past that mark. Fae have never been able to endure tattoos. Our bodies heal and spit out the ink. Of course, this is magic, and magic leaves scars, but...this was a different kind of magic. Something that came from the stars. I started to suspect her body accepted the tattoo just long enough for Bellicent to complete the transfer, and then her skin healed over it."

My heart pounded. "What convinced you that you were right?"

"This conversation right here." Gaven closed the distance between us, his bright eyes only inches from mine. Up close, he almost seemed taller and broader than he did from a distance, as if he had thrown off the mask that hid just how powerful he truly was. And that was when I noticed the fire that licked across the back of his knuckles where his fist was raised.

"You're an elite light fae," I said, swallowing. Just like my father had been.

"Yes, except I don't use my power to threaten innocents into submission."

"Is that not what you're doing now?"

"You are no innocent, King Ruari. So tell me, were you ever going to mention that the woman locked in our dungeons is none other than Bellicent Denare, the creature who has sucked the life out of so many others just so she could survive?"

I lifted my chin. I would not let him intimidate me. "I hadn't decided yet. I thought that if you knew, you might kill her."

"Any reason I shouldn't?"

"She's Kalen's mother, too."

The flames vanished, and I sighed in relief. Frowning, Gaven paced back over to the open door and shut it behind him. It was oddly comforting. If he didn't want anyone overhearing our conversation, perhaps he didn't plan on spreading this knowledge yet. Or maybe he just didn't want any witnesses when he burned me alive.

"Tell me," he said quietly. "How far gone is she?"

"I don't recognize her as the woman who raised me, but even back then, she was deep in the power's thrall. It doesn't...it doesn't take long to consume you."

"I'd hoped you wouldn't say that."

I tensed. "It's not her fault. She didn't ask for this. Based on the stories I've heard about her, from before, she would have hated the person she's become."

"So it would be a kindness, don't you think, to relieve her of this burden?"

His words were a punch to my throat. I sucked in a sharp breath. "You intend to execute her."

"Tell me there's another way. Give me another option, and I'll consider it."

I barked a bitter laugh. "Let her go."

"Is that what you want? To release Andromeda's most faithful follower? What do you think she'll do, Ruari? Fight on the side of humans and fae? Or will she join with the immortal creatures who wish to destroy us all?"

For a moment, I couldn't speak, or even breathe. His words weighed on me and then echoed in my ears. And I saw it all with brutal clarity. My mother—the essence that resided within Morgan's body now—had spent many days praying to the gemstone. I'd witnessed it countless times. Her knees would be raw and red after hours spent kneeling on the stone floor, and her face would be stained with tears. Those were some of the few times I'd ever seen any emotion from her other than disdain or irritation. She had prayed and prayed and prayed for salvation, and Andromeda had given it to her.

I closed my eyes. "She will choose the gods."

My words were her death sentence, I knew. Gaven could never allow a god's ally to live. Strands of regret wound through me, tangled with relief—because Gaven spoke true. Whoever Bellicent Denare was now, she wasn't who she'd once been. She wasn't even close. That woman—the queen of shadows—had died a very long time ago.

"What about your king?" I finally asked. "How will he feel about this?"

Gaven sighed. "I'm coming with you to fight, despite my reservations about leaving Endir without any of the Mist Guard. So I'll tell him in person. This is not the kind of thing to share through a communication stone. Which means...no, we will not have her executed yet. And in the meantime, perhaps we can get some information out of her."

My chest tightened. "That's why you came to me.

Not to find out what I know but to convince me to find out what *she* knows."

"Do you object?"

"I do if you want me to go down there and pretend you don't plan on killing her."

"Then don't pretend. Tell her whatever you like, just as long as you get some answers for us. You have until morning, and then we leave for Dubnos."

Gaven left my room while a dozen different emotions warred within me. None of this was right, or fair. Not that I knew what fairness would even be in this situation. On one hand, the clever fae was right. If anyone had information about Andromeda's plans or what it might take to beat her, it was my mother, who had been powered by the god's magic for hundreds of years. Through that gemstone necklace, Bellicent Denare had spoken to Andromeda's spirit, that essence stripped away and trapped there. There was no doubt in my mind she had told my mother wondrous and terrible things. But that did not mean she would share those things with me, or that I could look into her face and ask her to tell me when I knew her coming fate.

Permanent death.

I moved to the window and gazed out at the night-drenched realm. A moon burned through the dense fog, basking the city in a faint silvery glow. Over the past few hours, the mists had thinned so I could see the winding streets, the rust-colored rooftops, and the stone bridges that connected one hilly neighborhood to the next. Fae and humans alike strolled along the paths, clustering in squares with market stalls or wandering in and out of a bustling pub.

My heart ached at the sight of it. Once, Albyria's streets had been just like this. I'd only been a small child, running barefoot through the courtyard, laughing as the sun gifted us with its warming beams. My mother had chased me with her arms open wide. Then, she'd looked nothing like she did now. Her eyes had been bright, and I could have sworn there'd been a flicker of the human woman there...

But that was impossible. My mother was Bellicent Denare, not the poor woman whose life she'd stolen.

And I needed to find out what she knew. It was the only way to protect those people out there—the only way to protect Albyria, too.

With a heavy heart, I left my room and headed to the dungeons. The guards at the top of the stairwell leading down into the gloom were nowhere to be seen. Had Gaven told them to stand down to give me some privacy? Perhaps he thought she wouldn't speak unless she knew we were alone.

Still, a strange unease prickled the back of my neck.

The sensation only grew worse when I found a guard liberated of his head at the bottom of the stairs. I sidestepped his body and the pool of glistening blood to follow the path to my mother's prison.

The cell doors were wide open, and a key dangled in the lock. And of course, she was long, long gone. Bellicent Denare was free.

I found Gaven in the courtyard where he was directing warriors to the stables. His face remained blank as I stepped up beside him, though I could have sworn there was a slight hitch in his jaw. The courtyard was teeming with fae, warriors packing steel into sheaths and fitting bracers and gloves for the dangerous journey ahead of us.

"She's gone," I said in a low voice, careful to keep my words as vague as possible. I didn't want to raise alarm right before we were due to set off.

"Explain."

"There were keys in the cell door and a dead guard in the hallway."

He slid his sharp silver eyes my way. "And I'm to believe you weren't involved?"

"I have human blood. Scent me."

"Nice try, but you already told me that doesn't work. Any reason you aren't more alarmed by this?"

"I could ask you the same question."

"I *am* alarmed. But there's little I can do other than send some of our men into the mist to look for her. Perhaps she won't make it far."

"One thing I've learned over the years is to never underestimate Bellicent Denare." Even so, the thought of her out there by herself facing down countless beasts made me shiver. In Morgan's form, she would be strong and skilled at fighting. She'd have the ability to heal if she got into a bind. But she wasn't invincible, and those creatures knew how to kill fae.

I hated that I still cared.

"Well, there's nothing more we can do," Gaven said with a frown. "Continue your preparations. We ride for Dubnos at dawn."

Thirty-Eight
Tessa

Kalen's grand plan was to descend a dangerous mountain rather than taking the easier route through the Gaoth Pass. That was the way, he'd insisted, the gods would expect us to go. All the scouts had taken that path, and they'd vanished once they crossed the border. So instead of risking our lives that way, we were rappelling down a cliff face.

Fortunately, I felt right at home dangling off the side of a rock wall.

The rope slipped through my gloved hands as I hurtled toward the next outcropping below us, a familiar rush of glee filling my soul. A harsh wind whipped at my face, and my braided hair thumped against my aching back. Light, it felt good to be climbing again.

My boots hit an outcropping, landing me beside Kalen. I beamed up at him as Boudica darted around us on her brilliant black wings.

He chuckled. "Glad we didn't go through the sewage tunnels?"

It was the only other secret way out of Dubnos. It would have been the easier option, but I'd gladly chosen the cliff. I had no desire to sneak up on the enemy smelling of piss. "Oh, absolutely. This is the most fun I've had in days."

"And here I thought you were happiest in a library."

"If only we could scale down the side of a cliff *into* a library. Then I'd be in heaven."

His dark gaze raked over me. "I hope you're forgetting something. Otherwise, you wound me, love."

Despite the fate that loomed before us, I looked up at him with such a lightness in my chest that it took my breath away. "Well, the last time I was in a library, I did more than just read."

He practically purred in response. His need reached out to me through the bond, and I knew he could feel the same from me. It was all I could do to drag my gaze away from him and not climb his body like a tree. Now that we'd acknowledged the truth of our connection, sometimes I felt like I couldn't think straight. The thread between us tugged so hard that I felt compelled to erase the distance between us.

But we couldn't give in to it. Not here, not like this. Not when so many lives depended on us to find answers.

And so I let out a shuddering breath and wiped the beads of sweat from my forehead. As I did, my back flared with pain.

Kalen noted my wince and frowned. "We should take a break. It's still a long way to the bottom."

"We don't have time to waste. Dubnos needs us to keep moving."

"We won't find answers if your muscles give out. We'll rest for twenty minutes, and then we'll get back on the rope."

I wanted to argue and push past the mortal pain, but I knew he was right. Just behind the outcropping was a small cave with an entrance facing north, away from the eastern border. Once inside, Kalen gathered a few stray branches and started a fire. My tired body basked in the warmth of the flames, causing me to sigh in relief.

I hadn't noticed the cold until now. I'd been so focused on the rope and the rocks and the thrill of it all. Now that I sat still, the chill seeped into my bones. Even my breath frosted before me. The temperature had dropped significantly from when we'd left Dubnos.

Kalen handed me a canteen of water and a piece of dried meat before staring into the flames, his expression thoughtful. Boudica settled onto his shoulder. "It's getting colder, and the mists are getting thicker."

"I'm assuming that's not normal."

"It's happened before, but only for a few weeks at a time," he said. "Sometimes I forget the mists came from me. They've always felt like a living, breathing thing separate from myself, especially since I can't control them."

"What are you trying to say?"

For a moment, only the sound of the crackling flames filled the cave. "I'm not certain. It just all seems linked somehow. The mists, the creatures, the storm fae we faced in Itchen, my powers and yours. I don't know what it all means, but it does mean something."

I nodded. I'd had the same thought myself. But if

anyone had an explanation for all this, it would be the humans. "Any word from Niamh?"

"Not a one."

"Should we be worried?" Val's face flashed in my mind's eye, and panic threatened to weaken my resolve. The thought of her in danger terrified me. When she'd left for the mortal lands, I'd thought she'd be the safest of us all. And if anything happened to her… "It's been a long time."

"For all we know, the communication stones don't work in Talaven."

But Kalen did not sound convinced.

We spent the rest of our short break in silence, watching the dancing flames. A part of me just wanted to sink into the stones here and stay for hours, letting the heat chase away the eerie chill that lurked outside the cave. We would likely not take another break until we reached the bottom of the mountain, and then we'd be in enemy territory. There would be no more fires. No more warmth after this.

But then it was time. Kalen stood and held out his hand. I took it without a word, the grim dread in my heart reflected back at me through the bond. We walked onto the outcropping and grabbed the rope. And then we scaled down the cliff to where the enemy might be waiting for us.

Thirty-Nine
Kalen

Tessa's bravery would never cease to amaze me. She descended the rest of the cliff face without complaint. In fact, there was a glint in her eye despite the danger we might face. She was in her element out here, moving with dexterity and speed across the rocks. I'd known she was good—excellent, even. She wouldn't have survived so long stealing those gemstones if she weren't. But seeing it with my own eyes...moon be damned, she was breathtaking with her wild, fierce eyes and that curve of her lips as she deftly maneuvered past another jagged rock.

This woman was my wife. When all this was over, I would celebrate her the way she deserved.

We soon reached the ground, and as much as I wanted to keep watching her, I turned my focus to the dangerous path ahead. Eerie silence settled over us, and not a single shadow shifted other than Boudica, who swept by overhead. The mist was thicker than I'd ever seen it now, so thick the air felt wet when I tried to breathe it in. So wet it coated my face with a thin layer of water, as if I'd just dunked my head into a stream.

Tessa's boots thudded against the dirt as she landed beside me. Instantly, she had her hand on the hilt of the sword at her waist. She'd insisted on bringing the weapon instead of something lighter, determined she could scale the mountain even with the extra weight. A flicker of pride went through me. Of course she'd done it. In fact, she'd had no trouble at all.

I tapped my face just beside my eye and motioned in front of us, not daring to speak a word out loud. Understanding my question, Tessa shook her head. She couldn't see a damn thing. My enhanced eyesight pierced the mist —just a bit. Enough for me to spot a small hill rising on our left and a copse of trees draped across it. The enemy could be there. They could be anywhere. I couldn't see or smell a damn thing beyond that cluster of trees. Nothing but mist.

I motioned for her to fall into step behind me and then tapped near my eye again, hoping she got the message. *Stay back and don't lose sight of me.*

She frowned, and I knew she hated the idea of staying in the rear, but she moved behind me all the same and nodded that she was ready.

My breathing shallow, I crept up the side of the hill, listening to everything around us. A blast of brutal wind hit us as we climbed, bringing with it the acrid scent of smoke, the first real sign we'd had that the enemy was near. And much nearer than I'd hoped. If they were camping this close to the mountain, it would only be a matter of days before they came and wrought destruction upon us all.

Sorrow filled my heart as we moved closer to the line of trees just ahead. The fae of Dubnos had put their trust in me, the dangerous son of their once-worthy queen. Bellicent Denare had ruled the shadow lands with a kind and generous hand. Her reign had only been marred by the dark reputation of her husband. After my powers had brought the never-ending mist upon us, many shadow fae had packed up their bags and left. Those who'd stayed only did so because they thought my brutal power would protect them, even from the gods.

But I had not kept them safe from this.

I shook aside my dark thoughts as we inched below the canopy of trees. The silence struck me as *wrong*. There was no birdsong here, no scuttle of rabbits through the fallen leaves. Even the insects had fled this place. I stopped and held out my arm, squinting to see through the mist. Tessa tapped my back to let me know she was still there.

I could see only trees, but the scent of fire had grown stronger.

We continued on, moving like wraiths through the woods, our footsteps near-silent. Tessa had gotten better at stealth. Another sign she wasn't fully human.

Soon, we reached the other side of the small woods. The trees cut off at the edge of a steep cliff overlooking one of the many rolling fields of this kingdom. The mists were still thick, but a harsh wind scattered them here and there, giving me short glimpses of the field below and another tree-drenched hill. Just beyond it, to the left, orange flames burned through the night. Smoke twisted and danced, a shade darker than the mist.

At long last, sound drifted toward us. Tessa stepped up beside me and placed a gloved hand on my arm. She heard it, too. The murmur of voices and the scrape of swords against whetstones mingled together in a symphony I knew far too well.

There was a war camp up ahead.

Frowning, I led Tessa back into the thicket until we were hidden in a dense pocket of brush. My voice was barely a whisper when I said, "Stay here."

Her eyes widened. "Kalen, no."

"We don't know what we'll find up there. You should stay out of sight."

"I'm coming with you." As if to punctuate her statement, she pulled off her gloves and stuffed them into her pocket. "If Sirius or any of the others are there, your powers won't work. But mine will."

"Swear you won't do anything rash."

She flashed a tense smile. "Who, me?"

"Tessa."

"I don't want to die, Kal. I won't go rushing into an enemy war camp, swinging my sword. I can promise you that."

I didn't like the idea of her getting any closer to that camp, but I also knew she'd just follow me if I tried to leave her here. Stubbornness, yes, but it was more than that. I saw the fierce protectiveness in her eyes, that same feeling I had toward her. The bond had dug its claws in deeply.

Quietly, we moved back to the tree line and began our trek across the field, ducking to remain hidden in the tall grass. The distant sounds grew louder as we moved, and a new scent joined the smoke. It was unlike anything I'd ever smelled before—cloying and putrid and *wrong*, as if the air itself was thick with rot.

From beside me, Tessa almost gagged. She pressed a hand against her mouth and followed me through the grass and up the hill. When we reached the woods, the stench only grew worse. Her eyes watered as she gazed up at me, and I could see the question she was desperate to ask.

What in the name of light is that?!

I just shook my head. Unfortunately, we were about to find out.

The mists began to thin as we crept through the trees, and the glow of the bonfire was so bright after the darkness we'd just left that it almost blinded me. The stench grew stronger and the sounds grew louder until we neared the edge of the woods. I motioned for Tessa to get down on the ground. Wincing, she removed her hand from her nose and flattened her body against the dirt. Everywhere her hands touched, life turned to dust.

Her eyes glistened with unshed tears, but she did not flinch back.

I lowered myself to the ground beside her. Together, we crawled through the brush. Grass and brush turned black as we inched forward, Tessa leaving a trail of death in her wake. I tried to appear as if I didn't notice, as if the dusty path behind were nothing more than dirt. But still, I could see the shame on her face and the regret in her eyes. She was trying to control it—trying to stop her power from killing everything she touched—but that control still evaded her.

At long last, we finally reached the lip of the woods, where the small hill looked down on the war camp in the valley below. My fingers tensed on the ground, and absolute terror stole all the breath from my lungs. That was not a war camp. At least, it wasn't like any camp I'd ever raised in all those months I'd spent battling Oberon and his bloodthirsty kingdom.

A massive bonfire raged in the center of a clearing where the grass had been burned away, leaving behind a perfect circle of charred earth. The orange light cast eerie hues across a small cluster of dyed emerald tents that shuddered in the harsh wind—the color of the Kingdom of Storms. On a few flat stones, several storm fae perched, clad in leather armor and holding bows. With eyes vacant and hollow, they watched the rest of their camp.

A camp swarming with monsters.

Pookas prowled around the bonfire, the light glinting off their talons and fangs. Blood drenched their matted fur, blood that looked fresh. There were at least a hundred of them. And among them, wraiths danced in their tangled black robes, their bony feet leaving behind trails of black, poisonous sand.

But that wasn't the worst of it, not by a long shot. I saw five or six of those scorpion-like creatures we'd faced in Itchen hunkering in the darkness like mountains of death. There might've been even more, hidden by the dense mist.

Tessa sucked in a sharp breath.

Muscles knotting in my shoulders, I scanned the camp, searching for any sign of Sirius or the other gods. I would never forget him—his cruel, wicked face, and the way he'd looked at Tessa. But I did not see him among the fae nor anywhere else in the camp.

Still, this was not good. If these creatures swarmed the streets of Dubnos...I shuddered at the thought of all the blood painting the streets, and of the life draining from innocent eyes. The terror-filled end of all those trusting citizens who believed no one could harm them because they had the Mist King.

I swore beneath my breath and moved back, retracing my steps with Tessa by my side. As soon as we were far enough away to avoid being heard, I leaned down to press my lips against her ear.

"I'm going to attack that camp," I whispered.

Tessa hissed and pulled away from me. "Have you lost your mind?"

"Did you see Sirius or any of the others? My power should work without the gods nearby. I can stop that army of beasts from attacking my kingdom."

"Think about this," she whispered up at me. "Sirius could be hidden inside those tents. He could be waiting for *you* to show your hand."

I pressed my lips together. "You think it's a trap."

"I think it's a war camp with a terrifying variety of beasts, and those fae are readying themselves to march on Dubnos. Soon, no doubt. But they'll also suspect you've lost all your scouts and have come out here to investigate yourself. What better way to win than to take out the King of Shadows before the battle even begins?"

I clenched my jaw. Walking away from this when I might stay and prevent an attack on my kingdom from happening...it went against everything I was, everything I wanted to be as king. It felt like cowardice. It felt like loss.

But deep down, I knew Tessa was right. We'd seen no sign of Sirius, but that didn't mean he wasn't close enough to dampen my power if I tried to unleash it upon this army. *His* army. An army of beasts. I'd never before seen pookas so contained, so...calm. They were pacing around the bonfire, but they were leashed. The gods were able to control them. Or at least one of them was.

"I could take my sword against them," I murmured. "I'm powerful and fast."

"You're good, Kal. But there are too many of them, even for you. Even with me and my death hands by your side. They would either kill us or capture us, and then Dubnos would have no idea what was coming for them. We need to return to the city and warn them. We need to prepare for a fight. Because it's coming for us. May the realm never break."

She spoke with such conviction, and it wasn't fear or anger that fueled her words. The glint in her eyes was something else, something far more powerful—strength and clarity. She lifted her chin and spoke in a calm, steady voice. It was the way a queen might speak when faced with an impossible situation, in a voice that could capture the heart of an entire kingdom.

It had captured mine.

"All right," I answered. "Let's be swift. We don't know how soon they'll attack."

But as we turned to race over the hill toward the base of the mountain, a tall, hollow-eyed fae blocked our path. "Neither of you will be going anywhere."

Forty
Tessa

The eyes of the storm fae swept across us, his gaunt face highlighting the cutting cheekbones and a strong, jutting chin. His dark hair was pulled back from his face and melded into shadows behind him. He snarled, showing canines sharp enough to slice through flesh. And he had an arrow aimed right at Kalen's heart.

There was a buzz in my ears, and a heavy darkness crept into the corners of my vision. I stared down the fae, my own lips curling back. I had the sudden urge to rip his head off and tear the rest of him apart, limb by limb. My rage was so intense, my body shuddered from the force of it.

He had an arrow pointed at my mate. In the trees above, Boudica screeched.

"Run, Tessa," Kalen murmured, his hands tensing by his sides. He was itching to reach for his sword, I knew, but he wouldn't be quick enough. Not with a storm fae's arrow ready to fly. I had to remind myself the blow would not kill him. He was fae, and it would take more than a single arrow to steal his life away. That, of course, did not mean I would abandon him.

I held my hands up before me and narrowed my eyes at the storm fae. My fingers were still unbound, free of the gloves. Not that it would do either of us much good. I might have become proficient in destroying flowers and grass but nothing bigger than that. Certainly nothing as strong as a storm fae.

"She isn't running away from this, and neither are you." The storm fae jerked his chin in the direction we'd just come—the direction of the enemy war camp. "So start walking."

"No," Kalen said in a low growl, his voice lethal and dark.

The storm fae narrowed his gaze, his arrow still trained on Kalen's heart. "We have orders to keep the girl alive, but he said nothing about you. So you can come with us, or you can die. It's your choice."

"Are you one of Owen's?" Kalen asked.

"None of your concern."

"Does he know who holds the storm fae throne now?"

The fae before us huffed. "Toryn fled his kingdom. The throne is not his. It's ours now. And we fight for the gods."

I'd noticed this storm fae didn't wear an onyx gemstone like the others, at least that I could see. And that strangeness in his distant, hooded eyes made him look like he'd lost his grip on whoever he used to be.

Oberon had looked like that, right at the end. When he'd been screaming and running through the mists.

"He won't let you have it. Toryn, I mean," I called out.

The archer flicked his gaze my way. It was a momentary lapse, just a tiny break in his concentration. But it was enough for Kalen to draw his sword and duck.

The King of Shadows moved with speed and dexterity. He moved like wind, like smoke, like the very mist itself. One second, he stood beside me. The next, he'd ducked in beneath the enemy's arrow and shoved his blade right toward his gut.

But the storm fae danced back and whipped a dagger from his belt. The blades clashed together in a furious frenzy. I sagged in relief even as my hands itched to help. Kalen was an extraordinary fighter. All the years he'd spent avoiding his power, he had trained and trained until he became a whirlwind of brutal steel that could take down a dozen shadowfiends at once.

And so I did not fear for him even as the storm fae slashed his blade at Kalen's face. The King of Shadows met the enemy's blow with his powerful sword, and then he shoved him back.

Hands wrapped around my waist, and I was suddenly hauled from the leaf-carpeted ground. A sharp cry of alarm ripped from my throat as I twisted against the strong arms that yanked me to his chest. But his grip was tight and firm, and now he was running, fleeing through the woods toward the war camp.

Kalen's roar rent the quiet night. And through the bond—through that strange, overwhelming connection we shared—his fear punched me so hard it took my breath away.

Tears filled my eyes from the rush of his terror and pain, and instinctively, my hand stretched out toward him. But I could not see him anymore. The mists swirled in from the darkened sky and coated the woods.

"Tessa!" he shouted, his voice rough and raw. Steel rang only a second later as the archer kept him locked in the fight.

Everything within me screamed to get back to him, if only to stop his pain, if only to soothe the fear that rattled through us both, making it difficult for me to focus on anything but the force of nature threaded to my soul, to my heart.

"Let go of me," I snarled, twisting to face my captor at last. His yellow eyes gleamed in the dark, and his pale ginger hair was plastered to a sweat-drenched face. When I tried to wrench free, he clutched me more tightly.

With the shadows pulsing around us, it was impossible to tell how close we were to the war camp where hundreds of shadowfiends readied themselves for the upcoming battle. Shadowfiends and wraiths and more storm fae, all under the thrall of the gods. When Kalen and I had scouted the camp, we hadn't spotted Sirius, but he was likely there, too. And if this fae took me into that camp, I knew I'd never escape. Me against hundreds... those were impossible odds, even if my power obeyed me.

But one...one I could handle. I hoped.

Bracing myself, I shifted my head to the side and clamped my teeth on the enemy's arm. The storm fae flinched and loosened his grip. I knew it didn't hurt him, but the element of surprise was enough for me to wriggle out of his arms. I fell to my knees, my hands catching me before my face collided with the ground.

My power seeped out of me, and dust consumed the grass.

"You fucking bitch," the storm fae spat, striding toward me with a snarl. "I should rip off your head for that."

"But you won't. Andromeda wants me alive." Steadying my breathing, I rose to my feet. The storm fae was only inches away now.

He narrowed his eyes as I curled my hands, and then he reached for me. I danced back, light on my feet, even as Kalen's distant roars shook through me. He was still in the middle of a fight. There must be more of the storm fae in the woods. They must have surrounded him to distract him long enough for this bastard to steal me away.

But I was not a damsel in distress. I could not be *stolen*. Not anymore. I would be like the women in the novels I read, those brave souls who found the strength within themselves to fight back.

The storm fae smiled, revealing rows of sharpened teeth. "You truly think you can get away from me? You're mortal."

I reached for the sword at my side, but I was too slow. The storm fae moved as quickly as lightning across the sky, and then he was there. He grabbed my throat and shoved me against a tree. The scent of death gagged me.

"Don't you know what I am?" he hissed into my ear. "I am storm fae, and I move like the wind."

My heart pounded, and his fingers dug into my skin. The tree's rough bark scraped the back of my head, sending bolts of pain through my skull. I couldn't breathe. I could barely think. And through the bond, Kalen's terror churned my own fear, whipping it with a chaotic frenzy.

The enemy had been tasked with bringing me back, but whatever the gods had done to him had twisted him beyond repair. He was not going to let me live. And even if he did, I would not arrive in that war camp unharmed.

The way a hidden light gleamed in his hooded eyes reminded me of Oberon. Those sharp teeth, that unchecked cruelty. The strength of his hands when they closed around me. It was all him. For years, that cruelty had drowned me. No more.

Through the bond, I felt Kalen's worry, but I felt something else, too. Strands of his power reaching out to me. His magic hummed, sparking to life somewhere in the depths of him. As the storm fae choked me against the tree, I reached out through the bond and gave Kalen's power a gentle tug.

Life and death consumed me. A shower of sparks stormed my veins, stealing whatever remaining breath I held in my lungs. My skin burning, my eyes running, my ears ringing, I shuddered against the force of all that power and the awesome strength of it.

I lifted a shaking hand. The storm fae barely noticed. He continued to shove me against the tree with a deranged, wicked smile on his face.

And so I pressed a finger against his cheek and choked out, "Death."

The storm fae jolted back, releasing his grip on my neck. Instantly, sweet breath filled my lungs and chased the darkness away from my vision. I leaned forward, grasping my knees as I drank in the air, but I kept my eyes locked on the enemy's face.

He'd gone pale. Gasping, he collapsed to the ground. A tremor went through him as his eyes rolled back into his head. For a moment, nothing else happened. With a thundering heart, I stared down at the storm fae, horrified by what I'd done. He'd stopped moving. No more breath filled his lungs.

And then dust swarmed across his skin. *Ash*. Just like the Mortal Dagger had done. I watched as the dust consumed him from the inside out. The harsh breeze of the storm lands caught the flecks and blew them away until there was nothing left of him at all.

He was dead.

I'd done it. I'd actually done it.

I didn't know whether to sob from the horror of it all or celebrate that I'd survived. Maybe both.

But for now, I needed to find Kalen.

I raced through the trees. Branches and brush scraped against my fighting leathers, but I continued on, following the sound of singing swords. Through the bond, Kalen called to me. It was as if he knew I was free and searching for him now. I ran and ran and ran, trying not to focus on just how loud the fighting was. We were so close to that war camp. Anyone in it would have heard the chaos by now.

At long last, dancing shadows rose before me. Kalen was in close combat with two storm fae. Sweat and blood drenched his face, and for a moment, a new terror screamed through me. By calling on his power through the bond, had I weakened him? Could he heal?

"Kalen." I stumbled toward him with my heart in my throat. If I could just get close enough, I could help. All I needed was to press my finger against their skin and—

As if my voice had powered him, he spun through the air a shade faster. His sword sliced through the nearest storm fae's neck, and then punched through the leather armor of the next. Right through his heart. It was enough to kill them both instantly.

Heaving, he turned toward me and started to run with his arms open wide to catch me. But then a not-too-distant roar cut through the night, a sound that was blood-chillingly familiar.

The shadowfiends had heard us. And they were coming.

"Run," I whispered.

"Not without you." He started running toward me again, holding out his hand.

I shoved my gloves back on before he could touch my skin. When he reached me, I wound my fingers around his, and then we took off through the trees. We ran faster than I'd ever moved before. The world was nothing but a blur of darkness and of mist. Through the bond, his fear still reached me, but relief was wound around it like a thread of hope. If only we could make it back to the base of the mountain, we could leave this kingdom behind for the safety of Dubnos.

But then a horrified thought occurred to me. The shadowfiends—they'd always been able to scale the chasm walls. The only thing that had kept them from swarming Teine had been Oberon's barrier. There was no barrier here. So even if we reached the mountain and started to climb, they could follow us.

We wouldn't get away.

Burning tears filled my eyes, both from the mist and the new realization crashing over me. What were we going to do? How would we ever get out of this alive?

But more importantly, if we started the climb now and the shadowfiends followed, would they head on straight to Dubnos after they'd killed us? Would we be bringing death and destruction to an unprepared city before word could reach them about what was coming? They had no idea the gods had gathered an army of beasts.

"Kalen." I choked out his name as we continued to race through the night.

"I know," he murmured. "I know."

"What do we do?"

His hand tensed around mine. "Boudica has been in the skies above us. She saw everything, and she's flown ahead to warn Toryn. He's the only one who can understand her like I can. The city will know what's coming, and we'll do whatever it takes to give them time to prepare."

My heart rattled. "We won't scale the cliff and lead the beasts to the city."

"No. When we reach the mountain, I will turn and face the enemy. I will fight. For Dubnos."

Fight and die.

There were too many, even for Kalen. He knew that,

and so did I. And yet we could not climb. They'd only catch us and kill us, and then they'd set their sights on the castle above. A horrible understanding turned my stomach into a pit of writhing snakes. This was the end for us. There was no way out.

Through the trees, I spotted the wall of rock. The base of the mountain.

I turned my gaze to Kalen's tight face. "Your power. I felt it through the bond. It's awake, it's alive. You could use it against them."

"I tried," he said, his voice so tense it seemed as though he had to scrape the words out of his throat. "They're still muting it somehow."

I shook my head. But if I could feel it, if I could call upon it, then it had to be in there somewhere. Maybe with the bond I could unlock it somehow, just enough for him to blast through the shadowfiends that chased us.

Sucking in a breath, I turned my focus inward to the bond tethering his soul to mine. I reached out and searched for that all-consuming power. And there it was in a brilliant shade of sapphire—so vibrant and alive, glowing with the light of a star.

"What are you doing?" Kalen slowed to a stop.

"Just...trying something."

I held onto that thread of power and I pulled.

Pain exploded through my back. With a cry, I wrenched free of Kalen's hand and slammed into the ground, but I barely felt the impact. It was my back—burning, ripping, roaring, tearing me apart. It was as if a monster feasted on my flesh, its massive teeth digging into me.

Shuddering, I clutched at the ground. Dirt scraped against my fingernails.

And then something tore through my skin. It felt as if my shoulder blades had become swords, slicing through my fighting leathers. I turned and saw them, wide and gleaming white. They were beautiful. I flexed, and they extended to their full, glorious span. Wings. I had sprouted wings.

Forty-One
Tessa

A roar filled my head. It took me a moment to realize the sound was coming from me. Kalen knelt by my side, brushing the damp hair away from my sweat-soaked face, and my wings—oh, light, my *wings*—were gently pulsing against the wind. With every new beat, another blast of pain ripped through my back.

"Tessa, love, you need to get on your feet." Awe mingled with the concern in his voice, and I could tell through our bond that he wanted to soothe my pain, to take me away somewhere he could tend to me.

But there were monsters coming.

Grinding my teeth, I forced my aching body to stand, but my massive wings almost dragged me back to the ground. They were *heavy* and unbelievably strong. Teetering on my feet, I grasped Kalen's hand to hold myself steady, and then I met his eyes.

He smiled—actually smiled. "You are fucking breathtaking. Can you control them?"

"I don't know." I hissed as I forced the wings to move,

and a fiery pain licked my back. They'd torn through my skin and the back of my leathers, but enough of the material still hugged my waist and arms to keep my front covered. "A little."

"Do you think you might be able to fly?"

I choked out a tense laugh. "Absolutely not."

"Use my power to strengthen you." He lifted his head then and gazed through the woods. His throat bobbed as he swallowed. I knew what that look meant. The enemy would be here any moment. I didn't have much time to overcome this. Why did the wings have to come to me *now*?

"This is what we're going to do," he said. "You will use my strength to fly. I will stay and fight."

"I won't leave you behind to die," I told him. "Besides, I have a better idea. I'll fly in the opposite direction to distract them. You climb."

He swore. "Absolutely not. You can save yourself, Tessa. You can live."

"I don't want to live without you."

He dropped his forehead to mine and breathed. I held back the choked sob that rose to the back of my throat as I relished in the feel of him. Even though this was better than the alternative, I hated that we had to do this. I did not want to *leave* him.

But this was a chance at survival for us both. It was a long shot, but it was the only one we had.

"Kalen, I..."

"I know." He kissed me fiercely, and then backed away. "All right, we'll try your plan. Now go!"

I reached through the bond, found that thread of

power again, and gripped it fiercely. A part of me was afraid to find out what would happen if I pulled on it again. But I had to try. Steeling myself, I gave it a little tug.

That all-consuming power flooded through me, drowning my pain. I flexed my wings and forced them to shift behind me. My back still ached with every inch they moved, but I could think around it now, breathe around it. The crashing of the shadowfiends grew louder.

Praying to the stars and the heavens far above, I bent my knees, and I *jumped*.

My wings beat at the air to keep me aloft. Gritting my teeth, I spread them a little wider and forced them to battle against the wind. I rose, higher and higher, until I reached the canopy of the woods. Kalen gazed up at me, awestruck. With a slight smile, he turned and vanished into the shadows.

I spun in the air, wincing at the pain, and swooped low as I spun toward the war camp in the distance. My wings faltered, and the ground rose up fast. Gritting my teeth, I righted myself just before a tree slammed into my face.

"Come on," I whispered to myself as I fought against my wings. If I didn't get control, I'd crash, and Kalen would never get out of here alive. My fear for him flared within me, and suddenly, my wings rippled in the wind as my long-muted instincts took over.

Within moments, I passed the beasts, soaring only a few feet above the tops of their heads. Several storm fae were with them. They exclaimed and pointed up at my desperate rush through the woods. I had to twist and dive and dip to avoid slamming into the trees, often coming far too close to the ground for comfort.

But it had done the trick. The storm fae and the creatures had spotted me. They spun on their feet and gave chase. My back screamed as my wings pulsed behind me. With every moment I grew further from Kalen, the pain grew stronger. As I dodged trees left and right, I pictured his face in my mind. I called up Nellie's face and Toryn's face and every single face I'd ever seen in the shadow fae city. I could push through the pain, if only to give them a little more time—and to give Kalen time to scale the cliff.

Another tree line rose up before me, and I flew through it. Branches slapped my outstretched wings. More pain shot through me, this time from a thorny cut along my left-hand feathers. But I just kept moving. I soared across the field, dipping low to spin around the enemy's war camp.

There were still hundreds of shadowfiends lurking here and perhaps fifty storm fae with their hollow eyes and sharp teeth. No sign of Sirius or any of the other gods. Just behind me, the shadowfiends chasing me through the woods exploded from the trees and *leapt*.

There were at least a dozen of them, and they were coming right for me.

With a sharp cry, I pumped my wings and went up, up, up into the mists. And so did they. I had never seen a shadowfiend jump so high. They *couldn't*, or walls would have never done a damn thing to keep them out. But I knew what I was seeing. As soon as they were free of the woods, the beasts leapt into the air, pushing off with legs far more powerful than they should be.

And so I kept flying, letting my wings take me as high as they could. I didn't know how far would be enough to escape their grasp.

Suddenly, the mists vanished. I emerged from the clouds and rose above a blanket of darkness. High in the night sky, a crescent moon glowed brightly. My breath caught as I gazed around me. The stars were so clear up here. Hundreds and hundreds of stars—so many, I knew I would never be able to count them all.

It was breathtaking.

I slowed my wings, and they pulsed softly behind me. For a moment, the world seemed to still, and all the horror down below drifted away on a rolling wind. All around me, a blanket of dense mist engulfed the world, but there...far in the distance, I swore I could see light. Even amid all the gloom, there was hope.

And then the sky itself seemed to speak.

"Daughter of Stars," a feminine voice whispered on the wind, so soft I couldn't help but wonder if I'd imagined it. "I've been waiting for you."

"Daughter of Stars?" I asked, swallowing as I gazed around me. Where was that voice coming from? Was there someone else here?

"Dust of the earth, stars of the sky. Only you, who is forged from both dust and stars, can stop them." And then a sharp intake of breath. "But you must return to the darkness at once. The one made of mist and shadow needs you."

"Kalen," I said, my heart jolting.

I dove, spinning back into the shadows. My back screamed as I tucked my wings in close and plummeted toward the ground. I needed to draw the enemy further away to give Kalen more time to scale the mountain. Otherwise, they might think to look for us there. The storm fae might guess our plan.

I sailed, flying so low, my wings scraped the tips of the grass as I leveled myself, coming too close for comfort to one of the storm fae tents. The material whipped in the wake of my wings. It caught the storm fae's attention instantly.

Several of them shouted and rushed after me. And so I flew.

For hours, I let them give chase, leading them back across the storm fae lands toward the demolished Gailfean castle. When the crumbling ruins crept into view, I sucked in a breath and raced up toward the clouds once more before doubling back toward the mountain. Surely that would be enough.

Several more hours flew by, but at long last, I spotted a cave at the edge of a cliff. When I landed inside, Kalen was waiting for me. The wind whipped his dark hair around his face, lines of tension bracketing his mouth. I fell to my knees as pain dragged me down like a heavy iron chain. He was beside me in an instant, and his powerful arms lifted me to his chest. As he carried me into the cave, darkness took me.

I awoke curled against Kalen's chest. He'd tucked me close to him, and the solid strength of his body stilled my rising panic. I shifted against him, wincing at the pain in my back, but found the wings... they were gone.

"You're awake," he said in a rough voice. "Thank the moon." I pulled back to meet his gaze. He palmed my face, dropped his forehead to mine, and shuddered. "You were barely breathing."

I took a moment to inhale the familiar scent of him. He smelled so much like the mists. "I was afraid they wouldn't take the bait, so I led them very, very far away."

He let out a low, rumbling growl. "I hated you had to be the bait. In fact, I would take it back if I could."

"No." I shook my head. "It was the right thing to do. Has there been any sign of them behind you?"

We both turned to the cave exit, and I noted he hadn't built a fire this time. Even though the entrance faced north and away from the war camp in the distance, he clearly hadn't wanted to risk them seeing a hint of light. It would have wasted this entire effort.

"None so far. How far away did you lead them?"

I chuckled, though even that small movement hurt. "Some of them followed me all the way to Gailfean."

"Gail—no wonder you were gone so long."

"Sorry if I worried you. I wanted to buy you as much time as I could. How long have I been out?"

"A few hours," he said quietly.

Alarm flashed through me. "We should go. Now.

Before the shadowfiends start climbing up this mountain. We need to help the others."

He nodded, though his concern throbbed toward me through the bond. "You could really use some rest."

Sighing, I unwound myself from his embrace and stood on shaky legs. "We don't have that kind of time."

"I know."

Kalen led me to the outcropping outside the cave where the rope hung waiting, just where we'd left it. I tipped back my head and gazed up at the steep cliff. The top of it was impossible to see from here, but we'd only just scaled down, and I could remember exactly how far we had to go. It was a long way back to the top.

"You go first," Kalen said. "I'll be right behind you."

Just in case, he didn't say. Just in case my body gave out on me, and I slipped.

Calling upon the last dredges of my strength, I wrapped my gloved hands around the rope and began to climb. It was harder than I'd expected, even knowing just how exhausted my body was. Every inch felt like a battle. Every pause felt as if it might be my last. My wings were gone, but my back ached with phantom pain, as if they still pushed from my skin, making every movement that much harder.

And still, I climbed, Kalen just below me. Every now and again, I swore I faltered, and then I felt this push, this rush of strength in my bones. I knew he was somehow feeding it into me. I was too tired to call on it myself.

The moments crept by. This was taking far too long. Any moment now, the shadowfiends would hurtle up behind us and rip us from the sky.

But I would not give up. I would never stop trying, even when I wanted to lose myself in the sweet embrace of unconsciousness, just to get relief from the tormenting pain.

When I finally crawled over the lip of the cliff, Kalen only seconds behind me, Toryn stood waiting for us with Boudica perched on his shoulder. He offered me a hand and helped me stand before doing the same to his oldest friend, his fellow king. Before I could thank him, he tugged the both of us into his arms.

"Thank the moon you're back," he murmured, and I could have sworn his voice cracked.

"And yet," Kalen said in a rough voice, "I'm afraid we don't come bearing good news."

"I know. Boudica showed me everything." With a sigh, Toryn pulled away and motioned at the battlements and the city beyond. "I've already started the preparations. We will be ready for war by morning."

Forty-Two
Ruari

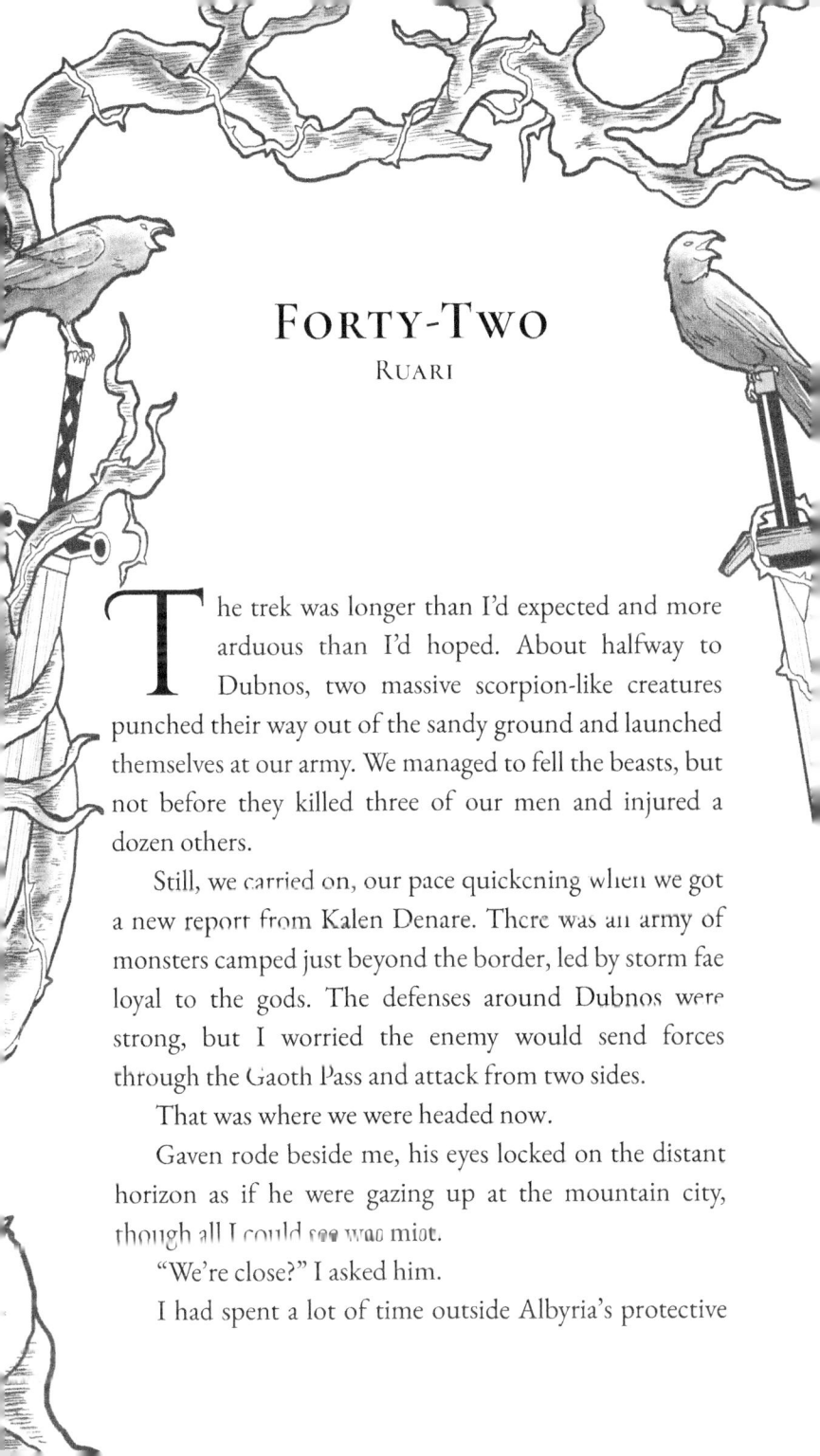

The trek was longer than I'd expected and more arduous than I'd hoped. About halfway to Dubnos, two massive scorpion-like creatures punched their way out of the sandy ground and launched themselves at our army. We managed to fell the beasts, but not before they killed three of our men and injured a dozen others.

Still, we carried on, our pace quickening when we got a new report from Kalen Denare. There was an army of monsters camped just beyond the border, led by storm fae loyal to the gods. The defenses around Dubnos were strong, but I worried the enemy would send forces through the Gaoth Pass and attack from two sides.

That was where we were headed now.

Gaven rode beside me, his eyes locked on the distant horizon as if he were gazing up at the mountain city, though all I could see was mist.

"We're close?" I asked him.

I had spent a lot of time outside Albyria's protective

barrier, secretly meeting with the mortals across the sea and storing all those supplies in my hidden cave. But I'd never ventured farther than the beach where the sun carried on, rising and falling, unlike everywhere else in the Kingdoms of Light and Shadow. Sometimes, I had sat on that beach, just me and the waves and the fish that nibbled my toes. I would watch the blue sky bleed into pink and orange and red, slowly turning inky as the stars appeared. I could have sworn a handful of times a whisper had drifted to me on the wind, a whisper from those brilliant stars.

Do not abandon hope.

I did have hope. I had hope that everything I'd done would help turn the tide when it mattered, I had hope that the mortal king was right, that as long as we followed the path the Druids had seen in their visions, we would be able to fight this.

We'd be able to win.

But despite the sunrises, the sunsets, and all the meetings and planning I'd been involved in, I'd never ventured further north. I'd never even seen Endir, much less Dubnos or the path that cut through the mountains, leading east to the Kingdom of Storms.

Which, according to Kalen Denare, was also now coated in mist.

Gaven slowed his horse as the vague shape of a mountain came into sight through the mists. "The Gaoth Pass is just around there."

The mournful wails of a war horn fell upon us. Gaven jerked on his reins, spinning in his saddle toward the sound. A moment later, a raven raced by and screeched out a warning. The muscles around Gaven's eyes tightened.

"What's wrong?" I asked. "That's to be expected, right? We knew the enemy would attack the city. They've planned for this."

"That was Boudica, Kalen's familiar. She never sounds that distressed, and something feels off," Gaven muttered, shielding his eyes as if to gaze into the sun itself. But then he shook his head and swore. "I'm taking a score of men up the mountain path to Dubnos. They might need reinforcements if the beasts have climbed the wall."

It was all I could do not to gape at him. "That will take hours, at best. And what about the Gaoth Pass?"

"I'll only take a score," he said. "You can take the rest of our warriors to the pass. And fight like the sun, Ruari."

I nodded grimly. "You can count on me. I swear it."

"I know." Gaven leapt off his horse and gathered other fae to join him on his trek up the mountain. And then I turned to the rest of the waiting army who would stay behind with me. They all looked at me expectantly, even the fae of Endir. The mortals of Talaven had not warned me about this fight, either. It seemed they'd kept a lot from me. Or they did not have any idea these events would come to pass.

For the first time in my life, my fate was blurry to me. A thrill went through me as I raised my voice to address the army. "Ready yourselves. It's time to fight. For Aesir!"

Their echoing cheer drowned out the thunder of my pounding heart.

Forty-Three
Kalen

I walked the battlements with Toryn by my side, watching the fae of Dubnos prepare for the worst battle they might ever endure. During the long years of my life, the city itself had only ever been attacked a handful of times, and it had never been anything we couldn't handle. We'd faced the storm fae, of course—just once or twice—when Toryn had first come to us. Then there had been an attack by a small band of light fae while I'd been out fighting Oberon near Itchen during our war. At the time, he'd believed I'd left my home city unprotected, too focused on destroying him.

He'd been wrong. And he had never reached Dubnos himself.

Pookas had never attacked us, not once in four hundred years. They'd been content with waiting for the solo traveler to wander too far out into the mists. That would change soon enough.

"Which god do you think is with them?" Toryn said,

referring to the strange collection of beasts that were coming for us. "Sirius?"

"It's likely Sirius. He is the God of Beasts, after all."

Now we truly understood what that meant. The pookas, the wraiths, and whatever these new scorpion-like creatures were, they came from the gods. We'd guessed it before, but this was confirmation.

Toryn sighed and palmed the stone wall, pausing our walk to gaze down at the shrouded war camp far below us. The mists were too thick now for us to see anything at all. "Perhaps it's all four of them."

My silence was the only confirmation he needed that I'd been wondering the same. We had no reason to suspect anything but the worst. Of course, the gods had wings. They could have flown after Tessa and me, if they'd wanted to. Perhaps they just wanted to lull us into a false sense of security before they attacked.

"I've been thinking," Toryn said, his eyes still locked on the mists below. "We've seen no sign of Andromeda. She wasn't in that cave beneath Gailfean. Only the four were. Where is she?"

"I wish I knew," I said bitterly. "She could be anywhere. The mortal kingdoms...or somewhere else in Aesir. She could even be in Teine or Albyria."

It was a troubling thought. If she was on the southern side of Aesir, she might be able to wipe out Ruari and his army before he could join us here. Then she would set her sights on Endir...I shook my head. I couldn't think like that. If Endir was in danger, Gaven would have notified me by now.

"True, but..." Toryn turned to me with a sharp glint

in his eyes. "She likely isn't with the others, right? I think that means the four gods aren't at their full power yet." When I frowned, Toryn held up a hand and continued. "Think about it. We faced Sirius in Gailfean. He was incredibly strong but not as powerful as we've been led to believe all these years. Nellie took him out so easily. And then there's the question of their wings. They're not using them, as far as we can tell. If they had their full power, why would they need beasts and storm fae to attack us? They wouldn't. Unless all the stories about them are wrong, their powers are at a low level."

"Hmm." I nodded. "And you think they need Andromeda with them to be at full strength."

"She's their leader. She was kept separately from them all these thousands of years, hidden in an onyx gemstone instead of in that cave. It has to mean something."

"You may be right." I braced my forearms on the stone ledge and leaned out into the mists. "Unfortunately, I'm not sure it does us much good. Unless we find her and stop her—and we don't know how to do that yet—she will reunite with the others eventually. Any issue with their power will be resolved then."

"I know." He joined me, leaning against the stone wall. He was the only real brother I'd ever truly known, other than Alastair. I was glad he was here beside me, at the end of everything. "But it might be enough for now, for this battle. We can save Dubnos today. And then we'll take on tomorrow as it comes."

I clasped his shoulder. "You're right. We will. I just wish Niamh were here, and Alastair. It doesn't feel right, fighting for this city without them."

"Me, too, Kal. Me, too. But we will see them soon."

After doing the rounds along the battlements where the archers readied themselves, I swung by my quarters, where Tessa was still sleeping like the dead. As soon as we'd reached Dubnos, she'd slumped over as if the full intensity of her actions had finally hit her. Quietly, I took the chair beside the bed and touched her cheek. She was warm. That was a good sign.

The first time I'd used my powers—*really* used them—I'd been wrecked for hours. My body had shut down, so taxed from the onslaught of all that magic rushing through me. No wonder she was exhausted. She likely hurt, too.

Her eyes cracked open. When she saw me sitting there, she smiled. "We made it back."

"Yes, we did. You were amazing."

Her smile dropped, and storm clouds swirled through her eyes. "How long have I been asleep? We need to get ready for the battle."

"We're getting ready. You don't need to worry about any of that. Sleep as long as you need."

She shook her head, and then she was on her feet before I could argue. "What's the plan?"

I frowned as she moved to the basin and splashed fresh water on her face. "The archers are on the wall, ready to loose a storm of arrows on the enemy if they try to scale the mountain. As for the rest...I was just on my way to meet with the others and make our final preparations. I wanted to check on you. You really should get back into bed and rest."

She turned to me with fire in her eyes. "I should help."

"You *have* helped, love. If you hadn't gone with me to scout, I'm not sure I would have returned. Now the city knows what's coming for them. You've done enough."

"That's not nearly enough, not with all those creatures out there. Not when you might have to fight a god. Your power isn't working, but *mine* is. I should be out there with you. I should fight."

My heart beat painfully. Always so brave. "And Nellie? Her powers work, too."

Her eyes narrowed. "I see what you're trying to do. If I don't think Nellie should be out there fighting, despite being one of the only people in the world who can harm a god, then I shouldn't be out there, either. Right?"

"Something like that."

"No. That's different."

"How?"

"Nellie has never fought in a battle. She grew up in Teine, protected by a magical wall. Oberon never laid a hand on her. I didn't let him. The worst thing that's ever happened to her was being locked up in a dungeon cell, but even then, she was safe."

I nodded and stood. "That's exactly my point. What you just did out there was impressive, but that wasn't a battle. True war is incomprehensible. It's bloody and violent. There's so much pain, so many screaming voices, so much fear, it reaches into your soul. And the smell, the horror of it...Tessa, you should not have to see this."

She swallowed, stepped up before me, and grasped my hand. Her fingers were still gloved, even now. "*No one should have to see this. But it is our fate now, and I will not turn away from it to spare myself pain. Not when I could make a difference. Not when this city might end up needing me. I know I have little experience with fighting, but I do have a dangerous power in my veins. It's one I hate, but it might be the only thing that can stop Sirius if he comes for us."

I closed my eyes, my heart tearing in half. All I wanted was to keep my wife safe. But she was Tessa Baran. She would never be satisfied hiding inside while the rest of us fought for our lives. I knew that because neither would I.

"I fight beside you, always." She palmed my chest.

With a shaky breath, I nodded. "May the realm never break."

The energy in the war room was muted. Fenella and Toryn stood on one side of the table, while the captain of the guard, Roisin, stood on the other side, flanked by Caedmon and Fenella's other cousin, Brigid. Caedmon had filled them both in on everything that had happened so far, so they understood exactly what we faced.

Druid Balfor stood quietly in the corner with a

pinched brow and terror in his eyes. I'd heard he'd been praying to the stars day and night since our return to Dubnos. It did not seem they were listening to him.

"Any word from my sister?" Roisin asked, her brow furrowed beneath her short black hair. Like her sister, Niamh, her muscular frame suited the armor she swore. "It's been weeks. She should be in Talaven by now."

I glanced at Toryn, who shook his head. "I'm afraid not."

"So Niamh might be dead," Roisin said softly, her hands tensing around the edge of the war table and her violet eyes glistening with unshed tears.

"They're not dead," Tessa said.

Roisin cut her eyes toward Tessa, fury in the tense lines that bracketed her mouth.

"If Val were dead," Tessa continued, "I would know it."

"You don't know a damn thing."

My shoulders tensed.

"Roisin," Brigid murmured before sweeping her silver hair over her shoulder. "I'm sure Tessa is right. Maybe they lost their communication stones, or maybe they don't work from so far away. I'm sure Niamh is fine, and she'll come riding in here any day now with news that can turn the tide."

Roisin scowled but said no more. The captain of the guard had always been fiercely devoted to her sister, sometimes to her own detriment. She was barely one hundred years of age, and they'd lost their parents not soon after her birth. It seemed to me she almost saw Niamh as her mother, not her sister, though she'd never admit to it.

"War is coming." I moved to the table and motioned at the section devoted to Dubnos and the border between my realm and the Kingdom of Storms. "The enemy could attack at any moment. We need to make our final preparations and ensure there is no way they can breach these walls. Most of the citizens of this city are not fighters. They will not survive if the beasts swarm this place."

Roisin dropped her scowl and immediately got to business. It was one of the things I'd always appreciated about her. She could be argumentative and tense a lot of the time, but when it came to the safety of our people, her determination was unmatched.

She pointed at the mountain wall that our city perched upon. "They have a long way to climb if they want to reach us. We have several hundred archers, a small cache burning oil, and nets of rock, so we should be able to pick them off before they get to the top."

Toryn moved some miniature swords to join the bows. "Some will still likely make it over the wall, but we have plenty of warriors who can engage in close combat."

I tapped a finger against the Gaoth Pass. "Just because they can scale the chasm doesn't mean that's what they'll do. We need to have soldiers ready here just in case they cross the pass and approach Dubnos from this side."

"Already there." Fenella moved some swords to the pass. "I sent them down the mountain path to meet up with Ruari and his fighters."

I gave them all an appreciative nod for making those moves without me having asked. We'd known each other for a long time and had faced endless danger side by side.

This wasn't our first dance with death, nor would it be our last if we survived.

"There's only two—well, three—things left to worry about," Roisin said, tapping the small section at the base of the mountain, the only weakness in our defense. "What if they find that gate into our sewers? They're beasts. I doubt they'd mind wading through filth if it meant they could breach the city."

"The storm fae have never discovered it in hundreds of years." I paused. "Still, you might be right. Things are different now. We should have a few warriors stand watch near the gate and then give us a signal if the beasts try to break it down."

Out of the corner of my eye, I spotted Druid Balfor pinching the bridge of his nose. "I do have something that might help. But please promise me, Your Majesty, that you will not get angry with me."

I narrowed my gaze in his direction. "What is it, Balfor?"

"I do have a small stash of valerian that could be used as a fog to sedate any beast that tries to breach the sewer gate, if it comes to that. It's not enough to stop this entire army, mind you, but it could provide a brief respite from an attack, just long enough to patch up the breach."

My hands dropped heavily to my sides. "I asked you for valerian before. You said you didn't have enough."

He winced. "Enough to take out an army? No. But it might be enough for this."

"There weren't that many storm fae when I asked you before," I said, my voice rising. "You forced me to use my power against them when we had an alternative all this damn time?"

"I am so sorry, Your Majesty," Balfor whispered, and then his lip began to tremble. "I do not believe in war."

"And yet war has come for you all the same."

Toryn cleared his throat to steer the conversation back to the task at hand. "We still need someone to stand watch and set off the valerian if the beasts find the sewers. And that's a—"

"I'll do it," Caedmon said, lifting his eyes from the table. "I was in Gailfean with you. I know what's at stake. I'll do it."

Beside him, Brigid nodded. "I'll go with you."

"You're certain of this?" I had to ask. "You understand the risks?"

"Far better than most," Caedmon answered with a tight smile.

With a nod, I moved another sword piece into place. "And so our plan is set. This will be a tough battle, but we might just have a chance of fighting off this army of beasts."

"Unfortunately, I think you're forgetting something important, Kal," Roisin said with a tense grimace. "What if the storm fae use elite powers against us? Or worse... what about the gods? Are they coming? How will we beat them?"

I exchanged a quick glance with Tessa. This was her domain, and she thought she could help, but the truth was, neither of us knew how she could use her powers against them. For now, we just hoped it wouldn't come to that.

"The storm fae will not be able to scale the walls, so we will focus on the beasts first," was the only thing I knew to say. "Now go to our people and pass out the onyx gemstones from Queen Tatiana. Get everyone inside somewhere. Anyone who wishes to wait it out in the castle may do so, including all our storm fae refugees. And tell them not to leave until they hear the ringing of the temple bell. That will be the signal that the battle has ended and it is safe for them to come out. We will fight for them with everything we've got. That's all we can do."

FORTY-FOUR
TESSA

My blood roared in my ears as I perched on the stone ledge of the battlements with my wings flared wide behind me. *My wings.* I still wasn't used to thinking of them like that, and every time they so much as twitched, a strange sense of *déjà vu* rushed through me, like something fundamental in the fabric of my reality had changed—something I should have understood but didn't. The seamstresses had taken my fighting leathers and stitched them back together, but they'd left two holes for my wings, just in case I wanted to use them in the fight.

"Should I do a sweep and see if I can spot where they are?" I asked Kalen, who had been brooding for the past hour while we stood watch.

"I just sent Boudica," he said quietly. "She's far less conspicuous."

"I could check the Caoth Pass."

"I want you by my side." He held my hand and kissed me with furious intent. When he pulled back, he took my face in his strong hands, and the look in his eye, something deep and fierce, made my breath catch. "Whatever happens today, I want you to know I love you. I love your grit and your stubbornness and your unwillingness to back down from a fight. I love the fierce love you have for your sister and how you would rip apart the world to keep her safe. I love the way you look at me, the way you taste and feel, and that glorious, defiant spark in your eye. I love everything about you, Tessa Baran. I will love you even after this battle, whether we're alive or our souls have been written into the stars."

My heart thundered as I gazed up at him, scarcely daring to believe it. They were the words I'd longed to hear. He loved me.

And I loved him so much, it was like a deep ache in my soul.

"Kalen," I breathed with tears in my eyes. "You're acting like you don't think we'll make it out of this alive."

His hands tightened on me. "We might not. And I needed you to know this before it all ends."

A tear slipped down my cheek, a hot trail against my cool skin. "I love you, too. More than I ever thought it possible to love anyone."

I climbed off the battlement and wound my arms around his waist, pressing my face against his chest. My wings draped awkwardly behind me, but he didn't seem to notice or care. He just held me like that until the knots in my shoulders loosened and the frantic pattering of my heart eased.

And then Boudica swooped in with a sharp caw.

Kalen pulled back as the raven settled on his extended

arm. He gazed into her eyes, and his expression soured. After a moment, he nodded and then straightened his crown. Darkness clouded his eyes.

"It has begun. The first squad of beasts are on their way."

Even though I'd expected them to attack at any moment, I gasped. "Where?"

"They're scaling the mountain. Twenty of them for now. It's time to sound the alarm." He gave his familiar a fond smile. "To the Gaoth Pass now to check this isn't some kind of distraction from the real threat. And then you can rest. Be safe."

Boudica launched into the sky before vanishing into the darkness.

Kalen leaned over the battlements. He pulled a deep breath into his lungs and focused on the wall that stretched down into the mist. Through the bond, I could somehow *feel* him reaching for his power. I knew what he was trying to do—stop the beasts before they reached us. But nothing happened. His power would not respond to him, even now.

Without another word, Kalen vanished into the turret just behind us. His boots thudded against the stone stairs, and a moment later, the low, eerie sound of a war horn echoed through the silent city. Several cries of alarm soon followed, and footsteps thundered as warriors and archers took up their assigned positions along the wall. They were all clad in black fighting leathers with a familiar sigil stamped into the center of their chests—the mask topped with a spiky crown.

I gripped the stone and leaned out into the mist, but I

could only see a few feet below us. How close were they? How soon would they come into view? And would we see them in time for the archers to loose their arrows? Our entire strategy relied on preventing the creatures from getting over this wall, but we would not be able to stop them if we could not see them.

I glanced over my shoulder. Kalen now stood at the base of the turret, exchanging words with the captain of the guard. Roisin pointed a trembling finger at the thickening mist, all her bravado gone. There was a gray sheen to her complexion. She looked like she was two seconds away from vomiting on the stones.

"The mists are too thick for us to see them coming." Her words drifted to me. "They'll swarm us before we can stop them."

"What about the oil?" I asked, moving to join them. "If you light the ropes now, it might give the archers enough time to loose a few rounds of arrows."

Roisin frowned. "But if we light them too soon, we'll waste all our oil, and then what? We'll be in darkness once again."

"I'll call Boudica back," Kalen said. "She can alert us when they're near."

"She needs to scout the Gaoth Pass." I held out a hand, motioning at the war horn he still held. "I'll do it. I'll sound the alarm as soon as they're close enough, and then you can send down the flaming oil. And some of those rocks while you're at it."

"I don't like it," Kalen ground out. "One of the beasts could see you and try to take you down. The oil could hit you. The—"

"Kalen. I can help."

He scowled at me, but he handed over the horn. It was heavier than it looked. As long as my forearm, it had been crafted from some kind of animal's horn. It had been sanded, polished, and painted a deep red that resembled dried blood. It hung from a leather strap that I swung over my head before tucking the horn into the front of my tunic.

"Be careful," Kalen murmured.

"I will." I forced a brave smile and stepped back. "Remember, I don't want to die. And I certainly don't want this to be the last time I ever see you. I'll be careful, and I'll be back before the shadowfiends even know I'm there."

His sapphire eyes flared. I knew he hated the idea of putting me close to danger, but I'd noticed in these past weeks that he never truly tried to stop me. He might voice his displeasure, but he didn't hold me back. And he never told me I wasn't strong enough to do it, either. Instead, I could see the slight lift in his chin and a glint of pride in his eyes.

With a deep breath, I took another step back, and my wings brushed the stone wall. "Be ready."

And with that, I turned, hopped onto the ledge, and leapt into the darkness. My wings caught the mist as I fell, spreading wide on either side of me. Pain flickered through my back, but it was a much duller version of the blinding rip I'd felt before. Steadying my rapid breathing, I swooped out from the wall and then circled back. Carefully, I slowed, aware that the wall—now invisible to me—was closing in fast.

The war horn thumped against my chest when I came to a sudden stop just inches from the wall. I swore beneath my breath and shoved my boot against it to put some distance between the stone and me. That had been too close. The mists were so thick now, the condensation stuck to my skin.

Glancing below me, I could see my scuffed leather boots and nothing more. This was bad. Even with the help of the burning oil, the archers above might not be able to see the creatures racing up toward them. Was this Sirius's doing? If darkness had fallen on the storm fae lands as soon as the gods had awakened, surely that meant they could control the mists, too. The mists and the beasts, plague and hunger. Even fear and death. They controlled so much and we so little.

I had to do what I could to help.

Bracing myself, I dropped a foot lower, gritting my teeth at the sharp tug of my wings against my back. Even though I'd soared through the skies once before, maneuvers like this were still foreign to me. And still, I lurched ever downward, inch by inch, closer to where I thought the reach of the arrows might end.

I hovered there, idly flapping my wings and searching for any sight of the beasts in the dark.

For a long time, nothing happened, and the muscles in my lower back strained from the repeated movement of my wings against the thick air. It was the only sound in the silence. Even the battlements above were still, so quiet I could have sworn they had been abandoned if I did not know Kalen would never leave his city unprotected.

And then a sound rose from the ground far below—

the click of claws against stone. My eyes burned as a swell of emotion rose within me. This was it. There was no turning back now. From this moment on, everything would change.

The clicking grew closer, louder, and the huff of heavy breathing joined the chorus. Still, I waited, my hands itching to bring the horn to my mouth. But I held off to time it just right. If I moved too soon, the archers' arrows would not hit their marks.

There was a rustling below me. Gently beating my wings, I edged back from the wall just as a mound of fur scuttled past me. It didn't give me any notice, even though I was only a few inches behind it. The beasts had no idea I was here. Yet.

With a trembling hand, I lifted the horn to my lips and blew with all my might. The sound was like a mournful wail, a shout of pain that echoed through the mountains. The beasts on the wall froze, but I shot away before they could turn their heads in my direction. A brutal wind slammed down on me, but I battled against it, pushing away as fast as I could.

And as I shoved against that wicked wind, thick with the stench of death and rot and pain, the beasts on the wall screamed as arrows rained down from the Kingdom of Shadow.

FORTY-FIVE
TESSA

Staying away from the wall to avoid the storm of arrows, I soared back to the city above. The burning oil lit the darkness, an eerie orange hue that cut through the mists. Kalen was pacing along the battlements, his jaw tense. When he spotted me, relief crossed his face.

I landed on the battlement, away from the archers. He rushed over and scooped me into his arms. I pressed my face into the crook of his neck, smiling.

"I was gone for ten minutes. At most," I murmured to him, relishing in the scent of his mist-scented skin.

He lowered me to the ground, wrapped his hand around the back of my neck, and kissed me fiercely. "One moment, knowing you might be in danger, is torture." His eyes hardened at the growing roar of the beasts that were scaling the mountain, and he turned toward the archers as they sent another round of arrows. "Stay with me. The fight will be upon us soon."

And so we waited. Toryn stood on Kalen's other side,

holding tightly to his spear. Fenella took up residence beside me with her two daggers, while I'd opted for that heavy sword. I'd had little time to train in the past weeks, but the weapon felt solid and comforting in my hands. Better this than anything else.

Better this than the death I carried in my hands.

Kalen had his own sword at the ready. And as a light wind pushed the mists away from his face, just for a moment, I drank him in. He looked like an agent of death himself, even with his power as muted as it was. Strength and terror pulsed from his body, beating with the rhythm of his heart.

And then a claw curled around the wall. A shadowfiend's glinting fangs appeared a moment later, just in front of an archer. The fae lifted his bow to shoot the creature, but its jaws clamped down on his body before he could release the arrow. The crunch of bone and the spray of blood felt like the slice of a sword through my heart. I flinched, gritting my teeth, but I forced myself to keep my focus on that creature. I would not look away.

Several of the archers screamed and stumbled back.

The beast moved to swipe at the nearest, but Kalen was in motion before those wicked claws could make contact. He was a whirlwind of shadow and speed. Even without access to his elite fae powers, he still had his strength and his skill with the blade. He swept his sword at the beast's neck and cut its head clean off. The severed head fell and vanished in the mist.

Thick crimson blood dripped off his blade as he turned to me. A slight smile lifted the corners of his lips, and I couldn't help but smile right back. Something stirred in my heart. For so long, for centuries, Kalen had hated what he was and what he could do, but there was nothing of that in his face now. No regret, no shame. Nothing but the understanding that his people needed him, and he would gladly fight for them.

Kalen turned as another beast hauled itself over the wall.

"Fall back!" he shouted to the archers when three more shadowfiends leapt onto the battlements. The archers scrambled away. And then he sprang into action, cutting through flesh and fur like a whirlwind of death. The mists swirled and parted around him, as if responding to his frenzied attack.

Fenella and Toryn stood on either side of me, waiting. The moment he started flagging, or too many beasts entered the fray, we would join the fight.

"The mists still move with him," I murmured to Toryn. "Do you think that means his power—the one that flattens anything in his path—is back?"

"I don't know," Toryn said, "but he would never use it in close combat like this. It could take out this entire wall."

On my other side, Fenella let out a hiss. I turned to see blood bubbling on her arm where she'd dug her own blade into her skin. Droplets splashed onto the stone. After a moment, she pulled a scrap of cloth from her pocket and wound it around her arm.

"I'm not healing," she said, her face paling. "Whatever is muting our powers, it's still out there, and it's worse than before. I was able to heal back in Gailfean."

Dread pumped through my veins, and several more

shadowfiends leapt over the wall. Their claws crashed into the stone, and chunks of crenel broke free, tumbling down the side of the mountain.

"To arms!" Toryn shouted as he raised his spear and dove into the fray.

Heart in my throat, I gripped my sword and rushed forward, Fenella by my side. A shadowfiend landed before us. Its fangs dripped with venomous drool. It turned toward Fenella first, and its claws clicked against the stone.

Fenella roared and slashed her daggers at the beast's throat, but it dodged to the side. I swung my sword at its back, but somehow, it sensed my presence and flicked out its tail. It slammed into my side, knocking me off my feet. Pain radiated through my backside when it collided against the stone.

I blinked away the pain and climbed to my feet just as the beast swung a claw at Fenella. She ducked low, and then danced out of the way before whirling toward the creature. Her blades flashed in the darkness. The creature backed up, swishing its tail at me once more, but I saw it coming this time. I slammed my blade down on its tail, cutting through flesh and fur.

The tail came clean off. A spray of blood coated my arms as the roar of the beast shook the stones. I swallowed down the nausea shoving up my throat as the beast whirled to me and screamed into my face. Its hot breath blew my braid over my shoulder, and the scent of that rot and the roiling death washed over me.

Heart pounding a frantic rhythm, I angled my sword and pointed the sharp tip at the beast's bulbous red eye. It took a step back. Fenella roared from behind it and drove both her daggers into its flank. The beast screamed, whipping toward her, its jaws widening. Through the sweat and blood, and maybe even fear, Fenella's hands slipped from the hilts, and she lost her daggers in the beast's flesh.

The shadowfiend whirled on her, snapping its fangs. The fear on her face shook through me.

Without even thinking, I leapt into the air. My wings sprouted from my back, and I drove my blade into the beast's neck.

Blood sprayed into my face. The beast stilled, and then its body dropped heavily on the stone battlement, shaking the wall. I landed in a crouch beside Fenella, tucked my wings away, and smiled. "See? Swords can be useful sometimes."

She barked out a laugh, but I could tell by the paleness of her face and the sheen of sweat on her brow that she was more shaken than she wanted to let on. I knew the feeling.

Another scream sounded behind me. My heart in my throat, I whirled on my feet to face the newest threat. But it was only the sound of another beast dying, this one to the brutality of Toryn's spear. Its tip shot right through the shadowfiend's eye and buried itself in its skull. The light in its eyes died a second later.

I braced myself, ready for the next group to claw their way over the mountain wall.

Fenella collected her daggers from the fallen beast's fur and came to stand beside me. We both gazed into the mists, our bodies tense, our weapons raised. Silence and stillness was our only answer.

Kalen frowned and motioned the archers forward before looking over the damaged crenels. They rushed to his side and threw some more lit oil down into the darkness. Something tightened in my chest as the minutes passed. Were more coming? Surely it couldn't have been as easy as that.

"How many was that?" Kalen called up to the fae still stationed in the watchtower.

The fae leaned against the wooden railing, his pale hair falling across his sharp cheekbones, and called back, "I counted twenty."

Twenty? Was that it? Somehow, that felt both far too few and far too many at once. But twenty, plus those taken out by the archers...how many shadowfiends had we seen in that camp? It was far more than we'd faced so far. Perhaps the enemy had realized they couldn't breach this city by sending monsters up the wall. And so they were holding the rest back.

As if our thoughts were in sync, Kalen spoke to the warriors gathered around him. "Haul the dead beasts over the wall. Send them back where they came from. Let's send a message to our enemies."

The warriors of Dubnos cheered. A breeze picked up their exuberant cries and spread them through the streets behind us. And then we got to work. Fenella and I dragged the beast we'd felled over to the wall and tossed it into the shadows. It vanished into a tumbling ball of fur and bloodied flesh, along with the others Kalen and Toryn had killed.

It did not take us long to clear the battlements, though remnants of the fight stained the stone. The beasts had taken out a handful of our archers. Several warriors collected them and carried them away while Druid Balfor looked on, his brow pinched. He followed them down the stone steps leading into the courtyard below and toward the Temple. Eventually, they'd be laid to rest in the catacombs beneath the city.

Silence descended once more. I watched as Kalen paced beside the crumbled bit of wall where the shadowfiends had launched their attack. He clearly didn't think this was over. Neither did I.

Fenella clasped my shoulder. "Nice fighting."

I gave her a smile. High praise, coming from her. "You, too."

"I owe you one. Again."

"Fenella, you don't have to—"

Her hand gripped my shoulder tighter. "My cousin is wrong about you. It doesn't matter if you're mortal or if you have a god's blood running through your veins. You will make an excellent queen, and I will gladly serve you."

I opened my mouth, trying to find the right words to say, but she turned away and started wiping off her bloody daggers. Conversation over. And so I smiled and drifted over to Kalen.

He slowed his pacing when I approached, but the tension in his face remained. "It won't have been this easy."

"I agree. I could fly down there again. See what the enemy is doing now."

"They might expect that now, since you already did it once. I won't risk you like that."

"Fair point. But there must be something—"

"Your Majesty!" one of the archers shouted. We turned toward the fae woman who was pointing down into the mist. "More beasts are coming!"

Kalen sprang into action. "Tessa, return to Fenella and Toryn's line. Archers, let's try something new. Light your arrows with the flaming oil and get ready."

Archers rushed into formation and lit their arrows on fire.

The creak of bows being pulled taut echoed through the silence, loud even over the thud of my boots. I slid in beside Fenella just as the burning arrows flew, carrying with them a storm of blazing death. From down the wall, beasts screamed as the arrows hit their marks. Flames flashed through the night, lighting up the mist.

For a moment, the sky was lit with orange. And then the light died, tumbling down the mountain and into the dark.

Moments passed in tense silence as we waited for the next assault. The anticipation was like a hammer against my skull, pounding in time with my frantic heartbeat. And I realized that was the point. This was the enemy's strategy. By now, we'd used up most of our oil. We had no way to anticipate when they'd make their next move. It could be at any time. They wanted to put us on edge—wanted to make us sweat.

A sound cut through the silence—*tap, tap, tap*. It was so loud, like a thousand fists were banging on a door.

"They're coming again!" the fae in the watchtower roared.

I gripped my sword and gritted my teeth. They were

indeed coming, and by the sound of them, there were far more this time.

"Nock!" Kalen shouted to the archers. Bows creaked, nearly drowned out by the roar approaching from below. "Loose!"

The arrows whistled into the mist, then thunked into flesh. Screams answered, but it wasn't enough. Not nearly enough. Dozens of the beasts burst through and landed on top of the wall. Their angry red eyes swept across the gathered fae, and then they charged.

Kalen began his dance of death. He swirled through the mist, his sword slicing one beast and then the next. But this time, there were far too many for him to take on his own. Gripping my hilt, I raced forward with Fenella and Toryn flanking me.

We joined the fray just as two shadowfiends landed on the battlements and tossed several archers into the mists. They screamed as they fell, the sound filling my heart with horror and fear.

And *anger*. That vicious, righteous, god-given anger churned through my veins like venom, urging me onward —urging me to rip these beasts apart. I shouted in rage as the nearest one went for Fenella. My blade cut through his throat before he could even get close.

Red stained my vision, not just from the blood now pouring onto the stones but from that vicious hate bleeding through me. Fenella and Toryn twisted toward another beast. They attacked it together while I faced another stalking toward me.

I bent my knees and readied myself for the attack,

narrowing my eyes and shooting the creature a wicked smile.

And that was when I heard it. The shouts and screams and terrified cries. Cries that were not coming from the battlements or the mountain wall.

They were coming from the city streets.

Forty-Six
Tessa

I cut down the beast as it lunged for me. I shoved my sword through its eye and into its skull, copying what I'd seen Toryn do with his spear. As soon as it was down, I ran to the edge of the wall—*away* from the attack—to gaze down on the courtyard and the city that spilled across the mountaintop beyond it.

A breeze pushed against the mists, as if the sky itself had sighed, and revealed the streets. My hand flew to my lips as I saw three glassy-eyed storm fae leading a band of shadowfiends out of the courtyard and into the city, where residents were fleeing.

Another group of enemies was heading right our way, no doubt to sneak up on us from behind.

My heart dropped when one of those shadowfiends pounced upon a man running toward the open door of an inn. Those massive teeth sliced through his neck, killing him instantly.

In the distance, the Temple bell began to peal. A signal to the city—the signal it was safe.

"No," I choked out, horror roiling through me. If the unarmed residents heard that sound, they might not realize what currently stalked through the streets, ready to cut them down if they left the safety of their homes. They might not hear the fighting along the battlement walls—some of the homes were far enough away...

I lifted the horn to my lips and blew.

But the bell still pealed, a clamorous sound. Would they be able to hear the war horn over it? Some of them undoubtably would. The horn had been built to carry sound far, but...some might not hear it. Some would trust the bell.

I cast a glance over my shoulder at the battle raging along the top of the wall. Kalen was deep in the fight, up against five shadowfiends at once. I couldn't distract him, not right now. If he shifted his attention, even for a second, he could be dead. Toryn was engaged with three others. I turned to Fenella. She was already running to my side.

I spread my wings and leapt onto the ledge before sheathing my sword on my back. I called out to her, "The storm fae are inside the city. Tell the others."

Her face blanched. "What are you going to do?"

I set my sights on the Temple's tower, halfway across the city. "I'm going to stop that bell."

"Fuck!" Fenella shouted when she saw a door on one of the nearby streets swing open. A few fae stumbled outside. A moment later, a shadowfiend was upon them.

Gritting my teeth, I soared over the rooftops, my eyes set on the tower. How had the storm fae gotten inside?

Who in the name of light would ring that bell? Was it a storm fae?

My stomach twisted as I flew closer.

Was it one of the gods?

I got my answer a moment later when I flew through the arched tower wall and landed in a crouch next to a cloaked figure whose face was hidden in shadows. Still, I recognized the burst of silver hair shot through with red. I'd only ever met one person with hair like that—one person I never would have expected to turn on us like this.

"Caedmon," I said quietly, rising behind him and folding my wings into my back so I could draw my sword.

He stiffened and let go of the bell's rope. With the sound as loud as it was, he hadn't heard me approach. Several more clangs followed as he turned to face me, pushing back his hood. His eyes flashed with defiance.

"I thought you might be the one to come for me." His lips flattened. "But it's too late, Tessa. The shadow fae are already leaving their homes."

"Why?" I asked, my palms slick around the hilt of my sword. "Why would you do this? To your own city? Your own people?"

He shook his head, his eyes a bit wild. "You don't understand, do you? You're all going to die. *We* are all going to die unless we join them. Because Kalen Denare has proven he does not have what it takes to win."

My heart pounded. "You opened the sewer gates for them. That's why you volunteered to guard it. Where is Brigid? Is she alive?"

"I am sorry," he said softly. "I wish it didn't have to

happen like this, but this is the only choice we have. Come with us, Tessa. You have a place by Andromeda's side. That's what Sirius said."

"I would rather die than join her."

I raised my sword, readying myself for a fight. Now that I'd turned him down, he would strike me with whatever weapon he had hidden beneath the folds of that cloak. He was a good fighter—one of the best I'd ever seen.

He had helped Nellie, shown her kindness even when she'd started shifting into a creature that would make many others turn away from her. He'd sat with me on the long journey, listening to my tales and sharing his. And he had helped the storm fae of Gailfean when all had seemed lost.

Tears burned my eyes, and that vicious, burning anger raced through me once more. Not at him—never at him. It was toward those fucking gods.

He smiled when I started advancing on him, the tower's rough stones scraping against my boots. "Your choice then. I'm sure I'll see you soon enough."

And then he leapt backward onto the ledge and vanished through the archway.

I sucked in a sharp breath and raced after him. Stumbling to a stop along the edge of the tower, I stared down at where Caedmon had fallen onto the back of one of the scorpion creatures. A roar filled my head as he slid down its tail and landed in the courtyard.

He tipped back his head and gave me a salute. And then he was off, racing to join the carnage in the streets.

I lifted my gaze. The bell had stopped ringing, but he

was right. The damage was already done. Some of the residents of this mountain city had trusted that sound. They'd left their homes, and now their bloodied bodies littered the square. The creature turned away, its talons clinking against the stone, and then it moved toward the wall where Kalen and the others still fought against the swarm of shadowfiends. The storm fae were kicking open doors and pushing inside the homes of those who hadn't taken the bait, and the stench of death and blood was so thick, I almost choked.

I took in the destruction, unable to breathe, unable to think, unable to do anything but lean against that arched wall. Some of the shadow fae archers had focused their attention on the enemies in their city streets and were firing shot after shot after shot, but again...it wasn't enough. It was too late.

The damage was done.

The enemy had gotten into the city. They were pouring over the mountain wall now. All our other fighters were stationed in the Gaoth Pass, too far from here to do us any good. We could call for them, but again...

The damage was done.

A choked cry spilled from my lips as my gaze snagged on the castle doors halfway across the city. Another scorpion had been led into the twin courtyard to this one, and it was slamming its massive pincer into the door over and over and over, the sound as loud as thunder.

Several archers trained their sights on the creature, but the arrows just bounced off its form, like they were nothing more than gnats toying with a giant. Half the city was hiding in that castle, along with the storm fae refugees, depending on its fortified walls to keep them safe.

Nellie was in that castle.

I knew she was strong—stronger than I could comprehend. But she was only one person against a storm of enemies waiting to push inside the castle walls as soon as the scorpion knocked down the door.

The mists swirled around me, still pushed by that incessant wind. I could see it all so clearly now. All that blood. All that death. The wicked lightning that crackled from the storm fae's fingertips. We would never win, even if we survived this battle. Sirius had yet to show himself—none of them had. It would only get worse after this. Grief pressed down on me, dampening the fire of my heart and snuffing out the rage that normally fueled me.

Now I just felt numb. Because this city was going to die—this *world* was going to die. And there was nothing I could do to stop it.

Forty-Seven
Ruari

The beasts swarmed us as soon as we reached the infamous Gaoth Pass, where the Kingdom of Shadows bordered the Kingdom of Storms. I'd smelled the rot far before we set our sights on the shadow-fiend army attacking Kalen's warriors. It was a terrifying sight to behold—an entire swarm of them with their vicious fangs and talons piercing through the flesh of centuries-old fae. I held my arm up to my side and motioned my own warriors forward, even as fear clenched my heart.

They raced into the fray while my second held back—my younger brother, Mykon, who had inherited my father's elite fae blood.

His throat bobbed as he surveyed the choked battlefield before us. The Gaoth Pass was a small, winding road that cut through the towering mountains on either side of us. On the right side, the rocky wall rose high. Somewhere beyond it, Dubnos perched on a cliff and looked down on where the storm-filled lands stretched east. On the left side, those mountains were even rockier, even more jagged. Only bandits lived in those dangerous hills, where venomous snakes and shadowfiends were known to prowl.

Mykon held up his hand. "Fire?"

I shook my head. "Fire from here, and we'll burn our own men."

Mykon growled as if answering the power in his blood, as if he needed to feel the heat and magic of it roaming across his skin for a moment. He would not release it, though. Not unless I gave him the signal.

"Stop playing with it." I moved my hand to the hilt of my sword. "Time to join the fight."

"I'm not playing with it," he said in a strange, faraway voice.

I shot him a quick look and noticed he was right—his fingers were free of fire. "Well, come on, then. Just stay near me and don't get yourself killed."

I started toward the battle, but Mykon gripped my arm and pulled me back. His eyes were frantic. "I can't call upon my power. Something is blocking it."

A chill swept through me, but I shook him off. "We'll talk about this later. Our people—"

"Ruari," a low, feminine voice said from behind me.

I tensed. I knew that voice. Dread crept down my spine, but I turned to Mykon and said, "Join the fight. Don't go to the front lines."

Mykon gave me a panicked glance before nodding and backing away from me.

And then I finally faced my mother.

She was wearing the same skin as before—Morgan's.

Her long silver hair now hung in a loose braid over her shoulder, where she'd strapped a fresh set of black fighting leathers over her muscular frame. Her silver eyes swept across me, haunted and strange and achingly familiar. Even like this, even in another stranger's body, I would have recognized her anywhere.

It was hard to imagine how Kalen hadn't. I supposed it had a been a long, long time since he'd seen her. And he did not know what it was like to watch her move from form to form, always changing her appearance but never those eyes. It didn't matter if they were blue or silver or bleeding red. They were always *hers*.

Swallowing, I dropped my hand to the hilt of my sword, still sheathed. "Mother."

She gave me a wicked smile. "My son."

Anger burned through me. At her, for putting me through this. At my father, for starting this whole thing in the first place, for turning her into who she had become. Deep down, I knew I wouldn't exist if he hadn't done it. I never would have breathed in the sun-drenched air and watched the birds flit through the skies, singing their songs of life. I never would have felt the soft kiss of mist on my face. I never would have seen a child smile.

A child, like my brother—*all* my brothers and sisters. They only existed because of this, too.

But still, I hated it.

And most of all, I hated the mortals who had pulled my strings all these years. They'd whispered the secrets of their visions with me, and yet they had not warned me of this.

"You killed the dungeon guard in Endir," I said, my

voice as hard as the steel I carried by my side. "I should have known not to trust you."

"You told Gaven about me when I asked you to keep my existence to yourself." She arched a brow, such a strange expression coming from Morgan's face. It was so familiar and yet so foreign all the same. "Perhaps it's the other way around. I cannot trust you."

I bristled. "Why are you here?"

She took a step closer, her eyes flashing. "Did you think I didn't know what you were up to all this time? Working with those ridiculous mortals and setting aside your little stash inside that cave?"

Heart pounding, I drew my sword, though what I planned to do with it, I still did not know. Because in spite of everything I'd seen and heard and been told, I could not hurt her, nor could I bear to see her bleed from someone else's hand. And she knew it. With a glint in her eye, she kept advancing on me.

"You've been working with the King of Talaven, thinking you could stop the gods' return, but you were wrong. Andromeda is here, and the others have awakened, and there is nothing you can do now to stop them."

I shook my head, refusing to listen to her. These were Andromeda's words, not hers. She wanted me to believe it was hopeless, but it wasn't. It *couldn't* be. We had done everything the visions had told us to do.

But...things were happening the humans had not told me about. At first, I'd assumed King Duncan Hinde was being secretive as always, but now I had to wonder...what if they hadn't seen any of this? What if something was off?

"You're wrong," I said, my voice coming out harsh and choked, despite the brave front I tried to show her.

She merely smiled. "Come with me, my son. Be my heir."

"Heir of what?" I couldn't help but ask.

"Of Gailfean. Of the Kingdom of Storms." Her smile widened, so wickedly familiar. "Of all of Aesir."

Chills rushed through me. I took a step back. "Gailfean? But didn't you hear? The city has been destroyed."

"Andromeda has left Gailfean to me. It's mine to do with as I please while they press on to the mortal realms, though I will have much rebuilding to do now. The city is empty, but we can bring it to life once more. You won't even have to deal with the gods. All they care about is Talaven." She held a hand out toward me. "Join me, Ruari. Be my heir. Be my son."

A knife of pain sliced through my heart as I stared into the silver eyes of my mother. I'd heard stories of those eyes and what they'd once looked like far before I was born. There were songs about her—tales told in pubs and around travelers' campfires, back in a time when fae could freely travel across Aesir. She'd had brilliant ice-blue eyes, such a similar color to the silver ones she had now.

There were other tales about her, too. Stories said the stars glowed brighter on the day of her birth. Many had believed it was a sign that her realm would prosper under her rule, that the stars themselves had blessed her reign.

Now I couldn't help but wonder if it had been something else entirely.

A warning.

From behind me, the sounds of the fighting cut

through my thoughts, reminding me of the here and now and everything that was at stake. My people needed my help. I lifted my sword and met the gaze of my mother for one last time.

"Never approach me again," I said to her in a snarl. "I will not join you in Gailfean, nor will I be your heir. Now get out of here before I order my men to cut you down."

She just continued to smile. When she stepped back, her form slowly blended with the mist. "When you realize your world will never survive, you can find me in Gailfean."

And then she was gone.

Forty-Eight
Tessa

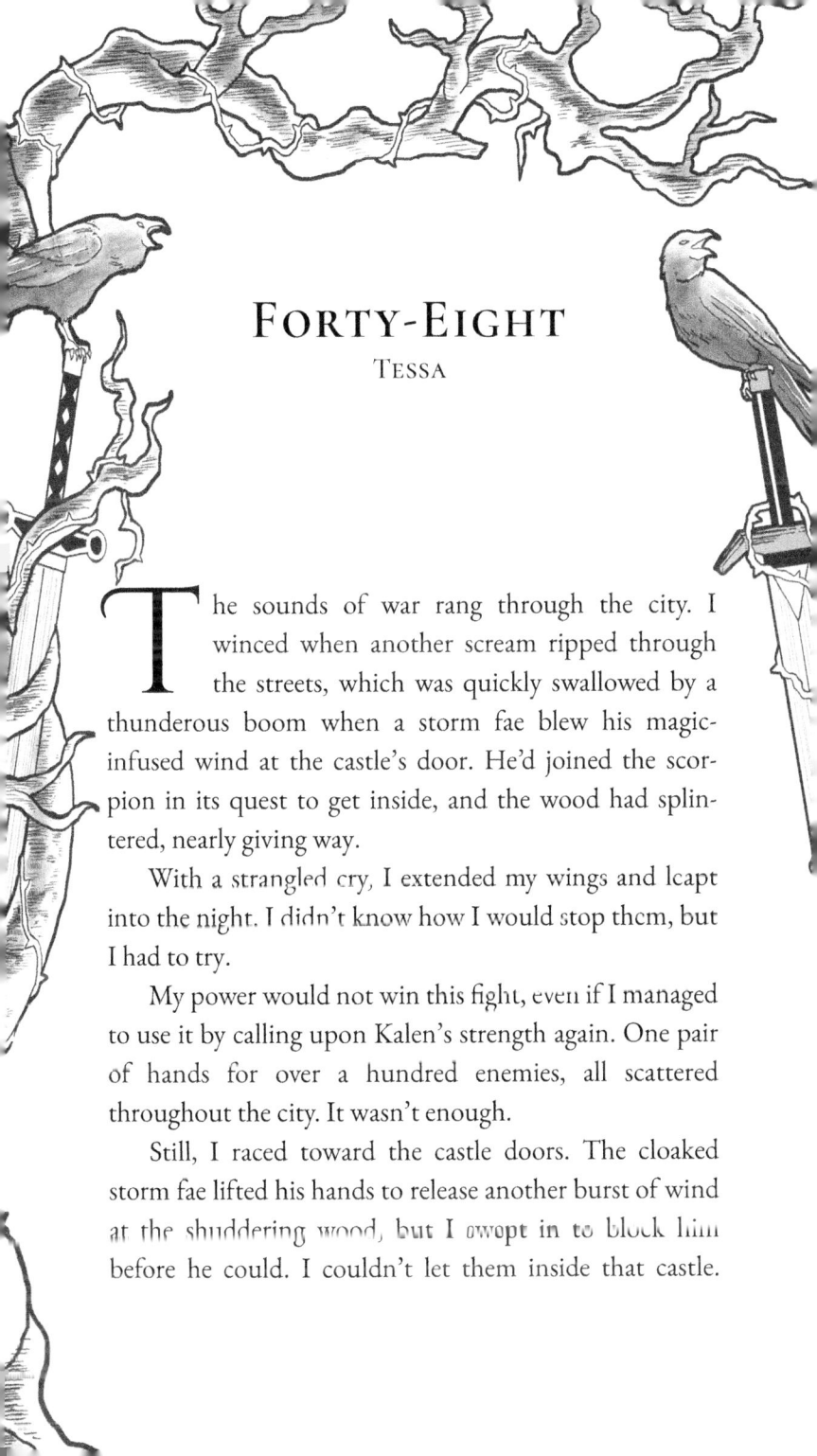

The sounds of war rang through the city. I winced when another scream ripped through the streets, which was quickly swallowed by a thunderous boom when a storm fae blew his magic-infused wind at the castle's door. He'd joined the scorpion in its quest to get inside, and the wood had splintered, nearly giving way.

With a strangled cry, I extended my wings and leapt into the night. I didn't know how I would stop them, but I had to try.

My power would not win this fight, even if I managed to use it by calling upon Kalen's strength again. One pair of hands for over a hundred enemies, all scattered throughout the city. It wasn't enough.

Still, I raced toward the castle doors. The cloaked storm fae lifted his hands to release another burst of wind at the shuddering wood, but I swept in to block him before he could. I couldn't let them inside that castle.

Half the city was in there, safely hidden away. And my sister. My heart squeezed at the thought of her face—both of her faces, wolf and human alike.

"No!" I shouted as I threw myself in front of the doors.

The blast of wind hit me square in the chest, throwing me against the cracked wood. My head slammed against it. Pain ripped through my skull. Black spots stormed my vision as my body tumbled, my wings curling up behind me.

When I hit the ground, my leg smashed into the hard stone. My ears ringing, I tried to blink away the spots just as a pair of boots moved into my line of sight.

The storm fae let out a low, blood-curdling laugh. "There must be something precious inside this castle, indeed."

I shook my head, my vision still blotchy, my ears still ringing, my body still screaming in pain. I needed to get to my feet. I needed to raise my sword. But try as I might, my body would not respond. The storm fae warrior gripped me by the back of my neck and hauled me from the ground. He slammed me against the door, and a broken beam sliced through my leathers and into my back.

Pain roared through me. Biting the insides of my cheeks, I forced the howl back down my throat.

Hissing, the storm fae swept a pair of red-tinged eyes across my face. "A mortal with wings." He took a sniff. "You're the one she's sent us here to look for."

"Then take me," I growled back, ignoring the blood

dribbling down my back. "Leave the people of this city alone and take me."

He flicked his eyes up and down my body, as if he were considering. "Tell me what's inside this castle that you're willing to *die* for."

I bit my tongue, but I saw no other option than to state the truth. "Innocents. They have nothing to do with any of this, and they don't need to die for your god to get what she wants. You came here for me, right? Well, you have me. Take me to her, and I'm certain she'll give you a great reward."

From across the courtyard, I heard Kalen's roar and felt the ripple of his fear and anger through the bond. He'd spotted me, then, trapped here by this storm fae and the scorpion. He was too far away to hear the conversation, but he might sense my intent all the same and see the resignation on my face. Because as I'd looked across this breaking city from atop that tower, I'd realized there was only one way to stop this battle.

We had to give Andromeda what she wanted, and what she wanted was me.

The storm fae leaned forward and sneered in my face. "Oh, don't you worry. I plan to take you to my god and get my reward, but this city will die, and there is nothing you can do to stop it."

My heart slammed into my ribs. "No, you don't have—"

He shoved me harder against that piercing bit of broken wood, forcing me to hiss through my teeth. "Kalen Denare is the only one who can stand against her. He and his city must die."

"Wait," I said, my voice coming out like a plea. "What do you mean? Kalen Denare is the—"

The storm fae shot his wind into my throat. I choked against the force of it, gasping for air as he sucked the very breath from my lungs. Shaking, I desperately fought for air, but he just kept taking it, pulling it from me until darkness dulled my thoughts.

I was distantly aware of the thud of my body against the ground when he loosened his grip on my throat. The tap of boots on stone sounded near my head, fuzzy and loud. Too loud. The storm fae laughed and kicked me in the gut.

Rage burned through me. I tried to find the strength to stand, but whatever he had done to me left me unable to move, to speak, to do anything other than take in tiny, aching breaths. I couldn't even blink, let alone see. The only thing that existed was a veil of mist drowning everything in shadow.

"How pathetic," he spat. "I thought Andromeda's blood would have more power than this. But you're just a weak mortal like the rest of them. I can't imagine she'll keep you around for long. And the funny thing is, you brought all this upon yourself."

His words sliced through my heart. Deep down, I knew he was right. I'd clawed my way through life, always fighting, always throwing myself from one bad situation to the next. My father might have been the one to blame in the beginning, but it had been me in the end. I was the one who'd gotten Raven killed. I was the cause of my sister getting trapped in that dungeon cell. I had even stabbed Kalen without any evidence to prove what Morgan had told me.

And it was I who had stabbed Oberon with the Mortal Blade.

I'd only brought this upon myself.

Myself and everyone I cared about.

The storm fae slammed his boot into my head, and the darkness finally consumed me.

"Daughter of Stars," a voice whispered in my mind.

I opened my eyes, jolted awake in a blanket of grass that danced in the breeze beneath the soothing sun. Alarmed, I climbed to my feet and gazed around. A large patch of charred ground stretched out behind me. I spun on my feet, spotting a city in the distance that glistened a deep burnished brown with hints of gold.

Like Albyria, but...not.

"Kalen?" I asked, frowning. Was this a dream? Did that mean the storm fae had dragged me out of Dubnos and this was hours—or even days—later? My hands curled as I tried to make sense of it. What had happened? Had the city fallen?

And then another question I did not want to ponder popped into my head.

Who had survived? Had anyone?

Soft voices drifted to me. I turned back to the stretch of charred ground to find two emerald-robed figures kneeling beside it. They were mortals, I could tell, though there was something different about them. Their weathered faces were lined with wrinkles, but there was something ancient in their eyes. Something almost...otherworldly.

One of them stood and pushed back her hood, her fingers brushing the rings along her jaw.

Druids.

Confusion rippled through me. What *was* this? And how was I here?

"The poor girl," the brunette woman said with a sigh. "Will she ever forgive us for what we've done to her? What we must still do to her?"

"I feel just as badly for the father. The moment he tossed his daughter over that wall will haunt him for the rest of his days, as short as they are."

My heart jolted, and I took a stumbling step toward them. "What do you mean?"

They had to be talking about me and my father. It was impossible to imagine some other girl had been thrown over a wall like I had. But how? And why? And where in the name of light was I?

The Druids continued speaking as if they hadn't heard me.

"Nevertheless, it is done now, and the path remains true," the woman said with a sigh. "Her power has sparked to life. Now we wait."

"How long?" the other asked.

"Twenty more years." She pressed her lips together. "And then it *truly* begins. The knife edge awaits us all."

The world shuddered beneath me, the dream twisting and turning and spinning me around. When the land stilled, I now stood on the bridge between Albyria and the Kingdom of Shadow. In the distance, I spotted a girl in an orange wedding dress with fear in her eyes. She was running toward the bridge, and her golden hair whipped the air behind her.

I swallowed and stepped to the side, waiting for her —*me*—to make the crossing that would change her life—change everything.

And then I spotted him. *Ruari*. The horned son of Oberon hunkered behind a boulder along the edge of the chasm, watching me flee. He did nothing to stop me.

After the girl—*me*—vanished into the mists where she would run into Kalen Denare's waiting arms, Oberon's guards tried to charge after me. Eventually, they gave up and vanished back up to the hill to their city. But Ruari remained. When he was certain they were gone, he finally stood and walked to the edge of the chasm. The wind ruffled his orange hair around his pinched face.

"Run, Tessa. Run as fast as you can. You're the only one who can save us," he whispered.

And then he seemed to look right at me.

A moment later, he was gone.

The world twisted around me once more. I didn't understand what was happening or why my mind was showing me these things, these memories. These glimpses into the past.

Everything stopped once more.

I gazed around the mist-shrouded woods. Again, a past version of myself appeared. This time, I was running from a storm fae with my braided hair bouncing on my back. My heart shuddered. This was no long-forgotten memory of the past. This moment had happened only days ago, when Kalen and I had scouted ahead to save Dubnos. As I watched myself facing off against the storm fae, I couldn't help but gape. Dirt stained my cheeks, and there was a wild look in my eye. I looked...powerful.

And strong. The armor hugging my curves highlighted the strength in my arms and the power in my legs. And then the past me—the wild, powerful me—whispered the word, "Death."

Dust billowed through the mist as the storm fae died by my touch.

I shook my head and glanced around, half-expecting Ruari to appear again or one of those Druids. I didn't understand why my mind had picked out these moments to show me right now. It was just like that time the god had played with Kalen's memories in my dream, only this time...I was alone.

"What is it?" I called up to the sky. "What are you trying to make me see?"

As if in answer, the world shifted around me. I landed on the battlement stones that stretched around Dubnos, and the sweat-soaked scent of war thickened the air. Kalen paced while the army—including me—waited for his orders. Blood stained the ground, and several chunks of crenel were missing. This moment was even more recent than the last. This was today, after the first wave of the attack. I'd been speaking with Fenella then, too far from Kalen to hear his words.

But now I stood beside him, and I heard every one.

"I never thought I would miss my power," he muttered. "If I had it, I would blast these creatures off this mountain before they could touch even one more of my people."

His power.

I took a step back as a strange, ridiculous thought sprang into my mind. It couldn't be possible. Could it? For so long, I'd been focused on my own powers...but more than once, I'd drawn upon Kalen's strength by using our bond. I'd used his strength and his healing—his magic-enhanced fae strength. Nothing had muted it in me, even if it had been muted in him.

Because I had Andromeda's magic in my blood.

Heart pounding, I whirled to face my past self, where I stood readied for the creatures that would come crashing over the wall any second now.

She had no idea what was coming for her. A grim determination lit her eye, but there was something else in her expression. Something she didn't want the others to see. Fear and guilt, still so heavy it weighed down her shoulders—*my* shoulders. It was the belief I hadn't yet shaken. That all of this was because of me.

It was the belief that if I hadn't stabbed Oberon or even fled the wedding that day by running across the bridge, none of this would be happening.

I've brought doom upon us all, but...if these memories were real, if I wasn't making all of this up, there was far more to it than I could have ever dreamed. None of it excused my past actions, but if I'd been influenced, if I'd been manipulated...

I'd been shown that moment with the Druids for a reason. They had started this. Not me.

So I strode right up to my past self and snapped my fingers in her face. "Snap out of it. You've used Kalen's strength. I bet you can use his powers, too. When those beasts come up the wall, blast them all to the underworld."

But my past self just stared straight through me now, the guilt still swirling in her eyes.

I snapped my fingers again. "Snap out of it!"

No response. Frustration rising within me, I dropped back my head and roared. This was a memory and nothing more, and I couldn't change the past. If only I had known this then, I could have stopped the enemy before they'd smashed their way through the Dubnos streets, killing so many innocent shadow fae.

"Wake up!" I screamed into her face.

Light slammed into my eyes. I gasped, blindly throwing myself to my feet even as I felt as if a hammer were splitting my skull. The world around me seemed to roar, and the acrid stench of smoke and death clogged my nostrils. Blinking rapidly, I tried to make sense of where I was now—where the dreams had taken me next.

That was when I heard his voice. It was the storm fae from the Dubnos courtyard, the one who had knocked me down. "Awake already? Seems I'll need to hit you harder this time."

Everything within me narrowed to a sharp point. My vision went crystal clear, like the glistening waters of the lake near Teine. The enemy storm fae stood just before me, not far from where he'd been only seconds before he'd knocked me out. How much time had passed? In my dreams, it had felt like hours, and yet...

He curled his hand as if ready to choke the breath from lungs once more.

"Kalen," I whispered, lifting my eyes to the battlements. The stone wall was a blur of steel, blood, and mist, and I couldn't spot him among the fray, though I could feel him there. I hoped what I was about to do wouldn't weaken him in any way, but I had to trust what I'd felt before. I had to trust those dreams.

They had not failed me yet.

The storm fae sneered and reached for me. "Your lover is not here to help you this time."

I breathed in the mist and let it coat my lungs as I called upon the power that flowed through Kalen—and me. Inwardly, I reached for it. I wrapped my mind around that thread and braced myself for the impact of all that brutal magic. I felt the darkness of it and its pure, unyielding might. And as the enemy fae stalked toward me, I threw that power right into his face.

It rushed from me with a violent recoil that threw me against the broken door, but the power also blasted the enemy across the courtyard. He collided with the stone fountain and then collapsed on the ground. From here, I could tell he wasn't breathing.

I flexed my fingers, fear and awe tangling together in my gut. It had worked. Against all odds, I'd fought this fae and won by using Kalen's powers—powers he couldn't access himself, powers he'd always struggled to control. I'd zeroed them in on one solitary enemy, and it had worked. It made no sense to me at all, but an explanation didn't matter right now. All that mattered was that I had a way to fight—*really* fight.

I was only one person, and the streets were full of the enemy, but I would do my fucking best.

With a deep breath, I yanked off my gloves and faced the scorpion creeping toward me. His talons hissed across the dirt as he shot his pincers right at my face. I ducked and then whirled, spreading my wings and ignoring another flash of pain in my back. It was still healing from where the storm fae had slammed me against the broken door, but I didn't have time to wait. I would just have to fight through the pain.

I shoved up from the ground and raced into the misty sky. As the scorpion reached up its pincers for me, its fangs snapping at the air, I loosed Kalen's power once more. It hurtled out of me, throwing me back several feet in the air. But it hit its mark with a powerful punch. The scorpion keeled over and landed on the ground. Dirt misted all around him.

Through the bond, I felt Kalen's attention snap to me, as if he'd finally realized what I was doing. I shifted in the air to stare across the courtyard where he stood on the top of the wall, surrounded by a dozen dead shadowfiends. His eyes were wild and bright, and his chest heaved with belabored breaths.

I lifted my hand to him and smiled, feeling the coil between us snap tight. It pulsed between us, almost as though it matched the beating rhythm of both our hearts. He gave me a nod, urging me onward. And so I turned, picked out a group of storm fae pouring into one of the buildings down the street, and flew.

Forty-Nine
Kalen

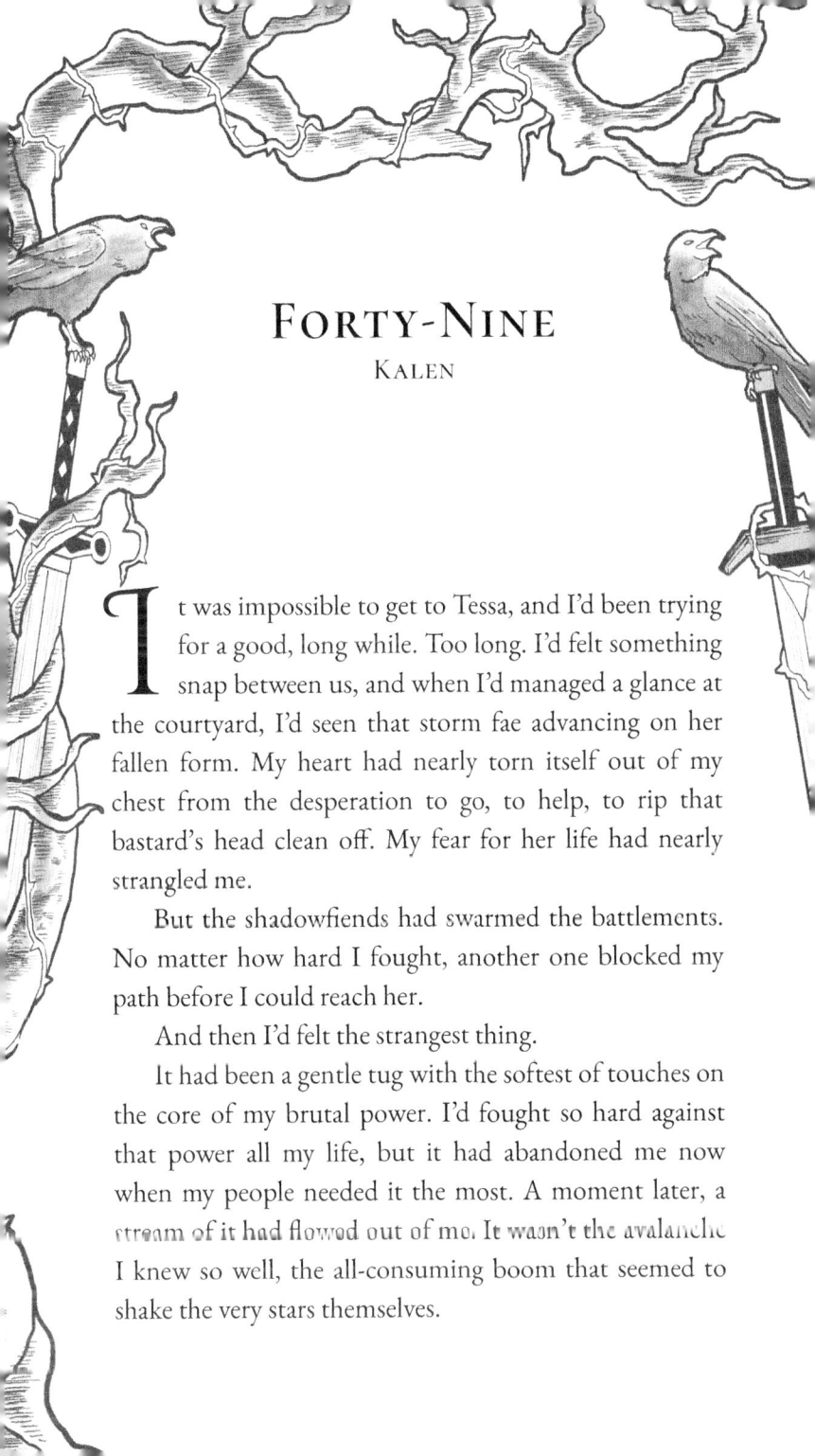

It was impossible to get to Tessa, and I'd been trying for a good, long while. Too long. I'd felt something snap between us, and when I'd managed a glance at the courtyard, I'd seen that storm fae advancing on her fallen form. My heart had nearly torn itself out of my chest from the desperation to go, to help, to rip that bastard's head clean off. My fear for her life had nearly strangled me.

But the shadowfiends had swarmed the battlements. No matter how hard I fought, another one blocked my path before I could reach her.

And then I'd felt the strangest thing.

It had been a gentle tug with the softest of touches on the core of my brutal power. I'd fought so hard against that power all my life, but it had abandoned me now when my people needed it the most. A moment later, a stream of it had flowed out of me. It wasn't the avalanche I knew so well, the all-consuming boom that seemed to shake the very stars themselves.

I'd understood at once what was happening. Tessa had somehow found a way to channel my power, and she was using it against the storm fae. In a momentary break in the battle, I'd stumbled to the edge of the wall to see her blast a scorpion into the ground.

Now she was racing through the Dubnos streets, taking out enemy after enemy. I'd never seen anything like it before.

"It's all clear!" Roisin called from the watchtower.

Relief shuddered through me as I lifted my eyes to the carnage along the battlements. Blood and gore caked the stones, and the stench of death was overwhelming. There were dozens of bodies, fae and pooka alike. We'd killed nearly a hundred of the creatures, but they'd managed to get their claws and fangs into at least twenty of ours. My heart ached at all the life lost, at all those men and women who would never again see the moon-drenched sky.

But this was war, and I was their king, and I could not show my despair. I had to be strong for everyone who lived. And this battle was not over just yet.

"Archers, to the wall!" I called out as I wiped the gore from my blade. "Stay in position in case another wave comes. Those with swords will split up. Half of you stay here to back up our archers. The other half head into the city. We're going to help Tessa clear these streets. Mist Guard, you're with me."

A moment ago, fear and dismay had painted every face along this wall, even Toryn's. But almost all of them had spotted what I had—that beautiful, winged creature soaring over the enemy and using my brutal power to stop them from killing more innocent civilians. Down in the courtyard, she landed in front of a pack of pookas, and a wicked smile curved her lips. I felt that tug again and then a soft release. My power blasted into the creatures, but it didn't stretch any further, like it usually did when I unleashed it.

A storm fae cried out from behind her. My heart lurched into my throat as he lifted a hand to throw his crackling lightning at her back. But Tessa shot up into the clouds, and his magic bounced off the stone and raced right back toward him. He had to duck to avoid the blow. It distracted him long enough for her to land on the street once more. The storm fae was dead before he could take his next breath.

"For the love of the moon," Toryn muttered beside me. "I've never seen anything like this."

Pride surged through me. The fighters on the wall gathered behind me, readying themselves for the next round of battle. And they all watched as the other half of my soul—their queen faced one of those monstrous scorpions. She easily destroyed the creature with no help from anyone.

I needed to reach her side. There were dozens more enemies out in the streets. Tessa was strong, but I would not risk her getting surrounded.

"This city," I called out loudly enough for every soul along the wall to hear me, "was once believed to be blessed by the very moon itself. So close to the sky, the Druids said, that the stars embedded their protective magic within the stones. The city has never fallen. And it will not fall today. For while the gods have muted our elite fae powers, they cannot mute the force of nature you're witnessing this day." I lifted my sword in the air. "Let us help Tessa Baran finish this. May the realm never break!"

The fae roared as I took off down the stone steps that led into the courtyard and the city beyond. The mists had cleared down here, providing a full view of the carnage left behind. The storm fae and their creatures had killed many unsuspecting fae who had ventured out of their homes when the Temple bell had rung. I cast a quick glance at the castle doors. They were broken and bent. But they still held, and Tessa had taken care of all the enemies in the courtyard.

She'd battled her way into the streets to protect the civilians hiding in their homes.

"Someone guard the castle doors!" I shouted as I raced through the courtyard. From the streets ahead, feral growls and gurgled screams drifted toward me.

Several warriors broke off from our group to stand watch by the castle, just in case more of the enemy spilled into the courtyard from the sewers. I pointed at the entrance to the sewage tunnel as we rushed past. Another handful of fae raced off to close up the breach.

Fenella and Toryn remained with me, one on each side, and soon, we reached the city beyond the courtyard. Tessa stood in the center of the street just beyond it, her wings flared wide behind her. They looked different now —the ends of the feathers gleamed the color of sapphire. She spun in a slow circle, her gloveless hands curled and shaking, as she eyed the storm fae surrounding her. She was trapped, and I understood at once why she hadn't loosed my power upon them yet.

The storm fae held captives.

FIFTY
TESSA

It had gone so well. I should have known it wouldn't be as easy as that. If it were just the beasts, it would have been over by now. They wouldn't be smart enough to put innocents between themselves and the magic burning at my fingertips. But the storm fae had seen me fighting with Kalen's power, and they'd understood.

Next thing I knew, they were dragging innocents out of their homes and clutching them against their chests. Shields—against me.

And now I was surrounded.

I held up my hands. "Let them go. I'm the one you want. Not them."

One of the storm fae sneered. "The entire city must die, including its king."

As if to punctuate his statement, he lifted a dagger to the sobbing girl's throat, but then blood sprayed before he could follow through on his threat. A spear shot through his neck, cutting off his breath. The storm fae loosened his grip on the girl, the light in his eyes blinking out as he fell.

The street exploded into chaos. Warriors rushed in from the courtyard behind us, led by a snarling Kalen and his Mist Guard. They were a whirlwind of death and mist as they swept through the circle of storm fae who had surrounded me. In the rush of it all, the innocents managed to spring free, and I motioned for them to follow me away from the fray.

They were crying and screaming and shaking like leaves, but they followed me off the path and up the steps of the nearest building. I yanked open the door and motioned them into the dark room. "Get inside and don't come out, even if you hear that bell ringing again."

"How will we know it's safe?" a pale-faced girl asked, her lower lip wobbling. She reached out to take my hand, but I quickly pulled it away.

"I will come back here and tell you myself." I started to shut the door but then paused at the look of utter devastation on her face. There was something in her eyes, something in the rawness of her expression, that made my heart twang. She reminded me so much of myself, of Nellie, and of Val—back before we'd escaped from Teine. Like she'd lost her hope. "Your king is out there fighting for your lives. He will not let you down. And neither will I."

"Your wings," she whispered as I turned to go. "Are you one of the gods?"

I gave her a slight smile. "No, I'm something better. I am the Daughter of Stars."

The name came to me as if I'd known it all my life, and the fae inside the building fell silent as I passed through the door to rejoin the battle in the streets. With a determined gait, I walked back down the steps and curled my hands. Kalen was locked in a battle with a storm fae. Fenella and Toryn had surrounded a pack of shadowfiends and were taking them out one by one. The streets were thick with fighting, dozens of shadow fae wielding their swords against the enemy.

A strange calm settled over me. Something about this moment felt so strangely familiar—so right. It felt like every choice I'd made, every path I'd taken, had brought me here. I was *supposed* to be in this street during the fight to save Dubnos.

One of the storm fae noticed me approaching the fight, and he rushed toward me with hands raised. I braced myself against the blast of wind he threw into my face. It batted against my armor and whipped my braid, but I held firm, my knees bent and my feet locked to the ground.

When the wind subsided, I met the fae's glare with one of my own and called upon the power. Not my mate's power this time, but the power that resided within me, desperate to be freed. I mingled it with Kalen's mist, which now seeped from my own skin, and let that mist carry my dark power toward my enemy. For a moment, nothing happened. He didn't see the threat for what it was. Instead, he sneered and started to blast his wind once more.

The mist reached his face. It writhed around him, clung to his skin, and seeped into his pores.

Shock flashed through his eyes, and he opened his mouth to scream.

Dust consumed him.

Kalen reached my side as the dust began to clear, his sword dripping with blood. Without a word, he put his back to me. I followed his lead and pressed my back against his. Our armor thudded as we linked our bodies and moved. We spun in a slow circle. He held his sword, and I curled my fists.

Two shadowfiends suddenly leapt out of the shadows, hurtling straight at us. Fangs bared, one of the beasts ran toward me. I opened my hands and sent another cloud of death mist toward the creature. It hit him only seconds before he could reach me. Kalen took on the second beast. His sword sliced through flesh and fur, killing the shadowfiend with brutal speed.

We continued on like that, fighting enemy after enemy together. With every street we cleared, my heart felt lighter, even as death clung to my skin. But we did not falter for even a breath. We persisted until the sounds of fighting faded to a dull murmur, until my soul felt spent and my body ached.

Until every last one of them was dead.

Cheers filled the city, from the battlements to the bloody streets, to the castle itself.

Even still, I did not rest. I took my tired body to the skies to do a sweep overhead. I didn't want to leave any shadowfiend or storm fae unaccounted for.

That was when I spotted the raven swooping through the gates, followed closely by a group of warriors who raced into Dubnos with a furious battle cry. And Gaven led the charge.

Relief soothed my frayed nerves as I rejoined Kalen and the others on the street. With a smile, I told them who'd arrived, and together, we went to meet our allies and celebrate the victory, as temporary as we all knew it was.

For now, Dubnos was safe. We had won.

Fifty-One
Niamh

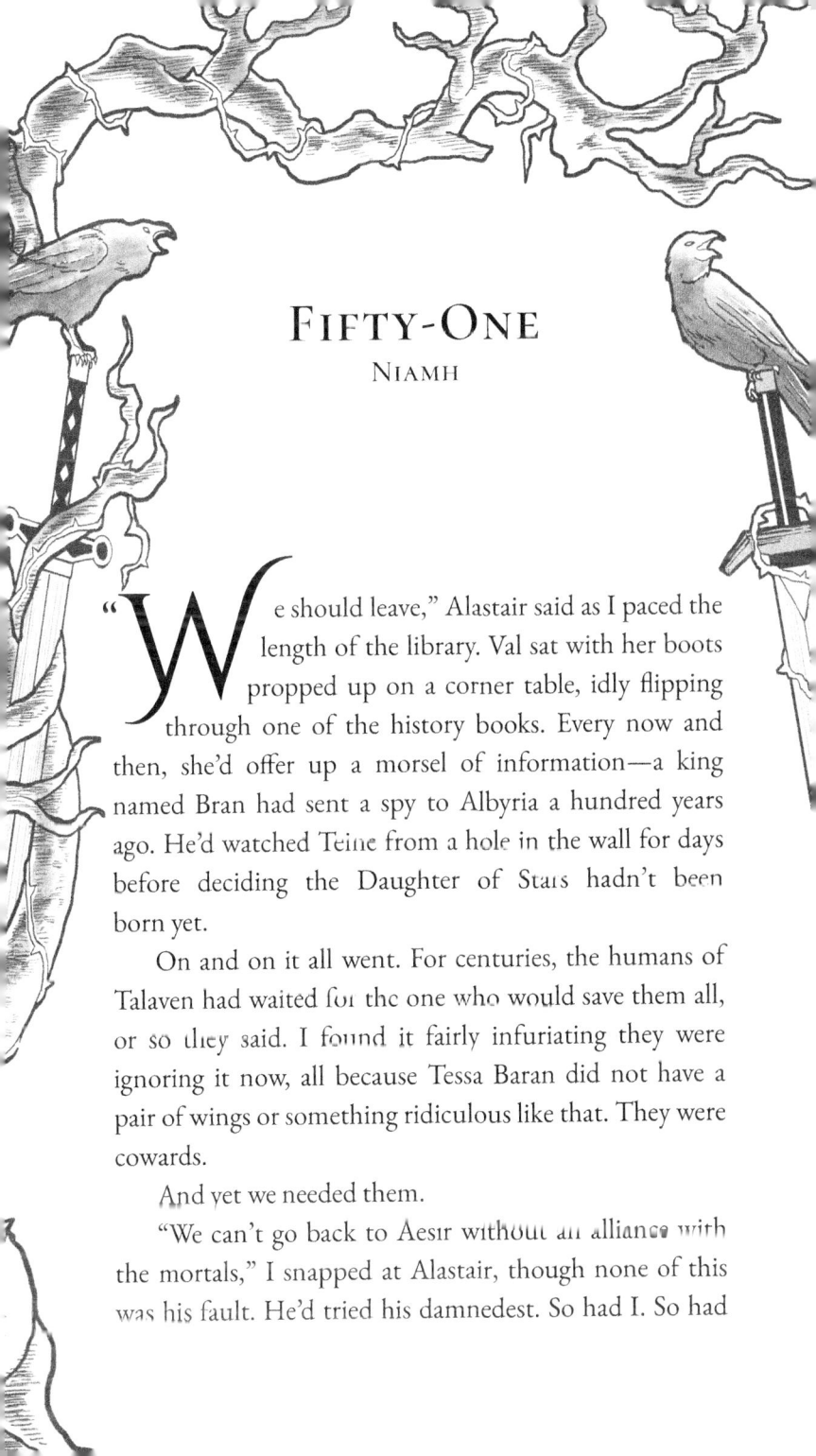

"We should leave," Alastair said as I paced the length of the library. Val sat with her boots propped up on a corner table, idly flipping through one of the history books. Every now and then, she'd offer up a morsel of information—a king named Bran had sent a spy to Albyria a hundred years ago. He'd watched Teine from a hole in the wall for days before deciding the Daughter of Stars hadn't been born yet.

On and on it all went. For centuries, the humans of Talaven had waited for the one who would save them all, or so they said. I found it fairly infuriating they were ignoring it now, all because Tessa Baran did not have a pair of wings or something ridiculous like that. They were cowards.

And yet we needed them.

"We can't go back to Aesir without an alliance with the mortals," I snapped at Alastair, though none of this was his fault. He'd tried his damnedest. So had I. So had

Val, in fact. But they wouldn't even listen to the pleadings of a human.

"We got what we came for. Information."

I clucked my tongue, still pacing. "We came here to find out how to banish the gods. All they've told us is some ancient prophecy, one where a winged girl saves this world from annihilation."

"And that's Tessa."

I slowed to a stop, my heart pounding. "But what if they're right, Alastair? What if she doesn't make the right choice? I won't deny she's special, but she's never shown any hint of power at all. She's just strong. That's not enough."

Val lowered the book. "That's not true. She killed a shadowfiend once, when she was a child. And she hauled both of us up the side of a chasm wall while using only one hand to hold on to the rope."

"She killed a shadowfiend when she was a child?"

"Yeah, I thought you knew. It traumatized her. Her mind locked the memory away because she couldn't handle it...but then she remembered while she was out there with you all hunting down Oberon."

I moved over to the table and sat down across from her. "She killed one when she was with us, too. With a sword."

Val just grinned, a sparkle in her eye. "She didn't have a sword the first time. Her father, the bastard, wouldn't let her have one. She used her fucking hands."

"Death by touch," I murmured, my heartbeat ticking faster. "Andromeda's power."

"I honestly thought you knew."

"That entire trip...it was so chaotic." I shoved up from the chair again, unable to keep my frantic energy tethered long enough to stay in one place for more than a moment. "We need to tell the king. If anything will convince him Tessa is on the right path, it's this."

"Ah." Val sighed and slumped in her chair. "I already told him about this when he was giving me a tour of the castle grounds. It's not enough. He said something about a knife edge. Tessa has to make some kind of choice, and we'll know she's made it if she shows her wings. He insisted the Daughter of Stars will have wings, and the feathers' ends will be sapphire instead of red."

"A knife edge?" Alastair asked with a frown.

"I don't know," Val said with a shrug. "I'm convinced she'll do whatever needs to be done."

Cheers from the streets filtered in through the cracked window. Val inched off her seat to get a better look, and the sun bathed her face in a warm, soft glow. She smiled a little, cocking her head.

"What is it?" I joined her by the window and looked down at the crowd. Hundreds of people had clogged the streets in joyous abandon. They were dancing and leaping and tossing confetti into the air. Curious, I shoved the window fully open and stuck my head outside.

"Hey," I called down to them.

A woman with sapphire ribbons in her golden hair lifted her eyes to mine and beamed. "Isn't it glorious?"

"What's glorious? What are you celebrating?"

She shook her head and laughed. "You haven't heard?"

"Clearly not," I said, getting a little annoyed now. If I'd heard, I wouldn't be asking, now would I?

"The Daughter of Stars. She's alive!" The woman's voice was gobbled up by the boom of a new round of cheers. Sucking in a breath, I eased back into the library and met Val's eyes.

"Did you hear that?" she whispered.

"They're talking about Tessa." Alastair crossed the room and looked down at the crowd. I could have sworn there was a tear in his eye. "The little dove did it. She fucking did it."

The library door suddenly flew open, slamming into the wall beside it. The King of Talaven strode inside, flanked by his ever-present guards. But for once, he did not eye us with suspicion and fear. He was beaming, his smile as bright as the stars he so painstakingly prayed to every night.

"We've had word from Aesir," he said in a hushed voice, as if he could hardly speak. "Our spies—"

"*Your spies?*" I couldn't help ask. "Are you telling me you sent some of your men to watch Aesir, and you didn't tell us?"

"They were already there. They've always been there. But no matter, that's not what's important. The enemy staged an attack on Dubnos—"

"*What?*" Alastair's shout was an eruption of sound, so loud and vicious, the King of Talaven jumped. I placed a shaking hand on his arm and tried to quell my own rush of emotion. An attack on Dubnos was bad, but the fae in the streets would not be cheering if they'd lost. They would not be celebrating the end of another fae kingdom...would they?

The king quickly continued. "But Dubnos survived, thanks to the Daughter of Stars. She saved the city!"

"Tessa did that?" Val asked, the crack in her voice betraying her emotions. "She saved Dubnos?"

"She did." Even the king looked emotional. He swiped a stray tear off his ruddy cheeks and beamed.

"And the fucking wings?" Alastair asked. "Are you finally going to admit she doesn't need them now?"

"She was seen swooping over the battlements on her great, glorious wings while she dispensed her brutal power on the enemy. They were tipped in sapphire."

Val gasped and whirled to me. "We need to go back. Now. She's going to need me."

I nodded. "We'll leave at once." And then I turned to the king. "Right?"

"It will take some time to ready the ships, but yes. I will bring my army together and send word to my allies." His eyes sparkled as he stood tall. "The knife edge awaited us all, but Tessa Baran chose to stay with Kalen Denare. She did not go with Andromeda. Instead of becoming the Daughter of Dust, she will be the Daughter of Stars. And so the time has come, and we will fight by your side. It's all worked. We will save this world after all. The stars be with us."

After the king left us, Val gathered up the books to return them to their shelves. There was a frantic energy in the way she moved, and her hands shook so hard, she almost dropped the books.

"Here, I'll do that." Alastair eased in beside her and unloaded her arms. She shot him a grateful smile.

He wandered off into the stacks. Steadying my breath, I stepped in beside her and gently placed my hand on her upper back. The moments when no one else was around were so fleeting, even now. Alastair would be back at any moment, and even then...it wasn't as if I had anything to say or do. I just wanted that breath of stillness with her. I wanted to help her calm down.

"You all right, Val?" I asked quietly.

Her throat bobbed as she turned to me. "I'm worried about Tessa. I know the king is excited that she's using her power and that she's found her wings, but all of this will be hard on her. I *know* her, Niamh. She's strong, but she can't do this alone. She shouldn't have to do it alone, either."

I smiled gently. "She isn't alone. She has Kal. And her sister and Toryn and Fenella are all there, too. They'll look after her."

She nodded. "I know. You're probably right. She's fine. It's just...she was there by my side when I was trapped in a grief greater than I could bear. If she hadn't been there, if she hadn't helped me...I would not be standing here before you. Do you understand what I'm saying?"

"Yes, I think so." My heart pounded painfully in my chest.

"And so I need to be with her now, just in case. Maybe she doesn't need me, but if she does, I do not want to there to be an entire sea's worth of water between us. If the king hadn't agreed to give us ships, I would have stolen one, fuck the consequences."

"You're quite something." I smiled. "Your hair matches the fire in your heart."

Val's tongue darted out to lick her soft lips. "You're telling me you wouldn't have done the same?"

"Oh, I absolutely would have."

Tension pounded between us, and I considered, just for a split second, throwing all caution to the wind and finding out just how soft Val's lips were. But I couldn't tell if she felt the same, and the last thing I wanted to do was ruin our friendship.

Alastair, of course, chose that moment to stomp back over to us.

"The books are taken care of. Let's go pack up the rest of our things. I'm eager to get back to Aesir."

Back to the fae lands, where danger awaited us all. The battle for the world loomed before us, but instead of feeling dread, a thrill went through me. I'd been born for this fight. I'd waited for it all my life.

"Let's go kill those gods," I said with a wicked smile.

Fifty-Two
Tessa

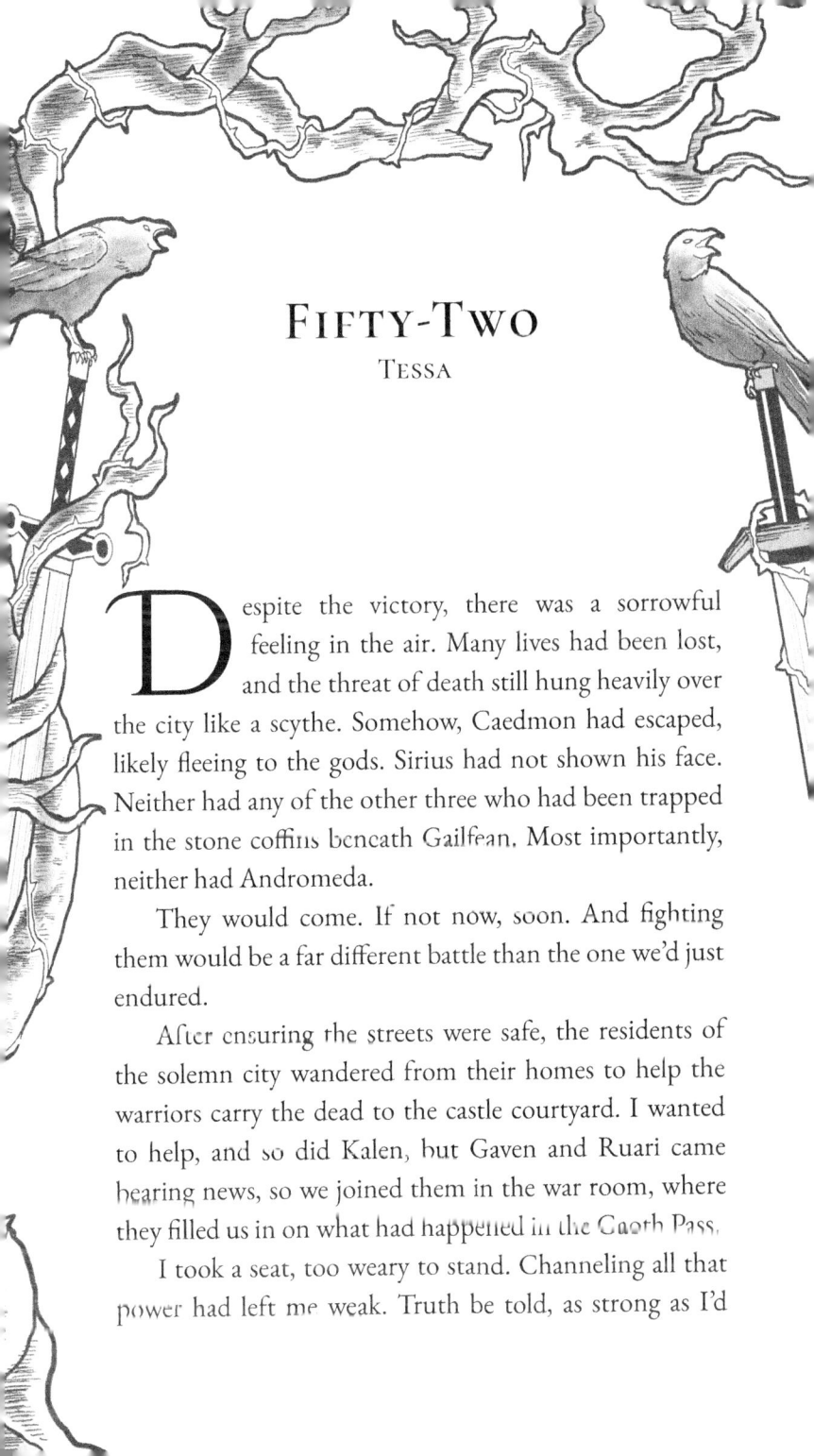

Despite the victory, there was a sorrowful feeling in the air. Many lives had been lost, and the threat of death still hung heavily over the city like a scythe. Somehow, Caedmon had escaped, likely fleeing to the gods. Sirius had not shown his face. Neither had any of the other three who had been trapped in the stone coffins beneath Gailfean. Most importantly, neither had Andromeda.

They would come. If not now, soon. And fighting them would be a far different battle than the one we'd just endured.

After ensuring the streets were safe, the residents of the solemn city wandered from their homes to help the warriors carry the dead to the castle courtyard. I wanted to help, and so did Kalen, but Gaven and Ruari came bearing news, so we joined them in the war room, where they filled us in on what had happened in the Caoth Pass.

I took a seat, too weary to stand. Channeling all that power had left me weak. Truth be told, as strong as I'd been during the fight, I knew I wouldn't have been able to go on much longer like that.

Ruari leaned against the wall with his arms folded over his chest. He eyed the wolf beside me. Nellie flashed her teeth at him, but he didn't so much as flinch. It was almost as though he could sense the truth about who she was, even though we hadn't told him.

Gaven took Kalen's offered drink and took a sip of the fion before speaking. "Ruari met your warriors in the pass, but they were almost overrun by the beasts."

Ruari nodded, running a hand down his tired face. Speckles of blood still painted his skin and his armor. No one had taken a moment to clean up yet. "There were even these monstrous creatures I'd never seen before."

"Large scorpions," Fenella cut in. "Right?"

He gave her a nod. "There were five of them and about a hundred shadowfiends. If we hadn't arrived when we did, your fighters would have been overrun, and then the beasts would have charged up the mountain path to the city."

"They really were trying to surround us on all sides," Kalen murmured.

And it had almost worked.

"Just before that, Boudica came screeching down at us," Gaven added. "I thought it was a cry for help, so I came this way. But it looks like you took care of it all yourselves."

"It wasn't easy." Kalen cut his eyes my way. "We'll need you for the next fight. This war is far from over."

"It's only begun," Ruari said in a rough voice, and

there was something in his tone that curdled my blood. "There's something I need to tell you."

Gaven slung his hands into his pockets and took a step away from the horned half fae. Interesting.

Kalen's eyes narrowed. "I don't like the look on either of your faces. Is this about your father, Ruari? Did he do something else before he died that's going to cause problems for us now?"

Ruari loosed a breath, but it was Gaven who spoke. "After you left, we discovered Morgan is in fact...well, I don't really know how to say this except as bluntly as possible. She's not Morgan. Your mother lives, Kal. She took Morgan as her vessel, and she lives."

Fuck.

Kalen's jaw clenched, and his eyes went hard. The bond between us snapped tight, and I could feel the avalanche of emotions that threatened to bury him. So much anger and so much grief, but there was a flicker of relief among it as well—something I knew he wanted to hide. I shifted closer to him and rubbed his back, but he didn't react to my touch.

When Kalen didn't respond, Gaven continued. "Somehow, she escaped the dungeons. We didn't spend long looking for her because we were readying ourselves to march to your aid, and we had to get moving. It wasn't until we reached the Gaoth Pass that she appeared again. To Ruari."

Ruari tensed as he met Kalen's eyes—his half brother's eyes, I realized. In a sense, anyway. "She waited to approach me until after Gaven had gone up the mountain to Dubnos. She was trying to tempt me into joining her in Gailfean."

"Gailfean?" Fenella asked with a frown. "Why'd she want you to go there? The city is nothing but rubble now, and it's not as if she has any past connection to that place. Right?"

She glanced at Kalen, but he didn't respond. He barely even breathed.

"She said Andromeda gave it to her," Ruari said, holding up his hands. "She plans to forge a new fae kingdom while the gods push forward to the mortal lands. That's what they're doing right now, by the way. All of this...I think it was meant to be a distraction, a way to keep us occupied while they go to Talaven. They don't care about Aesir as long as we don't fight them. They want the humans."

I sucked in a breath. "But the storm fae said this city had to die."

"No doubt they meant it," Ruari replied. "This kingdom is ruled by Kalen Denare, who is a great threat to them. Fortunately, they still underestimated us, but I'm certain they won't make that mistake again."

I cast a glance at Kalen. His face was still hard and unreadable. I knew this was difficult for him to hear, particularly the part about his mother. Not only was she alive, but she was serving the gods now. She was his enemy and his blood. I'd heard him speak of her before he'd known the truth, and I'd seen the look on his face when he'd thought Oberon had killed her. There was a deep love there. A centuries-old love.

Just then, a gray gemstone flickered from a small pile

on the war table. Niamh's solid, steady voice drifted into the room. "Kalen Denare."

I sagged against the table as Kalen snatched up the stone and lit a flame beneath it.

"Niamh," he demanded. "Are you all right? Where are you? Is everyone safe?"

"I'm fine. We're all fine."

"Val," I whispered, tears filling my eyes. I'd tried not to give in to the fear she might be dead, but it had still sat there in my gut, a constant presence these past few days. But she was fine. *They were all fine*. It almost seemed impossible to believe.

"Listen, we don't have long, so I'll be quick. The King of Talaven is readying his army. We're sailing to Aesir's aid with one hundred ships carrying archers, swordsmen, and battle-ready horses. Just hold out a little longer."

Kalen nodded, and I found myself gripping the edge of the war table. "Niamh, the gods are—"

"Yes, about the gods." Niamh's face began to waver on the stone. "There's something important I need to tell you, but I need you to sit down."

"Oh, fuck," Fenella muttered. "That doesn't sound good."

"Tessa was not the one who brought back the gods, and neither was Oberon," she said in a fierce whisper. "It was someone else, someone who made a bargain with Andromeda. It's a long story, so I won't go into all the details now. All you need to know is that Andromeda's soul—her essence—could not return without an anchor to this world. A tether."

An anchor.

"In exchange, this person was gifted eternal life. And as long as she lives, we can't get rid of Andromeda, though killing the anchor won't be enough to banish the gods again, either. You need something much more powerful."

A low rumble sounded in Kalen's throat, and a wave of grief washed over me. There was only one person in the world that could be, and Niamh was right. It wasn't me. It wasn't Oberon, either. Kalen had voiced this fear aloud to me a couple months ago. Since then, we'd both dismissed it. His mother was dead—or so we'd thought.

But now it all made sense. Kalen had been able to brush aside his vow so easily when it came to me. It wasn't because of our bond or his repeated insistence that Oberon had been his vowed enemy. Deep down, I'd always known there was more to it than that. I'd always suspected. It had been *too easy*. Because his mother, now residing in Morgan's body, had been the one this whole time. And so the vow still held.

Killing her would destroy him, no matter what she'd become.

"Niamh, wait," Kalen breathed when her face wavered once more. "You can't get on those ships. The gods are coming for the mortal lands."

The gemstone blinked out. For a moment, silence curled through the room like wisps of acrid smoke. Tension thickened around us. And then Kalen hauled back his hand and hurled the gemstone at the wall. It hit the stone with a crash and shattered into a thousand pieces, raining its shards on the floor.

Ruari propped his fisted hands on the war table. "I don't think she heard what you said, Your Majesty."

I lifted my eyes at his use of Kalen's title, but the king himself did not seem to notice. He was too focused on where that gemstone had shattered and the chip in the stone left behind by the impact. And then, after a brutal silence, Kalen turned to his Mist Guard.

"Try contacting Niamh again, and tell her what's coming," he told Gaven. "I'll be in the stables. I have to go kill Bellicent Denare."

I stayed behind in the war room to give him a few moments to be alone, watching Gaven try and fail to reach Niamh again. I didn't want to think about what that might mean. If they continued to board those ships and sail across the sea, what would be waiting for them on those rough waves? Did the gods have ships, too? How many storm fae had they convinced to fight with them? Did they even need an army to destroy the mortal ships? What about their wings?

And Val...oh, Val. She was stuck in the middle of all this.

Fenella and Gaven started bickering over what to do next, and so I left them to it. I found Kalen in the stables in the castle courtyard, gripping a stall door. The wood creaked beneath his hands.

"I'm sorry, Kalen." It was the only thing I knew to say.

"I knew," he replied in a rough voice. "Deep down, I knew it had to be her. She's the one who made me vow, and I wanted to believe this ended some other way, but I knew. I would never kill her unless I was compelled to do it. When she made me vow it, she knew it, too. All those things she's done and those lives she's stolen...I know it wasn't her choice. Not in the beginning, at least. All I want is to help her wring the god's influence from her mind until she's back to the woman she was before—the woman I know she must be beneath all of it."

I stepped up beside him and took his hand in mine. "I don't think she is that person anymore, Kalen. Andromeda changed her. I don't think there's a way to come back from that."

His hollow eyes met mine. "But you faced off against Oberon, and you saw a flicker of who he used to be. He tried to fight against it in the end."

"That's different," I said softly. "He's not the one whose body was filled with her power. Andromeda was keeping Bellicent alive, not him."

"Either way, I have no choice. I know where she is. As we speak, I feel compelled to go after her, and I can't hold myself back any longer. I have to go. Now."

"Well, then I'm coming with you."

"Tessa," he said in a low groan. "I have to kill her. You don't want to see me do this."

I slid my hands up his chest and gazed up at him with a lifted chin. "I told you I would never walk away from you, no matter what. That I would never leave you. And so I am going with you to stand by your side. I'll be there with you when it's all said and done. You don't have to face this alone."

He shuddered and pulled me to his chest. "I don't want to do this."

"I know," I whispered.

When I pulled back, he turned to the wall and grabbed two of the saddles. "Are you certain you feel up to this right now? You fought hard in that battle. I can feel your weariness."

It was true. Exhaustion throbbed through my muscles, particularly in my back. But I'd meant what I said to him. I made a promise to be with him always, and I could fight my exhaustion a little while longer. Anything so he would not have to face this alone.

"I'll be fine," I told him. "When we return to Dubnos, I'll rest then."

Fifty-Three
Tessa

The Mist Guard wanted to join us on the journey back to Gailfean, but Kalen ordered them to stay behind this time. The city was healing from the battle, and fear still stained the streets along with the blood. And even though Ruari insisted the gods had their sights aimed west, we had no way of truly knowing if they would send another army to attack Dubnos.

Once I'd mounted Silver, we set off with Boudica circling over our heads. Whatever unseen force had thinned the mists during the battle abandoned us now. A thick fog curled around us, obscuring the path ahead. We wound down the steep mountain path and briefly camped in a cave, warming our hands and feet by the campfire.

The vow tried to tug Kalen ever forward, preventing him from getting any rest along the way. I had to remind him and the vow over and over again that he would be no use in a fight if he raced to

Gailfean without pause. It seemed the vow could listen to logic—at least enough for a brief stop now and then.

When we reached the base of the mountain, we rode our horses through the Gaoth Pass. The bodies of dead shadowfiends had been piled on either side of the beaten path, and the stench was so thick, I almost lost my breakfast. But on we went, past the bodies and down the windy path until we reached the border into the Kingdom of Storms.

This time, it was impossible to tell where one kingdom ended and the other began. With the mist coating all of Aesir now, the lands were nothing but endless shadow, though something told me the storms still lurked in the skies above, unlike the vanishing eversun.

We slowed our horses to a stop at what felt like the edge of the world. "Do you think there are beasts still out there?"

"Yes. That won't have been all of them," said Kalen.

"And the storms? Are they gone, like the sun?"

"I don't think we're that lucky."

I nodded, hating the sharp stab of pain that went through me. "How does the vow feel about you walking into a kingdom full of night and chaos?"

"It doesn't particularly care," he said in a dark voice. "I'm to kill the anchor. Nothing else matters, not even my own safety. Not even yours, love. You can still turn back now. You can return to Dubnos and wait with the others. Be with your sister. Find a way to contact Niamh and Val."

I sat up a little straighter on Silver's back, my heart pounding. "You are not getting rid of me, Kalen Denare."

His eyes met mine, the sapphire gleaming in the dark. "I know. Stay close to me. But if something goes wrong, don't hesitate to spread your wings and get to safety."

There was no way I would leave him behind if something happened. "I would rather take my final breath than lose you, Kalen."

I thought he might argue, but instead, he nodded. "I could say the same to you."

He held out a hand, and I slipped my gloved fingers into his. That thread tightened around his heart and mine, and there was a part of me that never wanted to let go. But then we turned and faced the storms, and together, we crossed the border.

We rode quickly across the rolling plains. The mist streamed by us as our horses charged forward, taking us closer and closer to the crumbling city in the distance that was lit by a fiery glow. Neither of us said a word as we approached from the east, circling to the back gates instead of going in through the front. We had no idea if Bellicent would have any fighters or if she'd be pacing the streets alone. Ruari seemed to think she had no one with her, but one could never be too careful when it came to her.

The fiery glow turned out to be braziers that hung along the exterior walls, lit at regular intervals to bring some light amid the heavy gloom. When we were close enough for our sound to reach the battlements, we left our horses in the grass.

"Stay here," I whispered to Silver. He stomped his hooves but made no move to follow us into the remains of the city. Smart horse.

As we approached Gailfean on foot, I tucked myself into Kalen's cloak and hid my golden hair beneath the dark hood, just in case it stood out in the night. Kalen pressed a finger to his lips as we inched closer. His gaze was locked on the battlements above, but he made no indication that he spotted anyone up there.

The back gates hung open, half of the wood broken off. Even through the heavy mist, I could see the city itself was a shambles. Some buildings remained intact, but they were dusted by the ash that still fell from the sky all these days later. Most were nothing but rubble. The collapse of the castle had radiated through the rest of this city, likely destroying everything in its path.

My heart pounded as we stepped through the gate, my boots crunching against the pebbled ground. If we hadn't investigated those catacombs beneath the castle, hundreds of bodies would have been crushed beneath the falling stone and collapsing buildings. If we'd just been an hour later than we had been. That was all it would have taken. It was as if the stars themselves had aligned, urging us to leave the Great Hall and explore the queen's rooms. Once upon a time, I would have thought that was impossible, but I wasn't so certain now.

In the distance, another fire blazed. From here, it looked as though it came from the center of the city, where that glorious castle had once stood. Kalen met my eyes and gave me a grim nod. That was where we were headed, then.

Together, we crept through the broken city. A sharp wind whistled through the crumbling stone, but there was no sign of storms on the horizon. The acrid scent of smoke drifted from somewhere nearby, along with that rotting twang I'd caught scent of the last time we'd been here.

That wrongness permeated the air, and with every step toward that fire, it grew more persistent. Even the onyx around us seemed to glow, pulsing with life—and warning. Whatever Bellicent Denare was doing here, it did not bode well for us or for humanity. Just as Fenella had pointed out, this was not her home. She had no reason to come here, not one of her own.

We both slowed when we reached the bottom of a towering mound of broken rock near the remnants of the castle. The onyx stones were more numerous now, intermingled with the slate gray rock from which the castle had been hewn. A small path had been cut through the rubble, leading up and up into the gray haze.

Kalen motioned toward my gloves. With a nod, I removed them and tucked them into my waistband just as he drew his sword.

He took the lead, his steps careful and steady. I followed just behind him. Our boots on the stone were too loud in the eerie silence of the city. Long moments passed as we climbed. My breath grew heavy in my lungs, and exhaustion tugged at my bones.

At long last, we reached the top of the stone mountain. It was oddly flat at the top, and in the center of it, a massive fire roared. The flames flicked their orange tongues at the dark sky. Four onyx pillars stood in a row. Their bases were buried in the rubble, keeping them upright. A chain had been hammered into the center one, and the opposite end led to a pair of manacles. I frowned at those pillars. I'd seen them before.

And then I realized they weren't pillars at all. Those were the carved onyx lids to the gods' sarcophagi.

An eerie shudder went down my spine.

"Kalen," I whispered. "Something about this feels wrong."

"Stay behind me," he said, motioning toward the opposite side of the makeshift platform—away from the pillars.

But I could not stop staring at those chains—at the manacles. I followed Kalen and tried to piece together what this might mean. Those pillars had covered the stone coffins to trap the gods. I could still see the symbols that had been carved into them. But none of that had mattered in the end—not now, when Andromeda's arrival meant they'd awakened.

Something about this did not make sense. Had the gods carried their coffins out of the cavern when they'd escaped? But why? What would they need them for? More importantly, who was meant to go in those chains? They were a new addition, only added recently.

I slid my gaze back to Kalen, whose face was unreadable. The storm fae I'd faced in the castle courtyard had said something to me, and his words now echoed in my ears. He'd believed Kalen was the only one who could stop the gods. If he believed that, did Bellicent believe that, too? Did she intend to trap her own son?

"Kalen," I hissed, my heart pounding as the deep sensation of *wrongness* washed over me again. "I don't think we should be here."

But he kept his gaze forward, still inching around the edge of the platform. Through the bond, I could feel that he'd lost his grip on logic. The vow had consumed him now, forcing his every step forward, forcing him to hunt down his mother, who had to be somewhere nearby.

The familiar scent of lavender drifted into my nose. *Oberon's* scent.

I realized what that meant a second too late.

A knife pressed into my throat. "Drop your weapon, my son, or Tessa Baran dies."

Fifty-Four
Tessa

A low growl rumbled from Kalen's throat as he turned to face his mother and the dagger she pressed against my neck, hard enough that it cut the skin. Droplets of warm blood trailed down my skin, but I refused to show her my fear. All he needed was to distract her, just for a moment, and I could reach up and slam my hand against her face before she could slice my neck.

She'd be dust before she even knew what hit her.

My fingers itched by my sides.

"Mother." Kalen's hand tightened around the hilt of his sword. "Let her go. She has nothing to do with this."

"I think not," she snapped, though her voice sounded muted somehow, as if...her face was covered—protected from my touch. *Damn it!* "Now drop your weapon. I won't ask again."

"I can't," he said through gritted teeth. "Because I'm supposed to kill you. But you already knew that, didn't you? You've known it for four hundred fucking years."

She dug the blade deeper into my neck, and bright stars of pain flashed in my vision. Instead of answering, she said, "I'll give you one more chance to drop the weapon. It's up to you, my son. Andromeda would like to keep Tessa around, but not at the expense of my life. I'm far more important."

Kalen shook, gritting his teeth.

"Kalen," I whispered to him, forcing out the only words I could manage with that blade digging into my skin. "There are other ways."

I hoped he could read what I was trying to send to him through the bond. He didn't need his sword to stop her. Even with the cloth covering Bellicent's face, I could take her down by calling upon Kalen's power—she likely had no idea what we could do together. I just needed her to release the pressure on my throat. I could scarcely breathe, and my exhaustion muddied my vision. Still, I tried, but the thread felt too far out of reach.

With a mournful howl, Kalen ripped his hands free of the sword. It clattered onto the ground by his feet, and he slammed his boot against it. The sword flew into the mist, vanishing in the rubble.

He heaved, staring down at her. "There. Let her go now. Your business is with me."

"Go stand over there by the fire." She didn't release the pressure on my throat. More blood dripped down my neck. The pain compounded my exhaustion, making it difficult to think.

"Why?" he ground out.

"I just want to talk to you, my son," she said, her voice turning soft. "Deep down, I know you want to speak with me, too. It's been years. Centuries, even. And I know you still love me just as deeply as I love you. Let us talk and figure a way out of this. Do you truly wish to kill me? Because you don't have to. I release you from your vow."

Kalen shuddered, pain flaring in the depths of his sapphire eyes. "I know the truth about what you've done. You've become an anchor for Andromeda. So long as you live, she will be tethered to this world."

"Yes," she said. "She tricked me into doing that, and I want to find a way to undo it."

"You have a knife to my beloved's throat. I will not talk to you about a fucking thing until you let her go."

My heart pulsed as Bellicent tensed. And then she jerked me sideways, angling me in the direction of those four onyx pillars. "You're making this a lot more difficult than it has to be."

"Me?" Kalen let out a bitter laugh. "Let go of her now, Bellicent Denare. I do not know what it is you're trying to do, but your words taste and smell like bile. The mother I once loved is dead. Whoever you are, you're not her. And I will fulfill my end of the vow, no matter what you say to convince me otherwise." He stalked toward us, his eyes flashing. "Your greatest mistake was threatening the woman I love. So I will say it one more time, and it's not a request. Let go of my wife."

Bellicent sighed. "I really didn't want to have to do it this way." And then she raised her voice. "Andromeda, I need your help."

A heavy cloud of dread washed over the stones, a darkness so endless and whole that it made the Kingdom of Shadow's nights feel as though they'd been bathed in light. The fire gutted and sparked as a winged creature landed in a crouch between Kalen and me.

My breath caught at the vortex of gloom that spun around her. It sucked at something deep within my chest. She was tall and lithe, her long legs gleaming in the flickering firelight. Her cascading hair was the color of wine. Its strands flowed over pale shoulders that seemed to glow from within, and her eyes...such a deep, impenetrable black. But her face...it looked a lot like mine. And as she stared at me, it felt like every part of me began to unravel.

Even Bellicent tensed, a hiss through her teeth.

And before I knew what was happening, Andromeda pulled a sword from her back and shoved it into Kalen's chest.

The scream that ripped from my throat sliced my ears into ribbons, but that was nothing compared the pain in my heart—an all-consuming pain that buckled my knees. I struggled against Bellicent's hold, no longer caring about the knife at my throat or the god in my way.

All I cared about was him. The blood gushing from his chest. The horror in his eyes. The pain that flowed to me through the bond. It seemed like it might snap in half at any moment. Tears flowed down my cheeks as I screamed, and then screamed and screamed again. She'd stabbed Kalen.

She'd stabbed him, she'd stabbed him, she'd stabbed him.

"Kalen!" My voice came out a whimper as he tumbled forward, his knees hitting the stone. My heart shattered like glass. He was barely breathing. There was blood everywhere. He was dying, he was dying, he was dying.

Andromeda's voice was like ice as she turned to Bellicent and said, "Lock her in the chains."

I had to do something. As Bellicent dragged me across the stones, I tried to think around the horror that burned through me. I was stronger than this. I could destroy every last one of them. All I had to do was use Kalen's powers and get him away from here. Andromeda was muting his healing power, but Druid Balfor might be able to help him.

If I could just get him out of here, he would be okay.

He had to be okay.

I refused to accept anything else.

"If you blast me with that power, Tessa Baran," the god said in that voice made of ice, "you'll only end up hurting him."

She crouched beside him and gave me a feral smile. Too close. She was too fucking close to him for me to safely kill her. I tried to call upon the mist, but it evaded me.

Bellicent reached the pillars and snapped the manacles around my wrists. As soon as she stepped away, I whirled to peer between the pillars. Kalen still lay on the floor. His chest barely moved, but he was still breathing. He was still alive.

He couldn't die.

He couldn't die.

He couldn't die!

"Now," Andromeda said, striding away from Kalen. "Shall we have a little chat?"

"Fuck you," I growled, calling upon the power deep within Kalen's soul. I curled my hands and blasted it at her smug face, but...

Nothing happened.

"Nice try, but that onyx is acting as a barrier, and you cannot use his power. So here's your choice. Kalen Denare can live, or he can die. It is up to you."

"Live," I breathed, clenching my fists and slamming them against the stone. My knuckles screamed in pain, but I didn't care. "Let him go. Let him heal. I don't care what you do to me. Just please, let him live."

That feral smile returned. "First, you must vow never to use your power against me or Bellicent Denare. Or any of my fellow gods." Her eyes arrowed. "And you must vow to never again see Kalen Denare. You will remain with me until the day you die."

My heart pounded, and the storm fae's words echoed in my mind once more. Kalen's power was the only thing that could stop the gods. Bellicent must have learned this through the prophecy. At the time, it had made little sense. The gods could *mute* Kalen's power, and when I'd been in his firing line, it hadn't hurt me. So how could it possibly be the thing to kill them?

And why had Sirius seemed so intent on taking me that day? Not because Andromeda would care about her descendants. He hadn't gone for Nellie.

But now I understood. Kalen's power could kill them *through me* and only me.

"Ah, you understand now." Andromeda's eyes flashed. "It truly is a shame I have to separate you because a bond like yours is rare indeed. I did consider just killing him outright, as you wouldn't be able to channel his power then. But I also knew I'd never get you to make this vow if I did. And you, Tessa Baran, have far more power than just his."

My breath caught as the truth screamed through me. This god was scared of what I could do.

I curled my hands, and the chains rattled. But my magic just sizzled on my palms. Without access to Kalen's mist, I could only kill her by touch. I could not spray it toward her as I'd done to the enemies in Dubnos, not alone. Together, Kalen and I would be her end, but apart, we could not win.

"So let me repeat myself," Andromeda hissed. "He either dies or you make this vow. Your choice." Her eyes flicked to Kalen's crumpled form. "I would make it soon if you want him to heal. He doesn't have long."

"No." His word was so softly spoken I wasn't certain if I'd truly heard it at all, but then he continued. "Don't do it, love. You have to stop them. You're the only one who can."

A great sob shook my body, clanking the chains that hung from my wrists. Something in me cracked at the broken sound of his voice, in the defeat of his words. He would gladly sacrifice himself to save the world. He always would.

Chest heaving, I dug my fingernails into my palms. The puddle of Kalen's blood had spread, creeping across the stones like fingers, closer and closer to where I was trapped behind the pillars. Images flashed in my mind, Kalen's rare smile. The strength of his arms around my body as he kept me safe and warm. The rumble of his laughter.

The scent of his mist, both soothing and electric.

This vow would save him, but it would be the end of everything between us.

I would never get to look into those sapphire eyes again. The eyes that had saved me.

I felt like I was standing on the edge of a knife, and everything within me broke.

"No," he repeated, his voice louder and more insistent this time, as if he could read the path of my thoughts. He probably could.

"Kalen, I'm so sorry. I can't be the savior of the world," I whispered with tears streaming down my face. "Because for you, I would sacrifice it all."

And then I closed my eyes and said the words that would condemn me forever.

I made the vow.

Bellicent cried out, "Death has risen from the ashen remains of a great city. The time of the gods has begun."

EPILOGUE
TESSA

I was a broken thing when Andromeda released me from the manacles, shoved the gloves onto my hands, and carried me away from the ruins of Gailfean on her wings. My surroundings were a blur, and my heart was so numb that I had no fight left in me. She had stolen it from me, along with everything else. Bellicent stayed behind, calling after us that Kalen had already begun to heal.

At least he was alive.

At least I had not sacrificed everything for nothing.

And for that, I could not regret what I'd done, even if it meant I'd doomed us all.

At some point, I must have drifted to sleep or my mind became so numb I couldn't think, because the scent of brine twined with the cloying stench of rot jolted me awake. Andromeda clutched me tightly against her chest, and sick clung to the back of my throat. I wondered what would happen if I squirmed out of her arms. I would fall, but I bore wings myself. I could fly away from here.

If only I hadn't made a vow.

"Ah, you're awake." Her icy voice slithered through me as she held me tighter, her arms as unbreakable as steel. "Welcome to your new home."

The new home turned out to be Malroch, the storm fae city on the coast that Toryn's brother had been visiting. When we landed on the castle's spire, I let myself take in the whitewashed buildings, the streets lined with corals and seashells, and the swooping seagulls that filled the salt-drenched air with their song.

It seemed Toryn's brother had been busy. Soldiers marched through the streets, heavily armed. The mist was a heavy cloud overhead, but the streets were free of it.

From a small, small part of my mind, I knew it was an important observation, but I couldn't bring myself to care. Not when I'd never again see Kalen.

My eyes slid shut. This city was beautiful, but I couldn't bear to look at it.

"You're clearly exhausted. It's hard for me to remember you have human blood in you. I'll let you get some sleep, and then I'll introduce you to the others. You've already met my brother Sirius, of course."

Rage went through me, but it died like a spark beneath a heavy gust of wind.

"I can see we have a long way to go before you'll see me as anything but your enemy."

My eyes flipped open then, and I spat the words into her perfect, unblemished face. "Fuck you."

She tsked. "Right."

Andromeda spread her wings and soared down the length of the castle before swooping through an open window. We landed inside a richly furnished room, where a large bed took up only a quarter of the space. But the sight of all the plush carpets and chairs was marred by the chains and manacles attached to two bedposts. That and the heavy bars that slammed down on the window behind us.

As soon as she loosened her grip on me, I shoved out of her arms and stumbled back. "Not an enemy, right? That's why you intend to keep me chained to the bed."

Those deep black eyes bored through me. "I won't have you causing chaos."

"What's the point?" I shot back. "You made it so I can never see Kalen again. Or fight against you. Or do anything at all to save this world from your monstrous ruin."

"Taking this world is the only way my siblings and I can survive." She gave me an icy smile. "I don't care if you judge us for what we do, but you're no better. You could have turned down my vow and tried to fight against me. But you didn't. Because you wanted to save your mate and *only* your mate. So why don't you think about that while you sit in here and hate me for trying to survive?"

My mouth dropped open when she stormed out of the room. The slamming of the door reverberated through me. A moment later, bolts clicked into place, trapping me inside. I slid to the floor and palmed the carpet—soft and luxurious, but I could find no comfort here. The pain in my chest made it feel as though a fist gripped my lungs, making it impossible to breathe.

"Kalen," I whispered, the tears leaking from my eyes again. He was alive, but he was gone, and it felt like half my soul had been ripped from my body. I could not imagine an existence without him. The moment I'd first laid eyes on him, even when he'd been masked in my dreams, something in me had shifted.

I'd started to fight back.

I had to find a way back to him. I'd vowed that I would not use my power against Andromeda, but still…if there was one thing Kalen had taught me, it was that vows were not foolproof.

My breath went shallow as realization shuddered through me.

She'd made me vow to never return to Kalen's side, but she did not know about the marriage bond. Hardly anyone did. Fenella had sniffed it out, but Toryn and the others had been surprised by it. Could it override the vow I'd made to the god?

Maybe there was still hope. Maybe I could defeat Andromeda still.

As I pictured her face in my mind, that sizzling rage roared to life within me once more, stronger than it had ever been. Andromeda had done the one thing I could never forgive or forget. Kalen was the other half of my soul. I would rip this world apart to get back to him.

I would bide my time if necessary. I would watch and wait. I would learn their plans and make my own. And when she least expected it, I would take the God of Death in my hands, and I would turn her body to ash.

I did not care how long it took.

Lifting my chin, I stood. My wings flared behind me, the ends now tipped in red.

Glossary

Druids - religious fae leaders who worship the sky, the earth, and the seas

Familiar - a bonded animal; usually, only shadow fae have this connection

Fion - fae wine that tastes of silver and song

Gemstones - powerful jewels with magical properties

Gods - powerful, immortal beings who once ruled the world with violence, banished when humans and fae joined together to fight them: Andromeda, Sirius, Perseus, Callisto, and Orion

Joint eaters - monsters of the mist who can transform into any animal

Mortal Blade - a blade only a mortal can wield, and whoever is on the receiving end turns to ash

Pookas - the term shadow fae use for the monsters of the mist who feast on human flesh

Shadowfiends - the term light fae and mortals use for the monsters of the mist who feast on human flesh

The Fell - the time period when the five winged gods first arrived in the world

The Great Rift - the chasm separating the Kingdom of Light from the rest of the world, caused by the clash of powers between King Oberon and the Mist King

The Oidhe - the deal between the mortals of Teine and King Oberon

Valerian - a magic-infused herb that causes dreamless sleep

Wraiths - hooded creatures of the mist who leave behind trails of poisonous sand

Acknowledgments

First, I have to thank my husband. You offered to swap offices with me before I started writing this book, and it meant I got the better (and much warmer) room in the house! It made such a difference, so thank you, thank you, thank you.

To Nero and Vesta, the best pups in the world, for keeping me company every time I sit down to write.

To my writing friends, Christine, Anya, Alison, Jen, Marina, and Tammi, for your constant encouragement and daily chats.

To Sylvia Frost for the absolutely amazing cover design.

To my wonderful editing team, Maggie, Ash, and Anthony, for editing and polishing this book.

To Dian for another gorgeous artwork of Tessa and Kalen.

And to all the readers of this series, I appreciate you more than I could ever say.

Also by Jenna Wolfhart

The Mist King
Of Mist and Shadow
Of Ash and Embers
Of Night and Chaos
Of Dust and Stars

The Fallen Fae
Court of Ruins
Kingdom in Exile
Keeper of Storms
Tower of Thorns
Realm of Ashes

Demons After Dark: Covenant
Devilish Deal
Infernal Games
Wicked Oath

Demons After Dark: Temptation
Sinful Touch
Darkest Fate
Hellish Night

About the Author

Jenna Wolfhart spends her days dreaming up stories about swoony fae kings and stabby heroines. When she's not writing, she loves to deadlift, rewatch Game of Thrones, and drink far too much coffee.

Born and raised in America, Jenna now lives in England with her husband and her two dogs.

www.jennawolfhart.com
jenna@jennawolfhart.com
tiktok.com/@jennawolfhart